DIG

Also available by J. H. Markert

Spider to the Fly
Sleep Tight
Wicked Games
Mister Lullaby
The Nightmare Man

Writing as James Markert

The Strange Case of Isaac Crawley
Midnight at the Tuscany Hotel
What Blooms From Dust
All Things Bright and Strange
The Angels' Share
A White Wind Blew

DIG

A NOVEL

J. H. MARKERT

CROOKED
LANE

NEW YORK

Books should be disposed of and recycled according to local requirements. All paper materials used are FSC compliant.

Published in the United States by Crooked Lane Books, an imprint of The Quick Brown Fox & Company LLC.

Crooked Lane Books and its logo are trademarks of The Quick Brown Fox & Company LLC.

Library of Congress Catalog-in-Publication data available upon request.

ISBN (hardcover): 979-8-89242-415-8
ISBN (paperback): 979-8-89242-508-7
ISBN (ebook): 979-8-89242-416-5

Cover design by Amanda Shaffer

Printed in the United States.

www.crookedlanebooks.com

Crooked Lane Books
34 West 27th St., 10th Floor
New York, NY 10001

First Edition: March 2026

The authorized representative in the EU for product safety and compliance is eucomply OÜPärnu mnt 139b-14, 11317 Tallinn, Estonia, hello@eucompliancepartner.com, +33757690241

10 9 8 7 6 5 4 3 2 1

This novel starts with a character coming home after the sudden death of his father. I finished the first draft of DIG a week after my father passed away. My father, a Catholic Deacon, was one of the most well-known and respected stained-glass artisans in the country. He lived the last year of his life without legs, but continued designing windows until the end, from his wheelchair. In a newspaper article from the 1980s, he was quoted saying:

"I consider the gifts I have been given that allow me to be compassionate are bigger than the gifts that allow me to draw or paint or create art. I need them both, but if I were to lose my hands, I would not lose the other."
While he never lost his hands, he lost his legs, yet remained true to his words from decades before. After the surgery, he told me that he might be physically limited to his chair or couch cushion, but his compassion has no bounds. And he never lost his sense of humor: after the surgery when the nurse asked how tall he was, he said, "Two feet shorter than yesterday."

I think another word for dig, perhaps, could be perseverance, which any writer knows well. You dig and dig and dig until your achievement is there for the taking. Writers are always reminded to Show and not Tell. Perseverance was just one of the countless lessons I learned from my mother and father by watching them navigate through everyday life, from them showing through actions and never having to tell.

To all of you readers out there, keep persevering, keep digging.
And Dad,
This one is for you...

Have a wonderful day!

—Blue Bottles

PROLOGUE

Twenty Years Before the Sudden Death of Reverend Thomas Dodd

SUNLIGHT FILTERED THROUGH the glass honey jar on the kitchen windowsill.

Tiny black flecks of pollen, and even fragments from the bees themselves—all too small for the strainer to catch—floated in liquid gold.

Pure tupelo, she'd learned, could keep for decades without crystallizing.

To Amy's six-year-old mind, it looked like melted butter, but with a faint touch of green.

"It all adds to the flavor," Mr. Passafume had explained to her yesterday inside the sky-blue honey house, when he'd let her dip a finger and taste it straight off the honeycomb.

After a full day she could still taste the distinct flavor inside her mouth, floral and fruity and smooth.

"They're like little cheerleader pom-poms," she'd told Mr. Passafume about the tupelo trees' white flowers, which bloomed only during a two- to three-week window each year.

"So we have to be ready when they do," he'd told her, before pulling a wooden frame from the boxed hive, the honeycomb interiors full of rich nectar. "The bees," he'd explained, "fan the honeycombs with their wings to get rid of excess water, until it thickens just like they want it."

"Bees are smart," Amy had said, squatting, her face inches from the hives.

"Especially my bees," he'd said, next showing her the metal device that looked like a giant toaster, each wooden frame like slices of bread. Internal chains rattled the frames until all the wax caps broke, after which he scraped them with a wire brush to free any unopened cells, revealing golden honey within.

"We call it scratching," he'd told her.

Next came the slinging, which happened in another machine inside the honey house, like a washing machine on spin cycle, slinging honey from the open honeycombs and onto the interior walls of the extractor as the two of them stood side by side, hands on knees, watching the amber harvest drip and ooze into the mesh-covered vat below.

"It's magical," she'd said then, and thought again now, as sunlight made the honey jar glow.

But then, as always, the prized honey conjured her fear of the tupelo swamp itself, where the bee barges swayed creakily under tendrils of silvery Spanish moss, where the island spirits roamed freely, where gnarled tupelo trees soared mystic and bald cypress thrust upward from the dark, brackish water like ancient monsters.

C H A P T E R

1
Amy

"DIG . . ."

The male voice on the phone was familiar to Amy Barnes. "Reverend?" Amy placed the manuscript pages from the book she was writing on the history of Crow Island, along with the red editing pen, on the couch cushion beside her and stood. "Reverend Dodd?"

The voice croaked, "Tell Nathanial . . ."

Amy paced the living room, phone to her ear. *Tell Nathanial what?* She hadn't seen or spoken to Nathanial Dodd in eight years. She couldn't tell if the reverend was drunk—living in that massive plantation house by himself for so long now, he'd been known to imbibe—but this sounded different.

More urgent, unexpected.

"Dig . . ."

"Dig? Reverend? I don't understand."

"They're . . . real . . ." he said, with labored breaths.

"What's real? Reverend?"

"The birds . . ."

What birds?

Thomas Dodd called periodically to check in, as he did with many on the island, especially those with whom guilt still resided from the massacre. Despite what his younger son, Jericho, had done years ago, the reverend was still respected, but now he sounded delirious, and in obvious pain. She exited through the back door of her modest island house in leggings and a T-shirt from her evening run. She passed the empty swimming pool, refused to give it a glance after what had happened in it the other night, and hurried across the moonlit backyard, phone to her ear. "Stay with me, Reverend." Was it a heart attack? She'd never thought Thomas Dodd would be taken down by something as concealed as a human heart, no matter how badly his had been broken. He was healthy, fit, and strong. Only in his mid-fifties.

Amy picked up her pace. She was a late bloomer as far as running but now ran avidly as a form of grief therapy—she'd lost both parents and her twin sister, Bridget, all within a matter of minutes, on that fateful Fourth of July eight years ago. Running had become an addiction after she'd lost Chad, her husband of only two years, six months ago in a boating accident a half mile deep into Crow Island Sound. Amy lived in the middle of the island, in view of the eastern coast, right where the Devil's Backbone began to curl in upon itself; each morning she ran two miles south to the Rocks (where the locals liked to fish), and in the evenings, she'd run north toward the Sands. But having already slid off her running shoes and poured her nightly glass of Moscato, she'd rushed out of the house in flip-flops.

The Dodd House was only a quarter mile through the woods, a run she'd made countless times as a girl in only a couple of minutes, but with how leaden her legs now felt, it seemed farther away with every stride. On the outskirts of Crow Island Cemetery, she ran under live oaks and red cedars, longleaf pines and saw palmettos, forever aware of what lay beyond the acres of tombstones and mausoleums—the bee barges and honey house and tupelo swamp, where she'd almost drowned as a little girl.

Heavy breathing sounded over the phone, followed by a painful moan and then a loud thump.

"Reverend . . ." She felt sure Thomas Dodd had just collapsed. She exited the woods and sprinted toward Oak Alley, the Dodds' serpentine driveway, a hundred yards long and flanked on both sides by live oaks. As a little girl, Amy would race her twin sister Bridget down this driveway. Even by ten, Bridget had been in love with the Dodds' older son, Nathanial, and had always been in a rush to see him. Amy, more bookish and unathletic, would do her best to keep up, all while trying not to look at the tunnel of gnarled, overreaching tree limbs, the Spanish moss glistening like majestic crystals in the Crow Island breeze, moss she'd been told was really hair discarded from the island's Boo Hags.

Crow Island's twenty thousand acres was home now to just over one thousand residents and finally growing again after the massacre. The Dodd House was the original plantation home around which the island's economy had soared, first with indigo and then later with cotton in the early to mid-1800s. Amy knew the island well; as the only remaining member of her family after the massacre, she'd inherited it at age eighteen. She and Bridget had known they'd inherit what had been privately owned by their family since the decades after the Civil War, since the island's tupelo trees had made them rich enough to buy it, but she never could have predicted it would happen so soon, so suddenly, and with her as the sole survivor.

The Dodds' French colonial plantation home loomed with stately Greek columns and tall French windows. The front double doors were open to the night. Classical music played through the screen doors. Amy cautiously entered. Breeze circulated freely. She moved past the grand staircase, looked left toward the drawing room and then right toward the parlor. Every window had been opened wide, like the house itself was in the middle of a big yawn. The living room was clear, all those windows open as well.

Every room was empty and high ceilinged; her breaths trembled.

Settle down, Amy. Settle down.

The voice of her twin still followed her.

Eight years dead—*eight years murdered*—yet she could still hear it as clearly as the Crow Island Church bell. Amy stopped at the library. Inside, curtains billowed, shadows moved across the wooden floor. She turned off the classical music on the radio. With its floor-to-ceiling mahogany bookshelves and expansive book collection, the Dodd House's library had always been Amy's favorite room in the house. But now, as she entered, the old floorboards creaking underfoot, she somehow felt Jericho's suffocating presence in it. Her gut said *run*, as if she expected to find young Jericho Dodd standing in the shadows watching her with his mismatched eyes—one chestnut brown, the other Aegean blue. She held strong; Jericho was dead. He'd been buried deep, eight years ago.

On the far side of the room atop Reverend Dodd's desk, a stained-glass lamp glowed like a prism. Thomas Dodd's left hand rested limp on the floor beyond the desk, inches away from the phone. His fancy watch looked heavy against his wrist, his white button-down rolled at the cuff to just below his elbow. Blood leaked from a wound at his brow, where he must have hit it on the way down. His face was ashen, his eyes wide open and unblinking. His full head of salt-and-pepper hair, typically swept back and combed, was in disarray. It was Reverend Dodd, yet it didn't look like him. He was unshaved and gaunt, like he hadn't been eating.

Amy knelt beside him, checked for a pulse. Nothing. Holding his wrist was like holding a cold, dead fish, and she let go of it so quickly it hit the floor with a thud that made her nauseous. She put her ear to his slightly parted mouth and neither felt nor heard anything coming up from his lungs.

He was dead before he hit the floor, Amy.

She fumbled her phone, found Sheriff Kilbourne's number and called it. On Crow Island, Sheriff Kilbourne was every 911 department rolled into one. He answered on the second ring.

She told him to send help to the Dodd House. The reverend was hurt.

He's dead, her twin's voice in her head said. *Can't you see that?*

Amy wiped tears from her cheeks and sat back on her heels. Reverend Dodd's pale, clammy skin made his crow's-feet more pronounced, his wrinkles more furrowed, the laugh lines more noticeable, although she rarely remembered him laughing since the massacre. Contemplating doing CPR, she rolled him from his side to his back and straddled him at the waist. She leaned down, put her mouth to his cold lips—his breath smelled strongly of honey—and blew.

And that's when she noticed his right hand—or lack of one.

She screamed and crab-walked backward, panting.

Reverend Dodd's right hand was missing, and the stump that remained, just past the wrist, looked blackened and swollen and infected and . . . glistening with . . . honey?

She spotted a nearly empty jar resting sideways on the floor next to the bookshelves. It had a yellow circular sticker, which was how Mr. Passafume labeled early sample jars from his newest harvest. Typically, these weren't given out, even to the reverend, so how had he gotten one? It appeared Reverend Dodd had plunged his infected stump into the jar, as if to soothe his pain. When had he lost his hand—and how?

She surveyed the library for signs of blood and saw nothing, although the wound appeared to have happened in the past few days.

A siren approached in the distance.

She stood and backed away. On the middle of his desk rested a lone piece of paper with an uncapped red pen atop it. Perhaps he'd been putting together his next sermon.

At the top of the page, he'd written *In today's reading . . .*

But he'd stopped. To doodle?

All over the paper, birds had been drawn. Dozens of red birds, some seemingly in flight, some in clusters, others drawn as if perched atop an invisible electric cable.

They're real, he'd said over the phone. *The birds . . .*

Red birds.

But were they red because that was the color of pen he'd grabbed from the coffee mug, or had he meant to draw red birds? And they were crows. Crows had never been seen on Crow Island, not since . . .

You know what he means, Amy, said that little voice.

Amy hurried from the library and down the hallway toward the front door. She burst through the screen door, ran down the porch steps to the flower bed clearing and horseshoe driveway in front of Oak Alley, taking in full breaths of the humid, salty air.

Shadows moved on the far side of the house, near where the Dodds had had a series of parallel horseshoe pits. They were overgrown now, like much of the property. The reverend had given up on a lot of things after his wife died, after the massacre, after Nathanial left.

Amy followed the shadows to the side of the house and heard a dog growling. She saw not one dog but three, furiously digging in the moonlit backyard, each working on a separate hole, like they were in competition to find a buried prize.

"*Get,*" Amy hissed at the mutts.

One dog paused for a beat to stare at her but then resumed.

She clapped.

Two dogs looked up this time.

Sheriff Kilbourne's siren grew louder, and in its wake was the lone Crow Island ambulance. Headlights strobe-flashed through the trees of Oak Alley and grew brighter as they neared the house. This scared all three dogs into the woods behind the property but also gave Amy a good view of the entire backyard—it was dotted with at least three dozen more holes scattered about the grass and sandy beach soil that long ago had prospered with cotton.

Soil so famous for growing *anything.*

The ambulance stopped in front of the house, and two medics hurried to the veranda. The sheriff's car door closed, but Amy couldn't take her eyes off the holes—most of them a foot deep, some deeper and wider—and counted them.

Thirty-seven.

Unless she'd missed a few in the shadows.

Sheriff Kilbourne, his badge pinned to the white T-shirt he must have been wearing when she'd called, moved next to her, adjusted his hat. "What the hell happened here? Amy?"

She knew he was referring to the yard. "I don't know," she said without looking at him.

The dogs watched from the fringe.

"Reverend Dodd do all this?"

Amy shook her head. "Dogs." But then she noticed a shovel on the ground about twenty paces in front of her. "And yeah, perhaps the reverend too."

Before he lost his hand, she thought.

"Isn't this where they buried Jericho?" Sheriff Kilbourne asked.

"Yes," she said. "Somewhere around here."

CHAPTER

2
Nate

NATHANIAL DODD GOT the phone call from Sheriff Kilbourne halfway through his fifth tall beer.

He'd told none of his coworkers about the meeting he'd had with Principal Bates in the morning. The same principal who'd handed him a plaque last year for Teacher of the Year had delivered the news he might not be back next year for his fourth. Apparently, the parents of Sebastian Roark were pressing charges for an incident between Nate and their son back in April. An incident Nate thought had been reconciled by a phone call explaining things. "At some point there was a change of heart," Principal Bates had said. As Nate began his second beer, it had dawned on him that that change of heart had occurred the day the kids found out where he was from and asked about the massacre. He should have lied instead of dodging the question. It took the middle schoolers only a few minutes to figure out that not only had Nate Dodd been on Crow Island that summer eight years ago, but he was the older brother of the murderer, that monstrous boy killer named Jericho.

At the very least, Nate feared he'd be suspended. The Roarks were big donors, so it wouldn't be difficult to get him fired. Their son might have portrayed himself like an upstanding young man, but all the middle school teachers knew him to be a sneaky prick who didn't go a day without bullying those he deemed below him.

Nate had begun the day happy for the end of another school year, but excited mostly—he finally admitted it to himself—for the after-school celebration with his crew, specifically with Lauren Jenkins, one of the two sixth-grade homeroom teachers. But right around nine, at the beginning of his planning period, he'd gotten a text from Principal Bates, asking him to her office for a quick chat.

He'd known there was something off when she asked him to close the door. He'd been accused of causing physical and mental harm to the boy. He *had* grabbed the kid's arm, and had left a bruise when he'd pulled the kid halfway across the row of desks, no matter that he was reacting to a smaller student being bullied. The short meeting left him gutted. He could tell Principal Bates had been fighting her own emotions. She liked him. He'd been up front with her when she'd hired him about his past, about his hopes for a fresh start away from that island. She spoke of him highly. He was a good, young teacher, and his future was bright—until suddenly it wasn't.

But no matter the provocation, Nate had snapped that day in the classroom.

And his brother Jericho had snapped that day on the island.

So Nate was quiet and solemn throughout the day when he was typically full of infectious energy, and Lauren had asked him repeatedly if something was wrong. And every time he'd faked a smile and said no, he was fine. Just tired. But Lauren hadn't fallen for that. Which had prompted him to add that he was mostly bummed he wouldn't be seeing *her* every day, at which she playfully slapped him on the arm, when deep down they both knew there'd been an instant connection between them. It was just that now Lauren was single, and from what Nate had heard from coworkers, she was single because she'd broken up with her boyfriend of eighteen months two weeks ago. And they both knew, without saying, that tonight just might lead to something more than friendship.

Nate had downed his first beer quickly to relax at Puerto Vallarta, the teachers' go-to hangout on Fridays, while their group of seven went through multiple bowls of chips and salsa. Their margaritas disappeared just as quickly. All of them were in party mode except Nate, who felt the urgent need to bury himself, and his mood had brought

Lauren's down as well. So he ordered a second tall beer and did his best to pretend nothing was wrong.

Lauren was sitting directly across from him, and he could tell she wasn't buying it. He'd give her the hint of a smile that didn't last long, despite what her pretty face and stark green eyes and curly auburn hair typically did to him. He'd gone for months, hell, two years if he was being honest, wondering what it would be like to wrap her in his arms and kiss her. And up until this morning, he'd all but planned it out, imagined how tonight might go, never mind that his only true relationship had ended in such tragedy at the age of eighteen that he'd been reluctant to try again. Could he love another person like he'd loved Bridget Barnes? With Lauren, he sensed it might be possible.

It had become a ritual on the last day of school for their group to close the restaurant down. Six hours later, creeping toward midnight, as Nate realized he'd gone from melancholy to drunk without even knowing it, having finally begun to relax somewhere during beer number three, or maybe four, and was now reveling in the fact that Lauren, who'd stopped drinking hours ago, had teasingly insisted on driving him home—"Give me your keys, Mr. Dodd, you are not driving"—his phone rang.

He hadn't spoken to Sheriff Kilbourne since he'd fled the island eight years ago. His face must have shown panic, because across the table, Lauren, who'd gotten good at reading him, immediately asked who it was.

Nate hadn't spoken with anyone from Crow Island other than his father since he'd left. But it was the sense of dread he felt, increasing with each ring, that got him up from the table, had him heading toward the back of the restaurant to answer it. Like his conversation with Principal Bates in the morning, this one was quick, to the point, and mostly a blur afterward. He didn't expect to find Lauren standing next to him when he turned around. This wasn't the day he'd planned. But he'd been a fool to think he could ever pick up the pieces and move on from what had happened that day on Crow Island. Or that alcohol could bury the fact that he was possibly going to be fired.

Lauren placed a hand on his cheek, and he leaned into it. "Nate, what's wrong?"

His response was swift. "My dad's dead."

And I'm an orphan now, he thought, *at twenty-six.*

C H A P T E R

3
Sheriff Kilbourne

SHERIFF KILBOURNE PARKED his cruiser on the outskirts of Crow Island Cemetery and entered the woods on foot.

The only way to get to the tupelo swamp was on foot, and you had to walk through the ten square acres of Crow Island Cemetery to get there. But this morning what would typically be a peaceful stroll through ancient live oaks and ornately designed mausoleums was anything but, especially on the heels of what he'd seen last night at the Dodd House, with the reverend dead and missing a hand and all those holes dug in the backyard.

Mr. Passafume, who single-handedly ran the island's prized tupelo honey business, rarely asked for anything, so when he called Kilbourne's cell phone shortly after sunrise and said, "Lawrence, you need to get out to the swamp . . . now. There's something you need to see," Lawrence wasted no time. From the quaver in the old man's voice, Lawrence knew it was bad.

The phone call to Nate Dodd he'd put off for two hours last night had only lasted two minutes. His wife Tina kept telling him, "Dial already, Lawrence!" Tina had never been one to hold back, and now with both of them in their mid-forties and after twenty years of marriage, she had even less of a filter.

"Just rip it off like a Band-Aid, Daddy," their only child, five-year-old David, had said, the same phrase Lawrence had used the night before, trying to get David to down the last of the pink liquid antibiotic for his latest ear infection.

The swamp and bee barges came into view. His heart rate increased. As sheriff for the past fifteen years and fire chief for the past ten, he was accustomed to uncomfortable phone calls, but last night's to Nate Dodd, so quickly followed by the one from Mr. Passafume, had ushered in a sense of dread he'd not felt since the massacre. The actual anniversary—he hated when the locals called it that—was a month away, but for too many on the Backbone, himself included, it still felt raw. The vibes he'd felt last night in the Dodd House after they'd carted the reverend away had felt plain wrong. Off-kilter, like the air would get before and after a hurricane. It wasn't like the man's ghost was left behind, nothing like that, but more like the sudden emptiness in that old plantation house made them aware of what *had* been left behind.

All those holes in the backyard.

The red crows he'd drawn before he died.

Lawrence navigated the weedy downslope toward the swamp, where an old canoe—painted rust red and tethered by rope to a wooden post in the muddy bank—bobbed in dark, murky water. Walking around the swamp to the bee barges would have added another fifteen to twenty minutes of traversing through weeds and mud and brambles and bugs, so as much as he despised that canoe, he lowered himself into it and started rowing.

According to sixteenth-century island legend, the Creek Indian Malatche, in the dawn hours before the Spanish arrived, became possessed by a spirit and murdered dozens of his own Muscogee tribe by bow and arrow before piercing his own heart with a knife. The Spanish arrived to an otherwise abandoned island, where fires still smoldered and pigs and chickens and boars and deer roamed, healthy and well fed and, as one Spanish Catholic missionary had written in the few bits of correspondence left behind for the English to find two centuries later, *larger than any animals I'd ever seen*. Upon the bark of nearly every tree surrounding the island's central swamp, black crows had been painted, and atop the swamp's murky water floated four dozen empty fishing boats, bumping into each other, vacated except for the oars.

Where did all the Creeks go? Sheriff Lawrence Kilbourne thought as he rowed uneasily across the water. As for the crows painted on the trees—no sightings of crows over the next five hundred years had ever been recorded, hence the sarcastic name of the island. *Where did the crows go?*

A lifelong islander, Lawrence had never liked the tupelo swamp. Even as a teen, when his pals came to fish, he had stayed behind. The swamp still unnerved him, but he couldn't deny its mystical beauty, even now, as he coasted between the knees of ancient cypress trees, their veiny trunks thrusting from the water like the strained necks of buried monsters. Warm, fuzzy sunshine poked rays of golden glow through the canopy of overreaching boughs. Tendrils of Spanish moss glistened with dew. Morning mist hovered ghostily above the brackish water as if it were afraid to touch it, unlike the bugs that skittered atop the constantly moving surface, every so often devoured by fish jumping up, only to plop and disappear into ripples under the deep, dark, hidden depths.

Like he had as a boy, Lawrence wondered if it was his oar and canoe moving the water or if whatever was under the water was moving him. Even though he told his son David the stories weren't real, he'd always believed in the legends of the Boo Hags that lived in and around the swamp, legends that had unfortunately seemed more of a reality of late, as more and more islanders had been coming forth claiming to have seen one, to have witnessed one, to have felt one crawling into their bed at night.

The canoe rocked on a wave as if something had just passed underneath.

A bug grazed his left cheek, and he brushed it away.

A bee buzzed in front of his face, circled his body, and flew off.

The swamp air seemed extra thick, extra humid, extra stagnant, but the Spanish moss hanging from the live oaks along the banks twisted and moved as if a storm were coming through.

Hammering echoed from the direction of the honey house. Lawrence assumed Mr. Passafume was up there, waiting, if not working on something, maybe building a new hive. The man practically lived up there. The bee barges loomed larger the closer Lawrence rowed, the forty yards of woodworking stretching like a train trestle atop water that lapped against the stained wooden posts below. Swaying ten feet above the water's surface, the decking had been built around the dozens of tupelo trees on the southernmost edge of the swamp, at the best level for the hives to meet the flowers when they bloomed.

Lawrence allowed the canoe to coast toward the stairs at the far end of the barge and docked it, his mind reverting to Reverend Dodd. He navigated the rickety spiral of wooden steps leading up to the deck, wondering if the reverend had been sick, wondering what in the hell had happened to the man's hand. It had been weeks since he'd seen the reverend around the island, and come to think of it, the assistant pastor, Reverend Jennings, had led them in worship the past two Sundays, telling the congregation only that Reverend Dodd was taking some badly needed R and R. And now Nathanial Dodd was coming back into town after eight years gone, and Lawrence knew it would churn up dirt. Not so much because the kid was a prodigal returned, but with him being Jericho's brother, there was no way his arrival back on the island wouldn't cause waves.

The bee barge swayed when he reached the top of it, and the movement, as it typically did, made him nauseous. He glanced ahead but otherwise watched the wood planking as he walked, his mind already wrangling over what he'd seen on the decking just outside the honey house. It was too small to be a body but big enough for him to know it didn't belong outside something as "island sacred" as the honey house, its sky-blue walls lurid in the morning light, the pitched apple-red roof like something out of a fairy tale.

Large bees buzzed this way and that; Lawrence knew not to swipe at them. At least as far as the tupelo honey went, the blooming window had come and gone. Mr. Passafume had already secured the season's harvest in jars he kept hidden until it was what he called *go time.* Or what he had thought was hidden—less than two weeks ago, an entire crate of twelve jars had been stolen from his storage, and they'd yet to find the culprit.

The hammering was louder now.

Mr. Passafume, who everyone called Blue Bottles, protected the honey house like a priest would a cathedral and kept it padlocked—him with the only key—and he was hammering boards across the opening with an urgency that sent Lawrence's heart rate to high alert. He couldn't remember a time when the honey house had been breached. He wondered how long that door had been open before Mr. Passafume noticed it. Remnants of the old yellow door lay in a heap of wooden scraps near the barge's railing, upon which the words *DON'T LET THE HAG RIDE YA* were written in red paint.

"Morning, Lawrence," Mr. Passafume said with a glance over his shoulder, squatting as he hammered a final board to the threshold of where the honey house door had been.

"Morning, Earl," said Lawrence, taking in more of the senseless vandalism—the word *DIG* in red on the side of the honey house, letters nearly as tall as the wall itself. "Although there doesn't seem to be much good about it." He recalled the message Reverend Dodd had asked Amy Barnes to give his son last night before he'd died. *Dig* . . .

"Any morning we wake up on the right side of life is a good one, Sheriff." Mr. Passafume stood with an old-man grunt and looked satisfied that he'd sealed the opening up properly. If Morgan Freeman had a long-lost twin, it would be Earl "Blue Bottles" Passafume, his voice nearly as velvety smooth. He scratched at his short white Afro, wiped sweat from his dark, wrinkled brow, and nodded toward the decking to Lawrence's right. The word *JERICHO* had been spelled out on the planks in what appeared to be a conglomeration of red paint and twisted hair, the letters in all caps and a foot tall.

While the phrase *don't let the hag ride ya*—in reference to the island's Geechee Boo Hag legends—was a common one, *dig*, until last night, was not, and Jericho was a name that had been practically taboo since the massacre.

Lawrence squatted for a closer inspection of what had been used to make Jericho's name. His knees popped on the way down. His first guess was hair, or maybe weeds.

"It's Spanish moss." Blue Bottles squatted on the other side of the word. "And that ain't red paint. It's blood. Otherwise, I would have taken care of this in-house."

"Animal or human blood?" Either way, it was a lot.

"Human."

"How ya figure?"

Blue Bottles nodded to Lawrence's left, toward the trunk of the closest tupelo tree ten feet away.

A human hand, fingers down, palm to the bark and cleanly severed just past the wrist, had been nailed to the tree, about two feet above the bee barge's decking. Lawrence looked away, closed his eyes, took a beat to compose himself.

Just as he'd thought upon first glance, it was a right hand, a man's hand, and it had evidently been used to write the words all over the bee barge—the middle finger was stained red down to the first knuckle.

"'If your right hand causes you to stumble, cut it off and throw it away,'" said Blue Bottles as he stared absentmindedly at the hand nailed to the tree. "'It is better for you to lose one part of your body than for your whole body to go into hell.'"

"That from the Bible?" Lawrence asked.

"I believe so."

"When did you become a churchgoer?"

"I'm not. But if you live as long as I have, you pick up on a few things. Ideas who the hand belongs to?"

Lawrence said, "Yeah. I got a pretty good idea."

CHAPTER

4
Amy

Three Days Before the Sudden Death of Reverend Thomas Dodd

UNLIKE HER TWIN sister Bridget, who always had to be doing something with someone, Amy had always preferred the company of books and her imagination.

It wasn't until after her husband's death six months ago that she'd begun to feel what it was like to be truly alone. Her sister had been the first to fall victim to Jericho Dodd's axe on that Fourth of July afternoon; her parents had gotten axed seconds later as they'd fled. In the aftermath, Nate Dodd had hurried off to college and had yet to return, going on eight years later. Now that they were all gone, Amy too often craved their company, especially at dark, which was why since Chad's death she'd begun a regimen of swimming laps at night that bordered on obsessiveness, anything to take her to the brink of sheer exhaustion and help her sleep. Anything to take her mind off the fact that she was very much alone.

The cool, cleansing water put her mind at ease. When she emerged, it was like life arising anew. But just before her hand touched the pool's edge for the tenth lap, the earth began to rumble. It lasted for three seconds—she'd made it a habit when these tremors started years ago to count them, and none lasted longer than four.

The short rumblings had become so commonplace over the years that they no longer unnerved her, although of late the increased frequency was noticeable. But this was the first time one had occurred while she was inside the pool, and the suddenness caught her off guard.

Water splashed over the edge in a wave so strong it pushed one of the lounge chairs against the wrought iron fence. Before she could grasp the pool's edge, the water around her shifted, pulled her away from the wall, toward the center of the pool. She heard a sucking sound and then felt it beneath her feet, something pulling from the bottom, too reminiscent of what she'd felt in the swamp water as a young girl. Unlike the strong talon-like fingers she'd felt pulling at her ankles back then, this was more of a suction, but strong. Her first thought was of the giant sinkhole that had formed in the middle of Bull Street two weeks ago that had nearly swallowed Cody Jacobson and his golf cart and was still partitioned off with caution tape while Sheriff Kilbourne decided how best to remedy it. The thought terrified her. She attempted to swim to the side of the pool, but the rapidly declining water level made it difficult. Unlike most pools, this didn't have a shallow end. It had been installed by the previous owner specifically for diving and was a uniform twelve feet deep all the way across. Seeing the water level drop below the last rung of the ladder sent her into a panic. The walls grew higher by the second.

"Help," she screamed, the water now below her knees. She trudged through it toward the ladder, but she couldn't reach the lowest rung; the ladder had been installed with the idea that someone would be swimming, not reaching up from the bottom of a pool that had only six inches of water in it and a four-foot-long crack in the middle looming like a gaping wound, with muddy groundwater and soil burbling in just as the pool water rushed out.

She steeled herself against the cold damp chill and controlled her panicked breaths. Indecipherable whispers came from the crack in the pool floor. She wasn't alone.

As inexplicable as it was, she felt Jericho Dodd's presence in the pool with her.

When he was alive, they'd called it Jericho's residue, the unseen dread he'd leave behind in his wake. It was somehow in the air now, floating like toxin.

"Help," she screamed, trying again at the ladder, leaping, coming up short.

Her mind surged back to the memory of drowning as a girl, Mr. Passafume's strong hand beating against her back, his soothing voice pleading for her to come back, to come back . . .

Because she *had* gone somewhere. No matter how strenuously Nate and Bridget argued with her, she *had* drowned, and she *had* died, if only for a brief time, and during that time she *had* been somewhere else.

As mysteriously ambiguous as it had been, and still was, she'd experienced *the other side*, where the landscape was unexplainably full of lurid color, with bright-yellow grass and black trees with white leaves and black sand and waves that moved away from the shore, and she saw her nightmare of the Boo Hag, because that was where they lived. And every time Amy returned there at night, every time she had the nightmare, there were more of them over there, roaming that strange land in clusters, as if searching for a door they knew was there but couldn't see.

She heard something above. The iron gate to the pool creaked open, then shut with a loud, spring-locked clang. "Hello," she shouted. "Is somebody there?"

A distorted shadow stretched across the pool, and then it moved. A screeching sound reverberated around the circumference of the pool, like whoever was up there was dragging a heavy, metallic tool across concrete.

"Hello," she said again.

A tall figure squatted at the edge of the pool. "Hey, you good down there?"

Am I good down here? But she said, "I'm okay, but I can't get out. I need help."

"Looks that way, yeah," the male voice said. She sensed a reluctant tremor in his tone, a voice trying to sound deeper than it was.

It wasn't familiar enough to recognize. "Who are you?"

After a beat, he said, "Mitchell. Mitchell McBride."

"Mayor McBride's son?"

His brief laugh made her uncomfortable, like she'd pissed him off, but then he said, "Yeah, that's me." And then, "What have you heard?"

"Heard about what?" she asked, thinking this couldn't get any more awkward.

"About me," he said. "I know everyone is talking. I can hear it through the walls. Through the pipes. Through the ground."

Christ, she thought, having fully gone now from *Get me out* to *Leave me down here.*

"What's the *gossip*?" he asked.

Any normal person would have helped her out of here, no questions asked. She said, "Just that you had to come home early. From college."

"Nervous breakdown?"

"Yeah," she said, hoping that was what he wanted to hear. She'd heard about a nervous breakdown. Mental illness. And she also knew that his parents were doing whatever it took to hide the fact that he was home. She added, "Not that it's anyone's business." She bit her lip, waited. "Find me someone on this island who doesn't have issues, Mitchell, and I'll tell you where the money's buried."

"What money?"

She sighed, breath quavering. "Never mind. A figure of speech." She looked up. "Did you feel the tremor?"

"Yeah," he said. "But it wasn't a tremor. I assumed that's what they were too, like little earthquakes, but that's not what they are."

What else would they be? she thought.

"You know how hard it is to be perfect," his shadow called down to her.

"I can only imagine," she said, knowing damn well that up until the McBrides' only son came home from his junior year of college early because of a rumored on-campus incident, all the islanders had referred to them as the "perfect" family. The perfect mayor husband. The perfect Barbie-doll realtor wife. Mitchell, the perfect son, the straight-A student athlete with magazine-cover-model good looks. She added, stupidly almost, "Nobody's perfect, Mitchell." And felt weird calling him by his name; she knew who he was but had never spoken to him. She felt like she was looking up toward Buffalo Bill in *The Silence of the Lambs.*

"No," he said. "Maybe not. But I'm starting to think I can be."

He'd lost her. "Can be what?" *Just get me out of here.*

"Perfect," he said. "I'm beginning to see things clearly now. I know things I didn't before. I know my purpose."

Just as she was about to ask what that was, he shifted his position and reached a tool of some kind down to her, what he'd been dragging across the concrete, she thought. He lay down alongside the pool and extended a wooden handle down to her, and she grabbed hold.

"You ready?"

"Yeah."

Grunting, he pulled her up until he was able to grip her arm with his other hand and pull her free of the pool. Island air swooshed over her, along with a sense of relief. She lay there for a few seconds on her back, staring at the stars, panting.

"Thank you." When he gave no answer, she rolled to her side to look for him. "Mitchell?"

But he was already outside the fencing around the pool, walking into the darkness between the trees on the far side of her house, with what looked like an axe slung over his shoulder.

C H A P T E R

5
Sheriff Kilbourne

"Have a wonderful day," Blue Bottles had said before Sheriff Lawrence Kilbourne left the vandalized scene atop the bee barges, Reverend Thomas Dodd's severed hand safely concealed inside a Ziploc gallon food storage bag he'd for years kept folded up in the back pocket of his pants just in case of an unexpected evidence situation.

Given the circumstances, the words *have a wonderful day* had lacked Mr. Passafume's typical optimistic luster, and likewise, Lawrence's automatic response of "You too" had fallen flat.

It wasn't thirty seconds later that Deputy Justin Clampus radioed with another pressing matter and the day suddenly got a little worse.

"Sheriff," the young deputy said. "Where are you?"

"Leaving the swamp. What's up?"

"I know you're tied up, sir, but could you swing by Meg Roverson's house on your way back? She's really worried about Johnny."

Shit, thought Lawrence as he started down the bee barge steps. "What's wrong with Johnny? Weren't you just there yesterday?"

"Yes, sir. He could barely get out of bed. Just like some of the others who've been calling in."

"And now?"

"Now he won't come inside," Deputy Clampus said.

"And what's he doing outside?"

"Digging . . . with a shovel."

"You don't say?"

"Watching him as we speak. His hands are bleeding. Meg said he's been out there since yesterday afternoon. Apparently, not long after I left, he got up out of bed and went outside and started digging."

"Okay, fine. Tell Meg I'll be there in twenty minutes."

By the time Lawrence had settled into the canoe and started rowing back across the swamp, the bagged hand behind his seat so he couldn't see it, Blue Bottles had begun cleaning up the mess with a scrub brush and water hose, starting with the word *DIG* on the honey house wall. At this point, Lawrence wasn't sure what he was dealing with—it seemed that the reverend had died from natural causes, although he'd wait for the official report from the island coroner, Dr. Cheevers. Other than the missing hand, there seemed no sign of foul play. But having what was likely the missing hand pinned to the trunk of a tree the morning after made it all the more likely that they were looking at a crime scene. He'd taken his notes and asked his questions and snapped pictures with his iPhone. At which point Blue Bottles had gotten out his own phone and showed him the picture of the honey house door before he'd disassembled what was left of it and started boarding it back up.

The yellow door had been in shambles, busted through the middle, penetrated somehow in a way that made Lawrence think the perpetrator was trying to let something out rather than attempting to get in. But that wasn't what had Blue Bottles worried, and when Lawrence prompted him, the old man had said, "Take a good look at that door, Sheriff. Look at the marks. What's it look like did that kind of damage?"

And now that Lawrence made himself think about it, it was as clear as crystal. "An axe?"

Blue Bottles had put the phone back in his pocket. "Exactly." He nodded at the bagged hand on the decking. "And how do you suppose that hand was taken off?"

Lawrence's answer was to stare at the Spanish moss swaying from the trees, because he wasn't able to verbalize everything going through his mind. The hand had been cleanly cut off. And he'd seen enough axe wounds that fateful Fourth of July day to immediately notice one.

Since the massacre, axes were no longer sold on the island. Rose Bower refused to stock them in her store. Those who had axes either had them from years ago, before Jericho's Fourth of July rampage, or they'd bought them on the mainland. Either way, Mayor McBride, in the months after the bloodbath, had made it a rule that all axes be registered. It might have seemed nonsensical to some, but as Mayor McBride, in only his sixth month on the job, had pointed out, that Fourth of July hadn't been the only example of axe violence in the island's history.

Blue Bottles had said, "And I know that's Reverend Dodd's hand." Before Lawrence could respond, Mr. Passafume said, "Only man on the island I knew wore his wedding ring on his right hand. He switched it over after Samantha died."

Lawrence had nodded, acting as if he'd known that all along, when in fact he only knew it was the reverend's because it was a man's hand and the reverend was missing one.

He made a mental note to call Amy Barnes and let her know he'd found the reverend's hand. She wasn't an officer of the law, but he figured, since she'd come to Reverend Dodd's aid last night, that she deserved to know.

Then Blue Bottles asked, "What happened to the reverend? I saw your emergency lights flashing at his house last night. Along with the ambulance."

Lawrence knew Blue Bottles would keep his mouth shut. "Reverend Dodd passed away last night."

"Passed away, or murdered?"

"I believe he passed away, but we'll know more soon enough."

"Nate been notified?"

"He has," Lawrence said. "I believe he's on his way to the island."

"Poor kid."

"Yeah. Sucks." Noticing how little emotion Blue Bottles was showing upon the news of Reverend Dodd's death, Lawrence said, "But now that I've let that cat out of the bag, I do have a question of you."

"Shoot."

"Last night, when I surveyed the reverend's body, his, uh . . . stump was coated in honey."

"You don't say?"

"Couple weeks ago, you mentioned bottles were stolen from storage. You remember how many?"

"Twelve," he said. "Full case' worth of the newest yield. I haven't even gotten the purity results in. I'm expecting them today."

"Well, the reverend somehow had one of them," said Lawrence. "I know you and Thomas didn't see eye to eye . . ."

"He'd never steal from me," Blue Bottles said flatly. "Whoever stole the jars from me must have given one to him."

And then he dunked his infected stump into it like it was a salve or liquid balm, Lawrence thought, but he said, "Unless he wasn't in his right mind?"

"What are you saying?" Blue Bottles asked.

"Thomas, uh, looked a little worse for wear, like he hadn't been taking care of himself."

There was much more Lawrence would have liked to ask Mr. Passafume regarding his relationship with Reverend Dodd; the two had at one time been friends, if not close. But while some on the island had distanced themselves from Reverend Dodd soon after his younger son was born—because that boy had been wrong from the start—and others had done so after what Jericho had done on that Fourth of July, Mr. Passafume's break with Reverend Dodd had begun even earlier than that. In fact, Lawrence knew—and he was rethinking it now as he approached his cruiser—it had been before Jericho's birth. Lawrence recalled quite clearly Mr. Passafume's reaction—or stringent lack of one—to the news that Samantha Dodd, after years of trying for a second child, was finally with child again. It was as if Blue Bottles had known all along that Jericho Dodd would be different, that he'd be that monstrous, unhuman thing he'd ultimately become.

No, Lawrence thought as he started his car, Jericho hadn't become unhuman; he was what he was from the get-go, and in a way it was his mother who was his first victim, him killing her slowly over nine months and then for good on the day he was born.

CHAPTER

6
Nate

Seventeen Years Before the Sudden Death of Reverend Thomas Dodd

DON'T MAKE ME *hold him,* eight-year-old Nathanial thought as he eyed the crib across the room, his father reaching down to grab the infant that wasn't an infant.

That's what Bridget had said yesterday when she'd first laid eyes on his little brother, Jericho, now almost a week old.

"He's too big to be an infant," Bridget had said. "He's the size of a toddler." Nate had noticed Amy could barely look at Jericho. Bridget, on the other hand, had appeared unfazed, and had muttered, "He's very interesting, Reverend Dodd. Like an infant who isn't an infant."

It was better than the mean things Nate had been calling Jericho in his head since he was born and, honestly, in the months before he was born too, throwing insults at his mother's belly once he'd known she was pregnant, as many miscarriages and stillborn babies as it had taken. *Murderer* was his most common insult, as he knew that Jericho's birth had caused his mother's death, no matter how the reverend tried to sugarcoat it.

Your mother was weak. She'd been unwell for years, Nathanial. And that pregnancy took its toll . . .

Murderer.

All while Nate wondered why he hadn't seen his father cry yet for his dead wife.

Bridget, when Nate had spoken to her about it the day before, had said, "Maybe your father grieves on his own. Alone. Or he's so caught up with the baby," she had continued, "he hasn't had time to grieve."

Maybe that made sense.

When Jericho was born—when his mother *died*—he'd heard, from the room across the house, the unhuman cry upon Jericho's first intake of air. "Like something out of a horror movie," he'd told Bridget and Amy.

Dr. Cheevers and Reverend Dodd had been so secretive immediately after, hurrying that crying thing away and hiding it from everyone for the next five days before finally letting anyone see it.

It, not him, thought Nate. He'd been told that Jericho was a boy. They'd discovered that early on, even before Samantha Dodd had had to endure so many ultrasounds due to Jericho's rapid growth inside her.

And here Nate was, about to hold him for the first time, his father insisting on it.

The infant who wasn't an infant.

The murdering monster.

It made Nate's stomach hurt just thinking about him.

Please, don't make me hold him.

Reverend Dodd, forcing a smile—Nate could tell his father had mixed feelings about Jericho but would never admit it—lifted Jericho from the crib with a grunt and carried him slowly, both arms extended away from his body. "Nate, open your eyes."

Nate wasn't aware that he'd closed them, but when he opened them, there was Jericho, suspended in midair like the reverend was holding a boulder. Nate said, "What do I do?"

"Nothing. I'll rest him there on your legs."

The weight upon his lap was even more than Nate had anticipated. And other than in those first few seconds, when it had wailed like it was an alien, Jericho had never cried.

Weren't babies supposed to cry?

Maybe he and the reverend have a pact, Nate thought. *Thou shalt not cry, thou shalt not grieve.*

Whoever held Jericho never held him for long, Nate noticed throughout the day; they either put him right back down in the crib or pretended to be in a hurry and passed him along to the next person. Some grew pale. Others grew overheated. A few had broken out into coughing fits and immediately had to leave the room. Nate felt pinned to the couch cushion under Jericho's weight. Stuck there beneath his little brother, the biggest baby the doctor had ever seen, ever held, ever delivered.

Murderer.

He had too much hair for an infant, Bridget had said, and she was right. The amount of thick dark hair on Jericho's head was startling; it made him appear older. Downright scary. And the eyes, one brown and the other blue, the way they'd immediately fixed on Nate, had been so terrifying he felt a sudden urge to throw up. He looked away. But even as he looked away, he could still feel Jericho's eyes on him. He could somehow feel Jericho's thoughts, just as he could somehow feel the boy's heartbeat thumping through his legs, and suddenly Nate felt the urge to pee. To vomit. To scream. Terrifying dread. Nate's breaths became short, and he blurted out to the reverend, "Take him. Please. Take him! GET HIM OFF ME!"

CHAPTER

7
Amy

SHE BACKED HERSELF into the corner of the empty swimming pool. The cold tile walls stretched infinitely tall now that the water had vanished into the crevasse in the center of the pool, where dirty water burbled and muddy roots reached up like snakes from the massive ground below.

A hideous voice hissed from the jagged hole. Dig, Amy. Open the door, Amy, and let us in . . .

She couldn't close her eyes. In her nightmares she could never close her eyes.

Long, red, prodding fingers with white fingernails emerged from the crack in the pool. One hand, and then another, and then more of the creature revealed itself, two knobby red wrists connected to two sinewy red arms streaked with meandering blue veins.

No, *Amy pleaded.* No . . .

And then came the hair, the distinct white, stringy hair of the skinless Boo Hag as it climbed into the pool from the earth below.

Open the door and let us in, Amy. Dig . . .

The curtain of dirty white hair could no longer mask the red face and stark white eyes of the Boo Hag as it looked up and grinned.

Dig down deep, Amy, and let us *all* in . . . The horned one is coming . . .

Amy screamed, closed her eyes . . .

* * *

Amy awoke with a gasp of air, kicking at the bedsheets, at first certain the clammy, wet feeling on her skin was from the Boo Hag—too reminiscent of what she'd felt under the swamp water she'd drowned in as a girl—but as the seconds drew on, she realized, like always, it had only been a nightmare.

Another nightmare.

Her nightmare.

Versions of which had plagued her since childhood.

But instead of the Boo Hag emerging from the swamp water or from between the boards of the bee barge or from the honey house itself or from her closet or under the bed, the Boo Hag had come this time from the bottom of her own swimming pool.

She sat up against the headboard to mentally collect herself.

It was 9:05 in the morning; she was usually up by 6:30; she'd either ignored her alarm or had forgotten to set it.

At least her location in this nightmare made more sense, coming on the heels of what had happened inside her pool a few nights ago.

Morning sunlight shone through the bedroom window.

She felt groggy and discombobulated.

She shouldn't have taken the Ambien, but after last night's excitement at the Dodd House, seeing her first dead body since the massacre, she'd known she'd need it. She wouldn't have slept otherwise, and she'd lost so much sleep since the incident in the pool that she'd been desperate for it. Insomnia had become such a problem years ago that the doctor had prescribed the sleeping pills, but of late they'd become a necessary evil. The problem was, the deeper sleep the pills provided brought more vivid nightmares. When she was a girl, the doctor had claimed nightmares were worse for kids with overactive imaginations, at which point her father had laughed and said, "Oh, Amy has that in spades." He had flippantly dismissed her nightmares altogether, insisting that what she'd seen, or claimed to have seen, under the water during the thirty seconds she'd stopped breathing was all in her head, that she was simply a victim of her own imagination.

"She's always been that way," he'd said. "Isn't that right?" He'd turned to Mom for confirmation.

And Mom had said, "Oh, yes, she's always been that way."

Amy had wished *they* could have her nightmares. She'd wished the Boo Hags would visit *them* at night; she'd wished they could see that place on the other side and see how the creatures were mounting and multiplying and looking for ways to get through. She'd see if her parents would change their tune then!

Amy promised herself once again that she'd not take another pill. Promised that last night's would be the final one. But last night she'd had to get Reverend Dodd's mangled stub out of her mind. She wondered if Sheriff Kilbourne ever located the hand.

She'd fallen asleep with part of her manuscript on her lap, and now dozens of pages lay strewn across the bedroom floor. The manuscript was crap anyway. That was why she'd never been able to finish it. It was overflowing with the good stuff about Crow Island. With *only* the good stuff, which was the book her parents had always said she should write because they'd wanted people to come to their island and spend money. In the decade before their murders, they'd gone full throttle into turning Crow Island back into a resort for the wealthy and elite, just like it had been during the club era in the late 1800s and until the Second World War, when the Rockefellers and Morgans and Vanderbilts and Astors and Pulitzers and Goodyears came to relax and play golf and tennis and croquet and drink wine and smoke cigars and dine on fancy food. Her parents had envisioned a return to all of that, with plans of selling their bottles of liquid gold, their famous Barnes Tupelo Honey, by the caseload, starting at $100 a bottle. Owning a bottle of it, they said, would be akin to owning a Rolex (her father had two), or a bottle of the rare twenty-four-year-old Old Sam Bourbon (her father had three). Her mother claimed *their* honey—tupelo itself was rare, but Crow Island tupelo was even more so—was good for the skin, for the bones, and for your overall mood.

Amy rolled her eyes at it all.

Write something that will make this place shine even brighter than it does, they'd say. *Bury all the nonsense you've heard of the past.*

Oh, like slavery, she'd think.

Like the fact that their family had enslaved more individuals than even the original Dodd House did. Like the elite club era her parents so fondly wanted to return to wasn't 80 percent run by the descendants of formerly enslaved people, she'd think. Like 95 percent of Crow Island's Black Geechee culture hadn't been pushed out over the past half century by their family's land grabs and crooked paperwork and good ol' boy handshake deals with her father's *pals.*

And that was only the tip of the iceberg.

Her parents might as well have renamed the island Jim Crow Island, she'd often thought, had often almost told them so, and even more often now wished she had.

People don't want to hear about crime, dear, her mother had said in the days before dying by Jericho's axe.

People want to go where they'll feel safe, her father had said in the days before dying by Jericho's axe.

And all along, Amy—in her head, of course; her twin wouldn't have kept it in her head—was thinking that was bullshit because the island was *built* on crime. The island was built on violence. From the brutality of slavery to bootlegging and murder, enough blood had seeped into the ground to saturate it for centuries. Crow Island had been known for its extraordinary crop yields, producing double, with larger and more robust fruit and vegetables than any of the neighboring islands. Their indigo plants produced unmatched color during the early colonization period. The flowers grew taller, the trees sturdier, and when cotton was king, the fields, unlike anything seen before, would literally turn white. The fishermen claimed fuller nets, with a gluttony of fish and blue crab in the inland streams and coastal rivers. The hunters bragged about the island deer, which they swore wore larger antlers and provided better meat. And the honey, since her family purchased the island in the late 1800s, had been and continued to be—under Mr. Passafume's care—unparalleled.

Was there something in the water? What made the island so potent?

Theories had been bantered about—from unique weather patterns affecting only the easternmost island in the Atlantic to the island's Geechee culture and their centuries-old belief in spirits to the far-fetched theory of blood- and thus nutrient-rich soil—but nothing scientific had ever been proven. But that, she thought now, as she stood from the bed and stretched her arms toward the ceiling, was the actual stuff people cared about.

The creepy unknowns of it all.

The mysteries.

The why . . .

Because that place where the grass was yellow and the leaves were white and the sand was black and the Boo Hags grew in number . . . it was all real.

"And they're coming," she said in a whisper, realizing her broom was on the floor next to her bedroom door. And the door was slightly ajar instead of fully closed; she was sure she'd pulled it tight last night, as she did every night—it was part of her ritual, as was checking to make sure her broom was propped against the wall next to the door, bristles to the floor. And beside it, atop a small wooden stand, she always left her hairbrush and a colander from the kitchen. These items, to her, over time, had become a necessity. Boo Hags were not unique to this island, but like everything else nurtured around Crow Island—what the locals liked to call the Devil's Backbone—Boo Hags and spirits, not unlike the indigo and cotton and honey, seemed to inhabit this place in abundance.

It was why every home, hotel, and business on the island had, somewhere on its facade or porch or front door, the color known as haint blue, because it was believed *that* color, closely resembling the sky or water, kept the island spirits from crossing it. Just as it was believed the best way to stave off a visit from a Boo Hag at night was to leave a broom or hairbrush near the door, because they were easily distracted and infatuated by counting things. The bristles from brooms or brushes—or the colander holes—would keep them occupied, counting, and the hope was that the Boo Hag would still be counting when the sun came up, at which point they'd be unable to return to their borrowed human skin and would burn up in the sunlight.

But the broom on the floor wasn't the only item that had been moved overnight. The hairbrush, she found, was resting just outside the threshold in the hallway, and the colander was upside down on the wooden stand. The window across the room was open a crack. She closed it, locked it, stared at it. Boo Hags, according to legend, could enter a room many ways: through a cracked-open window, through the thin crease below a door, even through keyholes. She turned slowly, surveying her bedroom—Chad's side of the room still untouched and gathering dust—and wondered now if her sluggishness didn't have less to do with a sleeping pill hangover and more to do with an unwelcome overnight visitor.

Last week, Deputy Justin Clampus had stopped her in the grocery cereal aisle and nervously asked her for her opinion on something; they'd gone to school together, and while they'd always been friendly toward one another, they had never been friends, but ever since the tragedy he'd treated her with kid gloves. It was no secret what had happened to Amy as a girl under the bee barge. That was indisputable. As far as whether she'd really seen what she'd seen and felt what she'd felt under the water—and more importantly, had she really died for a short time and come face-to-face with a real Boo Hag?—the first thing Deputy Clampus did in the cereal aisle was make sure Amy knew he believed her. He'd always believed her. He believed in the island spirits. If he had wiped sweat from his brow one more time, Amy might have thought he was in awe of her. He asked her if she'd heard about all the reports of late, of islanders waking up sluggish and foggy headed and disoriented. She'd heard of a few but was intrigued to know more, and he then explained they'd had at least a dozen calls to the station over the past couple of weeks reporting signs of break-ins, signs of disturbances inside bedrooms, things being moved around and out of place, but the commonality that linked them all, Deputy Clampus said, was that the people affected were all so drained of energy they could hardly get out of bed. In Mr. Jacobson's case, he could hardly move until at least an hour after he opened his eyes. Amy didn't know exactly what Clampus was wanting from her other than some confirmation that yes, it sounded like those folks had gotten overnight visits from a Boo Hag. For which he'd thanked her kindly before going on his way. And this was why Amy had been extra vigilant over the past week, making sure her door was closed and the broom, brush, and colander were clearly visible should a Boo Hag make its way in.

Thinking now that one probably had, she instantly felt dirty.

She showered to wake herself up. While she washed her hair, she reasoned that she would have been more tired if a Boo Hag had ridden her. She would have been more drained. She convinced herself that all she was feeling were the effects of the sleeping pill and that if a Boo Hag had gotten inside her room, her defense precautions had stopped it before it was able to climb onto her bed. According to Gullah Geechee folklore, the Boo Hags were mythical vampiric creatures that sneaked into bedrooms at night and climbed atop a sleeping victim to steal their breath and energy, riding on their chest and feeding off their life force. They were depicted as skinless, red-fleshed entities with prominent blue veins and flowing white hair, similar to the hair that "grew" on corpses, which gave credence to the belief that they were vampires from the dead. Amy's nightmares had been consumed by them since she'd drowned in the swamp. Surely she would have known if one had pressed its mouth against hers and sucked her breath out. But just in case, as soon as she got out of the shower and dried off, she brushed her teeth and rinsed with mouthwash, and then she did it all again, brushing harder and swishing harder and spitting into the sink until her mouth was dry.

Back in her bedroom, she gathered the loose manuscript pages from the floor, added them to the rest of the manuscript resting on the bed. For the first time, she considered disregarding the book altogether. She'd guilted herself into writing it in the first place, diving in only after her parents had been murdered. In her mind, writing it was a form of penance for not missing them as much as she missed Bridget.

She needed to get back to writing for herself, like she had when she was a girl, when it didn't take bravery to be imaginative.

She put her contacts in and dressed in her running clothes, all the while thinking . . .

Dig . . .

And of the dozens of holes in Reverend Dodd's backyard, thinking . . .

Dig, Amy . . . Dig deep down into the island dirt and tell some ugly truths.

She carried her manuscript into the kitchen, tossed the entire thing into the garbage can, and felt immediately better.

She tied her running shoes and headed for the door.

A shiver coursed through her upon seeing her dead husband's cell phone on the counter. As it did every morning of late, it gave her pause. The urge to plug the phone in and charge it had never been stronger. Yesterday she'd gone as far as plugging the charger into the phone before stopping and placing the phone back down on the counter. What good would it do?

Amy picked up the phone.

Dig . . .

She started toward the outlet but then replaced the phone on the counter, facedown. Before she could second-guess herself, she opened the screen door and stepped out into an overly humid Crow Island morning, intent on outrunning her latest nightmare.

But the air was thick, and not just with humidity. There was also the hint of something disturbingly familiar.

She ran faster, in a futile attempt to outrun that too. And then her cell phone buzzed with an incoming call.

She stopped to answer it.

"Amy, it's Sheriff Kilbourne."

"Yes, Sheriff," she said, breathing heavily into the phone, thinking for sure this had to do with Reverend Dodd. "What can I do for you?"

"Are you busy?"

"Just out on my run."

"Would you mind running on over to the Roversons' house? Might need your help with something."

C H A P T E R

8
Sheriff Kilbourne

ONLY ONCE IN his career had Sheriff Kilbourne added bourbon to his coffee, and that had been the morning after the massacre, when he'd gone to bed shaking and rolled out of bed the next morning shaking worse.

But now, as he stood in Meg and Johnny Roversons' backyard watching twenty-eight-year-old Johnny dig into the ground beside their unattached garage like his life depended on it, maniacal almost, to the point where Meg had already gone inside crying because she couldn't watch him anymore, Lawrence needed *something* to help calm his nerves.

Minutes ago, he'd sent Deputy Clampus back to the station to pull, for the first time since its existence, the registry of men and women who owned an axe.

"And do what with it?" Deputy Clampus had asked.

"Check the blades for blood," Lawrence had told him, thinking *Specifically Reverend Dodd's blood*, and then he'd added, "And make a list of all . . . these people while you're at it."

"These people, sir?"

"All the ones like Johnny here, who've called us over the past three weeks worried about . . ."

And the rest went unsaid and assumed, because he couldn't bring himself to say *the ones who thought they'd been ridden by the hag.*

Deputy Clampus hurried off. It was taking all of Lawrence's willpower now, after the night and morning he'd had, to not go inside with Meg Roverson and steal a shot of the Old Sam he'd seen next to their toaster; he was lost as far as how to deal with Johnny, who was shirtless and sweating and digging into a hole that was now long enough to fit a car and nearly as deep. It was clear Johnny wasn't even taking bathroom breaks, because the crotch of his jeans was soiled. Every time Lawrence made a move to talk to him, Johnny made as if to hit him with the shovel, his eyes glazed over from exhaustion but fueled by an internal fire only Johnny could explain.

Lawrence looked at his shaking hands, and he feared Clampus had noticed earlier, which was no good thing. As sheriff and fire chief, he was supposed to be a pillar of strength. But he'd been shaking since he left the swamp. Truth be told, he'd been shaking since he got home last night from the Dodd House. You'd think that by now, after so many years on the job, he would react better to turmoil, better certainly than he had during the massacre eight years ago, when he had been near panic and had frozen under pressure in that four- to five-second window he could have shot Jericho Dodd and didn't.

Why was he even here?

Johnny Roverson wasn't harming anyone but himself, aside from freaking his wife out, but it wasn't like this was a crime. Although the words Meg had said to Lawrence as soon as he arrived—and he could see their truth—rang in his ear: *The more he digs, the crazier he gets, Sheriff.*

Lawrence thought of his family. Like this morning, when they'd told him goodbye before school, his wife and son—David a kindergartener, Tina the principal—kissing his cheeks simultaneously, one on each side, making a sandwich of his squished face. The thought of it now helped right his ship. But last night he'd tossed and turned until sunup, even after he'd made that call to Nathanial Dodd. Even after Tina had scooted over and held him, sliding her hand down toward the lining of his boxers, his hand gently catching her wrist to stop it. Their sex life had gone to a new level after David had come along, which seemed the opposite of what he'd heard would happen after a kid arrived. He'd never dug deep into the whys of that newfound intimacy, thinking if he brought it up that bubble might burst, but this wasn't something that could be so easily remedied. And when she'd asked if this was about finding the reverend's body, he'd shaken his head on his sweat-drenched pillow and said, "I don't know. Just some thread I can't seem to pull. Some thread I can't even yet see, Tina." To which she'd fallen asleep with her cheek to his chest, him running his fingers through her raven-colored hair that only in the past year had begun to show strands of gray.

Lawrence shouted across the yard, "You ready for a break yet, Johnny?"

Johnny didn't so much as flinch. If anything, the intensity of his shoveling increased.

A text came through on Lawrence's cell phone.

It was Clare from dispatch: *You done at the Roversons yet?*

In a few, he sent back. *What's up?*

Text bubbles percolated on the phone screen while she either typed or was thinking hard about what to say, and then: *Not sure. Got a call from Easy Perkins. Said she hadn't seen Mayor McBride in a few days. Or Beverly. Or the son, for that matter.*

Lawrence responded: *They're on the mainland for a week. Chip texted me a couple days ago. Said they were taking family time.*

He thought that was it, but Clare texted back, him wishing, when she had so much to say, that she'd just call.

Wouldn't he normally get someone to water their flowers? Easy said they usually do.

None of our business, he responded, thinking it was none of Easy's business either. *Maybe they forgot.*

Easy went over there.

Of course she did, he thought. He typed: *Why?*

Because she's Easy.

Clare Barnett tended to be long-winded. Every story, God love her, took twice as long as it should, and she left her most important thoughts dangling, not so much out of an inclination for unnecessary suspense but out of fear of verbalizing what was really on her mind.

Lawrence wrote back: *And?*

Clare responded: *She swears there's a footprint on the porch that looks like blood.*

Christ, Lawrence thought. Easy Perkins might be the island's gossip mill, or at least the grease that kept that wheel turning—it was part of the reason for her long-ago nickname—but as a retired nurse and one who'd worked day and night helping clean up from that day eight years ago, she knew enough about what dried blood looked like to make Lawrence feel uneasy all over again.

He texted back: *I'll check it out when I can.*

He pocketed his phone and heard footsteps to his left.

Amy Barnes hadn't been kidding when she said she'd run over, though he hadn't thought it would be literally. But while many on the island didn't own cars and most used electric golf carts to get around, Amy Barnes could probably outrun any of them.

She was barely breathing hard. "What's wrong, Sheriff?" she asked, but as she watched Johnny go at the ground with the shovel, it was clear she'd quickly figured it out.

Lawrence said, "Yesterday we got a call from Meg. She was scared to death because Johnny wouldn't get out of bed. We would have said it was more of a doctor's issue if we hadn't already gotten several calls like this over the past couple weeks. When we got here, not only could Johnny not get out of bed, he could barely move. Couldn't talk. All we got out of him was his eyes flicking back and forth. He looked scared to death, Amy."

"And the other calls you've gotten?" Amy asked. "Deputy Clampus mentioned them to me the other day in the grocery store. Are we thinking they got visits from a Boo Hag?"

The sheriff nodded, sighed in relief, glad she'd said it so he wouldn't have to.

Amy watched him for a few seconds, and they seemed to have a silent conversation as to why he'd called her over here. Amy Barnes, because of her childhood experience in the swamp, was about as close to an expert on such matters as they had on the island.

Amy approached Johnny and the hole he was standing in. He tossed dirt over his shoulder, and while Lawrence couldn't hear exactly what she was saying to Johnny, it was clear he'd heard her, because after only a few seconds, his pace began to slow, and after a minute he'd stopped altogether.

Amy stepped down into the hole, and she and Johnny faced each other in conversation. And while her back was to Lawrence and he couldn't see her expression, he saw clear fear on Johnny's face as he spoke. Johnny then dropped the shovel, the handle stained with the blood from his busted, blistered hands. Amy stepped out of the hole first and helped Johnny out next, careful to clutch his elbow and not his damaged hands. By then Meg had emerged from the house—she must have been watching from the window—and although she was still crying, a hint of hope touched her face as she walked her husband toward the patio door, telling him she'd get those hands bandaged up and thank God and we're gonna get you some food and rest, Johnny, and inside the door they went.

Amy waited until the door closed and said to Lawrence, "He was definitely visited by one. Or by something."

"But for him to be practically paralyzed yesterday, and then he goes and does this?" Lawrence gestured toward the massive hole in the backyard.

Amy seemed reluctant to divulge what had been discussed between them, like it was some kind of client-doctor privilege, but then she said, "He told me two nights ago, which is when the visit must have occurred, that he had a horrible nightmare. He felt like something the weight of a car was on his chest. He couldn't breathe. When he opened his eyes, he saw a devilish creature riding him. That's what he called it." A shift seemed to come across Amy's face. "A skinless creature with red flesh and blue veins and stringy white hair. It was small, he said, no more than five feet tall, which surprised him because of how heavy it was." Amy made eye contact with Lawrence, as if to hammer her next point home. "It spoke to him, Sheriff Kilbourne. After it took its mouth off his, after it had drained him to near nothing, it . . ."

"It what, Amy?"

"It leaned down toward his ear and said . . . *Dig*."

Lawrence felt a jolt run through the core of him as he recalled what had been written on the honey house wall. He said, "We found the reverend's hand." He should have stopped there but didn't. "Blue Bottles found it this morning, nailed to the bark of a tupelo tree outside the honey house. The word *dig* was written on the honey house wall. *Don't let the hag ride ya* on the bee barge railing. And then . . ." He paused as emotion hit him like a gut punch. He bit his lip, but his eyes filled with moisture all the same. "And on the decking of the bee barge, right outside the honey house, someone had written, in blood and twisted Spanish moss, the word *Jericho*."

"Jericho?"

"Yes," he said, "Jericho." Thinking, now that it dawned on him, that the message had been written right around the place where, at least a dozen times in Jericho's short life, he'd found that boy standing and staring at the honey house door and he'd either had to coax him down himself or call for Nathanial or Thomas Dodd to come get him, with Blue Bottles watching from afar because he always seemed to have a special, unexplained aversion to the boy.

To the man-child.

To that *thing*.

When Amy finally responded, a clear quaver of anxiety masked her voice. "What does this have to do with Jericho?"

"I don't know," he said, but he felt she had an idea, and he did too, because over the past twenty-four hours, at the Dodd House and the swamp and, shit, right here and right now in the Roversons' backyard, he could feel him. As little sense as it made, he could feel Jericho just like he'd been able to feel his presence in a room back then, without even seeing him.

"It's dread," Amy said. "Anxiety. I can feel it all over again, Sheriff."

"Yeah," he said, eyeing the nearby trees, the Spanish moss swaying.

"I felt it in the pool the other night. After the tremor."

"What happened in the pool?"

"Nothing," she said. "Never mind." And just when he thought she was going to drop it, and just as Deputy Clampus could be seen approaching up the driveway, returning with papers in his left hand, Amy told him what had happened to her in her pool the other night, how a sinkhole had opened while she was swimming and nearly swallowed her, how she'd been trapped until Mitchell McBride came to help her out.

"You sure it was Mitchell McBride?"

"I'm positive. Why?"

"Because Chip and Beverly told me they were going on a vacation and they were taking Mitchell with them."

"Unless I'm seeing things, he stayed behind," she said. "But that isn't all."

Deputy Clampus came forward and handed Lawrence two papers. "Sorry, Ms. Barnes. Didn't mean to interrupt."

"Justin, call me Amy."

"Okay," he said, breathing heavily, despite the fact that he'd driven over. To Lawrence, he said, with a nod toward the papers, "The lists you asked for."

"What lists?" Amy asked.

"List of those registered to own an axe," Lawrence said. "And the other"—he showed her—"a list of all those who recently had experiences at night similar to Johnny here."

Amy took a picture of the list with her phone.

Lawrence handed that list to Deputy Clampus. "Go house by house and see if any of the others on that list started . . . acting like Johnny."

"Digging?" Clampus asked.

"Yes, digging."

Amy looked at the picture on her phone. "I'll take the first half if you want the rest?"

Deputy Clampus said, "Done." And went on his way.

Amy asked Lawrence, "Can I see the other list. The axes?" Lawrence handed it to her. She quickly studied it, handed it back, and said, "Mitchell McBride isn't on there."

"Why would he be?"

"Because that's what he used to pull me out of the pool," she said. "The handle of an axe."

CHAPTER

9
Nate

AFTER A FOUR-HOUR drive from Atlanta the next morning, Nate caught the 10:00 AM Crow Island ferry out of Savannah. If Duff Hollaway was still in charge of the ferry service, his only other options getting to the island would have been noon and four, and as much as he dreaded his return, waiting would have been harder. Plus the morning ferry was typically the least crowded, and he wanted to hold off being noticed as long as he could.

With the addition of a few flecks of gray in his hair and beard, Duff looked about the same as he had when Nate left. If Duff had recognized him when he'd punched his ticket and boarded the double-decker catamaran-style boat, Nate hadn't noticed. Nate might still feel eighteen, but he no longer looked it. His face had filled out and he'd put on twenty pounds of muscle. And although his hair had begun to recede, he kept it short enough to comb with his hand, knowing he'd never grow it long and slick it back like his father, the look that had made him appear debonair and unapproachable, especially at those times Nate, in his childhood, had most needed to approach him. Ultimately, anything Nate had at one time wanted to say to his father had gone unsaid, and now it was too late.

Hard to mend broken fences when one side was gone.

Nate stood alone on the second deck against the railing overlooking the blue choppy water, pushing thoughts of his father aside for those from last night at his apartment and of how abruptly he'd left it with Lauren, who had only been trying to help. With anything. The driving, the funeral arrangements. Mainly, she wanted to help him through his grief.

If that was even what he was feeling.

He'd loved his father, but he hadn't liked him so often that it was tough now to pinpoint whether he was experiencing sadness over losing his only remaining parent or anger at having his life so suddenly disrupted. Bottom line was that Nate had never loved his father like he had his mother. Maybe that was why he hadn't cried yet; he'd used up all those tears when his mother died giving birth to Jericho, the second child she'd wanted so badly and for so long that it literally killed her.

Last night, when Lauren had spoken to him so affectionately in his apartment doorway, practically begging him to let her in—into his apartment, inside his head—what had he said so curtly?

I'll be fine. I'll be back in a few days; we can talk then. For now, I think you should go . . .

That's how he'd left it with the young woman who'd driven his drunk ass home. The woman he ate lunch with every day in his classroom. The woman he'd for the past two years wanted to ask out on a date, to maybe even marry one day, which was crazy because he'd never even kissed her and she'd had a steady boyfriend, but there it was.

That's how his mind worked, fast-forward and faster-forward.

Anything to keep it from going in reverse.

Back to the past.

He could have at least let her inside his apartment, but that would have only led to more questions about his meeting with the principal that morning, about his family, him stumbling through answers whose roots were tangled into one big, convoluted knot. Answers that might one day lead him to opening up about what had happened back then on Crow Island, the horrors that *really* kept him up at night.

Nate closed his eyes just as a dolphin jumped from the water in the distance, but the hurt look on Lauren's face stayed in his mind. How she'd backed down the hallway with moisture in her eyes, slowly at first, giving him an extra beat to reconsider because their night wasn't supposed to go like this, as if any second he'd say *I'm sorry, don't go*, before she'd turned away and walked fast toward the stairwell, him just watching her go.

Nate opened his eyes to the sound of seagulls. Waves rolled and foamed. Fellow passengers placed hands to their heads, either to keep their hats on or their hair from getting too windblown. The wind was always stronger near the Crow Island docks, which were visible now in the distance, shimmering above the glistening waves like a mirage. The lighthouse soared toward wispy clouds, overlooking Crow Island Sound like a watchtower. Waves pounded the run of boulders at the Rocks, water rising in clouds of windblown mist upon impact. Fishermen stood at the docks, poles hoisted, and even more lined the shoreline of the Sands, poles slanted out toward the water. In the background, the eastern ridge of the island jutted up from the sand dunes like a curved backbone, the towering trees watching like sentinels.

He'd dreaded his return but also missed the island. Minutes later the ferry coasted toward the dock, where a smattering of islanders awaited their arrival.

Nate had packed for only a few days and had everything inside the same backpack he used for school. He pulled his *Atlanta Braves* baseball cap down over his brow, hoping to avoid any immediate recognition. He descended the steps to the main level of the ferry and followed the two dozen passengers to the unloading zone, strategically waiting so he'd be the last to depart. Without looking at Duff, Nate nodded and said, "Have a wonderful day."

Duff grinned kindly. "You too, Mr. Dodd. And welcome back. My condolences."

"Thank you, sir."

So much for obscurity. It was a small island.

As Nate stepped out onto the dock, the breeze felt suddenly thick with something other than island humidity, something toxic yet so noticeable it caused his heart to race.

. . . give it a minute.

It was what they'd say about Jericho after he left any room—*Give it a minute.* For his residue to wisp away like invisible fog swirls.

Nate felt dread, closed his eyes until it passed.

It was nothing but a memory, that feeling in the air, just his senses playing tricks.

But then dogs started barking, all over the island, first a few and then what sounded like dozens, and then hundreds, a cacophony of noise that sent birds scattering from the island trees. Nobody else seemed fazed by any of it, which made him question whether he was really seeing and hearing this at all. He hadn't eaten since lunch the day before.

But why was everyone around him grabbing hold of the ferry's rails as if they were bracing for a collision?

Behind him, Duff said, "Brace yourself, Nate."

Right before the wooden planks beneath his feet started to sway.

And the ground began to shake.

CHAPTER

10
Amy

AFTER LEAVING THE Roversons' backyard, Amy had gone into the rest of her morning run with a newfound urgency, and so far she'd checked off every name on the list she'd split with Deputy Clampus as a positive.

Every man and woman on the list was outside digging. Debbie Kane was digging up the landscaping in front of her house. Will Paxton was digging so close to the foundation of his house that Amy wondered if he was planning to burrow under it. Tate Jacobs was in a small bulldozer, cleaving up massive amounts of soil beside his shed, including parts of his flower garden. Laura Lanning was sitting exhaustedly on her front stoop, elbows on her knees, staring out toward the street as Amy ran by. Amy hadn't stopped to talk to any of the others but felt the need to at least slow down and ask if Laura was okay. She looked like she'd just gone ten rounds in the boxing ring and lost.

Laura had answered, "Yeah, I suppose. Just taking a break."

"From what?" Amy asked, although it was clear enough from the long, trench-like hole running parallel to the walkway leading to the house along with the two shovels leaning inside it. Laura had been digging for days, Amy thought, after noticing a series of large holes leading around the house toward her gazebo.

But when Laura had said, "Digging," she said it like Amy had asked a stupid question, and maybe she had. Laura might as well have added *What else would I be doing?*

At which point Amy had moved on, fearing as she ran that the entire island was losing their collective mind. She slowed to a walk when she heard her phone sound with a text message from Deputy Clampus.

How's it going?

Amy replied: *So far every one of them is out digging.*

Same, he sent back. *Just heard from the sheriff that Johnny's break didn't last long. He's back out digging.* And then: *I think the island's gone crazy.*

Agreed, she sent. *I have one more house to go . . . Mr. Baines.*

Let me know thanks

Will do

Amy knew her parents would roll over in their graves if they knew she'd sold the island years ago. She loved the island and never wanted to leave it but had wanted nothing to do with the owning of it, so within months of her parents' and sister's funeral, she'd sold the island to the state of Georgia—who'd wanted to buy the land from her parents and grandparents for decades anyway—for a million dollars and with two stipulations: one, that their family's tupelo honey business go directly to Mr. Passafume, and two, that a long-overdue Crow Island Welcome Center be constructed on the three acres of land facing the ferry docks. On the same day she signed the island over to the Georgia governor, Amy had handed him the ideas and plans she'd drawn up of exactly what she wanted the welcome center to look like, which was basically an interactive museum. As promised that day, they'd broken ground on the two-million-dollar facility a year later, and it was completed nine months after that. Amy had been running the welcome center's day-to-day goings-on ever since.

Now, at twenty-six, when most of her peers were worried about careers and cars and rent, Amy never had to work another day in her life, yet work, to help her cope, was all she did. As she ran down Second Street, she knew her work was about to get a badly needed facelift. The island deserved to have certain truths to come out, certain truths to finally be written and revealed, because as crazy as the notion sounded, after this past week and with all the digging she saw now, she knew the island was fighting back somehow.

And that's what all this was about.

She ran the last three blocks of Second Street with her phone in hand, and when she reached Darryl Baines's house, she found him shirtless and digging as relentlessly as Johnny Roverson, but in his neighbor's yard, with his neighbor, Fernanda Gomez, screaming at him and threatening to call Sheriff Kilbourne. Darryl Baines seemed to be completely ignoring her until he suddenly stopped, leaned against his shovel, and shouted, "I can't stop, Mrs. Gomez. I gotta dig. And you should be digging too."

Mrs. Gomez stood with hands on hips, still fuming, it seemed, until she reached out a hand and said, "Hand me that extra shovel, then."

To Amy's astonishment, Darryl grabbed a second shovel from the grass to his right, walked it over, and politely handed it to her.

Just as Mrs. Gomez started digging, adding to the hole in her backyard that Darryl had already begun, the island started shaking.

And in the distance, the ferry had just docked.

CHAPTER

11
Sheriff Kilbourne

"STAY BACK," SHERIFF Lawrence Kilbourne said to Easy Perkins as she began to cross the road toward Mayor McBride's house, tying the belt of her cherry-red cotton bathrobe as she approached, undeterred. He said, "I got this."

She continued across the sand-gravel that made up most of the roads on the island like she knew he wouldn't stop her. If not for what Amy had said about Mitchell McBride, he would have considered this a wild-goose chase anyway. Although he wished she'd pull the bathrobe together tighter—he didn't need to see the black lingerie beneath it. Made him wonder who might be in the house across the street with her; he doubted she typically wore that outfit to bed. He and Easy were both Crow Island lifers, roughly the same age, and he'd had a crush on her when she was in eighth grade, but she was also a widow since the day of the massacre, when Richard, her husband of a decade, had been slain in the middle of Bull Street, heroically trying to block Jericho Dodd's progress toward the crowd.

She must have read his mind and fastened her robe as they approached the veranda to Mayor McBride's McMansion. She pointed toward the footprint. "Look like blood to you?"

The rust-colored, clearly ridged print—showing all but the heel of what was most likely a tennis shoe—sure as heck looked like blood.

"And look," she said, pointing toward the house now. "The front door's cracked open."

Sheriff Kilbourne knocked on the screen door, called through the mesh. "Mayor? Chip? Beverly?"

"I thought you said they went to the mainland," Easy said.

"I did."

"Then why are you calling out their names?"

Why are you still here? he thought, brushing his nose up to the screen mesh for a clearer look. The front door swayed even more open, like the unseen had just invited them in. Or maybe it had just been his breath.

"Their son came home from college early," said Easy.

"So I've heard."

"Had a nervous breakdown right in the middle of campus."

"Heard that too."

"Well?"

"Well what?"

She peered through the screen along with him. "It ain't right, Lawrence. The McBrides and their being embarrassed by it all."

Lawrence stepped inside the mayor's house and told Easy to stay outside. The modern home was high ceilinged and airy, with a front room that soared toward a balcony railing at the second floor. A ceiling fan spun above, something he thought they would have turned off upon their departure. Something in the air made him uneasy.

The screen door opened and closed, and there stood Easy Perkins.

"Jesus Christ, Easy. I told you to stay outside."

"And I told you something's not right."

"There's nothing to worry about."

"That why you pulled your gun?"

"Stay here." He made his way into the kitchen. The counters were messier than he would have thought, with them having a cleaning service and all—the sandwich bread left open next to a package of bologna and a jar of dill pickles. He entered the dining room and then the master bedroom, finding everything vacant, as expected, the bed made, as expected, and nothing, aside from the odd, earthy stench, out of the ordinary.

"Lawrence . . . in here."

Goddammit, he thought, stepping back out into the great room, following Easy's voice toward the hallway he assumed led to more bedrooms. Specifically, he thought, as he closed in on the first one to his left—the stench had grown stronger—where their son Mitchell must sleep.

Easy waved him on.

Lawrence said, "I'm about to cuff you, Easy, if you don't back out of my way."

She raised her hands as if surrendering.

He entered the bedroom and found a mess of ripped carpet and torn-up floorboards, discarded pieces of cabinetry and nails and tack strips and tools strewn about, all surrounding a bed that appeared recently slept in.

"It's the boy's room," Easy said from behind him.

"Yeah," he said in acknowledgment. "I figured." He closed in on the neighboring bathroom, the door propped open wide by a toilet leaking water from the base. All the destruction inside the bedroom had come from the bathroom; not only were the sink, toilet, and cabinet missing but a giant hole now resided in the floor, which was torn down to the skeletal joists and boards below. Next to the hole in the floor rested a jar of honey, nearly empty, with a yellow sticker dot on the glass, which told Lawrence this was one of Mr. Passafume's missing jars and made him wonder if Mitchell McBride had been the honey thief.

Dogs started barking outside, at first a few, then many. And then like clockwork, Lawrence thought, pausing to listen, came the sound of birds fleeing from trees.

"Here we go again." Easy braced herself in the door's threshold.

The house started to shake, as did the ground beneath them. Three to four seconds was all it lasted before everything settled again.

"They're getting closer together," Easy said.

"Yup," Lawrence muttered, somewhat immune to it now and mostly focused on the bathroom floor. He inched closer, the earthy smell making more sense to him now as he peered down into the hole, into the crawl space, into the wormy soil beneath the house.

Inside the muddy hardpack was the perfectly indented outline of a large tool, which appeared to have been embedded there for who knew how long.

Just as Lawrence was telling himself it couldn't be—that perfectly visible outline of a blade and long handle—Easy, who again stood by his shoulder, said, "That was an axe down there."

Lawrence finally holstered his gun, did his best to shrug off the anxiety coursing through his system. "Yeah . . . it was."

Down there in the mud.

Same shape as the one used by Jericho Dodd eight years ago.

CHAPTER

12

Eight Years Before the Sudden Death of Reverend Thomas Dodd

PORTION OF THE ***interview with Rose Bower, conducted by Sheriff Kilbourne in the days after Crow Island's Fourth of July massacre:***

Rose: *Go on, spit it out, Lawrence. Ask me what you came here to ask me. Why I sold a ten-year-old an axe.*

Sheriff Kilbourne: *Yes, ma'am. Especially after what was reported he'd said the morning of in the town square.*

Rose: *What? About the Boo Hags and the bees and Island of Horns?*

Sheriff Kilbourne: *Yes.*

Rose: *Because I didn't hear him say it. That was Mr. Hanratty, and we all know if he grew a third ear, that one would probably have a hearing aid in it too. But I sold it to him because that's what we do here at Rose's Hardware. We sell goods. The boy had cash. And he said it was for his daddy. Wasn't the first time he come in here to purchase a tool or a fishing rod. But what's that saying about hindsight?*

Sheriff Kilbourne: *That it's twenty-twenty.*

Rose: *That it's a son of a bitch, Lawrence. But let me now turn the tables on you. Are you or are you not glad, even just a little bit, that that boy is dead and buried? See, you're afraid to answer. How about this: Are you surprised by what Jericho Dodd did?*

Sheriff Kilbourne: *Are you?*

Rose: *No. And now that I've had a few days to think about it, there's not one of us here on the island who shouldn't have seen it coming.*

Sheriff Kilbourne: *Up until two days ago, Jericho Dodd had no record of violence.*

Rose: *And every tree branch is assumed sturdy until it snaps in a storm. Let's stop beating around Robin Hood's barn and get to the root of the matter.*

Sheriff Kilbourne: *What, that you're somehow interviewing me now?*

Rose: *Well, I did used to change your diapers, Lawrence, but no. Have you not noticed the calm?*

Sheriff Kilbourne: *What calm?*

Rose: *Since the tragedy. The lack of breeze. The calmness in the waves at the Rocks, and at the Sands, and at the docks? In the trees? And in the cemetery. In the tides. The calm after the storm, Sheriff.*

Sheriff Kilbourne: *What he did was no storm.*

Rose: *Sure it was. One that had been building for ten years. The sense of unease on the island that started the instant that boy was born. And the size he was? Those two-different-colored eyes. Ones that never seemed to look at you straight but worked double hard at looking straight* into *you. Be honest with me. Now that that boy is dead and buried, do you finally feel the calm?*

Sheriff Kilbourne: *I do.*

Rose: *Then why are we here talking about that axe?*

CHAPTER

13
Nate

Unlike his fellow passengers, Nate hadn't anticipated the three-second tremor and nearly went down on the ferry's plankway.

As soon as it ended, the rest of the islanders went about their business, as if earthquakes were commonplace on Crow Island. Nate felt dizzy under an aggressive sun. He moved aside as a man inside a small bulldozer navigated the ferry's off-ramp. Down the walkway, a middle-aged woman in a flannel shirt—her hands were dirty, as if she'd been gardening—pushed a wheelbarrow full of at least a dozen shovels toward what looked to be a newly constructed Crow Island Welcome Center.

As Nate walked the gangway, he stared down at the wooden planks, at the water and rocks visible through the cracks, and found himself stepping on every third board, just as he had as a boy, his stupid childhood way of avoiding crashing through. It was Trevor Sims who'd told him that every third board was sturdy. It was nonsense, but he'd started doing it anyway. Trevor had been one of the first slain by Jericho on that Fourth of July day, his head nearly severed on the corner of Main and Bull Streets just as the fireworks started. Nate shook the memory; he hadn't seen Trevor get struck, but he'd been close enough in the crowd to hear Mrs. McGivney's scream, and his mind had instantly gone to Bridget. The parade had just gone through. He'd been on his way back from concessions with an ice cream in each hand, chocolate for Bridget, vanilla for him, hurrying at first through the crowd with the ice creams, before the multitude of screams started and he dropped both cones and ran toward where he'd left Bridget near the front of the crowd on Bull Street.

Nate passed the woman pushing the wheelbarrow of shovels and heard a snippet of her conversation with the balding gentleman beside her, who, Nate noticed, had his right hand wrapped in bandages. He heard her say something about *They're happening more frequently now. What do you think it means?*

Nate assumed she was talking about the tremor. Another wave of dizziness came and went. He needed to eat. He was nauseous from a hangover and needed to get his feet on steady ground. Blurriness touched the edges of his vision. As he approached the welcome center, he contemplated sitting down for a minute on one of the benches.

Lauren had tried to get him to eat something last night, but he hadn't felt like eating. He'd been too abrupt with her. He made a mental note to text her and apologize.

No sooner had he taken his final step off the planks and onto the concrete surrounding the welcome center than a female voice spoke his name. "Nate? Nathanial Dodd?"

He looked up to his left. His legs turned to Jell-O. *Bridget?* Dizziness hit him full force. He dropped to his knees, stared up, saw her eyes, the curtain of wheat-colored hair.

"Nate . . ."

Could have sworn he saw a red bird, the size of a crow, circling the blue sky above her.

CHAPTER

14
Amy

IT HADN'T BEEN Amy's plan to meet Nathanial Dodd at the welcome center.

But after seeing the ferry dock, she'd found herself approaching the unloading passengers, walking faster when she saw the last man step off the ferry, baseball cap pulled low and backpack hanging from one shoulder, stepping on every third board like young Nate Dodd had always done. His confident walk and athletic gait hadn't changed. He'd filled out, in a healthy way. Amy had considered continuing on her run, if only to delay the awkward moment she knew would come when they crossed paths, but before she could stop it the words were out of her mouth.

"Nate? Nathanial Dodd?"

She hadn't given a thought to who he at first might think *she* was, with her running shoes and leggings, which had been Bridget's daily attire back then, while Amy had always dressed in baggier, less revealing clothes, when underneath it all their bodies had always been identical. In hindsight, it had been cruel calling out his name without warning.

Nate was out only for a few seconds before he tried to lean up on his elbows.

"I'm sorry," Amy said as she helped him to a sitting position. "I'm . . ."

"I know," he said, obviously embarrassed, quick to his feet as the crowd pinched closer. "It's just at first . . ." He trailed off, looked away, said to the onlookers, "I'm fine." He brushed himself off and said to Amy, "Thanks. I've rarely seen you without glasses."

"I finally got contacts," she said, walking Nate away from the crowd and toward where the sidewalk channeled to Bull Street, the main thoroughfare on the island. While Bull Street had been in existence since antebellum times, the current gridded pattern of streets, running parallel and perpendicular, north-south to east-west, all crossing in picturesque, Savannah-like town squares dotted by live oaks, hadn't been lain down until the 1920s. After a block of walking in silence, Nate said, "You mind if we veer off into the woods?" He looked paranoid, which wasn't like the Nate she'd known.

She attempted to break the tension. "What, you planning on abducting me?"

He grinned, didn't look at her—in fact, he was looking everywhere *but* at her—and said, "No, Amy."

As if she'd needed an answer to her stupid attempt at sarcasm. Nate had always said Bridget's sarcasm was one of the many things he loved about her, but sarcasm was one of the many things Amy, through grief, had grown into, finding herself, over time, not trying to be like her dead sister but picking up what little pieces she could along the way to never completely lose her, and *that*—her naivety and willingness to change and adapt and be strong—had been what her late husband Chad had most loved about her. As he'd often told her in their two years of marriage.

Like a turtle slowly coming out from beneath its shell, he'd say.

"Sure," she finally said to Nate, and as they veered off into the trees, it dawned on her why he'd suggested they move from Bull Street—they'd been within eyesight of Rose's Hardware on the corner of Bull and Winchester, where Jericho bought the axe before his killing spree. It wasn't really woods they were approaching, just what they'd always called taking the side roads, through the scattered trees between the gridded streets.

"Sorry about that back there," he said. "Just caught me off guard seeing you. I figured we'd . . . run into each other, just didn't think—"

"It would be the instant you stepped off the ferry?"

"That, yeah."

"I wasn't stalking you," she said.

That grin again. "That's not what I meant."

She said, "I was on my morning run and saw the ferry coming in."

"And thought you'd give me a heart attack?" Before she could respond, he said, "Kidding."

And that's how she'd preferred to remember Nate Dodd, as a kidder, like he'd been as a boy, and not who he'd started to become after his mother died.

"I've never passed out like that," he said as they crossed Benson Street and reentered the trees on the other side. "Just got lightheaded. Haven't had much of an appetite."

"I know the feeling." Amy had dropped twenty pounds after her family was killed, unable to get much food down during those initial months of grief.

"I assume you . . . felt that back there?" Nate asked.

"The earthquake?"

"Yeah, that," Nate said. "I lived on this island for eighteen years, and in Georgia ever since. I don't recall ever feeling one. How often do those occur?"

"Once a month," she said, "on average. They never last long." What she didn't say was how much the one a few minutes ago had unnerved her, that she'd gotten used to them until the horrifying incident inside her swimming pool. "Other than foundation cracks, they typically don't cause much damage. But we had one only a few days ago."

"So they're more frequent?" Nate asked. "That's the vibe I got from people at the dock."

"Yes," she said, "Unfortunately, they are becoming more frequent." She twisted the wedding ring on her finger. "You know I married Chad?"

"I heard," Nate said. "Sorry about . . . that must have been horrible."

"Yeah." She found herself again thinking of Chad's dead cell phone on her kitchen island. "I know you never liked him."

Nate watched her as they crossed Winchester and entered a half acre of scattered live oaks. "Even so, I'm sorry." He eyed the backyard of a nearby residence, where empty bottles—hand painted a half dozen hues of blue—hung heavy from the limbs of three dogwoods like giant, sun-dappled gems. Breeze clinked them together like wind chimes. In the background, tending to his flower garden behind the deck, stood white-haired Mr. Passafume. "I see Blue Bottles is still alive."

"He doesn't seem to age," she said, thinking that only Blue Bottles would be going about his day after what he'd found at the honey house this morning.

Mr. Passafume's ancestors had been among the first of the Gullah Geechee stolen from the windward rice coast of West Africa and sold into hard labor in the antebellum South. After the death three years ago of the island's resident root doctor, Madam Ma, who for decades had doled out medicinal herbal remedies from her small wooden shack in the shadows of the honey house, Mr. Passafume was the last of the Geechee descendants on the island. When not busied by the tupelo harvest, Blue Bottles spent his days tending to his garden, to his house, always smiling, collecting empty glass bottles and painting them various shades of blue, hence his nickname—hanging blue bottles from his backyard trees because they were good at catching and trapping bad island spirits. On closer inspection, Amy could see that he wasn't tending his garden now but hanging more blue bottles on the bushes alongside the back of his house.

Blue Bottles must have heard them. He turned around, waved, and shouted, "Have a wonderful day!"

"You too," she called back.

"He still does that?" Nate asked.

She laughed. "He even has pens now that say *Have a Wonderful Day* on them. He hands them out to everyone."

"They'll be a special place in heaven for Blue Bottles," Nate said, slowing as they crossed Guthrie, where a stray mutt dug furiously into the ground under a sprawling live oak. He'd made not just one hole but several, all in a cluster, as if he would dig to a certain depth before starting on another. The dog paused in his digging to growl and snarl at the two of them, eyes crazed.

"Whoa, boy," Nate said, cautioning the dog with an outstretched hand, stepping in front of Amy. They slowly backed away, took another angle into the trees. The Dodd House was visible a hundred yards away, but Nate's gaze was on the ground, at the dozens of freshly dug holes pocking the land like little craters, and thirty yards in front of them, four more dogs were digging into the dirt with an intensity that made Amy fear they were rabid.

In the distance, Mr. Jacobs was driving a small bulldozer in his backyard.

Mrs. Cranberry was in the middle of her backyard, digging.

Nate stopped to take it all in. "What the hell's going on here?"

"How much did Sheriff Kilbourne tell you last night?"

"Just that Dad died in the library," Nate said. "More than likely a heart attack or stroke. Said he'd explain more when I got here." The sudden anguish she felt must have been apparent on her face. "What?" he asked. "Amy?"

"Your dad called me," she said. "He . . . passed away while I was running to your house."

"Why you?"

"I don't know, maybe because I live close," she said. "But I think I need to warn you about your backyard." She gestured toward all the freshly dug holes in the ground. "It looks like this. There were holes everywhere. I think your father . . . he'd been out digging too."

"Why? Amy?"

"I don't know. But those were his last words before he . . . he told me to tell you to dig."

"To dig?" His voice trailed softer. "What the hell does that mean?"

"I don't know," she said.

A subtle breeze pushed across the island.

Spanish moss swayed from the branches of the surrounding live oaks.

The blue bottles hanging from Mr. Passafume's trees clinked together like they were singing. At first, she feared another tremor was coming, but the dogs hadn't reacted, and then the breeze died down.

When she looked at Nate, she found him staring at her. He asked, "The tremors . . . when did they start?"

She wanted to say something other than what the islanders had been speculating for years now but couldn't.

"Amy?"

She couldn't look at him. "They started a few months after the massacre."

Nate seemed to mull it over for a few seconds and then put it how she'd really been thinking it. "So they started after we buried Jericho."

"If you put it like that, yes."

CHAPTER

15
Sheriff Kilbourne

SOON AFTER THE tremor ended, and with a picture of the perfectly formed axe indention in the mud beneath Mitchell McBride's bathroom now in his phone, Sheriff Kilbourne had gotten a distress call from dispatch—Mary Winslow was panicked about something.

Probably the earth shaking, Lawrence had thought as he pulled up to the street curb outside the Winslows' ranch house. As had become his habit, he'd counted the duration of the tremor that had occurred when he and Easy Perkins were inside the McBrides' house moments ago: three seconds, maybe four.

He pulled out his cell, found the text chain he kept with his personal contacts from each of the neighboring coastal islands, and typed: *Another tremor.* He checked the time. *9:45AM, 3–4 seconds.*

Almost immediately, a text came in from his contact on Jekyll Island: *Nothing here.*

And then Ossabaw Island: *Same, nothing here.*

A few seconds later, a text came in from Sapelo. *Nothing, sorry.* His scientist contact from Sapelo Island always felt the need to apologize.

It was always the same. So far, in the seven years of checking in with the other islands, he'd yet to get a response back that anyone else had felt anything of relevance, which meant, as he'd known for years now, that these tremors were somehow unique to Crow Island.

In came a text from his contact in Savannah: *Nothing here, champ. Let me know if you need anything out there.*

Sheriff Kilbourne didn't respond; it wasn't that kind of text chain—the contacts didn't know each other—but more of his own experimental testing system.

Tybee Island came in next: *Nothing here.*

Now that he'd heard from both Ossabaw and Tybee, the two closest islands to the west, he'd call this one yet another iso. Crow Island had no bridge connecting it to the mainland and stuck out further into the Atlantic than any of the barrier islands. Ossabaw was bridgeless but for different reasons; it was a nature and wildlife preserve, a retreat for artists and poets and scientists. Tybee, on the other hand, was famous for its sandy beaches, historic sites, museums, and unique local culture. Some theorized Crow Island's crows had fled southwest for the nature preserve. The joke had always been that when the crows left, they'd flown northwest to Tybee because the beaches were better.

Lawrence pocketed his phone and shut off the car.

Before driving over, he'd tried calling the mayor to check in, but it went to voicemail. He'd then texted, asking if the mayor had gotten settled on the mainland, and Mayor McBride had texted back almost immediately: *All good here.*

He considered asking if their son Mitchell was with them but didn't. But as he approached the Winslows' porch, the trepidation he'd felt inside the McBrides' home, looking down into the hole in the bathroom, came back with a vengeance.

The Winslows were in their mid-sixties and retired, Mary from being a nurse and Patrick a plumber. Apparently, Mary had phoned the station, panicked because she couldn't find her husband, blubbering something about a shovel and *acting strange*.

Lawrence knocked, waited. And while he waited, three texts came in:

From Cumberland Island: *Nothing!* Clint, there, always used an exclamation mark.

From St. Simons: *Nothing here, Sheriff.* Holly never failed to call him *Sheriff.*

And from his wife, Tina, who should probably be added to the text chain, because she always reached out with the others: *You feel that one?*

He typed back: *Yup. Everybody good there?*

Yeah. Kids are used to it. And then: *Hamburgers tonight? David's request.*

Sure, he sent. *I'll grab meat and buns on my way home.*

He knocked on the Winslows' door again.

Tina responded: *Maybe if you're lucky those won't be the only buns you grab tonight.*

He smiled, pocketed his phone, thinking, *Jesus Christ.* Whatever horn-juice had seeped into her water after the birth of their son, it seemed to be in endless supply.

He made a mental note to remember the hamburger and buns.

His son David had told them the other day that a good hamburger—not cheeseburgers; the boy hated cheese—was his comfort food. The boy was wise beyond his years. But did David suddenly feel the need for comfort? Had the boy sensed his own unease this morning?

Suddenly, a woman screamed from behind the house. Lawrence followed the sound. The Winslows' backyard, beyond their vegetable garden, was marred by dozens of freshly dug holes. Some deeper than others, some shallow and abandoned. One near where the yard sloped off heavily toward the swamplands was large and deep enough for a body, and beside it, resting in the grass, was a shovel. From there, the property slanted steeply down toward a portion of the island's swamplands and salt marshes on the northeast side of Crow Island Cemetery. This estuary, a spawning ground for blue crab and similar to the infamously fertile Crow Island soil it abutted, produced more food than any estuarine zone along the eastern seaboard. Mr. Winslow, in his retirement, caught more blue crab than anyone on the island. His catches were coveted by every local restaurant as well as those in Savannah and Charleston on the coast and all the Georgia coastal sea islands in between. Nowhere could you find a juicier, meatier, and more succulent blue crab than those from what Winslow referred to as *his* salt marshes.

Sheriff Kilbourne spotted Mrs. Winslow halfway down the grassy slope, on her knees, weeping. Her eyes were red rimmed. "He just wouldn't stop, Sheriff. He wouldn't stop!"

Stop what? he thought. And then he figured it was digging all those holes.

Two gunshots sounded from somewhere across the island. Sheriff Kilbourne hunkered down, and on instinct pulled his own weapon for the second time that day.

He waited a beat, then asked Mrs. Winslow if she was okay, but she was now pointing out toward the swamp and salt marshes beyond.

He followed her arm, looked out toward where Mary Winslow was pointing.

Forty yards beyond her position, where dozens of ancient leafy green black gum trees soared from the brackish swamp water, Patrick Winslow's limp form, silhouetted by the sun, hung from a dark gnarled branch of one of the centermost tupelos, neck crooked in a noose, feet inches from the water, his body rotating slightly in the breeze as cordgrass and needle rush welcomed the incoming tide below.

CHAPTER

16
Nate

NATE WAS IN shock.

The tremors, so out of place for an island in this region, had been going on since Jericho's death.

Just when he was about to question Amy about it further, he followed her intense gaze toward a middle-aged man walking toward them down the center of the street with a gun in his right hand. Although he held the weapon at ease, down by his side, Nate, on instinct, stepped in front of Amy just in case the man fired.

"Mr. Delacroix," Amy called out to the man.

Delacroix, paying the two of them little attention, veered off toward a nearby house. As he reached the sidewalk, the front door of the house he was approaching opened, and out stepped another middle-aged man, this one balding with a gut pressing against his white tank top, as if to confront Mr. Delacroix.

Amy called out, "Mr. Torrence!"

But Mr. Torrence seemed unfazed by Mr. Delacroix's arrival—like he'd either known he was coming or sensed he might—but then looked panicked when he saw Delacroix raise the gun.

Nate slung an arm around Amy, and together they hurried low toward the nearest tree.

Mr. Delacroix fired.

The dogs scampered away from the holes they'd been digging.

Mr. Torrence had been blown back against the screen door, blood pumping from a red, flowering hole in the middle of his chest.

What the fuck? Nate thought. Was he really seeing this?

Amy fumbled with her phone.

"Call Sheriff Kilbourne." Nate had fled the island after so much bloodshed only to step right back into it within minutes of his return—he fought the horrifying flashbacks from the massacre. He started slowly toward the crime scene without a plan.

"Nate, what are you doing?" Amy called out.

He didn't know, but there was a man down, bleeding and hurt badly.

Mr. Delacroix, perhaps in a moment of shock over what he'd done, had dropped the weapon to the grass. His arm hung limply, fingers twitching.

Before Delacroix snapped out of his stupor, Nate kicked the gun away, spinning it down the sidewalk in scratches of metal on concrete. That woke Mr. Delacroix up. "Goddamn it," he hissed. "Give me . . . my . . . gun."

Amy hurried out from her spot behind the tree, telling Nate that the sheriff was on his way, before continuing up the porch steps to check on Mr. Torrence. Up and down the street, islanders had begun to gather in front of their homes, watching as Nate—a virtual stranger to them in a Braves baseball cap—struggled to keep the much-larger Delacroix from going after his gun. But Delacroix's determination seemed renewed as Nate, with his arms extended, stood between Delacroix and his gun on the sidewalk.

Delacroix had at least three inches and forty pounds on Nate. "The fuck out of my way, boy." He swiped at Nate, but Nate stood his ground, eyeing Delacroix in front of him, and in the background, Amy tended to the other man on the porch.

"What did he do to you?" Nate asked, feeling the need to stall until the sheriff arrived.

"Ain't your business." Delacroix eyed his gun on the sidewalk, and at the same time appeared like he'd just figured out who Nate was. Nate didn't recognize him; maybe he was one of the post-massacre arrivals, or "come heres," as his father had referred to them in his letters.

Nate took a shot in the dark. "You know Reverend Dodd?"

Delacroix paused. "What of him?"

"You respect him?"

"Course I do."

"What do you think he'd say, you trying to kill another man?"

Delacroix pointed back toward the porch, where Amy was sitting behind Mr. Torrence, the red, bloody flower on his chest expanding, soaking his pants. "That son of a bitch has been stealing from me for decades."

Just as Sheriff Kilbourne's siren and the accompanying ambulance came within earshot, Mr. Torrence, from his porch, shouted, "Fuck you, Steven." And then, after coughing up blood, "Fuck you and your whore of a wife too."

The whites of Delacroix's eyes went wide, the sclerae veined by thin trails of red that made Nate wonder how many days this man had gone without sleep. The man's hands looked blistered and scabbed; the palms of both had been wrapped with bloody gauze.

Lights flashing and siren wailing, Sheriff Kilbourne's cruiser barreled up the street. Delacroix had clenched his fists and raised them toward Nate. Knowing he'd need momentum, Nate made the first move, lowering his shoulder and plowing into the larger man's gut. Delacroix retaliated with a punch to the right side of Nate's head, and Nate's ear started ringing, the screams from the neighbors muted on the sideline, sucked down deep into a void of surging pain.

Nate swung back, landing a solid punch to Delacroix's right arm. The crazed man grabbed Nate by the neck and hurled him to the grass on the far side of the sidewalk. Delacroix retrieved his gun.

Sheriff Kilbourne's tires squealed; his car skidded to a stop.

Delacroix hovered above Nate, gun pointed at *him* now, and Nate thought, *I'm dead before I can even bury my father.*

Amy stepped into view and spoke. "Put it down, Mr. Delacroix."

Sheriff Kilbourne approached, his gun pointed at Delacroix's backside. "Put the gun down, Steven." His eyes darted from Amy to

Torrence's bloody body resting motionless on the porch and then finally to Nate.

Delacroix's eyes were puddling with moisture, like the realization of what he'd done was only just now kicking in and remorse was building.

Sheriff Kilbourne eased closer. "Lower the gun, Steven."

The gun shook in Delacroix's grip, and while he still limply held it in Nate's direction, he no longer appeared to be aiming. Delacroix said to Amy without turning his head, "Is he dead?"

"Yes," she said.

Delacroix's jaw quivered. A tear rolled from his right eye. "I'm sorry."

Nate cautiously made it to his feet. He assumed Delacroix was saying sorry for murdering Mr. Torrence in cold blood, but when Delacroix raised the gun and put the barrel of it inside his open mouth, Nate realized he could have been apologizing for what he was about to do.

Delacroix pinched his eyes closed, gunmetal clicking against his teeth.

Amy screamed, shielded her eyes. As did the neighbors.

Just as Delacroix's finger began to put pressure on the trigger, Sheriff Kilbourne's fist closed around the grip of his own handgun, brought it down hard on the back of Delacroix's head, jarring the gun from Delacroix's mouth before he could fire.

Delacroix dropped like a dead weight to the ground, out cold.

Sheriff Kilbourne was down on one knee, propping the weight of the man's slumped torso on the other, working his way through deep breaths, no spring chick anymore and showing gray around his ears. He said to Amy, "You okay?"

She sat on the sidewalk, stone faced, nodding.

Kilbourne looked at Nate. "Welcome home."

CHAPTER

17
Sheriff Kilbourne

*O*NE SHITSTORM AT *a time* was what Sheriff Kilbourne's predecessor, Sheriff Baisley, the old, grizzled World War II veteran, had told him on the day he was sworn in fifteen years ago.

Either nothing was going on or it was everything at once, and when it was the latter, *it's best to clean up one shitstorm at a time; otherwise you'll find yourself drowning in it.*

Sheriff Kilbourne had found that to be true. Unless, he thought as he stood outside the lone Crow Island jail cell, watching Steven Delacroix through the bars, all the shitstorms were somehow connected.

"Last chance," Lawrence said through the bars to Delacroix, who sat ten feet away on the side of the cot, staring at the floor between his boots.

This was the first murder on the island since the massacre, and within seconds of him seeing Jesse Torrence's bloody body, the memories of that Fourth of July hit him hard, and his heart, going on two hours since Delacroix's arrest out in the middle of Winchester Street, was still racing.

The PTSD was real, and he couldn't wait to get home to Tina and David.

And Steven Delacroix—business partner to the man he'd just murdered in cold blood—was still not talking, giving no reason why he'd walked two blocks over and shot him. Lawrence would seize both cell phones. Delacroix, the handyman, and Torrence, the developer, had been partners for fifteen years, their small company, Sea Breeze Rentals, responsible for a dozen or more of the beachfront rental properties overlooking the Sands.

Something had gone south.

"Fine." Lawrence moved away from the bars. "Suit yourself." And then he added, "You can rot in here, for all I care."

That at least got Delacroix to look up and finally acknowledge him.

While Lawrence had always liked Jesse Torrence, who was mild mannered and kind, he'd never much cared for Delacroix, an ex-Marine whose discharge from the military was rumored to be anything but honorable. An ex-husband to two ex-wives who'd claimed mental and physical abuse—but murder?

"I imagine you want a lawyer," Lawrence said. "That why you're not talking?"

"Don't need a lawyer," Delacroix said. "Been cheating me out of money for years."

And there it was. "So, what, you just shot him dead?"

"It was a lot of money."

"I don't care if it was pure gold shot right out of the world's biggest asshole, Delacroix."

"I learned some things."

"What things?"

"Small things, then big," he said. "And I just kept digging until I got to the root."

His use of the word *digging* gave Lawrence pause. "You talkin' the literal or figurative digging, Steven?"

Delacroix shrugged, stared at the floor, the hint of a smile, if not a full-on shit-eating smirk, punctuating a face Lawrence badly wanted to punch. Delacroix clasped his big, blistered hands together.

"What have you been up to, Steven, to get your hands all messed up like that?"

Delacroix spoke softly. "Been digging."

"You ever heard of gloves?"

Delacroix showed him the middle finger—"Ever heard of *fuck you*?"—and then leaned back on his cot. Delacroix had always been a jerk, but even from him this behavior was strange. He licked his lips. His mouth sounded dry, parched. "You tried this year's batch?"

"Of what?"

"The honey. What else?" he asked with a knowing gleam in his eyes.

"The honey ain't out yet," Lawrence said.

Delacroix grinned; it was clear he knew something Lawrence didn't. "Mighty fine. Mighty fine."

"You the one who broke into Mr. Passafume's storage?"

"No."

"Then how'd you get your hands on some?"

"For me to know and you to—"

"Cut the shit, Delacroix. Not in the mood."

After a few more beats of annoying silence, Lawrence started to leave, but Delacroix's voice stopped him.

"You believe in dinosaurs, Sheriff?"

"Huh? Dinosaurs aren't exactly a conspiracy theory. Unlike dragons or Big Foot or the boogeyman."

"That's not what I'm getting at."

"Then what are—"

"You think there was any ever here? On this island?"

"What? I don't know, maybe?" He stared at Delacroix's beat-up hands.

"What about monsters?"

"What's that got to do with anything?"

"I think I mighta found one," he said. "Found *something*. You know? Like a fossil. Part of one, maybe." For the first time since he'd been locked up, Delacroix seemed worried, scared.

"I'll look into it," Lawrence said, leaving his lone prisoner in their only cell, slamming the door behind him. Clare, across the room at dispatch, looked up from her desk. As Lawrence passed, she told him Deron Shackelford and Chris Weems, two of his volunteer firemen, were cutting down Patrick Winslow's body from the gum tree behind his property and that Mrs. Winslow was resting at her daughter's house down the street.

It was all bee buzz to Lawrence now that Delacroix's talk of fossils had stolen his attention. He'd get to Mary Winslow when he could and hopefully get some answers as to why her husband, seemingly of fine mental health, had done what *he'd* done. Some answers to why maybe he'd dug all those holes in his yard. Bottom line was that they now had three bodies in the morgue since last night. One heart attack. One apparent suicide. One murder.

Lawrence opened the station door with a little too much exuberance, suddenly desperate for air, but as soon as he sucked in a few deep breaths, even the reliable island air no longer seemed reliable. He coughed, like something had just burned his throat. The uncomfortable feeling dissipated, but not totally.

Ellison & Son was the only funeral home on the island, and they were about to get busy.

Again.

Lawrence drove to Steven Delacroix's house and parked in the driveway.

Before approaching the backyard, he shot Tina a text, warning her he'd be late. Next, he called Mayor McBride and left a message to call him when he got a chance, stopping short of saying what was really on his mind: *Shit is getting weird here.*

Delacroix's backyard was overgrown with weeds, not what you'd expect from a handyman and builder. Weeds climbed the picket fence. Weeds overflowed the flower beds and poked from the sagging gutters. Weeds sprouted from the cracks in the brick patio, where a mesh lawn chair with a ripped seat faced a rusted fire pit full of cigarette butts. Beside the chair rested four jars of tupelo honey—three of the jars were mostly empty, while one contained about a third of the glorious gold, like he'd been drinking it. All four jars were marked by a circular yellow sticker, which was what Blue Bottles placed on the newest yields. Which tagged these as four of the stolen bottles. Beyond the patio, the lawn resembled what Lawrence had seen behind the Dodd House last night, dozens of holes scattered about the grass, but beyond, where the backyard began to slope toward a ravine, a much-deeper hole had been dug near the fence line. This hole was sheltered by a four-legged pop-up canopy tent, with steel legs and a blue mesh covering, giving it the appearance of an excavation sight.

Lawrence closed in on the tent with trepidation. It was only the afternoon, but the sun looked like it was already setting.

Delacroix had piled the shoveled soil against the fence, covering it in places. The hole itself was wide enough for two humans standing head to foot and at least that far across. The pop-up tent covered the deepest part of the pit, which, by eyeballing it, he guessed to be six feet down at its deepest. That explained the damage to Delacroix's hands—he must have been digging at this hole for days. Lawrence looked up and found a larger, battery-powered light pointing directly down.

Do you believe in dinosaurs, Sheriff?

Lawrence turned the light on.

What about monsters?

He looked down and saw what Delacroix had spoken of—an off-white section of a large bone running diagonally across the bottom of the hole—three feet of exposed fossil, he guessed. And whatever it was, Delacroix was right about one thing.

Even mostly embedded into the soil, it was too big to be human.

CHAPTER

18
Amy

BY THE TIME Amy returned home, the ball of anxiety in her stomach physically hurt, escaping in beads of cold sweat across her brow, as invisible ants crawling up and down her skin.

The PTSD was settling in so deep she needed to scream, but she held it in as she hurried past the fencing around the pool—refusing to look at it, toward the memory of Jericho's presence coming up from the crack like a gas leak—but as soon as she closed the front door and stood with her back to it, she screamed so loud stars flashed across her vision. In her bedroom, she screamed into her pillow. It didn't take much to trigger the PTSD from "that day"—as good as she'd gotten at hiding it, it was always only skin-deep. But today was too much. Seeing Nate Dodd step off the ferry had nearly done it, but holding Mr. Torrence as he bled out on his porch had been next-level for her—she'd held Bridget on the Bull Street sidewalk in much the same way. The next several hours had been a blur, when she couldn't decide between fight and flight, trying to keep her shit together in front of Nate and Sheriff Kilbourne when deep down all she wanted to do was cry. But that was pure adrenaline, and now she was clean out of it.

Time might heal old wounds, but it doesn't fix them, Amy. Reverend Dodd had told her that the day her sister and parents were buried. *You come to me anytime you need to talk.* And she had over the years. Like Mr. Passafume, Reverend Dodd was safe to talk to. She'd hugged him that day inside the church, wrapped her arms around him like she'd never hugged her own father, because he was the fancy icing on the cake while Reverend Dodd was the cake itself. Not only had he enfolded her in his warm embrace that day, but he'd held her like she was one of his own, hugging her for seven wonderful seconds.

She'd counted the hug to keep from crying, as back then it had been a daily chore to show the rest of the island that Amy Barnes, the last remaining Barnes on the island—the reason she'd kept her last name after marrying—was still standing and ready to take what had been passed down to her.

She considered calling Nate to see if he'd settled in at the Dodd House, but she didn't want to bother him. And every time she looked at her phone, it drew her attention to Chad's phone sitting on the kitchen island, daring her to charge it and start scrolling. She didn't know what had urged her to dig it out of the box of his things a couple of weeks ago, and she'd nearly charged it and opened it then. But ever since, she'd viewed it as a testament to her willpower that it was still resting there, next to the bowl of fruit, untouched.

Maybe it wasn't her willpower at all but the fear of what she'd find. *Did you really love him, Amy? Or did you love more the idea of not being alone? The idea that someone out there loved you—the shy, sheepish nerd who never went anywhere without her face in a book.*

She quickly sat up in bed when she realized she hadn't cleaned all of Mr. Torrence's blood from her hands and arms. Blood stained her shirt; she removed it, tossed it to the floor like it was diseased. She kicked her shoes off, saw a spot of blood on her left sock. She took it off, panting, and then removed the other sock. Then she saw blood on the right knee of her leggings and peeled those off next, kicking them across the bedroom floor to near where she'd discarded the shirt. She breathed in rapid gasps. Her chest felt tight. Her heart raced like it might leap from her throat, and then that too started to tighten up.

She closed her eyes, did what Blue Bottles had taught her to do as a little girl, to let her mind's eye take over, even if only for a minute or two.

"And do what?" she'd asked when, to her father's chagrin, he had come to her bedside in the days of recovery after the drowning incident in the swamp.

"Do what you do best," he'd told her from the bedside chair her mother had reluctantly brought in for him. "See what everyone else can't, Amy. Let your imagination rain. Let it pour."

She recalled that day, feeling sick from whatever germs she'd picked up from the swamp water, nodding as she stared at him, believing him, loving him.

"He gets me," she'd told Bridget.

Her twin had smiled and said, "Good." And she'd meant it, like she was glad someone else did. What Amy hadn't told Bridget was that she felt somehow connected to Blue Bottles now.

"Your imagination is a gift," Mr. Passafume had told her.

"Do you see it too?" she'd asked back then, not fully aware of what she meant by *it*. But he'd nodded, and he'd patted his calloused yet soft and gentle hand on her head.

And her mother from the doorway—she must have been watching, spying—said, "Okay, Mr. Passafume, I think she needs to rest now." And Amy remembered being mad at how abruptly her mother had dismissed the very person Amy had wanted to see.

She was only now realizing why it had angered her, but she kept her eyes closed for another minute, slowing her breaths, imagining and remembering . . .

. . . the crescent sun over there . . . the ocean that moved away from the beach . . . the black sand . . . the trees whose branches were shaped like thorns, whose boughs looked like antlers . . . whose leaves were white with red veins . . . and . . . and . . . the crows . . . they were red over there . . . the deer were black and they had massive antlers swirled with red and orange . . .

She opened her eyes, better now.

Because those fantastical things made her smile.

But they didn't always stop there, her memories of that place.

Mr. Torrence's blood had dried under her fingernails; rust-colored spots of dried blood stained her left elbow and right wrist. She stepped into the shower, turned the water to near scalding, and scrubbed until her skin was pink, the last vestiges of Mr. Torrence's blood circling down the drain. And then she began digging at the blood under her fingernails, eventually becoming so fixated she feared she would open wounds of her own, have her own blood circling into the drain, and the shower water had turned cold.

Shivering, she turned the water off, stepped out and dried herself. In the bedroom, instead of pajamas, she dressed again in clothes for her morning run, already anticipating a long night of mental wrangling and little sleep, because she wasn't going to take a sleeping pill. She was convinced now more than ever that during her deep sleep last night, she'd been visited by a Boo Hag. Before leaving her bedroom, she caught her reflection in the dresser mirror and did a double take, long enough to realize how easily Nate had momentarily thought she was Bridget.

I am you and you are me.

It was something they'd say to each other as kids before falling asleep every night, each lying on her side, staring at each other from their respective beds like there was a mirror between them. Silly, but fun. When they tried, they could look identical in every way. And despite their differences in personality, they'd rarely fought. And even though Amy had often felt like the third wheel, it wasn't until months before the massacre that she'd ever resented Bridget's all-consuming relationship with Nate.

Ever since sixth grade when Bridget and Nate had held hands roller-skating during the field trip to Savannah, it had been the two of them. Amy knew that as teenagers they'd begun having sex in the months before Bridget was murdered, as she'd walked in on them one afternoon when their parents were on the mainland, opening Bridget's door without knocking, catching sight of Nate's bare ass between her sister's legs. To her knowledge, Nate never found out Amy had walked in on them, but Bridget's eyes went wide, and she quietly flicked her fingers at Amy as if to say *Go on, nothing happening here, close the door on your way out* before putting an index finger to her lips. Amy had backed out, quietly closing the door, pretending it was all no big deal, when in fact she'd go several days after that unable to sleep, even though all she'd wanted that day—in the middle of the afternoon—was to borrow her twin's calculator because the battery on hers had died. But what had bothered her more than any of it wasn't the fact that they'd naïvely pinkie-promised to steer clear of boys when they were seven; it was that the entire scene she'd walked in on—the dust motes floating through the sunrays at the window, her sister's long legs bare except for her footies—had hammered home that Amy herself was eighteen and had yet to even have that first kiss. That first note passed to her in class. That first dance offer from someone other than her closest male friends, two of whom were gay.

She opened the fridge in the kitchen and took a deep swallow of Moscato, straight from the bottle, which she'd never done before. She took another swig as she remembered that Reverend Dodd was dead, and then another drink as she recalled the fatherly hug he'd given her eight years ago. Wondered how Nate Dodd had ever thought this man cold or indifferent as a father when he could give a hug like that.

Don't think it, Amy. Quit digging. It's not true.

Of course it is, she thought. *He was hugging Bridget that day in the church. He might have been physically hugging me,* she thought, *but what he was really doing when he held me those extra seconds was hugging Bridget one last time. Hugging who he'd always assumed would be his daughter-in-law, the mother of his future grandchildren. He was hugging my twin sister.*

I am you and you are me.

Moisture returned to her eyes.

And so did a memory from that place, which she'd long ago begun calling the *other side*, because if she remembered it too long the Boo Hags showed themselves . . .

. . . first one, with red skinless flesh and meandering blue veins and long, white, stringy hair, and then two, and then three and four . . . all roaming with their crooked, creepy gaits, as if lost, and the more of them that arrive the more it appears like they're moving in a flock, like birds, and they're searching for something, Amy . . .

. . . open the door . . .

. . . let us in . . . let us all in . . .

. . . and then a shadow looms, a shadow in the form of a man with a head full of shadowy horns . . . and then the shadow man's face reveals itself to be a Boo Hag with hooked horns growing from the strings of white hair . . . he's older, bigger, stronger, he's the hag with horns and his face is inches from hers, and his skinless flesh is bright red and glistening and his nostrils are flared and his mouth opens wide enough to devour her . . .

And Amy opened her eyes, found herself braced against the kitchen island, panting.

What was happening to her? What was happening to the island?

Dig, Amy . . .

Whose voice was that? She knew, but how was it possible? Jericho was dead. Jericho never talked. Why did it feel like he was inside the kitchen with her?

She looked out the window above the sink.

It was growing dark too quickly for a summer night. It wasn't even seven, and the sun appeared to be setting as a haze moved across the island.

She spotted Chad's uncharged cell phone on the counter and wondered what he'd been doing out that night on the boat. Was it really routine maintenance? That late?

She could hear Bridget's voice now: *You hadn't believed him then, Amy, so why have you let time sugarcoat it? Why have you let time enable him again?*

Damn straight, Amy thought, placing the wine bottle atop the counter.

Just before she picked up his phone, someone knocked on her front door. She froze. Who would be visiting her this late?

But it wasn't late, she reminded herself. Maybe it was Nate. She hoped it was Nate.

She opened the door to find Mr. Passafume in his pajamas—loose purple silk covered in different phases of the moon—and sandals that revealed bare feet as ancient as tree bark.

"Mr. Passafume?"

"Can I come in?" he asked, looking frazzled and as solemn as she'd ever seen him, so far removed from the boisterously exuberant bundle of joy he was for everyone across the island that Amy was struck dumb by it. "Amy?"

"Oh, yeah, please." She moved aside. "Come in."

He stepped inside, closed the door behind him, and faced her. "I did it."

"Did what?"

"A hundred percent purity." When she didn't respond right away, momentarily confused by what he was talking about, he added, "The honey. It's one hundred percent pure."

CHAPTER

19
Nate

*O*PEN THE DOOR, *Nate! Open the door and let little brother in for a hug.*

The bedroom door rattled. The knob twisted, shook.

Those footsteps coming down the hall seconds ago had been real—Nate had felt the weight of each one of them from his bed. The shadow looming at the crack beneath the door was real. The dusting of fresh brown soil, gently pushed under the threshold upon Jericho's arrival, was real, as was the steely screech of the axe blade he'd dragged down the hall with him—like Marley and the chains he'd forged in life—the axe he'd used inside every nightmare to dig himself out of the backyard grave.

You're not real. You're dead. You're not . . .

Nate awoke disoriented on the living room couch, sweating, breathing rapidly as the nightmare faded. The fact that he wasn't inside his childhood bedroom helped moor him to reality. He wasn't eighteen, and Jericho was dead.

This he would tell himself after each nightmare had seized him in the days after the massacre, in the nights after the private backyard burial, where Nate and his father stood witness, taking turns filling in the massive hole they'd dug to fit Jericho's dead body—all six feet four inches and 250 pounds of him—along with the axe he'd used to murder all those islanders.

Jericho had been ten years old yet was already the size of a large man, and as much as his father had tried to play it off, it was more than just the benign, inoperable tumor on his pituitary gland. The boy wasn't normal. He wasn't human.

He couldn't have been.

Like the boy himself, the tumor had grown in ways the doctors and surgeons had never seen before, spreading throughout his brain like water through foundation cracks, like tentacles burrowing for more areas to grow inside that oversized cranium.

Nate stood from the couch. When Amy had asked him hours ago if he would be okay entering the house on his own, when they'd awkwardly parted ways at the beginning of Oak Alley, he should have told her that entering the house alone was the last thing he wanted to do. That back on the island was the last place he wanted to *be*. That every night he'd slept inside this house after burying Jericho, the nightmare of his dead brother crawling from the grave and entering the house, pleading for a hug, to be *loved*, to be human . . . it haunted him. But Nate had balked at her unmentioned offer to come back with him, fearing she'd view him as weak, because this really should have been nothing, entering the house he'd left as an eighteen-year-old and returning as a grown man of twenty-six.

The sole heir.

He, like Amy Barnes after the Fourth of July tragedy with her family, was now the only survivor of his, the last Dodd standing from the horrors Jericho's life had brought upon the island. It had just taken eight more years to kill the reverend, as Nate was sure it had ultimately been the weight of Jericho's existence that had done it. But after he and Amy had witnessed Delacroix killing another man in broad daylight, they'd been too stunned to discuss it.

Amy had asked for his cell phone. He'd handed it to her mindlessly, staring off toward the trees as she keyed in her number and handed back his phone.

"Call me if you need anything," she'd said.

He'd responded with a cool "Yeah," turning away from her before she'd turned away from him because she looked too much like Bridget. He'd been so exhausted that he barely remembered entering the house, barely remembered staring out the window at all the holes his father had dug in their backyard, barely remembered falling asleep on the couch in the great room, wondering why all the windows had been left open. Had his dad known he was about to die? Had he left the windows open so his spirit could get out? He'd heard of such things but never thought his father, a true believer in heaven and hell, would fall prey to it. With how adamant Samantha Dodd, especially during her pregnancy with Jericho, had been about keeping the windows closed and locked, it seemed like a slap in her face to have opened them all.

Nate approached the closest window and closed it. Before he'd dozed off, the breeze inside the house had felt good, calming even, after the day's events, but now, as night had set in, he felt uneasy. He began entering every room and closing the windows, starting upstairs with the six bedrooms whose windows opened to the second-floor breezeway galleries. All except Jericho's old bedroom at the end of the hallway—he found that door locked, just as it had been when he'd left. The key was in his parents' bedside drawer.

As Nate worked his way downstairs, his brother's nightmare voice still chased him.

Open the door, Nate . . .

On the nights when the nightmare went longer—torturing him well into his college years before finally fading—Nate's bedroom doorknob rattling was only a precursor to the door being blown open and Jericho standing there with his mismatched eyes, hulking, a dirty shovel, entangled by shredded roots, over one shoulder, the blood-stained axe leaning over the other like a lumberjack's, grinning, his teeth stained with dirt, his face with grime, his clothes eaten away by whatever feasted on such things underground.

Nate stepped off the curved grand staircase to the foyer. He'd loved this house as a boy and had been taken in by its stately charm and beauty, his mother spending quality time with him to explain every detail used in the construction of it—she'd been the main cog in the wheel that had kept the old house from falling into disrepair. No task, from painting to plumbing to keeping the gardens alive and vibrant, had been too large for Samantha Dodd to at least attempt, and Nate had always been her sidekick.

And nowhere was she more content than when tending to the garden outside. Nate had learned everything from her. That the overall plantation design was structured to beat the sweltering summer heat. That the wraparound veranda wasn't there just for aesthetics but, during the time before central air, provided interior shade and allowed the original owners, the original Dodds, to be outside and away from the grueling sunlight. The entries and exits and doorways and fireplaces all had symmetry. The tall French windows caught the breeze and provided relief from the humid climate, and the house's high ceilings let heat rise away from the living spaces. The raised foundation protected it from flooding. She'd pointed out every architectural intricacy, from the garçonnières and keystones, the rosettes and medallions and onlays, the wainscoting and door capstones and moldings, to the porticoes and interior plasterwork. Even during her times of depression, the gardens and grounds had been impeccably landscaped, and Nate had watched her in awe. But as Nate grew older, he realized the house's history was a double-edged sword, with beauty and charm on one side and what the plantation house had represented on the other—power and dominance, authority and subjugation—and he'd had trouble getting over the fact that his ancestors had owned slaves, right here on this island.

Next, he closed windows in the billiards room, the kitchen, dining room, the cigar room, and both drawing rooms, with haste, not lingering in any of them longer than necessary as the dark of night seemed to be growing darker, the shadows in each room endless. He saved the library and parlor for last, reluctant to enter the room where his father had passed away, and the parlor, where his mother had died giving birth to Jericho.

At the end of the hallway, the parlor had changed noticeably. He could smell it before making out clearly what was in it. His father, for the entirety of Jericho's life, had left the parlor locked and untouched, off-limits to all of them, as if it were sacred, and something about it had always bothered Nate, just like the fact that the two of them had never discussed how much his mother's death had bothered *him*. How his mother's death had changed them both.

In all of Nate's earliest memories, Thomas Dodd was a powerful beam of light. He smiled and joked, and he was fun. He'd been perpetually upbeat and positive during Samantha's years of depression, during the years of miscarriages, and then the stillborn baby had turned her quiet. Those times broke Nate's heart, when it got to the point some days where she was too depressed to come out of her room, too sad to spend the time with him around the house and gardens. But Thomas Dodd had never wavered. He'd been extra supportive of her soul-crushing determination to have another child, and Nate had always admired that about him, he was a rock, but then soon after Samantha Dodd became pregnant, again, with the one they would call Jericho, Nate noticed a change in his father that wasn't subtle. He, like Samantha in the years before, went quiet and distant, and to Nate it felt at that point like he'd emotionally lost both parents. While his mother was physically changed during the pregnancy, his father's metamorphosis seemed to be more emotional. His father's smiles went away, and his mood declined. He became more strict and too often quick to anger, like he was taking whatever was bothering him out on Nate, and it became even worse after Jericho was born. It was around that time, too, when Blue Bottles stopped coming over to visit. Blue Bottles was a family friend and then suddenly he wasn't, and Nate had always wondered why. And then it had gotten so bad, especially after Jericho was born, that Blue Bottles and Thomas Dodd could hardly look at each other.

But now the double glass doors to the parlor were propped open like welcoming arms to the rest of the house, and the entire room had been converted into an indoor garden of potted flowers and hanging baskets. The sweet fragrance of the blooms brought Nate back to when his mother would lead him by the hand through the outside gardens, pointing out each flower to him, encouraging him to put his nose right into the unfurled petals and smell.

Nate entered the renovated parlor and inhaled the fragrant air, the room now a haven of soft leaves and vibrant color, a sign that, despite the fact that he'd rarely seen his father mourn his late wife, he'd missed her more than Nate had ever known. Nate wiped tears from his cheeks as the smell of flowers and soil and gardening suddenly overwhelmed him. He stepped from the parlor, and aside from during those first months after his departure from Crow Island, those first few weeks of college as a newly arrived nineteen-year-old on UGA's campus, he'd never felt this alone.

He took his phone from his pocket. Amy had sent him a text earlier: *All settled?*

He responded: *Getting there. Took a nap. Dad left all the windows open. Closing them now. But all good, I think.*

Let me know if you need anything.

Will do. And then: *Thanks. Talk soon.*

Amy came back with a smiley-face emoji that reminded him he needed to check in with Lauren, who was the queen of the smiley-face emoji. But first he entered the library to close those windows and immediately saw where his father had fallen and hit his head.

Spots of dried blood marked the hardwood floor. It was jarring, seeing it, not knowing why he'd thought it all would have been cleaned up. It wasn't a crime scene. Sheriff Kilbourne had told him on the phone that he'd take care of things. He'd meant having the body picked up by the funeral home, not cleaning up what was left behind. One by one, Nate closed and locked the four library windows. He grabbed a roll of paper towels and a bottle of Windex from the kitchen pantry and cleaned the blood spots from the library floor. Before leaving the library, he spotted the paper on his father's desk and saw the crows he'd drawn in red ink all over the white page. Nate was sure he'd seen a red crow earlier, just before he'd blanked out near the docks, but had his father seen them too? Nate had chalked it up to being dizzy, delirious even, because red crows didn't exist.

Neither did Jericho, Nate thought, *until he did.*

Suddenly, he didn't want to be inside the house anymore. He left the library without turning off the light. He knew what he needed to do. Not only had his father asked it of him with his dying wish, but Nate had felt it as soon as he'd come within sight of the Dodd House—that intense urge to dig. Truthfully, it had formed before that, when he'd seen the dogs digging just before Delacroix walked down the street with his gun. Those dogs had been digging with such ferociousness that he'd entertained the idea of joining them. To not only physically dig into the ground but dig into some previously unanswered questions and uncover truths.

To go out to the backyard and dig.

He needed nourishment first; he couldn't take the chance of passing out again. He couldn't remember the last time he'd eaten. He opened the fridge, found the fixings for a ham and Swiss sandwich on wheat, and ate it while he paced the kitchen, washing it down with a lone Coors Light he'd found between the milk and orange juice.

He'd never checked in with Lauren.

He took out his cell and typed: *Hey dummy, I made it. Sorry about last night. I was kind of a dick.* But he didn't send it, knowing that if he did, he and Lauren would be on the phone for an hour, texting back and forth, and as gloriously normal as that sounded, he couldn't do it.

Not yet.

The outdoors was calling him . . . *now.*

He finished the beer and placed it on the counter. He resisted the urge to send the text but left it typed and unsent. He'd send it later. He placed the phone on the counter next to the sink and headed outside, grinning. Typing the word *dummy* had at least made him smile. Lauren had called him that once, jokingly, during a Middle School team meeting, and it had sounded so juvenile at the time that they'd both cracked up, and ever since it had been what they'd called each other—flirtingly, he'd realized weeks ago. *Oh, and Lauren, I just ran into my old flame's twin sister,* he thought, searching through the foyer closet for the box of work gloves. *For a second, I thought it was actually her, risen from the dead—her name was Bridget, by the way—minus the gaping wound my brother Jericho cleaved into her chest with that axe.*

But I'm okay. All good here.

After Nate found gloves, he headed outside with a flashlight. The motion sensor light clicked on when he walked out the front door to the wraparound porch, the haint-blue ceiling above gleaming like a summer sky.

His mother had repainted that ceiling every year, always with a close variation of the same color, ranging from robin's-egg blue to Aegean, and it appeared as if his father had kept up the tradition. The color, haint blue, in all its various shades, was meant to mimic the sky or water, according to Gullah Geechee culture, to ward off haints and evil spirits. Apparently, spirits had an aversion to water. His mother had begun to keep saltshakers on the windowsills of every room during her pregnancy with Jericho, because she'd heard that those evil entities hated salt. Reverend Dodd hadn't fought her on the saltshakers but had been quick to remove them in the weeks after her death. Just as he'd done with the masking tape she insisted they keep over their bedroom keyhole, the small burlap bags of gunpowder and sulfur she'd hung from the veranda next to the wind chimes, and the plastic coverings she'd taped over every chimney opening in the house in the beginning months of her pregnancy.

Nate arced the flashlight beam over the backyard terrain, left to right and back again. He could tell by the paw marks which holes had been dug by the dogs, so he sought out the ones that looked shovel driven and manmade, and of those, none were deeper than a few feet, none wider than a manhole cover. But why had his father stopped and started on so many? Was he looking for something particular? Had he repeatedly lost the nerve once he got to a certain depth?

Nate navigated the untouched spaces between the holes and approached the tree line at the edge of a bluff overlooking the rest of their property, where instead of the cotton fields and production barns and slave quarters down below he now saw at the edge of his flashlight beam acres of meadows and grasslands dotted by trees where red-tailed hawks, bald eagles, and songbirds soared. Down below, on the wall of the bluff, was a rope ladder leading from the fields up to where he now stood. Thirty yards down and to the left would be the large, circular metal grate inside the rock wall that acted like a windscreened door to the old supply tunnel leading into the house. He and Bridget and Amy had often run through that old tunnel as kids.

Nate looked at the two massive live oaks on either side of him, then down to the ground. His father had begun a hole here as well, perfectly centered between the trunks—only two or three shovelfuls at most before he must have lost his nerve. Nate used the sharp tip of the shovel blade to draw an X into the dirt, right below where his father had begun digging and stopped.

"X marks the spot," he said, before plunging the blade into the ground, crunching through root and sandy dirt, fiercely determined now to dig until he'd uncovered what had been chasing him now for eight years.

Determined to end *his* nightmares once and for all.

To prove to his mind that Jericho really was dead down there, and that they hadn't buried him alive.

CHAPTER

20
Amy

AMY HAD NEVER seen Mr. Passafume so shell-shocked, so full of negative energy.

The two of them sat at her kitchen table, each with a glass of iced sweet tea. But the more she listened to Blue Bottles explain the significance of why he was here—he'd finally reached 100 percent purity with this year's tupelo yield—the more enthralled Amy became. As old as he was, he was amazingly clearheaded, recalling dates from decades ago with as much ease as if they'd occurred yesterday.

97% purity in 2017
95% purity in 2001
96% purity in 1993
94% purity in 1985

"When we get into the years and decades before then," Mr. Passafume said, pausing as a thin ribbon of tupelo oozed from the counter jar Amy had handed him—a jar from last year's batch—twisting the jar, like the pro he was, just as the sliver of honey dripped into his tea so that no more came out. "It was a matter of guessing," he continued. "By taste." He stirred the honey into his tea. Ice clinked against the glass. "By sight." He wrapped his long, bony fingers around the glass and brought it to his lips. There was an indentation on his ring finger hinting that he at one time had worn one. He swallowed a gulp of tea, placed the glass back down on the table, and sighed. "That's good."

"The tea?" she asked. "Or the honey?"

He smiled for the first time since entering her house thirty minutes ago. "The combination, Amy. The marriage." He lifted the honey jar to his nose, smelled it, eyed it. "Ninety-two percent."

"You remember from last year," she said, acting unimpressed.

"I can tell." He closed his eyes as if still savoring what he'd swallowed seconds ago, even diluted by the tea. "Cinnamon . . . with a touch of anise. A smidge of jasmine." He opened his eyes, smacked his lips. "Of tangerine." He pointed to what was left inside the jar, the rich honey easing down the inside of the glass, reshaping into the pooled meniscus atop what remained. "Soft. Light. Buttery as it coats the tongue. Meant to be savored like a fine bourbon." He placed the glass down again on the table. "As they say in tupelo country, Amy, the honey is the money."

It was one of his famous sayings.

He'd first told her that when she was five. While Bridget had never shown much interest in the process, Mr. Passafume had taught Amy everything, even allowing her inside the honey house with him on numerous occasions, when it was otherwise off-limits to everyone but him. And then Amy's father, as he did so often after noticing her alone with Mr. Passafume, would call her away from whatever tutorial he'd be giving her, claiming it was time to go.

Mr. Passafume said, "I can tell purity by taste, to within a few percentage points. Nineteen seventy-eight was a pure year. As was Nineteen sixty-four."

"And you were how old then?" she asked.

He wore a short-lived grin. "Nice try." He lowered his hand to the table, intertwined the fingers of it with his other one.

Amy leaned forward. "Mr. Passafume . . ."

"Amy?"

"Yes?"

"You're plenty old enough to call me Earl."

"I think that would be a little weird."

"Try it."

"Earl . . ."

"Well?"

"Not bad."

"Your question?" he said.

"It seems that a hundred percent purity would be something to celebrate."

"Yes . . . it probably should be."

"But?"

He looked at her. "Let's just say it was always something your parents pressed me on."

"My father in particular?"

He nodded. "Yes. He was quite adamant we achieve this in his lifetime. I guess I missed it by eight years." And then to her: "Sorry. That was cruel."

"No, don't be," she said. "But can I ask you another question?"

"Yes."

"How did my parents treat you?"

"They paid me well."

"That's not what I asked."

"But that will be my answer."

"I didn't understand it then," she said. "But now, in hindsight, it seems my parents never approved of me spending much time with you."

He watched her. She watched him, raised her eyebrows, awaiting an answer. He said, "There wasn't really a question in there."

"Okay, then why? Why did it seem like they didn't trust you alone with me?"

"Amy, my dear, I was hired help. I was not family."

"Of course you were. Did they think you were, what, overstepping some boundary?"

"Why did I come over here today?"

"Not to brag about your honey's purity. Because you're frightened about something," she said, then added, "Earl. What is it that scares you about this?"

"Do you understand how impossible this all is?" He looked at her, his wrinkles more furrowed, his hair seeming whiter, his voice atypically engraved with anxiety. "It means that every single bee, every single bit of nectar created, was taken from—"

"From the tupelo blooms alone," she said, cutting him off, realizing herself how impossible it was, knowing that most beekeepers would agree anything over 60 percent constituted a good-quality tupelo. The rest would come from other flowers like gallberry and wildflowers. And while honeybees were known to bypass those flowers whenever tupelo trees bloomed, to think that this year the bees swarmed *only* to their island tupelos and completely disregarded any other flower was too much to fathom, even for Crow Island, whose tupelo had for decades been envied by those who harvested the swamps in Georgia and Florida. An impossibility in purity, they'd say. Some kind of fool's gold, they'd claim. As if the island had an unfair advantage. "But nothing should surprise us anymore with this island," Amy said to Mr. Passafume, who'd finished his tea and stood slowly from the table, prompting her to say, "Wait a minute. Where are you going?"

"Back home," he said, checking the old pocket watch she'd always known him to wear. "It's late."

"It's not."

He looked at his pocket watch again. "No . . . I suppose it's not." He looked out the window toward the dark. "It just seems late."

"You're worried about what's happening on the island, aren't you? I heard about someone vandalizing the bee barges. And the honey house." He'd turned his back on the way toward the front door, but she followed closely. "And all the digging. What's going on, Mr. Passafume? You know more than you're telling."

He stopped at the front door and turned on her. "Perhaps."

"You can't just dangle the carrot."

"I need to go," he said. He gestured toward his face. "*This* needs beauty sleep."

"How old are you?" she asked bluntly, not joking this time, not saying it in jest as she had so many times in her life.

"Old enough, Amy."

It was an answer he'd given often, but now it annoyed her—a feeling she'd never felt toward him until now—and she couldn't stop the barrage of questions that had been festering for years. "Why are you the only one allowed inside the honey house? Why is it always locked? Why are our bees so smart? Why have you never been stung?"

"Why have *you* never been stung?"

This gave her pause, long enough for him to open the front door and casually step outside to her small, covered porch. "Good night, Amy. I'm sorry to have bothered you with this." With an arthritic hand clutching the rail, he slowly navigated the steps to the grass.

"Mr. Passafume," she said. "Do you feel him . . . again? Jericho. Do you sense he's somehow out there . . . again?"

He nodded solemnly, sadly, but not with the confusion she might have expected.

"I watched you around him, Mr. Passafume. Most everyone was leery of him, a little freaked out by him, maybe, but you . . . you seemed scared of him. Even when he was an infant, you seemed scared of him. Like you knew what he was, or what he was gonna be."

He started to walk away without answering.

"What was he?" Amy asked. "I deserve to know."

"What makes you think I know?" he asked, stopping to face her.

"Because you seem to know everything," she said, and his familiar smile returned, but she remained undeterred. "What was it that was so important you had to come tell me about the honey tonight? Mr. Passafume?"

Moisture glistened in his eyes, like he might suddenly cry. "You're not the only one who's alone, Amy. Why can't it just be that?"

He'd never looked so sad as he did right now in his pajamas and flip-flops, and here she'd unintentionally pushed him away with her questions. Yet even knowing this, more questions came to mind. *Why did you never try to squash my imagination like everyone else? Every time I mentioned the* other side, *you seemed to understand it—why? Why do you never visit the mainland? Why are you afraid of the docks? Why do you secretly wear a wedding ring at home yet claim to have never been married? Why did you never have kids? Have you ever seen a red crow?*

She verbalized her next thought. "Why was Jericho so captivated by the honey house? He wandered from the Dodd House all the time.

They'd find him in the woods next to the swamp, sometimes atop the bee barges, staring at the honey house like he was trying to figure it out. Like he desperately needed to know what was in there."

"The hives," Mr. Passafume said. "That's what's in there, Amy."

"But is that all?"

"And the machines."

"Please tell me you feel him too. And I'm not going crazy. Jericho?"

She'd known him long enough to know he too was trying to make sense of the current state of things before he offered any opinion. He looked wearily at her. "Amy, my dear, I'm tired."

"I am too."

"I'll offer you this," he said. "I am scared, Amy. Days ago, a full crate of honey jars was stolen from my storage. And those jars are out there, the 100 percent ones."

"I can understand being upset," she said. "But why does that scare you?"

"Those years I mentioned earlier, the years with the highest tupelo purities?"

"Yes?"

"Look into what happened those years," he said. "Do some digging of your own." He forced a smile. "Have a wonderful day, Amy."

But it lacked his typical gusto.

"You too."

He walked away, through a noticeable nighttime haze of dust motes, and then disappeared into the shadows.

C H A P T E R

21
Lawrence

WHILE TINA PUT David to bed, Lawrence sat alone at the kitchen table, nursing a two-finger pour of Old Sam Bourbon on ice.

Tina would read David a story, and then Lawrence would do the final tuck-in. Tina's story time took longer now that David was five and reading at an advanced level, the two of them now deep into *The Lion, the Witch and the Wardrobe.* They jokingly argued about where David's brain had come from, but Lawrence knew the truth: Tina had always been the brains of their marriage. She was the looks too, which had led Lawrence to occasionally ponder what exactly he'd brought to the table.

He sipped his Old Sam and started cleaning the remnants from their quick dinner, laughing at the memory of how eagerly David had buried his face into the first hamburger bite. Tina, laughing, had said, "Easy there, champ." It had set the tone for their meal, for conversation about their last day of school, giving Lawrence a needed diversion from his day.

Between sips of bourbon, he put the leftover lettuce and tomatoes—both island grown and luscious—into Tupperware containers and started in on the dishes. What was it that his own father had told him about love? *Love starts with them in your arms and ends with your arms in a sink.* By the time he finished, the ice had melted in his bourbon.

"He's ready for you," Tina said as she entered the room.

Lawrence dried his hands off on a towel. When he slid by Tina, she grabbed his wrist, pulled him toward her, tiptoed and kissed his lips.

"We'll detox later."

It wasn't a question; he'd get David to bed and then the two of them would discuss his day. She'd made it her job, as long as they'd been married, to not let him be weighed down by too much at bedtime. Said it was bad for his heart, just like the nightly glass of red wine was good, she claimed, for hers.

She smacked his ass and left the room.

They'd tried for a decade and a half to have a child and had all but given up even before the massacre, which had left everyone on the island too shell-shocked to do much of anything. When that fateful Fourth of July was two years in the rearview mirror and after one of their many arguments over adoption, something Tina had for years wanted to pursue and he'd always fought, Tina had conceived. His swimmers, which the many doctors had warned weren't potent enough, had managed to do their thing. She'd cried when she told him he was finally going to be a daddy. He did, after all, believe in miracles. And while he'd told Tina, around the time she'd become pregnant, that he'd begun going to church and praying more, he'd never told her about the time he'd gone to the tupelo swamp in the middle of the night to visit Miss Madam Ma, who for decades, as the matriarch of the island's dwindling Geechee community, had offered remedies not perceived as viable options by the doctors at the Crow Island Medical Center.

Lawrence, at the time, had become convinced he was cursed, as they'd long known it wasn't Tina who was infertile. And while Tina had never once hinted at blame, he could tell it had been wearing on her by the year. He'd come back from the swamp that night wearing around his neck an amulet Miss Madam Ma had sewn and stuffed with tiny herbs and crushed roots. Lately, whenever he entered David's room to tuck him in, he wondered if that amulet had indeed been the reason they'd finally conceived. He'd showered after returning from the tupelo swamp that night and made sure to conceal the amulet beneath his pajama shirt when he crawled into bed. He'd told Tina the only lie of their marriage, that he'd had to work extra late. She'd turned her back to him. He knew she was pissed; she'd circled this day on the calendar as one where she could be the most fertile. She didn't stay mad for long that night. The thirty minutes that followed had been etched in his mind ever since, her more passionate and aggressive than ever, him more agile and into it than he'd been in years, him also making sure, during the sweaty, grunting throes of it all, that he kept his shirt on, kept that amulet concealed.

"What are you thinking about?" David said from his bed across the room.

Lawrence snapped from his reverie, felt embarrassed. "Oh . . . nothing."

"Not true," said his perceptive son. David patted the mattress beside him. Lawrence sat. David said, "So the shit really hit the fan today?"

Lawrence laughed. He tucked the boy in, leaned close. "Let's just say Daddy has a full plate. But don't worry."

"Why'd you get the blue paint out of the garage?"

"You don't miss a thing."

"Nope."

"I'm going to repaint the porch ceiling."

"Tonight?"

"Yeah, maybe tonight."

"To keep the Boo Hags out?"

He looked away for a few seconds, then back to David. "What do you know about Boo Hags?"

"That they're like vampires," David said. "And they need energy from humans to survive. They climb on our chests at night and suck out our breath."

"David . . ."

"Yeah?"

"Who told you all this?"

"Tony."

"From school?"

"Yeah. He said his dad got ridden by a Boo Hag and now he won't stop digging in the yard."

This gave Lawrence pause. Tony's dad wasn't on their list, which meant he hadn't reported it, which made him wonder how many more were out there who'd had apparent Boo Hag visits but didn't report them. And why was the frequency of these events rising so rapidly?

As if David had read his mind, he said, "Tony thinks it's the earthquakes."

"Does he now?"

"Yes." In David's hand was a small unicorn figure Rose Bower had given him the last time they'd gone into her hardware store. Recently, David had been claiming unicorns were real, and Lawrence didn't feel the need to tell him any different. *He's a boy. Let him daydream, let him fantasize.* "Boo Hags sneak around during the day wearing somebody's skin," David said. "At night, they hang the skin up on a hook, like it's a coat or a jacket, and they go out at night and steal our breath. Then they go back and put the skin back on before the sun comes up."

"And what happens when the sun comes up?" Lawrence had heard it all before but wanted to see what all his son knew.

"If they aren't back in their skin, they burn up in the sun," he said. "Boo Hags don't like the sun. I think that's why it's starting to get darker earlier."

"What do you mean?" Lawrence asked, even though he'd noticed it this evening, a thick haze that had seemingly ushered in dusk earlier than normal.

"The Boo Hags are making the days shorter."

Lawrence sat at his son's bedside, one cheek on the bed, one cheek off. "David . . . have you seen one?"

"No," he said. "Except pictures Tony drew. He has nightmares of them. But I'm not scared."

"Why not?"

"Because Captain Swirls will kill any Boo Hag that comes near me."

"And who is Captain Swirls?"

"He's a unicorn," David said, showing him the one in his hand, before closing his fingers over it again. "I dream about him when I'm in the deep sleep. He's big and white and has a long horn that's swirled with all the colors of the rainbow."

"Captain Swirls sounds like a great friend to have."

David pursed his lips as if to think on it. "He is."

Lawrence kissed David's forehead, left his lips there long enough to smell the berry-scented shampoo Tina had used in his hair. He smiled thinking of David's use of *shit hitting the fan*. "And David, we don't say the word *shit*."

David leaned up, whispered, "You do."

"But you don't."

"Then why'd you laugh?"

"It was funny," he said. "But your mother wouldn't think so."

"Okay." David settled his head back into the pillow. "Daddy?"

"Yeah?"

"Why is everybody digging?" he asked.

"I don't know, son."

"But you're gonna find out?"

"Yeah, that's my job to find out."

Truth was, just yesterday, Lawrence had gotten his shovel from the garage and had begun to dig a hole in the middle of his backyard, before Tina, from the deck, called out, "What in the world are you doing, Lawrence?"

To which he'd grinned like a goof and lied for the second time in their marriage. "Found a dead bird needed burying."

"Bury it at the fence line then, not out in the middle of the yard."

He'd fired off a sarcastic salute, filled the hole back in, and returned inside, wondering what in the hell had brought him out there in the first place.

Just some itch he'd badly needed to scratch.

"I think they're all looking for something," David said. "Something big."

"Is that so?" Lawrence ruffled the boy's hair, hoped he'd let it drop, but he didn't.

"I bet Ms. Rose at the hardware store runs out of shovels," David said. "We can't have the hardware store running out of shovels."

"No, we can't," Lawrence said. "But how about I drop by first thing in the morning and make sure Rose has enough."

This seemed to appease his son. David finally closed his eyes. Lawrence turned off the bedroom light and thought that was that until David's voice stopped him cold.

"Why doesn't anybody think I look like you?"

"Well, you know," Lawrence stammered, thinking, *Where did this come from?* But it was true. David mostly resembled his mother, and there wasn't much about David that reminded anyone of Lawrence. "Genetics is a funny thing, David. Some kids look more like one parent than the other. Some resemble both. If we were to have another one, maybe he'd look more like me."

"Or *she* would."

"Right. Or she," Lawrence agreed, still unnerved over the abrupt question. "Although I'd hope not," he said, as a joke.

"Hope not what?" David, as astute as he was, didn't get it.

"If we had a girl," Lawrence said, "I'd hate for her to look like me, right? I'm not the most handsome boy at the party."

David stared at him from the bed. Didn't agree or disagree. "But you're not gonna have another one, are you?"

"No," he said, "I think we stopped at perfection. That help answer your question?"

David shrugged, still seeming troubled by something.

Lawrence approached the bed. "Did somebody say something to you about this?"

David stared past Lawrence toward the hallway. "No."

"You know adults often joke, right?"

"But not all jokes are funny."

"No, not all jokes are funny."

David motioned him closer, whispered in Lawrence's ear. "Unicorns are real."

Lawrence ruffled David's hair. "Yeah. I'm sure they are, champ."

At the bedroom doorway, David's voice stopped him again. "Daddy?"

"Yeah, buddy."

"I think I look like you."

"Me too."

"And we're both handsome."

"That'll be our secret," Lawrence said. He waited at the doorway until his son closed his eyes. He left the room wishing this age with David would never end.

Lawrence poured two fingers of Old Sam neat and joined Tina in the living room, where she was stretched feline-like out on the couch, shoes kicked off, sipping red wine. He lifted Tina's legs at the ankles like a gate, sat down on the opposite end of the couch, and then lowered her legs onto his lap. He rubbed her feet and started talking. She already knew about the holes in Thomas Dodd's yard, so he started into the rest of it, and halfway through his telling Tina had closed her eyes, drifting into a deeper level of relaxation. She moaned gently as he massaged her feet. He knew she wasn't casting aside the horrific events of his day, but whether she had answers for him or not, the whole point of the nightly detox was to not let the bad stuff build up inside him. Her father had never talked, he was always stressed, and one day when Tina was a teenager, he'd dropped dead of a heart attack in the kitchen.

Tina placed her half-full wineglass on the coffee table and slid her right foot from his grasp. At first, he thought she was getting up to go to bed, but when she lowered her foot toward his crotch, nudging it gently, he knew she had other plans on her mind. As much as he typically liked where this was heading, he wasn't in the mood. In fact, something about the gesture had inexplicably pissed him off, coming so soon after his weird conversation with David. He knew it wasn't fair, but he suddenly felt cross toward her, and anyway, he had some painting on the porch to do. "Not tonight, Tina."

"Oh, okay, that's fine." She didn't seem hurt by his apparent rejection, just confused. "Long day." She sat up on the couch and kissed his cheek. "Maybe tomorrow."

"Yeah." Why couldn't he look at her? What was going on? *You know what's going on, Lawrence. It's the same old question that's been bubbling up since David was born.*

"Everything else okay?" she asked.

"Yeah. I'm fine," he lied, for maybe the third time in their marriage.

"No man is fine when he says he's fine, Lawrence." She stared into his eyes until he finally gave in and looked into hers. "We good?"

Goddamn, he loved her. "Yeah," he said.

But he wasn't good. His skin had popped out into gooseflesh. His heart raced. He sipped bourbon, but that only made it worse. Made him hotter, made him want to go outside and put a quick layer of haint-blue paint on the porch ceiling to keep the Boo Hags away, made him want to go into the backyard and continue digging that stupid hole he'd started yesterday. But that was crazy talk. And why did the damn air feel like Jericho had just passed through?

Dig, Lawrence. Dig deep. Dig until you upturn truths and get to the roots.

"Lawrence, you don't look good. Do I need to call an ambulance?"

She grabbed her phone from the coffee table, but before she could use it, he grabbed her wrist. "Don't!" He'd grabbed her much harder than he'd intended.

She pulled her arm away as if burned. "Jesus, Lawrence."

"I'm fine. I'm sorry. Just got a little overheated."

She backed away, gave him space, but the sudden fear he saw in her eyes scared him. They'd argued before, but he'd never seen fear in her eyes. He'd never given her a reason to look at him that way, and he didn't know from what deep well it was coming now. "I'm going to bed," she said, without looking at him. "You coming?"

"I'll be there in a minute."

He watched her go. *Don't do it, Lawrence. But you've always wanted to know. Ask her. Get to the root, Lawrence. Why did she start fucking you like she was a porn queen back then, and then continue doing so even after David was born?*

"Tina?"

She turned, looking nervous. "Yeah?"

"Do you love me?"

"What? What kind of a question is that, Lawrence? And how dare you ask it."

"Do you?"

"Of course I do," she said, standing stunned, eyes glazed with tears.

"So all that . . ."

"All fucking what, Lawrence?"

Fucking, he thought, grinning. "You aren't faking? You really want me as much as you seem to?"

She shook her head, turned away, and a few seconds later slammed their bedroom door.

He sat there, methodically sipping his bourbon until it was gone, thinking damn, how quickly this night had turned.

Shit is still hitting the fan.

But he had some business to take care of, some digging to do. Outside on the porch, as dust motes floated through moonlight, he opened the paint can, dipped the brush into the deep, rich color of blue, positioned the step stool in the back corner near the house, and started painting over what he'd neglected to repaint now for two years.

Four hours later, after pausing multiple times in his painting to check out mysterious movement he'd heard in the surrounding trees, he returned inside.

Without cleaning the dried paint from his hands, and for the first time in their twenty-plus years of marriage, Lawrence slept on the couch.

Before falling asleep, he'd wished for David's dream of Captain Swirls, but instead he had a nightmare about Jericho wielding that axe during the Fourth of July parade.

He woke up in the middle of the night, sweating, fearing that Jericho, as nonsensical as it sounded, since he was dead and buried, somehow wasn't finished.

CHAPTER

22

Fifteen Years Before the Sudden Death of Reverend Thomas Dodd

AMY DIDN'T WANT to go to the honey house, but Bridget wouldn't listen.

They'd been warned: *Never go to the honey house alone.*

Not so much because of the bees, Amy thought, but the bee barges and the dark swamp water below, where the haints and the Boo Hags lived. Unlike Bridget, she believed in the legends. But it wasn't the only reason she'd been so hesitant. Lately, she hadn't enjoyed being around Bridget and Nathanial, ever since they'd begun holding hands and she'd become the third wheel. She was slowly losing her best friend to a boy.

Amy followed the two of them through the warm spring air toward the swamp like an afterthought, lost in their giggly wake. She hated the bugs out by the swamp; like everything on Crow Island, even the bugs seemed bigger.

Amy had been reading *Harry Potter*, book one, for the second time, when Bridget pulled her from the living room chair. "Come on," Bridget had said. "There's a world that exists beyond your imagination, Amy. It's called outside. Don't be such a nerd."

That's what had broken her resolve, being called a nerd, even though she was. Until then, Amy had always thought it was their differences that truly bonded them as twins. Now she feared, as they grew older, that those same differences would place a wedge between them. In this case, the wedge had a name, and as much as she liked Nate Dodd, she resented him for that, especially now as he led them through the bug-infested woods toward the swamp, toward where Nate swore he'd seen a bright-purple snake atop the bee barges earlier in the morning. Bridget looked over her shoulder, reached her hand out to her twin, and the three of them became a chain as they neared the bee barges, where tupelo and gum trees loomed and ancient cypress soared centurion-like from the dark, murky swamp water, their shadows blending into endless shade.

Nate was probably pulling their leg about the purple snake, but Amy knew, if something strange was to be found on the island, outside the honey house was where it would be. She'd never told anyone, because they wouldn't have believed her anyway, but a few weeks before when she'd been atop the bee barges with Mr. Passafume, she'd seen a rabbit in the trees, and she'd sworn it was sunflower yellow, with a tail as red as a ripe strawberry.

Lately, Nate had grown more serious and quieter. Two nights ago, when the three of them had been outside roasting marshmallows, he'd started to tell them something about his father and the honey house, but then he'd shut down, saying, "Never mind," and it hadn't come up again. But now, as they approached the woodworking of the bee barges, Amy wondered if this trip wasn't somehow related to that *never mind.*

The bee barge's framework held the decking, atop which rested the sky-blue honey house with the bright-yellow door and apple-red roof. A curl of wooden stairs spiraled upward toward the bee barges, atop which the hives had been strategically placed along the floor of the decking. The creaky steps swayed underfoot as they climbed them. Bridget squeezed Amy's hand. Nate's pace slowed as they reached the top of the bee barge, the three of them in the middle of all those honeybees.

As Amy followed Bridget and Nate across the wooden planks, she watched her feet instead of the bees buzzing and flying between the hives and the trees' white flowery blooms, gathering glorious nectar for honey and crawling in the deep wrinkles of the tupelo's gray, ashy bark. She saw a shadow moving beneath the boards that she didn't think was hers. There was something down there—something moving and clicking against the underside of the decking. To steady her nerves, Amy imagined Mr. Passafume explaining the bee barges, that the platforms had been built high enough to avoid the floodwater and low enough for the white blooms to hover enticingly over the hives. That the Europeans had brought honeybees with them in the 1600s. That Native Americans had used honey to sweeten their water. That a strong hurricane could destroy a season's tupelo yield. Swamp water was important in keeping the trees' feet wet and the soil nutrient rich, he'd explained, pointing toward the tupelos on the far banks, the trees fanning outward at the waterline and below like a pair of bell-bottom jeans. "And those over there have knees," he'd said, pointing toward the ancient cypress trees on the opposite bank.

A wind gust moved the deck beneath their feet.

Bridget screamed, "Nathanial!"

Nate was on his knees, staring straight ahead toward the locked yellow honey house door thirty feet away, softly saying, "Dad . . ."

Even though no one was there.

Nate was crying. Something told Amy he was no longer concerned about the purple snake he claimed to have seen earlier in the morning. He was here for something else. Bridget knelt beside him, consoling him, but then Nate stood abruptly and hurried back toward the stairs.

The barge swayed violently now that the three of them were running.

Amy, again in the rear, looked over her shoulder toward the honey house and at first saw nothing out of the ordinary, but then she thought the door had gently started shaking in the frame. All around the barges, bees buzzed, and breeze blew, and Spanish moss spun from gnarled branches.

Amy followed Bridget and Nate toward the stairs.

The entire bee barge framework groaned as they hurried down.

She looked down again, saw the shadow passing between the spaces of the floorboards below, and then heard something hard hitting the underside of the decking. Something had come up from the swamp, and the shadow had horns. That's what was thumping against the underside of the decking as she moved, as it followed her . . .

. . . horns on boards . . . horns on boards . . .

With some of the steps still slick from morning mist, Amy hit a wet patch and went down, grabbing for the wobbly rope railing but unable to get a firm hold before falling down toward the dark water and the horned shadow in waiting.

CHAPTER

23
Amy

THE AIR FEELS strange.

It feels wrong, she thinks as she walks across a field of bright-yellow grass, ankle deep, where a lone, unmarked tombstone rests out in the open. Up above, purple birds, as big as condors, soar across a dark-blue sky dotted with pink clouds. Ocean waves crash in the distance. Between the tall black trunks of towering, white-leafed trees, whose branches grow crooked as antlers, she sees the ocean waves somehow moving away from the shoreline, where dozens of red crows pick green insects from coal-black sand.

Everything is wrong here, Amy thinks, as a black deer with a massive rack of red-and-orange antlers charges across the land before disappearing over a tree-lined ridge in the distance.

It's the other side, Amy.

This is where the imagination lives.

I'm dreaming . . .

No, I'm dead.

She approaches an old barn. The double doors are open as wide as welcoming arms. Something is moving in there, sounds like cornstalks whispering in a cornfield.

She steps inside.

They aren't cornstalks but rows of skins.

Hundreds of human skins hanging like costumes from hooks in the roof beams. Skins with faces and hair and arms and legs sagging limp and shriveled with no stuffing in them, no bones or muscle or tissue . . .

The Boo Hags have hung their day skins up for the night, and they're out on the hunt.

Breeze blows inside the barn, and the skins twist from the hooks.

From the far side of the barn, the rows of skins part and a shadow looms, moves closer, reveals itself with its red, sticky flesh and long white hair and two horns and deep dark wells for eyes, and then it begins to run.

And Amy runs from the barn, and now, across the great expanse of yellow grass, hundreds of Boo Hags roam, searching for something, some in thickly populated packs, others in small clusters. They claw at the air like they're ripping it to find something.

And then they spot her.

And they all swarm.

And Amy screams.

CHAPTER

24
Amy

AMY AWOKE WITH a gasp on the living room chair, knocking her phone from her lap to the floor.

When she picked it up, her phone read 2:32 AM.

She'd dozed off for only an hour, but long enough to bring something back, because that's what it felt like, as if something from her nightmare had come with her.

She moved from room to room and checked that all the windows and doors were closed and locked, and they were. Unlike in the bedroom, where she had the broom and hairbrush and colander, in each of the other rooms, next to each entrance, she kept jars full of marbles she'd collected all through her childhood, nearly two thousand in total. She made sure all of them hadn't been moved, and it appeared they hadn't.

She was just being paranoid.

But before falling asleep in the chair, she'd been researching the history surrounding those highest yields of purity Mr. Passafume had given her. She'd written her findings on a notepad, and they didn't look any more believable now than they had earlier.

The year 2018 was a no-brainer. She didn't need to look that up to know it was the year Jericho had gone on his killing spree, but now she knew it coincided with a 97 percent purity rate in that season's tupelo yield.

In 2001, when the purity rate hit 95 percent, Cory Jepson walked into Crow Island Bank and shot three of the tellers before turning the gun on himself. Later in the year, Catrina Bayers was arrested for setting fire to three different beachfront properties. In all, the arrests that year were double compared to the years before and immediately after.

In 1993, when the tupelo yield hit 96 percent purity, the island was rocked by a run of three suicides in the six-month period following the tupelo harvest.

In 1985, domestic violence incidents quadrupled the previous high, with none more brutal than when Sally Bates put her husband Billy into a three-year-coma by beating him near to death with the rolling pin that she'd then used—bloodstained—to flatten out her latest batch of sugar cookies, telling the sheriff back then that she'd "had enough of her husband's bee buzz."

Every instance of high tupelo purity coincided with higher rates of violence and erratic behavior. And the 100 percent purity of this year's yield went a long way in explaining the behavior on the island now for anyone who had partaken of it. But it didn't explain all of it. Amy knew the island's history, specifically the bad stuff her parents had never wanted her to write about, and now she felt the urgent need to do just that. And although those decades before the 1980s didn't have the scientific testing available now, she would be willing to bet the purity had been high in 1946, the year of the fire that ended the Crow Island club era, considered arson, and before that in 1924, when the Crow Island Gentleman's Club was closed for the entire month of August after two factions of gangsters, one from Chicago and the other from New York, all there as comrades, suddenly turned on each other following a two-week period of handshakes and partying and started shooting, leaving three dead and ten wounded and blood all over the Greek columns at the facade of the clubhouse. The newspaper picture Amy recalled vividly showed not only broken bottles of bootlegged whiskey but also crates of that year's tupelo honey busted up and splattered along with the blood.

How deep did she want to dig? To the beginning of Jim Crow? The Civil War? Slavery? Back to what really happened to the Creeks before the Spanish arrived? And to the Spanish before the English arrived?

Crow Island was replete with violence in any era, but was there proof that honey purity had anything to do with it? It was far-fetched, maybe, but why else would Mr. Passafume hint at it?

What had her attention now was Chad's cell phone on the counter. Her scattered brain couldn't concentrate on any task for long. She couldn't stay focused.

Anxiety overwhelmed her.

Why haven't you ever charged Chad's phone?

Go on, she thought, *prove your friends wrong. Prove that he did love you for you and not what you'd inherited.*

"What good would that serve?" she screamed across the kitchen, realizing that her emotions were scattered as well. She wasn't usually this quick-tempered. She wasn't usually this ready to listen to the voice in her head that she liked to pretend was Bridget but was really her old friend self-doubt. "Chad loved you," Amy said aloud, as if coming to her own defense. *He was kind and supportive when you needed it most.*

He'd gotten her through her grief. He'd tried to win her over for almost two years before she'd agreed to go out with him. Unlike Bridget, she'd never been much enamored by boys, and knowing Chad's reputation as a jock and a player and not the intellectual she'd foreseen for herself, she'd for a long time not responded to his advances. Because the two of them together made no sense. They didn't *go* together. Not like Nate and Bridget had gone together. The questions resurfaced. *What did he see in me? And did he see it before the massacre? Before I lost my family? Why did he come on so strong during my grief? Was it genuine?*

She stormed down the hall to her office with an urgent need to dig into something other than her dead husband's memory and headed straight for her manuscript. And then she remembered it was in the garbage. *It can stay there,* she thought. *Because it isn't the true history of the island if it doesn't include all of it.*

Not all that happened on this island was good, and you know it. Your family wasn't good, and you know it.

History may bury the bad seeds, Amy, but it doesn't mean they're gone.

Jefferson Barnes III, her grandfather on her father's side, had told her, even as a little girl, that she had a kind, old soul. Grandpa Barnes had been eighty-seven and on his deathbed at the time, but his grasp on her right forearm that day, as if urging her to one day dig deeper, had felt like that of a man in his prime. *History may bury the bad seeds, Amy, but it doesn't mean they're gone.*

Amy stared at an old newspaper clipping from back when the island thrived—one of the many periods it had thrived—and saw her grandpa as a little boy, dressed in a tuxedo and standing next to *his* father, Jefferson Barnes II, who was also wearing a tuxedo and a top hat, with a half dozen other white men, none of whom were looking at the camera, a shot taken perhaps unbeknownst to all of them. The picture was black and white, and dated, as much as she'd been able to decipher, back to the early 1920s, during what Amy considered to still be in the heart of the opulent "club era," where the Crow Island Gentleman's Club, started in the late 1880s, had, like the Jekyll Island Club miles away, been favored as a winter retreat for wealthy northerners. This picture, apparently taken before a party they were about to enter, also included Langdon Dodd II, the great-great-grandson of the island's original plantation owner of the same name. Langdon stood next to Jefferson Barnes, the two seemingly deep in conversation, and while Jefferson was tall and lanky like she'd envisioned Abe Lincoln to be, Langdon Dodd was shorter, stouter, but no less impressive looking as the two men stood, the center of attention of the suited men around them.

Her grandfather had handed her this picture that day, tapping it with an arthritic index finger to punctuate whatever point he'd been trying to make. Back then, she'd assumed he'd been tapping the picture in general, but in the past couple of weeks, after the picture had resurfaced along with her research, she believed he'd been tapping a certain part of it, if not a certain person: the African American man leaning casually against one of the clubhouse's stone pillars off to the side. Although this man wasn't dressed like the white members, he gave off an aura of importance, of status.

Who are you? Amy thought, again studying the man. *Why was my grandfather pointing at you?* Or had he been pointing to the clubhouse, which had burned down in the summer of 1946?

She focused on the man again. Could he be the thread that, if pulled, would unravel things? *And isn't that what you want, Amy? To dig and dig and dig until you get to the dirty roots?*

To really wake this island up.

Open the door, Amy . . .

It's already awake, she thought, pushing away from her desk, from the picture. *Because life isn't always what it seems. And maybe when Reverend Dodd hugged you that day, he was pretending to hug Bridget one last time. That's not putting an ugly face on a thing; that's just getting down to the bare-bones truth, and often the truth just hurts.*

Taking the black-and-white picture with her, she stormed back into the kitchen. Without giving herself time to change her mind, she attached the charger into Chad's iPhone, plugged it into the wall socket next to the coffeepot, and waited.

Dead. Dead. Dead.

And just as she was about to lose her nerve and yank the plug from the wall, a small charge showed on the dark display screen, a tiny red sliver of battery:

1% charged. 2% . . . 3% . . . 4% . . .

He needed your money to start his boating business. Can't you see that?

5%

She touched the screen, prompting the security code she knew was on there.

Four digits.

It had always been their anniversary, 0529, for May 29, and with shaking fingers she keyed it in. It failed. She keyed it in again. It failed again. He'd changed it. Why had he changed it? She keyed it in a third time. It not only was declined again but temporarily locked the phone.

"Fuck!"

She tossed the phone back on the counter and turned away, subconsciously knowing she'd just locked herself out on purpose so she couldn't pry, couldn't creep, couldn't dig.

She looked back to the picture, to the Black man standing on the periphery of it, and held it inches from her face. *I know you.* She peered closer. *I know you . . .* And then, "Holy shit." It looked like a young Mr. Passafume. At first she thought it was him, but after factoring the math she knew it couldn't be, so maybe it was his father. Or an uncle or grandfather. The likeness, minus age and some wrinkles, was uncanny.

Her cell phone rang with an incoming call. Startled, she looked at the screen and saw it was Nate Dodd. What did he want in the middle of the night?

"Nate?" she answered.

"Amy . . . can you come over?" He sounded rattled. "I'm in the backyard. There's . . . something you need to see."

CHAPTER

25
Amy

AMY HURRIED OUT the door with a flashlight.

It was the time of night raccoons and possums roamed, but it was a dog furiously digging in the shadows to her right that startled her. The dog stared into her light beam, and from the crazed look in its eyes, she feared it was rabid. She picked up her pace, hoping the dog wouldn't follow, breathing easier only after she'd put thirty yards between them. As she ran, her mind chased history, recalled legends and stories, of which none was more popular on the island than that of Adeline Drew, an African American woman who, as the story went, was ridden by a Boo Hag one night and went crazy and killed a half dozen white men with an axe. It wasn't the first time a parallel had been drawn between what Adeline Drew and Jericho Dodd had done, over a century and a half apart, but it was the first time it had dawned on Amy to dig into what else was going on the year Adeline Drew went on her murdering spree and then, as the legend went, disappeared into what would later become the honey house.

As Amy ran, ghost legends chased her, grasping at her sudden vulnerability alone in the dark, and the closer she got to the Dodd House the more she realized it was the same vulnerability she felt whenever Jericho was around, how she'd *feel* his presence in the room before she saw him. And there he'd be, standing still as a statue, staring with those mismatched eyes. *He's got a crush on you, Amy,* Nate would say, he and Bridget snickering.

That's why Jericho was always carrying a book, they said. *He's trying to impress you, Amy,* and they'd laugh, but Amy's laugh carried an undercurrent of unease, because maybe he *was* trying to impress her. The boy, they'd been convinced, wasn't even human. How could he even learn *feelings*? Even near the end, he still couldn't tie his shoes, when he was one of the larger people on the island. That's why he always wore Velcro shoes. And half the time, when Jericho would pick a book from his father's library, he'd hold it upside down.

Nate had told her to meet him in the backyard, so she bypassed the front porch and followed the brick walkway to the grass behind the house. A motion sensor light clicked on when she entered the area, exposing the same holes she'd already seen, but no Nate. Dust motes floated through the humid air. She then noticed a light in the distance, near the tree-lined bluff overlooking where the cotton fields and warehouses used to be.

She used her flashlight to navigate the fifty yards through the trees, turning it off as she neared the lantern Nate had hung from the low limb of a sprawling live oak. A few feet away Nate leaned on a shovel, peering down into a hole he'd dug deep enough to bury a small car.

He looked up, casually raised his left hand, and beckoned her closer.

His eyes looked crazed in the lantern glow.

This was where they'd buried Jericho eight years ago. The island had refused his burial in Crow Island Cemetery, and Reverend Dodd, forever guilty over what had happened, hadn't fought it. It was under this tree overlooking the old cotton fields where Jericho liked to sit and do what he did best: stare. And watch. And wait—they never knew what for—but he must have been waiting for something, if not just the end of his life, which had come abruptly that night inside the jailhouse.

"Watch your step," Nate said.

Amy looked down, felt sick to her stomach, like she was walking on tainted, evil ground, just like Jericho had been in life. An evil monster who'd murdered her family.

Nate said, "I'm sorry. I didn't think how hard this might be for you."

"I'll manage." Amy stepped over another hole. Nate was eerily pale, and his face was covered in dirt. His hands and fingers were bleeding. "Nate, your hands . . ."

He looked down at them, as if noticing for the first time how beat-up they were. "Oh, yeah." He looked at her. "I've been digging."

She didn't know what to say to that. How focused on the digging had he been to have neglected those hand wounds?

"He's not down here?" Nate finally said.

"What do you mean, he's not down here?"

"Jericho."

She forced herself to investigate the massive hole, and while she saw chunks of dirt and soil and debris, she didn't see a casket.

"We buried him in a plain wooden box," he said. "It was big. He was big." Nate wasn't speaking like himself. It was like all the digging had reduced him to these simple, truncated sentences. He removed the lantern from the nearby tree limb and held it closer to the hole. "Look. There are remnants from the casket we buried him in, but it's all splinters. Normal decay wouldn't have done that. It's like it was blown to pieces underground. Like . . ."

"Like what?"

"Like he broke out."

"Nate, you need to go inside and clean up," Amy said. "You're a mess. You need to sleep. Jericho is dead. He didn't—"

"Then where is he, Amy? Why isn't he down here?"

"Maybe this isn't the right spot."

"It is, though," he said, scratching his sweaty brow, streaking it with dirt, with blood. "I helped bury him, Amy. I tamped the last shovelful down. I had nightmares for years that we'd buried him alive. I could hear his heartbeat through the ground, through the walls, through my bedroom door. I had one just this evening. I can't sleep. So I came out here to dig, and he isn't fucking down there." He hurled the shovel like a spear into the hole and looked up at Amy. "*He isn't down there.*"

Amy hunkered low, playing it like she wanted a closer look in the hole, but truthfully it was either that or collapse—she felt like a baby deer trying to stand for the first time.

"But that isn't all." Nate lowered himself down into the hole, the lip of which came up to his shoulder. He looked up at her again. "The axe is gone too."

"Nate . . ."

"We buried it with his body, inside the casket. Maybe the casket decayed into bits of nothing, along with his bones, which I don't think is possible, mind you, but the axe? The handle, possibly, yeah, maybe the worms and the mites and the minerals and the whatevers gnawed that part up, but what about the blade?"

"I don't know, Nate, but you're scaring me. Let's go inside and leave this be for now." Her words were shaky, and she couldn't escape the memory of Mitchell McBride and the axe he'd thrown so casually over his shoulder the other night. The McBrides, according to the registry, did not own an axe.

So how had Mitchell gotten one?

Nate laughed—a short punch that froze her heart, because she sensed a little insanity creeping in. "Wait till you see this," Nate said, grabbing hold of a blue tarp she hadn't noticed until now. "This was what I really wanted you to see."

As much as she wanted to look away, she didn't.

Nate pulled the tarp aside and smoothed his hand over something hard down there. He grabbed the lantern and held it closer to what he'd just revealed, and in the hazy glow, she saw what looked to be a portion of a bone.

A skeleton.

But it was too big for that.

He'd unearthed a good five feet of bone, two feet wide at least, running north-south and parallel to the house. And while he'd uncovered most of it on either side, enough to be able to tell the bone was rounded and tubular, like it could have been a leg bone or an arm bone, he hadn't dug deep enough to show exactly how big around it was.

"Looks like a dinosaur bone," Nate said. "Or something else. There's no telling what once lived on this island before the Native Americans."

Amy nodded, speechless, still grappling with the fact that, if indeed this was where Jericho had been buried, where was *his* skeleton? Where were *his* bones?

And more pressing, where was that damn axe?

She reached down into the hole, offered Nate her hand, hoping he'd take it. "Nate, please . . . come inside."

He flashed a grin, eyes starkly white against the dark dirt on his face. "I can't stop now, Amy. I think this is what Dad wanted me to find."

"I don't know, Nate."

"This bone goes somewhere, Amy. It belongs to *something*," he said, smearing blood and sweat across his brow. "I gotta keep digging until I find out what it is."

CHAPTER 26

153 Years Before the Sudden Death of Reverend Thomas Dodd

THE ISLANDER THEY called Sheriff trekked through slick mud on the banks of the swamp, his gun pointed at the door of the crude wooden structure the woman must have built under everyone's eyes.

Under the cover of darkness.

That's when the Boo Hags liked to work.

After the bloody carnage Adeline Drew had left behind in town—the body count now up to seven men killed with the axe she'd dropped into the swamp as she'd fled—it was widely believed she'd not only been ridden by a Boo Hag but somehow possessed by one.

It was the Africans who did it, thought the sheriff, *bringing those Geechee spirits on the boat with them from Africa, and now the island is infested with them.* What else could explain what she'd done?

The sheriff approached the wooden hut on the hill overlooking the swamp, two fellow islanders on either side of him holding bull's-eye lanterns so they could see. He'd known Adeline Drew for some time and never thought her capable of this, killing those men while they slept and slithering out the doors like a sneak thief.

Dozens more islanders stood on the opposite side of the swamp, waiting as they'd been told, their torches rippling in the breeze, pitchforks and guns poised, some shouting for Adeline to come out with her hands up, come and take what she deserved—they wanted her head on a pike, and they wanted it displayed in the town center.

The sheriff motioned for them to quiet down as he approached the closed door to the hut. He jiggled the knob and found it locked. He knocked on the door and insisted she come out, but she didn't answer. There were no windows, so he couldn't look inside, but they'd all witnessed her hurrying in there—wobbling, rather, as pregnant as she was.

Growing impatient, he pounded on the door of the hut, waited a few seconds, and then pounded again. He stepped back when he felt the door rattling beneath his fist. He thought it was from the impact, but he'd stopped pounding and the door was still rattling.

"You doing that?" he called through the door. "Huh?"

No answer.

That pissed him off, so he raised his leg and put his boot to the door. Once, twice, three times until it began to splinter near the knob. A minute later he opened the broken door and motioned the men on either side of him to give him some light.

"Adeline Drew," he announced. "I'm coming in."

He entered, raised the light, turned in a full circle, saw nothing but bare, windowless walls and a floor that was solid with no trapdoor in it.

"Bring her out," one of the men shouted.

The sheriff's voice was weak with confusion and a pinch of fear. "She ain't in here."

"What?"

He found his voice this time. "She ain't in here." He surveyed the small hut again, smelled fresh wood and nothing else.

And then he heard a baby crying.

He stepped toward the noise, held out the light before him, and couldn't believe what he was seeing on the floor next to the back wall.

A newborn baby, still inside an intact amniotic sac.

What his mother called *en caul*, a baby still inside the water bag.

The sheriff had never seen such a thing but had heard of superstitions that came along with it, like how the sac protected the baby from harm, but even more, he thought—knowing most of the islanders out here had been dead set on drowning her baby when it was born—this baby could have special abilities and be destined for greatness.

C H A P T E R

27
Sheriff Kilbourne

IT WASN'T UNCOMMON for Tina to sleep in on the first day of summer break, but Lawrence wondered if her sleeping in on *this* first day had more to do with their fight last night than it did her typical post-school-year winddown, which would inevitably include last-minute emails, phone calls, and some well-deserved lounging while she nursed a pot of coffee and started her first summer book.

Lawrence had slept fitfully on the couch, awakening with a crick in his neck. He'd hoped Tina would come out of the bedroom and apologize. For what exactly, he didn't know, which led him to believe maybe he should be the one saying he was sorry. Had he really questioned her love for him? *What had he been thinking?* His shoulders ached like hell from painting the porch ceiling last night, but after he swallowed three Advil and took a hot shower, they'd begun to loosen up. By the time he dressed, he'd decided that if she was up, he'd apologize immediately, and if not, he'd make it up to her with flowers and a good meal later.

If the island hadn't killed itself overnight, that is.

Maybe yesterday had all been a nightmare.

Tina wasn't up. Or, at least, she'd yet to emerge from the bedroom, even though David was at the kitchen table eating a bowl of Lucky Charms. Lawrence ruffled David's hair as he chewed his cereal.

David said, "Mom hasn't come out yet."

I can see that, thought Lawrence as he made a single cup of coffee, wondering if his son remembered their bedtime conversation from last night as wholeheartedly as he still did.

"Is she sick?" David asked.

"No, she's not sick," he said, although it would have been easier to say that she was.

"So she's mad at you?"

"Why would you say that?"

"Because she's not sick."

"Those my only two options?"

"And she's not asleep."

"How do you know she's not asleep?"

"Because I tapped on her forehead."

"Interesting," he said, thinking maybe he should try that.

"And she told me to go ahead and fix my cereal. So that's what I'm doing."

Lawrence tilted his coffee mug toward his son in acknowledgment. "Well done."

"Thanks." David winked. It wasn't a wink done voluntarily but rather one they'd come to notice of late that was more of a tic. Tina had questioned David a few weeks ago, doing her best not to draw too much attention to it, but noticed the boy did it more when stressed about something. He took another bite of cereal, did the wink-tic again.

Always with the right eye. Lawrence smiled but otherwise ignored it. Their pediatrician predicted it would go away with time, but Tina, who typically wasn't a worrier about such things, had been seeming uptight about it, especially the first time she'd seen it.

David slurped the remaining milk from the bowl. "Is she?"

"Is she what?" Lawrence asked, fitting his sheriff hat on his head.

"Mad at you?"

Lawrence thought about lying but said, "You don't miss a thing, do you?"

"Nope."

Lawrence coaxed David off the chair and walked with him down the hallway. "Adults disagree from time to time," he told his son. "But you've got nothing to worry about."

"Prove it."

Fine, he thought, opening the bedroom door, finding Tina still in bed with her back to them. He and David walked around the bed, and Lawrence, not totally sure how he was going to *prove it,* as David had demanded, knelt at the side of the bed next to his wife, his face a few feet from where Tina pretended to sleep. Lawrence felt sure she would have gotten out of bed as soon as he pulled from the driveway, but now he decided, with David as the judge and jury beside him, to push the matter. With his index finger, he gently tapped his wife's forehead, as David claimed he had done earlier. He even looked at David as if to say *Is this how you did it?* and David nodded. Tina opened her eyes, amused as far as Lawrence could tell.

For David's sake, Tina said, "Morning." But she couldn't look him in the eyes.

Lawrence leaned in, kissed her lips, and stood. He nodded at David and softly said, "See?" He ruffled David's hair and moved around the bed, thinking he'd made the first move, a nonverbal way of apologizing, but she sure hadn't kissed him back. In fact, what she'd done had been the equivalent of trying her best to *not* kiss him, or *un*kiss him.

Before Lawrence left the room, David said, "Don't forget to ask Miss Rose about the shovels."

CHAPTER

28
Amy

AMY MANAGED TWO hours of sleep after returning from the Dodd House overnight, before thoughts of Chad's cell phone returned.

She'd fallen asleep, still dirty from last night's dig with Nate, with an intense paranoia over why her late husband had changed the passcode, only to wake up feeling it even more intensely. A quick shower helped, but even as she stood beneath the hot water, she felt like she was wasting precious time. Now *everything* seemed pressing.

And where had Jericho's axe gone, if it was no longer buried in the ground?

She dressed in her running gear and hoped a good run would calm her down.

Chad's phone was completely charged. The four passcode boxes stared at her, blank like her guesses, which made her doubt how well she'd known him. What could he have switched it to? She typed in her name, and then punched in the number 1, like maybe she was his number one, but it didn't work. Next she tried the word *babe*, but that didn't work either. She felt foolish for not knowing and gave up for now.

Fuck him, she thought, and then felt guilty because he wasn't here to defend himself. Chad had been fished from the water after having been lost at sea for two days, his body, according to the dockworkers, nibbled on and covered in muck. Amy remembered now how they'd been unable to look at her when they'd told her they'd found him, then shielded her from the more gruesome truth of what condition his body had been in. But now, more than ever, she wanted to know. Had a shark eaten half of him? How badly was he mangled? She'd agreed to a closed casket, to never see his body, because she'd trusted everyone. But now . . . she would have liked proof he was even in there. She'd never thought of it then, so why was she thinking it now?

She considered starting her complete rewrite on the history of the island, but her mind felt too scattered.

But research, she could do.

Dig, she could do.

And while last night she'd discovered correlations between tupelo purity and island violence, she decided that, after her run, she would dig even deeper into the island's past to see if anything else jumped out at her. But once she started pulling books from her shelves and old, laminated newspapers from her old-school filing cabinets, and even more after she logged in to her welcome center account and scrolled through even older newspapers stored on microfiche, she decided her run could wait. Especially after discovering that during the year of Adeline Drew's murder spree, according to the *Crow Island Gazette*, that year's cotton yield had been unlike any they'd seen before. And for Crow Island, Amy thought as she scrolled through the article, that was saying something. She'd seen these old pictures of that season's yield before—of the cotton in the fields, which usually hit six to eight feet tall, towering to at least ten feet and fluffier and larger than anything the islanders had on record—but now, after what she'd learned of the tupelo purity, it held more significance. She doubted back then that they'd kept as detailed records as Mr. Passafume did with his honey, but after an hour of searching, she found a handwritten note from Lucius Dodd, dated 1837, describing the cotton fields that summer, and in his perfectly sprawled penmanship, he'd written *The fields looked like the clouds had fallen atop Crow Island, with the plants soaring as high as the tallest cornstalks.* After scrolling newspaper headlines for thirty more minutes, she came across a headline from November 6, 1837, that read *Tragedy at the Cotton Mill.* Amy knew of the horrific event, where the seamstress, Justine Baker, had stood from the table where she'd been sewing cotton-stuffed pillows going on seven hours straight and without any warning started stabbing her fellow seamstresses with a pair of shearing scissors she'd spent the previous half hour sharpening under the table. She killed two and injured seven others before she was contained by a group of women. What Amy hadn't known, and discovered farther down the article, was that Justine Baker, later that night, in her jail cell, threw up on the floor and later admitted to ingesting some of the cotton before stuffing each pillow that day. And when asked why she'd done it, she said, "Which part?" And then went on to say, "The cotton just looked too delicious to resist, and the scissors—well, I felt the ground needed a good watering of blood."

Justine Baker, forty-three at the time, spent the rest of her life in a Savannah insane asylum for Women.

Now that Amy was putting two and two together, she didn't need to look up anything on the arrival of the Spanish on the island centuries ago, when the Creek Indian chief had gone on his killing spree, leaving dozens of bodies to be found by the missionaries and even more missing from their boats in the swamp. But she recalled reading what a Spanish priest had said upon arrival, about *the indigo plants covering the island in dollops of magnificent purples and blues, like something from a Renaissance painting.*

Colors unlike any I'd ever seen before . . . Amy remembered reading.

From her desk, she retrieved the black-and-white photograph her grandpa had given her, with the mystery man she was convinced now was Mr. Passafume's father or a close relative, and she tucked it in the waistline of her running shorts.

She stepped outside to a morning where sunlight battled a thick, noticeable haze, where dust motes floated like embers from a nearby fire. Except she knew what it was from—the digging. On her way to Mr. Passafume's house, she called Sheriff Kilbourne and told him about what Nate had discovered last night—the massive bone in the yard—and also what he *hadn't* discovered: Jericho's bones or coffin remnants or, most pressing, Jericho's axe. And while Kilbourne said he didn't know which unnerved him more, he'd look into both. She considered telling him about Mr. Passafume's visit last night, about the 100 percent purity, but decided she'd let Blue Bottles do that himself. She did, however, ask the sheriff to recheck the McBrides' house to see if there was any sign of Mitchell staying there while his parents were gone. She knew it was him who'd rescued her from the pool the other night, and she was certain now that he'd used an axe to pull her out. Kilbourne said he would pay the house a visit as soon as he left the hardware store—he evidently had some questions for Rose Bower—but then prodded Amy for more. Said he could tell she was mulling something over.

"The axe," she said as she walked. "It was old." After a beat of silence, she said, "Sheriff, what is it?"

"I don't know," he said. "Just that I was inside the McBrides' house yesterday. Mitchell's room and bathroom were torn apart. The bathroom, all the way down to the joists, and underneath it all, he'd . . . he'd dug deep under the house, and there was the impression of an axe in the mud."

"Same kind of axe Jericho used?" she asked.

"Yes," he said. "I'll get back over soon as I leave here."

"Thanks, Sheriff," Amy said, unable to drop the line. "Do you think . . . ?"

"I don't know," he said. "I just don't know."

They promised to be in touch.

Next, she dialed Blue Bottles. He answered after one ring.

She warned him she'd be on his porch in less than five minutes. "I've got something to show you," she added.

"Oh . . . okay," he said, sounding confused and old.

"I've been digging, Earl," she said. "I've been digging into what you told me last night about the tupelo purity."

"With increases in violence?"

"Yes."

"And?"

"I don't think it's limited to the honey." She spotted his house a hundred yards away through the trees. "It's the island itself. It gets hungry and thirsty and it needs to feed."

"On?" he asked, but something told her he already knew.

The Boo Hag's voice from her nightmare chased her.

Open the door, Amy . . .

"Blood," she said. And when he didn't respond either way, she said, "You weren't at the parade that day."

"What parade?"

"You know what parade," she said. "Fourth of July. You were the only islander not there. You said you were on the bee barges when it happened."

"Because I was."

"But what did you see?" she asked loudly over the phone.

It was silent for a few seconds before he said, "The front door will be unlocked. Just come in when you get here."

CHAPTER

29
Sheriff Kilbourne

OFFICIALLY, ROSE BOWER was a grandma ten times over; unofficially, as the island's grandma, she watched over everyone.

Lawrence parked at the curb in front of Rose's hardware store and removed his hat out of respect as he pushed open the wooden front door.

The bell chimed overhead as he entered.

Pushing seventy, with a healthy white updo of curls, Rose looked up from the counter, where she leaned over the bucket of knickknacks she'd hand out to any kid who entered her store. A few weeks ago, she'd tossed David that plastic unicorn he now carried everywhere he went. "I didn't do it," Rose said, tongue in cheek, as she did every time she saw him, and it had become his custom to give her a different, equally cheeky answer.

"If I thought you had, Rose, I'd be coming in with backup." He leaned against the counter, mirroring her pose.

"What can I do you for, Lawrence?"

"When are you gonna start calling me Sheriff?"

"When hell freezes over."

He surveyed the store from where he stood. "Shelves are looking a little slim, Rose."

"Should have some deliveries today."

"I assume you've seen what's going on across the island. All the digging?"

"I have. That why you're here? You need a shovel?"

"No, but my boy, you know how he is . . . he's worried you've run out."

"Put his mind at ease and tell him there's more on the way," she said. "What's a hardware store without shovels, Lawrence?"

What's a hardware store without axes? he thought but didn't say.

"Island has lost its collective mind," Rose said. "And I didn't sell the gun to Delacroix. If that's really why you're here."

It wasn't.

Lawrence thought she might never forgive him for questioning her about selling that axe to Jericho Dodd eight years ago. Rose didn't sell weapons, so he knew she hadn't sold the gun Delacroix had used to kill Mr. Torrence yesterday, but the fact that she knew about it meant the entire island knew, and the silence now lingering between them hammered home that Mr. Torrence's murder had been the first since the massacre. Rose had never backed down from selling that axe to Jericho, but the island was well aware she'd never sold another. And had, in fact, shipped back the remaining axes she'd had.

"I'm really just here to avoid doing what I should be doing," Lawrence said, patting the countertop to signal his departure.

"You know what they say about procrastination, Lawrence?"

"What?"

"Don't."

"Nice." He placed the hat back on his head and turned away. "Thanks for the advice."

"Why'd you really come in here?"

"See about the shovel situation."

"Could have just called."

He looked back over his shoulder. "Then I wouldn't have gotten to see your lovely face."

"Shoo, fly," she said, motioning him toward the door. "Speaking of a lovely face, give this to your boy." Lawrence caught the small Matchbox car she'd tossed him. This one was a bulldozer, which he thought poignant. Rose said, "Good thing he got his looks from his mother."

Lawrence smiled. "At least he got *somebody's* looks."

Rose laughed behind him. Lawrence forced a smile, but something about what she'd said, in the wake of what David had said last night, had landed like a hollow thud in the pit of his stomach. Without turning around, he called out, "See ya, Rose."

"Have a good one, Lawrence."

He stopped at the door. "Say, you haven't seen Mitchell McBride around, have you?"

"No, sir," she said. "Heard the entire family was on the mainland. Why?"

"Just curious," he said. "Amy Barnes said she'd seen him."

He tipped his hat and left the hardware store just as someone else was walking in, and without paying attention to who it was, he held open the door for him.

Had he taken a second to identify the man, he wouldn't have, as he wasn't one of his favorite people on the island. Lawrence kept his emotions in check and said, "Morning, Caleb."

"Morning, Sheriff," said Caleb Jones as he slid past him and into Rose's Hardware, damn near looking the other away to avoid eye contact. At six foot two, Caleb was a couple of inches taller than Lawrence, as he had been all through their school years, but ever since Lawrence had been sworn in as sheriff, he liked to think he towered over Caleb, who was now an accountant with his own firm. He was also the man Tina had dated for two years back in college.

The only other man Tina had dated, other than Lawrence, for any length of time.

Lawrence and Caleb had never been friends as kids, other than being teammates on a few ball fields, but they hadn't been enemies either. It was just that, knowing that that man had once kissed and done God knew what with Tina back then, he considered him his nemesis. And while they'd always been cordial around one another, both knowing the other had at one time loved the same woman, it wasn't until lately, Lawrence had noticed, that Caleb seemed to always go out of his way to avoid him.

But how long had that been going on? Lawrence thought as he stood on the hardware store steps, the door closed.

Let it go, he heard Tina telling him last night. But he couldn't. Seeing Caleb now was just too much of a coincidence to ignore. And maybe . . .

Just *maybe* Caleb Jones *was* that splinter Lawrence had been feeling under his skin of late, the splinter he'd only just begun to dig out.

Lawrence forced himself toward his car, replaying the scene from a minute ago, when Caleb Jones had slid by on his way into the store. Had the son of a bitch winked at him?

Let it go, Lawrence.

But he couldn't.

He got behind the wheel of his car, started it, and then revved the engine twice, because he was suddenly that juiced. Caleb had winked at him on his way into the store. But it hadn't been any ordinary wink. It was something Lawrence had been seeing from Caleb Jones ever since they were kids, something he'd seen but never really paid much attention to until now.

Lawrence had never been much good at math, but finally he'd added something together that perhaps should have been added years ago.

Caleb Jones had an eye tic just like David.

Or, rather, his son David had an eye tic just like Caleb Jones.

C H A P T E R

30
Nate

Eleven Years Before the Sudden Death of Reverend Thomas Dodd

"JERICHO, LET'S GO."

Goddamn it, Nate thought as he stood atop the bee barge, twenty feet behind his little brother, who at seven was already taller than Nate at fifteen. *Fucking weirdo.*

But Jericho just stood there like the hulk he was becoming. Acting like he hadn't heard, when Nate knew he had. He had ears like a mouse. No, that wasn't true—they were more like bat ears, by the size of them.

Eating them out of house and home.

Nate had caught him eating a bug the other day, or at least trying one he'd picked from the garden weeds he'd been sitting in.

His father had called from his church office thirty minutes ago. Couldn't get away, he'd said, and then asked Nate if he minded going to the honey house to retrieve Jericho. An anonymous someone had called in to the station saying they'd seen Jericho wandering off into the woods again, which meant he was heading to the bee barges and honey house. At least three times a week they'd find him there, standing atop the decking and staring at the yellow honey house door.

Nate had been about to go over to see Bridget, but yeah, sure, of course, he'd go get his freak of a brother. *Oh, by the way, Dad,* Nate had thought right after ending the call, *I caught Jericho last night sitting next to his bedroom lamp, pinching the skin on his arm and holding it up to the light. Analyzing it like it wasn't real. Or, like, maybe it wasn't* his *skin.*

Add that to the list of abnormalities.

And now as Nate stood behind Jericho, wishing and hoping he'd just turn around and follow him back home, it dawned on him that the skin Jericho had been holding up to the light last night had been at around the same part of his arm he'd freaked out about hours earlier at dinner, when he'd spilled salt on it at the table.

Jericho had been asked to pass the salt. He never talked but those ears could hear, and he could evidently understand, mostly. And somehow the rubber stopper inside the bottom of the Mickey Mouse shaker came out and the salt poured out over his right forearm. He screamed like a baby—and deep down, maybe he still was, Nate had thought, despite his size—but it was more like he'd been burned. Dad had, of course, treated him with kid gloves, telling him it was okay and that everything was fine, all while not hiding as well as he used to the fact that he couldn't look at him anymore. Nate had noticed that months ago, how as the years went on and Jericho got bigger, his father had been having more and more trouble looking at him, and Nate wanted to say *See, I'm not the only one.* But Nate couldn't deny the fact that Jericho's skin where the salt hit it had turned a bright shade of red and the redness stayed there most of the night.

Nate checked his phone, raised his voice. "Jericho, let's go! I don't have all day." He knew Jericho would come eventually. When they'd walk home together, Jericho would stay several paces behind, which was fine by Nate, Jericho walking in his shadow and not the other way around.

But then, all of a sudden, that yellow honey house door started rattling, like it was experiencing its own little earthquake, which Nate knew was nonsense—the island didn't have earthquakes. Or maybe Blue Bottles was on the other side of the door, locked in. But that made no sense either. He'd just unlock it. Unless someone had padlocked him in, but if Blue Bottles was at the swamp, they'd know it. And even though Blue Bottles traditionally ignored Jericho, in this situation they found themselves in, with Jericho so infatuated with the honey house it was like he was hypnotized, Blue Bottles would usually at least help coax him away. Although there had been that time a year ago when Blue Bottles had attempted the opposite, to see if Jericho would go closer. He'd even opened the door, as if to let Jericho in, but ultimately, Blue Bottles had closed the door and helped Nate talk him away.

But the honey house door was still shaking, and Nate didn't like it.

He hadn't been a fan of the swamp since Amy Barnes had drowned in it. And maybe even earlier than that, because Nate could have sworn—and maybe he'd just dreamt it; early memories weren't reliable—that his dad had at some point in Nate's childhood come out here at night and not come home until the morning, covered in honey and dirt.

Of course he'd dreamt it, Nate would think when the memory surfaced, because that was ridiculous.

And now Jericho was pointing at the honey house door.

"Jericho, I'm gonna count to . . ." Nate's voice trailed away, because the door had stopped shaking so suddenly it was if someone were holding it still on the other side, and out from the thin gap at the doorway near the top left corner, something was emerging.

Jericho didn't budge, but Nate took a couple of steps forward to see what it was.

It was a bee.

Just a big fat honeybee, Nate thought, trying to rationalize it but also wondering how that plump, colorful bee had made its way through the thin little crease, and then thinking even further, *Was that what was shaking the damn door?*

Jericho clamped his big hands over his big ears, turned away from the bee like he was scared of it, and only then started walking away from the door.

Nate let Jericho pass him, for whatever reason not wanting him to walk behind him, and noticed for the first time the thin bandage wrapped around Jericho's right arm, where the salt had apparently burned him last night.

As Nate followed Jericho around the swamp, he stared at the bandage on his arm.

And that made him think again about the spilled salt and the red marks on his brother's skin.

And then that made him think of what had happened right after dinner, when their father was getting ready to clean up all that spilled salt but Jericho had stopped him with a grunt. He'd put on a pair of surgical gloves he often wore because he didn't like to touch certain things, then proceeded to count each and every piece of salt, on the table and then what had fallen on the seat and floor.

The counting kept him occupied for almost three hours.

CHAPTER

31
Nate

NATE SAT UP, shirtless, disoriented and muscle sore on the library couch. Dried dirt covered his chest, arms, and blistered hands. He'd dug through the night, even after he'd promised Amy he'd stop.

The grandfather clock across the room showed one in the afternoon. When had Amy left? She'd helped him dig for at least three hours after he'd showed her the massive bone out by Jericho's grave, the two of them upturning earth, casting it aside into heaps that towered over the trench, following the bone as it ran like a pipeline toward where his father and the stray dogs had been digging in the backyard, toward the house, in the direction, he remembered thinking, of the library on the back side of it. That was why he'd slept in here. He'd finally come inside, leg weary and brain tired, yes, but also still somehow juiced and wired and curious—no, more like paranoid—about whether the bones ran not only through the backyard but under the house.

Across the floor rested the sledgehammer and crowbar he'd retrieved from the garage last night when he'd contemplated digging into the library floor. That's when he'd fallen asleep. And now here he was, in pain all over but also kicking himself for the time he'd lost sleeping. The damn bone was heading right toward the house, toward the library. Right underneath this floor, he thought, with a yawn. And then, after Amy had gone, he remembered the second bone he'd discovered running almost parallel with the first. It hadn't been as large in circumference but was still alarming in size.

Nate stood from the couch and stretched his arms toward the coffered ceiling. It went a long way to loosening him up. Thinking of his excavation site got his adrenaline pumping, his synapses firing. He started a pot of coffee in the kitchen, considered a shower, but instead stood by the coffeepot as it percolated, inhaling the aroma.

He noticed his iPhone on the kitchen island, and the screen was shattered. He plugged it in, got nothing, and stepped back to recall what could have happened. For some reason this didn't alarm him like it would have before he'd returned to the island. While seeing his phone not working would have typically freaked him out, he felt oddly calm about it. Time away from the phone would mean more time to dig. And the more he dug, he felt sure, the more he'd understand things. About Jericho. About that fateful day. About what had happened to his father, the king of being kind to everyone but him.

Toe the line, Nate.

You showed everyone in your congregation your smile, your laugh, Nate thought, *so I know it was in there, but why couldn't you ever show me?*

And why haven't I cried yet? When his mother died, he'd cried for days, for months. Her death had flipped such a switch on his emotional state that his life would forever be viewed as Nate before his mother's death and Nate after. Or, he thought, as the coffeepot dripped, another way to look at it: before Jericho was born and after. That's when Nate's life truly turned, because you couldn't have one without the other.

His life, her death. Her death for his life.

He leaned against the kitchen island and remembered how his phone had shattered. Lauren had texted him. She was worried about him, and rightfully so—he'd promised to contact her when he got settled and he'd never done it. Because he'd never really gotten settled. He'd promised himself he'd text her as soon as he took a break, but then he'd passed out on the couch. By then he was pretty sure he'd already taken the shovel to the phone anyway, because it wouldn't stop ringing. It hadn't been Lauren calling; if it had been, he would have picked up, because he loved her. He really felt like he did love her, he remembered thinking last night, even with Amy digging by his side, looking so much like Bridget. It had been an unknown number. An island number. He'd picked up once and heard a male voice say, "I know what your father did. And deep down, so do you."

Nate had stood there panting, sweating, doing his darndest to recall the voice.

"Who was it?" Amy had asked.

"Nobody."

"Didn't sound like nobody."

"Wrong number," Nate had said, dropping the phone back down to the grass, where it landed faceup. "Let's keep digging."

And they did.

But the phone rang a minute later, same number. Nate answered again, this time with anger. "What do you want?"

"It only took one swing of the axe after I sharpened it."

Nate hung up, dropped the phone to the grass.

Amy said, "Call them back."

Nate shook her off, said, "Let's keep digging."

The phone rang again, same number.

He let it go to voicemail, and he could tell by glancing down at his phone that whoever it was had left a brief message. After a minute, when he couldn't take not knowing, he listened to it. It was short but no less ambiguous: "If your right hand causes you to sin, cut it off and throw it away."

He tossed his phone down, confused.

"Same person?" Amy asked.

"I think so."

When the phone rang again, Amy dropped her shovel and started toward it, as if to answer it, so Nate had stabbed it, shattering the screen, once, twice, and then three times, because whoever it was on the other end was a psychopath.

And now he had no way to get hold of Lauren.

And while he wanted to be left alone to do his work, part of him needed to see her. Needed to be grounded by the calmness of her voice, the realness of her. Lauren would have reminded him why he'd returned to the island in the first place. To bury his father. While he poured fresh coffee from the pot, he remembered he was supposed to meet with the funeral home today to discuss funeral plans, but how could he do that when he still had so much work to do?

The coffee burnt his tongue, but the pain from it fully woke him up.

"Why'd you tell me to dig, Dad?" he asked aloud, staring over the island and down the hall toward the room where his mother had died giving birth to Jericho, the same room his father had turned into a sanctuary in her memory since Nate had been gone.

He told you to dig, Nate thought, *so you'd find exactly what you found out there.*

He somehow knew there was something giant underneath the ground.

Tears welled in his eyes, and he knew it was from seeing that room constructed in his mother's honor. His mother's pregnancy with Jericho still conjured anxiety. Like she'd contracted a virus instead of conceiving a child. The island had viewed her during those nine months like she was infected by something. For the first four months of her pregnancy, Samantha Dodd had thrown up every morning. She'd begun to show within weeks, while the rest of her had grown gaunt.

Nate remembered the whispers at the food market at around five months of pregnancy, when she'd looked nine months already . . .

. . . *that baby inside her is sucking her dry* . . .

. . . *taking everything and leaving her with nothing* . . .

. . . *killing her slowly* . . .

. . . *there's no way there's only one baby in there* . . .

. . . *it has to be triplets, at least* . . .

. . . *they must have used fertility treatments* . . .

. . . *do you think it was an accident, after all these years* . . .

. . . *I know how long they'd been trying* . . .

. . . *I hear the poor thing suffered four miscarriages in between* . . .

. . . *I heard five* . . .

His mother's mental health was none of their business.

Nate hadn't understood enough back then about miscarriages and life in general to show the sympathy he'd felt, always wondering why his mother had turned so solemn and depressed, year by year, him knowing she wanted nothing more than another child but not getting why he wasn't good enough. Why wasn't she satisfied with it being just him, just the three of them? And the reverend going along with whatever gave her hope, her sampling all the religions known to man in her most irrational days, thinking *that* was the problem, until Thomas Dodd, growing weary himself, ultimately changed the Crow Island Baptist Church to nondenominational.

As badly as the words about his mother hurt, the truth of them hurt worse, and as much as he'd wanted to defend her back then—and still did—his own frustration toward her would grow, and grow, much like his little brother inside her, until, at times, he'd begun to resent not only him, his brother who wasn't even yet born but had already stolen the mother he knew, but her nearly decade-long insistence, no matter the emotional or physical cost, to have another child.

The last three months of the pregnancy, she'd gotten so large, her back pain so incessant, her blood pressure so high, she'd been ordered by the doctor to stay in bed, which was where she'd given birth to Jericho, in the makeshift bedroom inside the first-floor parlor, and also where she'd died during the delivery, during the C-section. At night, during those last three months of her pregnancy, Nate had been able to hear her through the floor vents, privately crying, and he never knew if it was from physical pain or depression or both, but no matter how many times he'd walked downstairs and crawled into bed beside her and read to her from his books and secretly wished his little brother would die so that his mother could be returned to him, she never got better.

In fact, every second Jericho was inside her, she grew worse.

Because he *was* killing her slowly. The gossip wasn't wrong. Nate had felt the foreboding through his mother's every exhale, through her sweat and tears. His father would never admit it, but Nate just knew he'd felt it too.

Jericho was *never* right. He'd never been human.

Nate remembered Jericho finally taking his first steps at eighteen months, just when they thought he'd never walk. Just when Thomas Dodd had begun toting him around in the Radio Flyer because he was too big for the stroller. He'd been sitting on the library floor staring out the window, and then he suddenly stood and walked out of the room. Nate had been watching him that day. It was the most peculiar thing. There was no wobble to his gait, no uncertainty to his steps . . . he just stood and walked out of the room like any adult might.

And babysitters, Nate thought—nobody lasted more than one time because of how uncomfortable Jericho made them feel, him staring at everything, staring at them, never talking.

It was like he'd come out fully grown but only half baked.

He wasn't right from the get-go.

And Nate, in hindsight, had somehow known *that* even before his little brother was conceived. He'd been seven on the night he'd heard his father sneak out of the house in the middle of the night. He'd waited at his second-floor bedroom window for his father to return, seeing him two hours later stumble, as if drunk, back through Oak Alley, holding the folds of his bathrobe closed, Nate knowing he'd gone to the tupelo swamp, where that old, shriveled Geechee woman lived, where the Boo Hags and the plat-eyes and the haints roamed. Nate had hurried downstairs, watching as his father tiptoed into the drawing room to remove his muddy shoes, his face pale, his hair in disarray, a look of shock in his eyes. And then the wind had blown, and ash sifted from the fireplace, dusting the brick hearth and wooden floorboards with black and gray soot that stuck to him like mud, as if a great breath had just come down through the chimney.

Nate had stood at the door's threshold, thinking *You're not my father. You're an impostor* . . . Looking down at his own feet, he wondered why *his* shoes were muddy too, wondered why he even had them on at all. Hadn't he just come running down the stairs?

All the while the chimney dust floated upward and his father stood inside the growing ash plume, which puffed as if it were alive, as if it had substance, enveloping him like dirty fog, and that's when Nate had gone running up the stairs and closed his door and hidden under the bedcovers, where he remained, shivering, all night. He remembered his father's shell-shocked, gaunt appearance the next morning and how he'd drunk his green tea loaded with so much island honey it dripped down his chin, and how intently he'd stared at his wife, at her stomach specifically, like Jericho was already in there growing.

Nate dropped his coffee mug. It didn't shatter on the hardwood floor, but hot coffee splashed across his shoes, wetting the cuffs of his jeans as he found himself standing in front of his little brother's bedroom door. He didn't remember walking upstairs, just like sometimes he'd arrive home after teaching school and only vaguely remember the drive. That didn't make him crazy; it just meant he was tired and had a lot on his mind. He and Lauren had had a conversation about it. They'd had conversations about everything. He remembered how badly he'd wanted to talk to her about his suspension from school, the probability that he wouldn't be asked back because of that incident. About how he now understood why the incident had happened, where that sudden rage had come from, that need to defend the defenseless. And now his phone was broken, and he couldn't reach out to her. He couldn't even use the landline here to call, because he didn't know her number.

Dummy, he thought with a smile.

Nobody knew any numbers anymore.

And what was he doing standing outside Jericho's door?

It was locked, as it should be. The notion he'd even unconsciously wanted to open it made him nervous. He turned quickly toward the top of the stairwell, feeling like someone had just been there, watching him.

He was being paranoid.

Nate stepped over the coffee spill and made a mental note to clean it up later.

Anxiety coursed through his bloodstream, as it did every time he thought of the honey house. *Why'd you go there, Nate? What did you see inside the honey house as a boy?*

He had to get back to work. He'd wasted too much time dillydallying, and the digging he'd been doing all night, that physical exertion, he now realized, had been the only thing to calm him. He changed into a pair of cargo shorts and a UGA T-shirt and returned to the library.

The first board was a bitch to pry from the subfloor, but he soon found himself developing a rhythm, and within a half hour he'd dug deep enough to switch to the sledgehammer.

CHAPTER

32
Sheriff Kilbourne

Sheriff Kilbourne shouldn't have been preoccupied by his home life, but here he was sipping iced tea at Mary Winslow's kitchen table, staring with her out the bay window toward where her husband had hung himself, knowing he needed to go investigate the mayor's house again for their son Mitchell, but all he could think about was Caleb Jones and his eye tic.

Lawrence tried to focus. To do his damn job and save the drama for later, because Mary Winslow, now a widow, was clearly suffering.

As islanders, they were short on all the departments the mainland would typically have in the investigation of someone's death, and because Crow Island had no bridged connection to anywhere, Lawrence was often left to his own devices. So while his team of three volunteer firefighters was cleaning up the mess from yesterday's Delacroix-Torrence homicide, and with his only deputy, Justin Clampus, watching over Delacroix at the jailhouse, two neighbors, both of them shrimpers by trade, had volunteered to cut Winslow's body down, and they'd managed to lower him to the cordgrass minutes before the tide had come in.

Lawrence sipped tea. "Do you mind recalling . . . any events that may have led to . . ."

"Him hanging himself?" Mary asked, her gaze on him now instead of the salt marshes out the window. She was in her sixties, with hair already turning white, but her olive-green eyes still clung to the youth of yesteryear.

Lawrence placed his unsteady hand over her trembling hands in the center of the table, and both sets of hands seemed to calm. She smiled at him. This gave him strength to be blunt. "Why'd he do it, Mrs. Winslow?" She wiped her eyes, composed herself, but didn't answer. Lawrence focused on the holes in the yard and took another path. "Mr. Winslow dig all those holes out there?"

"I dug the holes," Mary answered. "I dug every one of those holes, Sheriff."

This wasn't what he'd expected. "Why?"

She shook her head slowly. "I don't know, really. One night, a couple weeks ago, I just . . . started digging." She pointed out toward the yard, lowered her arm, looked at Lawrence again. "You ever felt like you had a splinter, Sheriff, but you couldn't see it?"

Lawrence nodded, probably too enthusiastically, because damn did he ever.

"But you knew it was in there," she said. "Hiding somewhere under the skin, waiting for someone to come looking. Or . . . or . . . like when you walk through a cobweb and no matter how much you pick at the busted frays, you can still feel it on you."

"What are you trying to say?"

"At first I just started mindlessly digging." She nodded toward the window. "As you can see. And then that wasn't enough. Like the physical digging was just the precursor for what was really hiding."

"Hiding where?"

"In the dark, Sheriff." She swallowed hard, like what she was about to reveal was going to be a real humdinger. Dread poured into the room like invisible smoke. "Patrick had his secrets," she continued. "And maybe, deep down, I'd always known. Maybe I'd sensed it. He had an addictive nature once he latched on to something."

Lawrence fidgeted in his chair, drank more tea. The tremor in his hands had returned. He waited.

"Patrick wasn't who the island thought he was, Sheriff." She pointed to her chest. "Wasn't who *I* thought he was either. Sure, he could catch blue crab out there like nobody's business, but wasn't that more to do with the island's nature than any true talent? The blue crab were there in perfect abundance. They practically crawled into his nets. A blind chimpanzee could have caught them."

Lawrence said carefully, "Who exactly was he, Mrs. Winslow?"

She stared blankly out toward the salt marshes, perhaps the sea beyond, to whatever might be in store for her over the horizon. "A fraud."

"How so?"

"He gambled away our entire savings," she said, her eyes settling again on Lawrence. "Every bit of it. Sports. Horses. Blackjack. Online cricket from India. I loved him." She smiled, but it faded into something desperate and agonizingly sad. "But I'd always had a feeling that I didn't love *all* of him. And I never knew why. I ignored it, for years, for decades, through three children . . ." She teared up, wiped her eyes. Her jaw started quivering.

Lawrence said, "What exactly did you find?"

"He emptied our savings. Our retirement. Our kids' inheritance," she said, staring out the window again toward the salt marshes. "He was almost four hundred thousand dollars in debt. I killed him, Sheriff. He was the one to put the physical noose around his neck, but . . . just two days ago, I told him I was going to the authorities. I was gathering everything I needed to bring to you, all the while thinking of giving him a chance to change. But he couldn't. It's who he *was*, Sheriff. That's who I married. I married a fraud."

"Gambling's not exactly a crime, Mrs. Winslow."

She looked at him. "False charities are. Fake fundraisers for cancer are."

Lawrence leaned back in his chair as reality dug in. Mr. Winslow was known all over the island for his blue crabs, but even more for the millions of dollars he'd raised over the decades for various charities.

Before Lawrence could verbalize it, she said, "All of it was siphoned into his gambling debts. He was clever. Just not clever enough to get away with it forever. I couldn't stop digging. And the more I dug, the more I uncovered. I confronted him, told him I was going to report him. And then he did what he did, and that's that and what's the point now?"

Exactly, Lawrence thought.

And the image arose of Mrs. Winslow kneeling, distraught, on her lawn yesterday, amid all those freshly dug holes, crying and screaming *He just wouldn't stop . . . He just wouldn't stop!*

And all the while, Lawrence had assumed she was talking about the digging. He wouldn't stop digging, when it was she who'd dug the holes. And she who'd been consumed by finding the truth.

Lawrence was finding it difficult to breathe.

"You okay, Sheriff?"

He nodded, placed his hat back on his head, touched his clammy brow.

"I'm sorry to drop this on you," she said.

"You did the right thing," Lawrence said with a certainty that belied his own inner turmoil.

Before he left her kitchen, Mrs. Winslow said, "The island . . . something's happening. It feels like it did when that boy was alive."

Like many islanders, she avoided saying the name of Jericho Dodd.

"Can you feel it too?" she asked.

Lawrence sure did, but wasn't going to admit it.

She was staring out toward the salt marshes again, toward the gum trees and cordgrass and needle rush. "So many crabs." She laughed. "This island has never done anything half assed, Sheriff Kilbourne."

Lawrence watched her, wanted to hug her, but found himself backing away. But she wasn't wrong. The island, as far back as records went, had grown everything in abundance. A hundred yards away from the Rocks, where the Creeks used to throw their oyster shells by the millions, were ancient rings, now archaeological mounds. The live oaks back in the colonial days had produced superior hulls for ships. And the size of the island's fruits and vegetables!

Sheriff Kilbourne tipped his hat, looked away from her. "The island sure does know how to grow things."

"I don't think it was ever meant to be inhabited," she said bleakly. "I think that boy was sent here to show us that. He would have killed us all if given the chance."

Lawrence didn't have a response, at least not one he could formulate into any coherent thought, so he went on his way, Jericho on his mind.

Once outside, he started coughing in the dusty haze.

After he settled that down, he couldn't help thinking, as he'd done too often to count over the years, about not only how goddamn big that boy Jericho had grown by the time he'd killed all those people, but how big he might have gotten had he still been alive.

CHAPTER

33
Amy

THE FIRST THING Amy had noticed before entering Mr. Passafume's house, beyond the sound of all the blue bottles softly clinking together like wind chimes from the trees in his front and back yards, was that he had no holes in his yard.

Like he was the only person on the island *not* digging, either physically or emotionally, which meant, perhaps, that Blue Bottles was the only person on the island still thinking rationally.

Amy liked to think she was too but didn't trust some of her recent sudden compulsions. But no matter how much pressure her parents and grandparents had put on the old man during tupelo season, Amy had never seen him rattled until recently. Had never seen him angry. Had never seen him anything other than mind-numbingly kind. *Have a wonderful day! You too!* The man oozed positivity and compassion, and that's what Amy needed now, she realized, as she sat at Blue Bottles' kitchen table sipping iced tea enriched by a careful dollop of tupelo honey he'd dripped from the jar of last year's yield resting on the windowsill above his sink, suddenly wishing now that she hadn't forced the old photograph on him.

As Mr. Passafume studied the black-and-white photograph, she stared at the honey jar on the windowsill. The thick tupelo, even minutes after he'd placed the jar down, was still settling in a golden hue toward the bottom of the jar.

He slid the photograph across the table toward her, removed his bifocals, and placed them folded on the table next to his tea. "Why do you care about this picture all of a sudden?"

"I plan to rewrite my book."

"Why?"

"Because it sucks," she said. He laughed, but in it she sensed an undercurrent of worry. "And I need to write the truth."

"And what is the truth, Amy?"

"Besides this island being founded on greed and cruelty, that something sinister is happening on this island, and I think this picture is a clue. That this island is somehow cursed." She leaned with her elbows on the table. "Something happened to the Creeks before the Spanish arrived. Same thing maybe that happened to the crows. Where did they all go?"

"A mystery that'll never be solved," he said.

"You're always quick with your answers."

"I see no need to delay."

"And the English," she said. "When they came, I don't think the Spanish, those that remained, simply rolled over and gave it to them. Where did the Spanish go? I don't think it was all from disease, as our history claimed." Amy gained steam—Mr. Passafume had yet to contradict anything she was saying. As the only ancestor left of the enslaved Africans and Geechee stolen centuries ago to work the indigo and cotton fields on Crow Island, Amy had always figured he'd known more than he was willing to reveal. "And where did all the slaves go after the Civil War, Mr. Passafume?"

"Like many after the war, Amy, they returned to the islands, took up residence in the very homes they'd worked in before the war."

"But the white owners came back."

"Yes, they did," he said, showing for the first time, a hint of hidden anger. "What was given to them, however briefly after the war, was quickly taken back, yes."

Amy pointed to the picture. "And soon thereafter the club era began. The Crow Island Gentleman's Club. The rich islanders—the rich *white* men—gathered into a tightly knit group. The elite of the elite would visit. Northerners poured in on vacations. From every picture I've ever seen of the Gentleman's Club, I've yet to see one where these white men weren't being served by island Black people, or Black people ferried in from the mainland."

"What good will any of this do, Amy?"

"My point is, from the pictures of the older days, *nothing* seemed to change. The former enslaved still served."

"They were paid wages."

"But where did they all go, Mr. Passafume?" she asked. "We know the Gentleman's Club burned down after the Second World War. And soon after that, Black people on the island, aside from those who worked with you on the bee barges, began to trickle away. Where did they go, and why?" When he didn't answer, she said, "And we know what the past fifty years of modern development has done to the Geechee community, pushing them off land that was rightfully theirs through bogus contracts and lies and deceit and bureaucratic bullshit. But before all that. Where did they all go? Your ancestors? During the club era? By the time the club burned to the ground . . ."

"Yes," he said stoically. "By then my parents' ancestors and their friends and families were virtually gone." His voice reverberated with repressed anger. He leaned forward, and in a serious tone she feared was now directed toward her for unearthing all of it, he said, "Call it a slow-burn, generational genocide."

Unashamed, she said, "I checked those years you gave me on the high-tupelo yields. They all match years of high violence."

"I've heard it referred to lately as cluster violence."

This gave her pause, because the term made sense. "I think this island hid a lot of crime and death and cruelty and injustice and painted over it all for centuries with extraordinary yields of vegetable and fruit and cotton and blue crab and fish and—" she paused, the tupelo jar again stealing her attention at the windowsill. "And honey."

He sipped his tea, said calmly, "What do you want with all of this, Amy?"

She looked at him. "You knocked on my door last night plainly scared about something."

"A brief moment of weakness," he said. "I'm sorry." He removed a pen from the rubber-banded cluster on the middle of the table and slid it toward her. "Have a pen."

"I want the truth," she said, ignoring the *Have a Wonderful Day* pen. "This island isn't right. And those episodes of violence aren't limited to the honey. There are instances that coincide with the greatest cotton and indigo yields as well." This didn't seem to surprise him, and that drove her on. "It's an island of fool's gold. It's an island of . . ." He watched her. She finished: "Of wrong."

No matter how much he tried to hide it, his facial twitch showed he was hiding something.

She said, "I think the soil needs human blood on cycles. It drinks. It feeds." Out of nowhere, another idea came to her. "Just like the Boo Hags need to feed. I see them in my nightmares. I see them gathering on the *other side.* I noticed, even now, that whenever I bring that place up, you can't look me in the eyes. Because you *know* it exists." She waited for a response, but he wouldn't look at her. Moisture had come to his eyes. She looked at the ring finger on his left hand. There was an indentation on the skin, as if a wedding ring had recently been on it. She'd noticed this for years, as readily as she'd noticed how often he looked at his old pocket watch, but had always thought it was none of her business. But now that she'd begun digging, she thought maybe it *was* her business. "I think you put a ring on your finger every night when you go to bed," she said. "And you take it off every morning. Why?"

His jaw trembled. She'd never seen him shaken before. She felt horrible for causing him such distress but couldn't stop. "I think you were married at some point." She stood abruptly from the chair and walked down the hallway and entered the old man's bedroom. Just as she thought, a ring rested on the bedside table, next to his reading glasses and a hardcover copy of Stephen King's *Skeleton Crew.* She had no business doing so, but she picked up the ring and marched it back to the kitchen. She placed it in front of him and awaited an answer.

After a beat, he glared at her. He slid it on his ring finger, flexed his fingers, curled his hand into a fist like he was about to strike something but then left it there on the table, a withered ball of skin and knuckles and age.

"Every Sunday morning, for as long as I've known you," Amy said, "you make a bouquet of flowers from your garden and you walk them *through* the cemetery, and you place some of them at the grave of Hannah Jane Jones Passafume, who lived from 1876 to 1903. She died of typhoid fever. It says so on the marker."

"A distant relative."

"I've looked around that grave," Amy said. "That isn't the only Passafume buried there. There are at least a dozen more throughout the past hundred and fifty years. Why is that the grave you leave flowers on?"

A mixture of sorrow and pride masked his eyes. "What do you kids call it nowadays, on social media? Creeping? Is that what this is? You just *have* to know?"

She swallowed over the lump in her throat, fearing she'd for the first time in her life ticked off the one person, aside from Bridget, she might have loved the most. She nodded, because she *did* need to know. "But you don't leave all the flowers at that grave."

"You know that I don't."

"You take half of them into the honey house."

"And I place them in a vase in the back corner."

Amy closed her eyes; a memory flashed so unexpectedly it startled her. She opened them with newfound clarity. "I saw a grave over there. On the other side. On the island of—"

"Amy . . . please, don't."

"Until now, I couldn't see what name was on it," she said. "It was just a slab of concrete. Mr. Passafume . . . please, look at me."

He did.

She said, "It said Adeline." He didn't deny anything, but something told her he knew exactly what she was talking about. Amy continued, "Adeline Drew. Everyone knows the legend."

He nodded solemnly. "It's a legend, Amy. A story passed down from generation to—"

"There was a flower," she said, cutting him off. "When I was there. In my dream. My visions of that place are always dreams before they become nightmares, before the Boo Hags come. But I've seen flowers, *your* flowers, at the base of Adeline's tombstone. Over there. It was one from *your* garden," she added. "Mr. Passafume? Earl?"

"Amy?"

"My parents and grandparents and great-grandparents were pillars of a community that I believe now was rotten to the core. People who poisoned this land with hate and death, and the land is fighting back." She didn't know where that thought had come from, but it made sense. The tremors. The digging. And then it dawned on her, as if the tupelo-laced tea she was drinking had enlightened her with a clearer vision of both the future and the past. "The day you pulled me from the tupelo swamp," she said, "we'd gone there because Nate swore he'd seen a purple snake come out of the honey house. But he got weak-kneed atop the barges and nearly fainted. That's when we hurried down and I fell."

"What's the question, Amy?"

"Did Reverend Dodd ever go into the honey house?"

"I don't know," he said, but looked away.

"Nate thinks he went in there alone one night."

"He told you this?"

"And that's the real reason we went to the swamp that day," she said. "Not just because he claimed to see a purple snake. Maybe he had. I've seen one myself over there, in my dreams. But Nate was confused about something he might have seen . . . or thought he'd seen, with his father. Bridget and I talked about it."

She switched gears. "Why were you so scared of Jericho?"

"I wasn't scared of Jericho."

"You avoided him. The mere sight of him angered you. You stopped talking to Reverend Dodd after Jericho was born. You used to be friends."

"People change, Amy."

"Nate saw it in you before Jericho was born," she said. "He noticed you'd stopped visiting even before he was born. His mother adored you. You and Samantha Dodd spent countless hours in her garden, planting and pruning. You were like a second father to her, Mr. Passafume. Nate loved those times. If you're wondering why Nate turned sour on you, it was because he thinks you abandoned Samantha Dodd during that pregnancy."

He clenched his jaw, stared at her, full of emotion. "I did abandon her, and there's not a day that goes by I don't regret it. But at that time, I couldn't bring myself to enter that house."

"You *knew* Jericho was going to be wrong, didn't you?"

He swallowed a heavy gulp of tea and stared at the windowsill above the sink, where the honey in the tupelo jar had finally settled.

"And the Boo Hags I've seen in my nightmares since I drowned in that swamp," Amy said. "They're not just evidence of my wild imagination. They're not just stories and legends." She pointed toward the kitchen window at the hundreds of blue bottles hanging from the trees surrounding his property. "You believe it too, because those are not out there for decoration, Mr. Passafume. We all know why they're there. You aren't the only person on the barrier islands to have a blue-bottle tree. You have them there to catch the haints and the Boo Hags, hoping they'll crawl into the bottles so the sunlight every morning will burn them up. But you *are* the only person I've known to have that many. What are *you* afraid of?"

He leaned forward, elbows on the table. "After all you've been through, you still want to know? You want me to tell you how secretly awful your family has been since they took over this island after the Civil War? While I sweated and toiled in the summer sun, out on those bee barges, inside that honey house, all so that your family could rake in the fruits like gold, season after season after season? You want to know how awful those racists were to me and the people I loved? You want to know what I was doing when Jericho did what he did that Fourth of July afternoon? You want to know if the legend of Adeline Drew and that honey house is true?"

She nodded, teary-eyed and shaking.

"Yes," he said, looking her directly in the eyes. "It is true. But you don't know the half of it. Nobody does."

She reached across the table and squeezed his hand. "Help me dig deeper."

"Why?"

She felt crazed, full of sudden tension. "Because I need to know."

"No." His hand slithered from her grip. "You don't."

The sound of a helicopter suddenly emerged outside, loud, like it was directly over the house, then faded into the distance. It paused their conversation, but then Amy pointed to the black-and-white picture her grandfather had given her on his deathbed, her fingernail tapping atop the Black man in the corner of it. "Who is this? Mr. Passafume? You've been dancing around everything else. Who is this man? He looks like a younger version of you. He looks just like you."

"Because it is," he hissed, then stood abruptly from the table.

CHAPTER

34
Nate

NATE SAT ON the library floor, staring into the hole below his dangling feet, where the smell of mud and freshly turned soil wafted.

With no watch (he couldn't recall where he'd left it) and no phone (he'd crushed it), he'd lost all track of time. His father had never placed a clock in the library, which was his place to unwind. The library had been his sanctuary, and Nate was tearing it up, board by board, the dirt he'd dug up now resting in small mounds all around the hole in the floor and subfloor.

He'd finally found the bone he'd been tracking; he'd been right about it traveling like a pipeline beneath the house, through the hole he'd dug in the library, and now catty-corner toward the hallway beyond. Nate peeled off his gloves, wincing, his hands covered with busted blisters. The question now was whether to skip to the hallway and go into the floorboards there or go to the kitchen, as it seemed that that was where the bone was heading. Something big and ancient had crawled up and died beneath this land, and he wasn't going to stop until he found where it began and ended. *Don't start something if you know you won't finish, Nate.* He could hear his father's voice now. *Do the job right.*

All those chores, all while Jericho roamed the house and yard like a brainless zombie, helping with nothing, doing nothing except make people anxious.

Just as Nate was about to drop back down into the hole to retrieve his shovel, someone knocked on the front door. He didn't initially respond, but after the third series of knocks, Nate figured they might not go away until he answered it.

Standing up from the floor and walking through the house, he realized how sore he was from all the manual labor. He still hadn't showered, and it showed. He smelled of body odor and dirt—his fingernails were caked with it.

Nate opened the front door and found Blake Ellison on the porch. The island funeral director from Ellison & Son Funeral Home backed away, as if afraid, when Nate stepped out to him. Sweaty and shirtless, Nate said, "What can I do for you, Mr. Ellison?"

Mr. Ellison, dressed in his typical suit and tie from the 1980s, swallowed hard and said, "You, uh . . . missed our appointment this afternoon."

Nate looked at his wrist, to the watch that wasn't there. "Is it already afternoon?"

"Four o'clock." Mr. Ellison, who had to be in his sixties by now, looked especially nervous, off his game and in a hurry.

Nate said, "Sorry. Lost track of time. Let me jump in the shower and I'll be right over."

"No need." Mr. Ellison held out before him a fancy wooden box, no bigger than a shoebox, artfully engraved on top with the Ellison & Son insignia (*since 1897*). "I'm sorry for your loss."

"What's this?"

"It's your . . . your father's ashes."

"Wait, what?"

"Thomas's ashes," said Mr. Ellison. "It's what I was going to give you this afternoon. I was worried when you didn't show. You didn't answer your phone."

"It's broken."

"Or the home phone."

"Must not have heard it," Nate said, thinking he *had* heard it a few times but ignored it, too busy working under the library floorboards to answer it. Nate accepted the box, thinking how strange it was that

Mr. Ellison, on his island golf cart—marked at the front with the Ellison & Son insignia—had driven the great Reverend Thomas Dodd over in a wooden box, when Nate had always figured his father's funeral would somehow involve every person on the island. Despite what Jericho had done, everyone, to his knowledge, still loved his father.

Mr. Ellison must have read Nate's mind. "Your father, he came to me several weeks ago. We'd always joked about his funeral one day having to be outside because the church might not hold everyone wanting to come."

Doesn't seem like much of a joke, Nate thought, holding the wooden box, unable to look at it but thinking it didn't seem to weigh very much.

Mr. Ellison continued. "He'd always said he wanted this song and that. Not that I'd be in charge of his funeral, mind you, but . . ."

"I get what you're saying," Nate said, feeling like he needed to let Mr. Ellison off some hook. "Looks like he changed his mind."

"Yes. A few weeks ago, he came to me and said he wasn't going to have a funeral whenever he died. He just wished to be cremated and scattered next to his wife's grave."

The lump formed immediately in Nate's throat. Reverend Thomas Dodd had always loved a crowd, and oftentimes—Nate could tell when he was in the pulpit—reveled in the limelight. He never shied away from being the center of attention. It wasn't like him to go silently into the night.

Mr. Ellison said, "He didn't want to trouble you."

"Trouble me?"

"Said he didn't want to be a bother to you. Making the arrangements and all. All the food and planning and decisions."

"Okay . . ."

Mr. Ellison stood straight and honorable. "Your father was a good man, Nathanial."

Nate nodded; deep down he knew as much but had never been able to get over the fact that his father had always been so hard on him. "Mr. Ellison, was Dad sick? Did he know he was going to die?"

"I can't speak to the physical health of your father, but . . . I will say he hadn't been himself of late."

"For how long?"

"Weeks. Perhaps months, in hindsight. You could tell by the way he carried himself. He moved about like he was fighting a wind nobody else but him could feel."

"That doesn't sound like him," said Nate. "Maybe he had cancer or something. Knew it was coming."

"Could be," said Ellison. "Or he was just dotting all his *i*'s and crossing his *t*'s."

"He said that often." Nate grinned, then said, "But I heard it was a heart attack."

"As did I," said Ellison, who looked to be pondering his next words. "Or a broken heart."

Nate stood silent for a few seconds.

Mr. Ellison, perhaps thinking he'd overstepped, said, "I'm sorry, I shouldn't—"

"No, no, it's okay."

"Like our recent earthquakes here," said Ellison. "You can't always see the cracks. The fissures, before . . . things that are stressed just start to break."

Nate said, "Thank you. For bringing this by."

"My pleasure," said Ellison. And then he added, "I didn't know about his hand. Poor thing. I don't know what happened. It was a shock when I got the body to see him missing one."

Nate looked up from the box of ashes in his hands. "What are you talking about?"

"He was . . . missing his right hand. I'm sorry, I assumed the sheriff had told you."

"No," Nate said. "He didn't."

"I'm terribly sorry," Mr. Ellison said.

Nate waved it away. He wasn't as shocked over the news as he probably should have been, and he chalked that up to exhaustion. But he *was* kind of pissed nobody had told him—not the sheriff, not Amy. And then he recalled the random phone call from the previous night, when he'd been in the back yard digging, a voice claiming it had only taken one swing of the axe, and now that call made a little sense.

Nate noticed dirt on the funeral director's hands and on the cuffs of his sky-blue suit coat.

Mr. Ellison must have noticed Nate staring. He raised his arms a bit, eyed the dirt on his hands, wiggled his fingers in a way that creeped Nate out. "Oh, this . . . I've just been out in the yard. A bit of digging."

Nate said, "You doing okay?"

Mr. Ellison nodded but looked on the verge of tears. "Just not myself lately. Found out some disturbing things, in fact . . . about my son." He wiped his cheeks, left wet dirt smears under his eyes, then shocked Nate by offering more: "He's been stealing things from the caskets before we bury them. Can you believe that? Valuables and whatnot. Things the family put in there with them for eternity. He's been stealing them and selling them online."

Nate almost asked how he'd come about the information but didn't. It was obvious. Mr. Ellison had found a thread and started pulling.

He'd been digging.

"I just can't . . ." Ellison wiped his eyes again and let out a loud, heavy breath. "You think you raise them right and . . . I don't know . . . But Lou Ann and I are going away for a while. Things just aren't right here on the island. You can feel it, can't you?"

"Feel what?"

Nate knew what but needed to hear someone else say it. Ellison didn't, and maybe it was out of respect for the ashes of the man Nate now held in his hands. But he could tell what had been on Ellison's mind.

It felt like it had when Jericho was in the room, except worse. And it seemed the air was getting thicker with it by the hour. Thicker with Jericho.

Mr. Ellison turned and walked sadly to his golf cart.

Nate watched him pull away, down Oak Alley, just as the Crow Island emergency helicopter sounded in the distance, a blip hovering over the trees atop the Backbone and growing larger. Something about the helicopter didn't seem right.

Nate returned inside anyway. He placed his father's remains on the kitchen island. He'd deal with that later.

For now, there was too much work to be done.

He retrieved his sledgehammer and shovel and crowbar, eyed a spot on the wooden floor in front of the oven, and started prying up the boards.

CHAPTER

35
Sheriff Kilbourne

LAWRENCE DIDN'T HAVE time to run home.

Not with the town losing its mind and the mayor not returning calls, but he couldn't let David's eye tic drop. This thread had to be pulled now. He coasted into his driveway, shut off the car, and approached his house like he was heading to a drug bust. He entered the kitchen, softly closed the door behind him.

Paranoia propelled him now, he knew that, but still he moved on, through the kitchen, down the hallway, like a sneak thief. He peeked into David's room, found him asleep on his bed, taking his midday nap with the little unicorn in his hand. He found Tina on the couch, her back to him, typing away on her laptop, AirPods in her ears—the reason, he assumed, she hadn't heard him come in. That and he wasn't expected home anytime soon.

But it wasn't her laptop she was on. Not her emails she was apparently scouring.

It was his.

He moved into her periphery. She jumped in her seat and quickly closed his laptop. She removed the AirPods from her ears, fumbling one across the floor. "I didn't hear you come in."

"I see that," he said, not pleasantly. "Why are you on my laptop?"

"I . . ." she stammered, and then put it back on him. "Why are you home?"

"I live here, Tina." He nodded toward his closed laptop. "Find anything good in there?"

She looked on the verge of apologizing or making up a quick excuse, but then got suddenly defensive and stood from the couch. "You're the one acting crazy, Lawrence."

"Yeah? How so?"

"How could you ask me what you did last night?" Her tears were instant. "Huh?"

Maybe this wasn't much of a fight compared to what most couples had, but it had reached a point of intensity that surpassed any they'd ever had, and the foreign territory, he could tell, was emotionally ripping them open. He still went for it, went straight to the root, straight to the question that had been haunting him now for hours even though his mind had yet to admit it, had yet to even give it air to breathe and become anything other than the nonsense it might be. "Is David mine?"

She grew pale, and without warning slapped him across the face and stormed past him.

It stunned him only momentarily. He followed her down the hallway and into the kitchen, feeling guilty already for asking it. But then she stopped suddenly and turned around and faced him and boy did he see it then, written all over the worry lines in her face, what he had always seen as crow's-feet around her pretty eyes but now saw as more. It wasn't so much David, or having a kid in general, that had aged her these past five years—it was a secret she'd been holding on to since their son was born. Since he was conceived.

And she had yet to deny a thing.

"I'm right, aren't I?" Lawrence said, visibly shaking. "He has the same eye tic as Caleb Jones."

She folded her arms, looked away and then back at him, as if with a new resolve. "You refused to adopt, Lawrence. For *years* you refused."

"So you went off and . . ."

"It was one time, Lawrence. One. Time." She pointed down the hallway toward David's room and hissed. "And I'm not calling that boy in there a mistake. And not even a lapse in judgment. I knew what I was doing, and I gave us what you—"

"What, Tina? What I *couldn't*?"

"What you *wouldn't*."

That was true. He'd been stubborn. Refused to have a child that wasn't biologically his own, and now look at them. "Do you love him?"

"What? No . . ." Red-faced and crying, she screamed, "I love *you*, Lawrence. I love *you*."

"How could you?" he asked, drained of the intensity that had lured him into the house minutes ago.

She didn't back down. "And we both wanted a child so bad, Lawerence. It was slowly tearing us apart. You remember what it was doing, turning us inward, turning us *quiet*. And that's worse than fighting, Lawrence. The silence."

He shook his head, knowing she was right, but how could she?

"He's ours. David is ours. No one knows."

"I know . . . and I'm pretty damn sure Caleb Jones knows."

"He's never suspected—"

"That why he can barely look at me? Do you have secret playdates with the real daddy?"

"Goddammit, Lawrence, no," she said, crying. "But your praying wasn't working. Your going to church wasn't working. Your sneaking off into the tupelo swamp for your voodoo bags wasn't working." This drew a reaction from him, and she must have noticed it. "Yeah, I knew all about that. I didn't say anything because I felt sorry for you, Lawrence. For us. So I did something about it."

"You cheated on me," he said with rage, suddenly wanting to arrest Caleb Jones, to kill him, to slice his dick off for sticking it where it had no business going—and then he remembered he hadn't yet gone back to check on the McBrides' house for Mitchell.

"It was consuming us, Lawrence. The desperation."

He moved past her, aggressively brushing her shoulder, spinning her unintentionally into the wall, not hard, just enough to shock them both.

"Where are you going?" she asked.

"I don't know." Suddenly, obsessively almost, he began to think—no, worry—about what she might have found lurking inside his laptop, because she'd been digging too. But there was nothing incriminating in there. Nothing he could think of. No porn. No messages with secret lovers. He didn't lie, cheat, or steal. He opened the door.

"Lawrence, this is stupid."

"I saw his tic, Tina. I'd seen it before, but today I really noticed it, you know? Then I started thinking, started *digging* . . ."

"Mommy," David said from the hallway, but it was background noise.

Tina stepped toward Lawrence, as if for a consoling hug—God how he needed one—but he backed away from her, into the screen door. She said, "You don't look good, Lawrence. Something has gotten into you. Something is happening to the island, and it's . . ."

"It's what, Tina? Making me imagine all this?"

Before she could respond, distant chopper blades grew louder, sounding as if the chopper—the sole Crow Island emergency helicopter—might be directly over their house. Only Deputy Justin Clampus had a license to fly it, but what was he doing up there now when he was supposed to be back at the station watching Steven Delacroix?

Tina heard the helicopter. "What's going on out there?"

"I don't know." He was too mad to think. Being mad at her was ripping his heart to shreds. But when you dig and you find what you were looking for, you gloat, right? You give them the bone you dug up and make them chew on it.

"Right?" he said aloud, verbalizing the question in his mind.

She looked up, shook her head, confused and scared.

"Daddy . . ." It was David again, but Lawrence's mind was back on the helicopter outside, and the fact that it seemed to be sputtering. Lawrence grabbed his hat from the counter, couldn't bring himself to look at the boy, and stormed outside.

The air felt weird, toxic almost, as if loaded with an invisible current.

The hair on his arms stood on end. He checked his phone, found it dead, completely dead, when previously it hadn't been close to losing charge. He tried to radio the station but found that dead too.

He got inside his car, and within two blocks, his engine cut off.

Up and down Bull Street, the electricity blanked out.

The helicopter turned sideways into the wind, the chopper blades slowed, and then it started plummeting toward the ocean.

CHAPTER

36
Amy

BECAUSE IT IS . . .

The words echoed inside Amy's head now with as much force as when Mr. Passafume had hissed them moments ago. But if he was the same man as the one in the black-and-white picture, it would put him well over a hundred years old.

The sound of the helicopter had lured them outside before she could ask more. Seeing the lone chopper always reminded Amy of their isolation. Aside from that and the ferry, there was no way to get off of the island. Three times, bridge networks had been designed to connect Crow Island to the mainland—the first in 1911, the second in 1919, and the third attempt in 1940—and all three had ended in tragedy shortly after construction started. Workers fell off piers and drowned. Bridgework collapsed. Storms demolished frameworks. In all, sixteen people had perished in the three separate attempts to link Crow Island to the mainland by bridge before it was ultimately decided it was not only impossible but irresponsible to even try.

Did the island itself refuse the bridges? Did the island kill those people?

Maybe the island *was* alive, she thought now as she spotted the chopper in the sky. The island had a heartbeat and soul, and it was pissed off about something.

Maybe for being inhabited in the first place.

Her phone vibrated in her pocket as if she'd just gotten a burst of texts, but when she pulled it from her pants, it went dead. She pushed the power button, held it down, but to no avail. And then the helicopter suddenly sputtered. The chopper blades cut off; it went first into a tilt, then into a tailspin and an angled descent toward the horizon. A collective gasp sounded from every islander outside watching it plummet toward the Sands, where the beach would typically be full of people.

"Oh dear God," Mr. Passafume said under his breath.

Amy sprinted toward where the helicopter was headed for a crash landing. As she ran, she realized all the power on the island had shut off, and the air, although eerily silent, felt electrified. The hair on her arms stood on end, as if current pushed across the island like a tsunami wave.

In the distance, as the helicopter began to more violently spin to its demise, the pilot—it had to be Deputy Clampus—jumped into a whirling freefall. Seconds later the chopper crashed into the ocean. Amy pushed herself through the streets, through the woods and over the trails, until emerging onto the grassy field sloping down toward the Sands. The few who'd been on the beach—by the numerous craters in the sand, it was obvious they'd been digging—had had ample time to take cover and were coming out from behind whatever shelters they'd sought. The ejected pilot crawled like a wounded soldier from the water, through the wet sand, and Amy was the first to reach him. It was Deputy Justin Clampus; his legs were shattered so badly his left femur stuck out through his torn pants. Blood trailed behind him across the sand as he crawled toward her, his face a blackened smear of blood and ash and dirty sand.

"Pic . . . pictures," he said in a garbled voice. Blood oozed from his mouth. "Film . . ." He collapsed face first into the sand. Amy helped him roll to his back and gently placed her hands on each side of his face to help him focus. His blood-filled eyes settled on her. "De . . . develop . . . the film . . ."

What film?

Mr. Matthew Folsom, a well-regarded CPA on the island, hurried up the beach toward them with something in his hands. He was shirtless, and his swim trunks were soaking wet. "I was, uh . . . swimming.

I saw the helicopter hit the water." He held up a camera. "He tossed this before he landed. I retrieved it before the tide took it."

Amy looked down at Justin Clampus, his open eyes unblinking now. He was dead. She closed the young deputy's eyes, nodded toward the camera in Mr. Folsom's hands. "Hold on to that for Sheriff Kilbourne."

"What's in it?" he asked.

"I don't know. But my guess is he was up there taking aerial shots of the island."

"Why?"

"I don't know. But you really shouldn't be out there swimming alone. Mr. Folsom?"

"Oh . . . right," he said, in his own zone. "I wasn't alone. My brother was with me."

"He's still out there?"

"Yeah . . ." And then he looked at the camera in his hand. "You think he saw me do it?"

Amy's heart lurched. "Saw you do what?"

Mr. Folsom stared catatonically toward the sky. "Did you feel it?"

"Feel what?"

"Right before the chopper lost power," he said. "Like a wave of something in the air. Static electricity. I think it short-circuited the island. I think he's fully awake now . . ."

Amy couldn't yet process what he'd said. She surveyed the beach, the waves calmly floating in, rolling out, knowing that by tonight, if not sooner, pieces of that helicopter would either come ashore or drift farther out to sea.

"Yeah," Mr. Folsom said. "I think he saw me." He looked at his hands—hands that looked blistered like so many across the island. "Red-handed, I guess you can say."

Just when Amy thought he might take the camera and run with it, Mr. Folsom gently dropped the camera in the sand beside her and started walking back up the shoreline toward the grass.

Amy looked out toward the ocean again, toward the section of water from where Mr. Folsom had just emerged. She squinted for a tighter focus and saw what looked like a body floating atop the waves.

C H A P T E R

37
Nate

Fourteen Years Before the Sudden Death of Reverend Thomas Dodd

JERICHO WAS FOUR years old when Nate, at twelve, first saw him hitting his head against the bedroom wall.

Nate was brushing his teeth after dinner, eager to get to the Barneses' house to see Bridget and having even squirted a burst of his father's cologne on his neck, when he heard something thumping against an upstairs wall. He followed the sound down the hall to Jericho's room and stopped at the open door. Jericho, in blue pajamas with sailboats on them, sat up in bed, his back against the headboard, methodically knocking the back of his head into the wall, hard enough to dent the drywall. Nate was surprised their father hadn't heard and come running, but sometimes after dinner he liked to put on his earphones and close his eyes on the library sofa and allow Mozart to take him away.

Nate rarely stepped foot in Jericho's bedroom but forced himself to go in. "Jericho, stop," he said softly, shuffling closer to the bed. Jericho continued rhythmically thumping his head into the wall, eyes blinking with each impact. "Stop it," Nate said louder, inching closer, Jericho mumbling something Nate couldn't make out. "Jericho, stop it."

Nate snapped his fingers. He clapped, and that didn't work either. Jericho seemed to be in a trance. The bedside lamp flickered. Nate had seen lights flicker before when Jericho entered a room, but this was different. Nate stopped beside the bed, close enough now to hear what Jericho was saying, and it sounded like "Bees, bees, the bees . . ."

Nate looked around the room, saw no bees. And then it dawned on him that the bees might be inside Jericho's head, or at least that he might think they were. Sometimes Jericho clasped his hands to the side of his head as if in pain. Maybe hitting his head against the wall was to combat the bee buzz. Nate placed a hand behind his brother's head to soften the blow. The forcefulness and weight of Jericho's head made Nate queasy, and instead of Jericho's head hitting the wall, Nate's hand was being smashed in between. Just as Nate was about to remove his hand, Jericho eased, not in pace or rhythm but in intensity. Nate absorbed a few more blows with his hand while Jericho calmed down. "No more bees." Nate didn't know what else to say.

"No more bees," Jericho repeated like an echo, saliva dotting the corners of his lips. And then suddenly he stopped altogether.

Nate's reddened hand felt pain at every knuckle. He said to Jericho, "You okay?"

Jericho blinked.

Nate took that as a yes and then hurried from the room to throw up.

CHAPTER

38
Nate

NOW THAT'S THE *shit,* Nate thought, staring down into the kitchen floor.

And there it was.

Another part of the bone he'd tracked from the yard, through the floor of the library, and now into the kitchen. Under the kitchen, rather, because he'd had to strip it all down to the joists, just as he had in the library, before he'd been able to start in with the shovel.

He wiped his sweaty, dirt-crusted brow and again heard the helicopter flying above the house, as if circling the island, and thought it must be hard to fly through this air, which seemed to have become thicker with whatever they'd allowed to escape from the ground.

Nate just knew it was *Jericho* in the air.

The air was thick with it. Thick with *him*. With Jericho. And this all seemed like life-or-death now. Like Nate *had* to do this, or else. Just like Jericho must have understood he had to beat his head against the wall every time he felt the bees buzzing in there.

The sound of the helicopter changed, as if the blades had given out somewhere over the island, but Nate had lost interest.

The lights in the house flickered, once, twice, and then the power shut off.

Nate stood, placed his hands at the small of his back, and stretched like an old man. Outside the kitchen window, it was clear the Dodd

House wasn't the only residence on the island to lose power, and with the waning sunlight, the sky had an eerie orange glow. He looked down into the kitchen floor and decided he'd gone as far as he could inside the house. He imagined the bones branching out like an underground spider web but was convinced this largest bone was tracking like a pipeline toward the veranda and Oak Alley.

Before it got too dark, he needed to hunt down some candles.

And some matches.

He'd seen some earlier inside his mother's memorial parlor. He'd only glanced in there earlier, but now as he navigated the room full of her favorite flowers, some on tables scattered about the room, some hanging in baskets from hooks in the ceiling, others growing on fancy wrought iron trellises, he realized the room was more of a shrine, complete with floor drains for easy watering. His father had spared no expenses constructing this room.

The plants looked dry. Nate spotted a watering can on the floor near the room's entrance and spent the next hour watering the flowers, meticulously, obsessively—like he'd done with the digging—until every flower dripped, until every soil bed felt saturated, until the room sounded like a rain forest.

He closed his eyes, listened to the water trickle, and only then did he realize how tired he was. But he had work to do and the clock was ticking. He spotted six candles where the reverend had placed them, stationed around the room, each in front of a photo album propped on wooden stands. He removed the nearest photo album, this one from his parents' early years, pre-children. It shocked Nate to see that his father had taken the time to organize all the old pictures into albums. He flipped a page, saw a much-younger Thomas and Samantha Dodd holding hands, standing atop the decking of the bee barges with the sky-blue honey house in the background. This, Nate knew, was rare. His father didn't like going near the bee barges because of how allergic he was to their stings, but then something else about the picture struck him. A memory flashed of his father inside the honey house, late at night, the same night he'd seen him coming home from the tupelo swamp, shoes muddy, the ash devil spinning from the chimney like it was alive.

You didn't just see him come home, Nate. Your shoes were muddy too. You followed him.

You followed him to the swamp. You followed him up the spiraling wooden stairs to the floating barges. You followed him to the honey house. You called out, "Daddy?" But he didn't hear you.

And then he went inside.

And you followed, stopped at the door, and you watched.

You saw what he was doing inside the honey house, Nate.

For eighteen years, he'd blocked it out.

"And we weren't alone," Nate said aloud, standing unsteadily in the darkened parlor, the plants still dripping water. The memory had come to him so instantly and without warning that he'd already begun to question it. But the memory was also half baked in his mind—it hadn't come back in full. It had ended abruptly with him, as a seven-year-old boy, stopping at the honey house's open door.

The door hadn't been locked that night. But he couldn't remember the rest. As much as he wanted to know what he'd seen inside the honey house that night, he also *didn't* want to know.

Because maybe your father, as perfect as he seemed, wasn't perfect. He wasn't the saint the island thought he was. So dig into that, *Nate.*

He knew that the next morning, his parents had been quiet at the breakfast table. Nate remembered being scared of both of them. In hindsight, Nate would have described his father as *shelled*. Used and abused, disheveled and unshaven, when by breakfast he was typically clean and put-together. Mom wouldn't even look at Dad as she took tiny bites of her honey-dabbed toast, gently touching her stomach like she knew a baby was already growing in there.

A monster, Nate thought. And somehow his father was responsible. He'd gotten her pregnant that night as if he'd done a deal with the devil. Not just planted the monster inside her but brought it back with him from the swamp.

No, he thought, that was crazy.

But was it?

His mother, within days, had begun that painful, nine-month downward spiral to her death, checking the locks and windows every night, leaving deposits of sand under doors, placing brooms and hairbrushes next to entrances, hanging colanders above doorways. But by then it was too late, Nate thought. The Boo Hag had already gotten in, and it was growing inside his mother. Because his father hadn't been alone inside the honey house that night. He hadn't been alone inside the drawing room when he'd stood amid the spinning ashes.

And nine months later Jericho had entered the world.

C H A P T E R

39
Sheriff Kilbourne

THE POWER WAS out across the island.

His only deputy had just perished in a helicopter crash.

Mr. Folsom had apparently killed his brother and left him to float out in the ocean.

But all Lawrence could think about was Caleb Jones.

Could he arrest someone for committing adultery? For screwing his wife? Even if it was just one time? *I am the sheriff,* Lawrence thought, on foot now, since the cars and golf carts had been rendered useless by whatever had pulsed through the air minutes ago. The air seemed thick with what Lawrence could only think of as despair; it grew hazier by the hour and had developed a distinct orange-yellow hue, what he imagined it might look like after a nuclear bomb went off and the dust settled.

Lawrence pounded on Caleb Jones's front door and waited, knowing he shouldn't be here. But this root needed to be pulled right now. After knocking again with no answer, Lawrence made his way around to the back of Caleb's house, where he encountered a freshly dug hole in the ground, big as a swimming pool and at least four feet deep in parts. Lawrence pulled his gun as he neared the outer edge of it. "Jesus wept," he said, looking down into the pit and the newly uncovered bones within, bones too big to be human. Unlike the isolated bone Lawrence had seen in Steven Delacroix's backyard excavation, this was a network of bones curved parallel toward another bone central to it all.

"I think that might be part of a rib cage." Caleb's voice sounded from the back porch.

Lawrence spun quickly toward the voice, pointed his gun toward Caleb, who was sitting on a rocking chair with a shotgun across his lap.

"Go ahead," Caleb said. "Shoot, Sheriff. Isn't that why you came here? To kill me?"

As much as he wanted to pull the trigger, if for no other reason than to scare him, Lawrence lowered his gun. "No, I ain't gonna shoot you."

Caleb did that involuntary eye tic he'd handed down to David, and Lawrence held in his fury. "How long you been working on this hole?"

Caleb said, "About two weeks."

Lawrence noticed Caleb was talking funny, like his current disheveled condition went beyond exhaustion and had entered the realm of delirium. Lawrence had been so focused on the eye tic earlier at the hardware store that he hadn't noticed the man looked like he hadn't slept in days. "Why the shotgun?"

When Caleb didn't respond and instead stared toward his unattached garage beside the hole he'd dug, Lawrence snapped at him. "Caleb . . . what's with the shotgun?"

"That McBride boy was snooping around the garage earlier. Had to chase him away."

"You don't say?"

"I do say."

"You sure it was him?"

"Sure as shit, Sheriff," Caleb said. Something about hearing Caleb call him *Sheriff* gave Lawrence a new sense of authority, and then Caleb added, "And he had an axe on him."

Lawrence stood suddenly rigid. "Was there blood on the blade?"

"Didn't get close enough," Caleb said. "Why?"

"Anybody else with him?"

Caleb stood with a grunt. "No. He was solo." He navigated the porch steps like an old man and passed Lawrence on his way toward the hole he'd dug. But instead of heading toward the hole, he walked around it toward the garage.

Lawrence said, "Where you going?"

"Follow me," Caleb said over his shoulder. "Got something to show you."

"What?"

"I caught one of them."

C H A P T E R

40
Amy

UNLIKE MOST ISLANDERS, Amy had never been a lover of the ocean.

The unpredictable nature of the waves had always frightened her.

But whether the man she assumed was Terry Folsom was dead or not, she couldn't leave him out there floating out to sea. From the bizarre moment she'd shared with Matt Folsom after he'd emerged from the surf with the camera he'd retrieved from the helicopter, she'd gotten the vibe that he'd drowned his brother out there. But she had to make sure.

Maybe the nightly laps in her pool had trained her for this, or maybe it was pure adrenaline, but she fought the waves with reckless abandon, chopping her arms tirelessly through the water toward the man's body, only to find him dead, just as she'd feared, and then the two of them, just as she'd also feared, started floating farther out to sea. So she linked her left arm around his right and started her impossible trip back to shore. She refused to let go, refused to stop, even as her shoulders burned from the exertion and her lungs felt on the verge of bursting from fatigue. Once she made it to the shore, she gripped Terry Folsom's arms and backpedaled deeper up the beach until she collapsed into the sand, leaving the body ten yards from where Deputy Clampus had died.

She hated to leave the two dead men on the beach for the island birds to pick apart but didn't know what else to do. She had to get the film in that camera developed; it was clear Deputy Clampus had been up there in the chopper taking aerial shots of the island, but what had he seen for him to so desperately demand she develop them?

She wiped wet sand from the camera and headed back into town. Her clothes were soaked and smelled of the sea, but she wasn't chilled—the air felt like a furnace. Her clothes were already drying. By the time she made it to Bull Street, where every storefront remained darkened by the power outage, her skin was coated in grime, a combination of sea salt and the unavoidable dust motes polluting the air. The street was vacant. It was too early for the sun to be setting, but that's exactly what was happening across the island.

A block away, the sinkhole from two weeks ago loomed large inside the yellow caution tape surrounding it. Beyond the sinkhole was the storefront of Dennis Wagner Photography. As the island's main photographer, Dennis was always working, but she doubted he'd be in there now, in the dark. But as she approached the front door, she noticed it was open. She showed herself in, called out Dennis's name. She spotted candlelight flickering in the back of the store and followed it. "Mr. Wagner?"

"Back here," he called out, and then, "Amy Barnes! Perfect. Come, come . . ." Mr. Wagner wasn't as old as Blue Bottles, but he didn't seem too far behind. But while Mr. Passafume still moved with an agility that belied his age, Dennis Wagner, who looked like a modern-day Albert Einstein, grunted with every movement, each shuffled step taking maximum effort, and his posture seemed to grow more stooped every year. With a bent elbow and arthritic hand, he waved her over. It was almost like he'd been expecting her. He said, "I was about to come to you, and here you walk in like the angel you are, my dear."

Amy slowed her gait, suddenly leery about what he wanted to show her.

He moved one of the dozen scented candles he had lit on a shelf behind him to a nearby table. The conglomeration of scents made Amy nauseous, but she inched closer.

"Wild berry," he said of the scent he'd moved, his face inches from the flickering flame. "It was Janine's favorite. I wonder what she would make of all this catawampus of madness going on out there." Every time Amy saw Mr. Wagner, he used a word she'd never heard before, and she loved him for it. He gestured toward the enlarged picture next to the candle and tapped it with a crooked index finger. "Look. What do you see?"

"That's Discovery Bank," she said. "Across the street."

"Look closer. Look at the far-right window."

Amy leaned down closer to the candle glow, and when she saw it, she gasped, covered her mouth, and stepped back into a cart of supplies. There was an obvious glare at the window in the picture, but beyond the glare stood an even more obvious monster from her nightmares, at least the profile of one on its way to the bank's open front door.

A Boo Hag with red skinless flesh and long white stringy hair.

She believed in the Boo Hag spirit, but this, unless someone dressed up in costume had been playing a prank, appeared to be flesh-and-bone real. Sinewy like the ones from the other side, like the ones trying to get through.

"It can't be," she said, incredulously looking at the photograph again, but deep down knowing it was true, because they'd all been digging, and the door was opening, and she didn't know what that meant but . . .

"But it is," Mr. Wagner said, sliding another couple of pictures out from under the first. "I went over there last night, not long after I snapped that photo you see there. It was gone by the time I'd gone in, but it made a wreck of the bank. Maybe it was looking for something or it was just its nature to vandalize. Or who knows, maybe it needed some cash. But it was there and it's not human." He showed her the other two pictures. One looked like a pile of animal dung formed into a foot-tall cone. "The smell of that was toxic." He didn't need to explain what that was, but the next picture he did. "They've long faded by now, but what does that look like?"

"The ridges of a footprint."

"Yes," he said. "But not one from any human I've ever seen. It was wet, with red, sticky residue. Look how narrow the foot is. And with a very high arch. And those are toes, yes, but look at the dots in front of each toe. What do those look like to you?"

"Claws," she said. "Those are from claws." She'd seen them in her nightmares. The Boo Hags had long fingernails and claws at the toes.

Mr. Wagner smiled. "I remember a drawing you did when you were in elementary school, Amy, for the island junior art contest. Of these devilish monsters. Your parents weren't too proud of it, but you were. That's what I saw across the street last night."

She was too stunned to respond, and couldn't match his apparent excitement when he asked, "Now, what did you need from me?"

C H A P T E R

41
Nate

When Nate left Crow Island in the days after the massacre, he had sworn he'd never return.

And as much as he hated the tupelo swamp, he felt drawn toward it now. After seeing the picture of his parents taken decades ago outside the honey house door and remembering that he'd followed his father there that night as a boy, he knew he needed to return if he wanted the rest of his questions answered. If he wanted the rest of his memories dug up from the deep.

But his mind was anything but focused, and with every step he took through the weirdly encroaching haze of orange-yellow motes toward the woods and swamp beyond, he fought the nearly equal pull to go back home and continue digging.

Because he was making some serious progress on that underground fossil.

Part of him knew he was stalling, his mind throwing out roadblocks to keep him from doing what he was about to do, from going to where he was about to go, and he fought it, even as jittery as he now felt walking through this weirdly polluted air toward the woods, like the air was chewing, the leaves were chewing.

He reminded himself again to stay focused, but then he spotted the house of Dr. Cheevers on the outskirts of the woods and without thinking veered toward it. He told himself that one little detour wouldn't hurt, especially if it answered a long-standing question about Jericho's birth.

He approached the doctor's quaint little wooded abode and pounded on his arched door. Ten seconds later he heard footsteps on the other side and saw movement at the nearby window, where a curtain opened and closed. The door opened as wide as the chain would allow, and in the crack, white-haired Dr. Cheevers, who had to be retired by now, peered through. His eyes were bloodshot, which, as evidenced by the bourbon or whiskey in his hand, was alcohol induced. Alcohol, Nate thought, wasn't a bad idea.

Dr. Cheevers, after recognizing who he was, unlatched the chain and opened the door wider. "Nathanial, what can I do for you?"

Nate could tell the doctor was analyzing him from head to toe. His clothes were filthy and his hands were blistered and bloody and his own eyes were probably bloodshot from exhaustion. Nate tamped the anxiety and dread and full-throttle *That's the shit* attitude coursing through his system and calmly said, "I need to know what the big secret was when Jericho was born. Between you and my father."

"I don't know what you're—"

"Yes, you do," Nate said. "And I don't have a lot of time." *I need to get to the honey house,* he thought, and added, "I need to know why you and my father kept Jericho hidden the first five days of his life."

CHAPTER

42
Sheriff Kilbourne

"WHAT DO YOU mean, you caught one of them?"

Caleb Jones propped his shotgun against his leg long enough to pull a pack of cigarettes from his trousers pocket and light one.

Lawrence watched dubiously. "When did you start smoking?"

Caleb took a drag like he was inhaling medicine and then exhaled. "Two days ago." He coughed like an amateur. "They don't seem to like the smell."

"Seems like you don't either."

"At least that's what Donnie Potts told me." The lit cigarette dangled in his lips as he spoke. "Donnie keeps incense going by his bed. Either that or a cigarette, and so far he hasn't gotten visited."

Lawrence didn't need to ask *visited by whom*, and he now had an idea of what was in Caleb Jones's garage, or at least what he thought he had locked in his garage.

Caleb confirmed it as he started toward the garage door. "It's a Boo Hag, sheriff. I wasn't buying in to the madness until I saw one snooping out here. My garage was open. I closed it in. Simple as that. And you know what the legends say. They're skinless and red fleshed when they go out at night. Then they wear a human's skin during the day so they can move about in sunlight. Well, this one is definitely skinless."

Lawrence had also heard that if you could find the human skin the Boo Hags hung up at night and pour salt inside it, they couldn't put it back on. That it would burn them when they tried to wear it. And something about that made Lawrence wonder if he and Caleb would be better off with a bucket of salt apiece instead of the guns they now held.

Caleb nodded toward the garage door, which looked like it had been pulverized with a hammer or mallet from the inside. "See that? It was trying to get out last night. Haven't heard much from him during the day. I think it's asleep. But I know what you're thinking—this can't be real. Boo Hags are spirits. They aren't flesh and blood. But I'm telling you, sheriff, that's what's in there, and I think it has something to do with all that digging."

Lawrence had thought the same but wanted to know where Caleb's mind was, and he was kicking himself for having gotten so distracted by his own digging, but Caleb was the second person now to have seen Mitchell McBride walking around the island with an axe he'd apparently dug up from the ground. "How so?"

"Don't know exactly." Caleb took a soft drag on the cigarette and exhaled. "But I think we unleashed something from the ground and it's irreversible. We might be able to put the dirt back, but this dust . . ." He made as if to grab the yellow-brown-orange motes floating through the air. "There's no getting it back in the ground, Sheriff. Maybe the Boo Hags are drawn to it. Or maybe, somehow, we made them real. Dug them out of the ground or something. Or . . ."

"Or what? I can guess what you're thinking, and you won't be the only one."

"I think Jericho's back, Sheriff. I don't know how to explain it, but there it is. I think Jericho is back, or maybe he never really died in the first place and that relief we all felt when he was buried was only short-lived. Just none of us wanted to admit it."

"The earthquakes?"

"Yes, the earthquakes."

Lawrence was fully focused on the garage now, and could have sworn he'd just heard something skittering in there. "Let's get this over with."

"Stay behind me." Shotgun in one hand, Caleb bent down and wedged the garage door open with the other. He hoisted, lifted it higher. Lawrence gave him a hand. Without electricity, and with the door being warped and dented, lifting it was a bitch, but once they had it open to around five feet high, Caleb ducked under, and Lawrence followed.

The garage smelled like swamp water and dirty animals. Except for some tools and yard supplies, the garage was empty, and mostly covered in shadow aside from the faint, angled beam of daylight coming in from the open door. With sunlight fading so quickly, Lawrence knew it would be completely dark soon, and the thing that was curled up in a ball like a sleeping dog in the far corner wouldn't be so small anymore once it stood up. He could tell it was breathing: The alien-like, textured flesh at the visible rib cage moved in and out. In the shadows, its dirty white hair looked as gray as a used rayon mop, and between the strands, a lone white eye watched them, the tiny black pupil clearly tracking them.

Caleb stopped halfway across the garage floor and held out his hand in caution. "Don't go any closer. It's on a chain hooked to the floor pipe back there."

"It's watching us."

"Yes, it is."

Suddenly Lawrence wanted a cigarette.

And then the thing spoke in a hushed hiss. At first the word was indecipherable, but when it spoke again, clear lips moving to enunciate behind the splayed strands of white hair, Lawrence heard it clearly.

"Jericho . . ." it hissed, grinning now, with crooked white teeth and purple gums.

"Did you hear what I just heard?" Caleb asked, cigarette dangling as he raised the shotgun toward the Boo Hag.

Lawrence nodded as the Boo Hag shifted and then lengthened, making it to its feet, and what seconds ago had been curled into a harmless ball was now unfurling to something six feet tall at least, sinewy, muscle corded, and gangly. They both stepped away as it turned toward them, took one slow step, and hissed the word "Jericho . . ."

Quick as a snakebite, it sprinted toward them, mouth wide open, and the next thing Lawrence knew, blood and guts and bone had been blown across the walls and Caleb stood there, breathing heavily, the sound of his shotgun blast still echoing in the sheriff's ears.

"Holy shit," Caleb said. The cigarette had fallen from his mouth onto the garage floor, inches away from a splotch of Boo Hag bloody goo. He grounded it out under his boot.

Lawrence said, "I thought it was chained and couldn't reach this far."

Caleb nodded toward the cinder block wall. "It's smarter than I thought."

Lawrence followed his gaze, where it was clear the thick chain had been gnawed through and the Boo Hag had been waiting for the right time to strike.

CHAPTER

43
Amy

AMY COUGHED AS she hurried through the increasingly polluted island air, the motes so thick she could feel them on her skin.

It was dirt, yes, but not only dirt. Mixed in with the fine, grainy, orange-brown particles floating in the air was the taste of toxicity and poison, of dread. And she sensed Jericho around every corner. Behind every tree. Crawling out every recently dug hole across the island, and he was laughing. The only time she'd ever seen him smile—only days before the massacre—had been at her, and the memory sent chill bumps across her flesh, mixing with sweat and grime and salt from the ocean.

She clenched her jaw, forced her mouth closed, but breathing through her nose was just as bad. With every breath she felt like she was ingesting sickness, and she feared it would cause delirium if she allowed it. She needed to find Sheriff Kilbourne and tell him about what she'd witnessed on the beach, and even more about the pictures she'd seen inside Dennis Wagner's Photography. One of *her* Boo Hags had somehow made it through. She didn't even know what "through" meant but was as convinced of that as she was that these Boo Hags were somehow *her* doing. She'd had nightmares of them for years; therefore, they were hers. They were her responsibility, and this was her island, and it was up to her to stop them, because . . . the air had a smell to it too, and the smell was familiar. Not only familiar, she thought as she found herself approaching Matt Folsom's property in the middle of the island, but distinctly noticeable.

You know this smell, Amy. You've been there.

It's as fruity as it is gut-wrenching. As delicious as it is toxic. It's air from the other side because it's starting to come through. It's a dream world, Amy, and there's an army of Boo Hags and they all smell like Jericho. They smell like dread and anxiety, and they skitter and they've located the door and . . .

The earth started shaking.

Ten yards deep into Matt Folsom's property, which had the nicest, lushest lawn and most finely pruned landscaping in all the island, she braced herself against the trunk of a sprawling live oak. She closed her eyes and counted. But unlike the other tremors, it didn't stop at three or four seconds but at nine.

The longest one yet.

She opened her eyes, surveyed. The island had stopped shaking. She noticed that even though Matt Folsom had apparently lost his mind drowning his brother in the ocean, he had no holes anywhere in his yard. He hadn't been digging. His yard still looked as pristine and manicured as it had before anyone's shovel first turned earth under to begin all of this.

She felt a prick at her palm, as if she'd just brushed her hand over a thorn. On the other side, the rocks had thorns, and the grass blades had thorns and the trees had thorns too, horns and thorns growing from the dark bark like appendages. Because weren't thorns like little baby horns? Didn't thorns grow into horns? But when she analyzed her palm, she saw no marking, no blood from a recently pricked wound, and the tree looked like any other island tree. It was just in her mind. Just as on the day she'd drowned, before she'd gone down the stairs, the sound of horns running across the underside of the bee barge's decking that she'd been running across the top of had been in her mind, and there had not been a hag with horns down there in the swamp to pull her under, following beneath her like a devilish shadow, *horns on boards, horns on boards*, like the sound of a stick dragged across the vertical slats of a picket fence.

She remembered the shadow down there, moving along with her, directly below . . .

. . . tick-tick-tick-tick-tick . . .

Thorns on boards, Amy. Thorns on . . .

She shook it away, focused on Matt Folsom's front porch, on the screen door. The main door was wide open. Candles flickered through darkness on the other side. She shouldn't be here. It wasn't safe. He was a murderer. But she needed to dig. She needed to *know*.

The branches are antlers over there . . .

She called through the screen door, "Mr. Folsom?"

She had no plan, no idea what she would say to him, other than ask him straight to his face *Why did you just kill your brother and leave him to float out there in the ocean?*

To her surprise, he said calmy, "Door's open."

She opened the screen door, stepped inside the small foyer, and smelled upturned soil and mud. She smelled cigarette smoke to her right. She turned. Matt Folsom sat in a recliner, feet propped up, completely naked, his skin pale and flabby. In one hand he held a lit cigarette and in the other a handgun, pointed directly at her. She knew nothing about guns, but this one looked big and heavy and extra powerful, like it took effort to even hold it up with one hand. She discreetly shuffled a few inches back with one foot, as if to start her getaway, before hearing the gun click. It was too late; she'd unknowingly placed a foot inside this bear trap.

And he might not have touched a blade of his perfect grass outside, but as she surveyed the living room and hallway, it was obvious he'd dug up virtually every inch of the floorboards. There were piles of boards and dirt and nails and mud everywhere.

"What do you want?" he asked.

Why did you kill your brother? But it wouldn't come out. Because just as she was about to verbalize her thoughts, she saw two empty honey jars beside his recliner, both with a yellow sticker. "Where did you get those?" she asked, nodding toward the honey jars.

"They were gifted to me." He licked his dry lips. "Never tasted anything like it in my life. You ever had an orgasm, Amy Barnes? Knowing how Chad was with the ladies, I'm sure you have. But that's what it was like, swallowing that honey. Except it didn't stop there; it went straight into the bloodstream. Straight into my heart." He tapped his chest with the gun and then touched the barrel to his right temple. "Straight into my brain." She should have made a run for it but felt frozen, and before she knew it the gun was on her again. "Mitchell McBride. That boy ain't all bad. Despite what some are saying."

Amy swallowed audibly. "How did he get it?"

"How you think he got it? Stole it. Said the Boo Hags told him to. Just like they told him to dig. Told *me* to dig. Just like they told him to visit Reverend Dodd."

Amy had been looking anywhere but at Matt Folsom until then. "When did he visit Reverend Dodd?"

Folsom shrugged, took a long drag on his cigarette, exhaled and waited until the gray-blue smoke dissipated before answering. "Weeks ago." He laughed. "Drove that man batty. Made him confess. Made him wear his own little proverbial crown of thorns."

At the word *thorns*, Amy flinched. "What are you talking about? Confess to what?"

"The reverend's great sin." Folsom shifted in the recliner, kept the gun on her. "You know Mitchell found Jericho's axe?" He raised his eyebrows. "Can you believe it moved underground? It took eight years, but tunneling through dirt and rock and mud takes time. But it did. Like a baton passed at a track meet. He used it to cut the reverend's hand off. Reverend begged him to do it."

The only thing on Folsom's body was the watch on his left wrist, and he checked it now. Amy was shivering. Folsom said, "Time for me to clock out, Amy Barnes." He finished his cigarette, flicked it into the open pit before him. Amy watched it land, and for the first time noticed part of a bone down there in the dirt, a thick bone like the one in the Dodds' yard. He went on. "Earthquakes are only gonna get worse, and I don't want to be around to see what's next, not without more honey. Go on now."

Now she felt sure he was about to shoot himself. "Mr. Folsom, please don't. You can work things out with Sheriff Kilbourne."

"You've got five seconds, honey," he said with a quick chortle, before a crazed look overtook his shadowed eyes. "One, two . . ."

She turned and ran out the door.

His crazed voice chased her. "I was born naked, Amy Barnes, and I shall die the same!"

Just as she rounded the porch, the gunshot sounded, and blood sprayed against the window to her left.

She kept running.

CHAPTER

44
Nate

As an eerie dusk settled low over the island, quickly darkening the forest to deep shadows, the tupelo swamp appeared to be glowing.

Spanish moss moved in gentle whispers, showing like radiant crystals in the strange, waning light. Thick, colorful bees buzzed through the air. White butterflies fluttered, as if playing in the haze.

The bee barge swayed beneath Nate's feet.

Movement.

There was always movement at the swamp.

Movement under the decking.

Just like he'd felt movement under the water's surface minutes ago, when the canoe cut through the murky chop of algae and oily grime coating the waves.

Him thinking *The swamp shouldn't have waves.*

Him thinking *I can't believe what I just heard at Dr. Cheevers' house about Jericho.* Him thinking *They should have killed him then. They should have killed him right away.*

His hands shook as he slowly made his way across the bee barge. His flashlight flickered. The strobing effect only added to his anxiety. Forty yards across the decking, the honey house loomed, and the door was open to the night.

The door was never open.

It shouldn't be open.

It was open that night, Nate. Wide open, and your daddy went in there.

A memory flashed in snippets: his father standing beneath lantern glow, his shadow mixing with another shadow . . . the shadow laughing . . . and the shadow grew and stretched from wall to wall and ceiling until the light went out . . .

Nate moved slowly toward the open door of the honey house.

There were shadows in there now.

Something moved in the shadows between the cypress trees on the far bank of the swamp. Something big. Something heavy. More movement behind the tupelo trees to his left.

Why was my father missing a hand?

Shadows moved behind the honey house door, or what used to be a door. There was someone in there. He followed the flashlight beam.

It was Mr. Passafume. But what was he doing?

"Mr. Passafume," Nate called out, his voice weak, his breath somehow coming out in plumes of steam as if it were cold out. But it wasn't. The air was humid and warm.

The air was . . . Jericho.

Now only twenty yards from the honey house, Nate stepped in something sticky and looked down. The floorboards glistened with golden, gooey honey. As he got closer to the honey house, he noticed vines with prickly thorns had sprouted from the doorway, spiraling in threads of purple and gold with small white blooms interspaced throughout, spreading out across the front of the honey house as well and beginning to creep toward the pitched red roof.

The colors, he thought, were so luridly rich, like wet paint.

Amy always spoke of the colors in that place . . .

The other side.

They'd never believed her.

"Mr. Passafume," he called out toward the open door. He smelled honey and nectar and flowers, but when he aimed the flashlight inside the honey house, Mr. Passafume was nowhere to be seen.

The old man had seemingly vanished. But there was nowhere for him to go.

Nate aimed the flashlight from wall to wall, heard the collective bee buzz growing louder. On the floor, dozens of bees were stuck to the floorboards, wings slowly moving in a spill of thick honey. The wooden manmade boxlike hives along the floorboards and on the shelves weren't the only hives now taking up space inside the small, square house: Dozens of natural hives and nests clung to the spaces where the walls met the ceiling and even more adhered to the wooden rafters, where hive after honeycomb hive hung alien-like in their various sizes and designs, seemingly fastened to whatever surface they touched, one as uniquely formed as the next, clusters hanging down like stalactites from the ceiling of a cave and rising like stalagmites from the floor, all of them covered by bees.

A bird fluttered above him. He ducked, saw only the shadow at first, but then the bird landed on the floor and watched him with black, oily eyes. It had a brown-orange beak and stark-red feathers—a crow, a red crow, and its talon-like feet made tiny imprints in the honey-slicked floor.

And then it flew out the open door, leaving him alone with the bees.

The strobing flashlight beam made their movement more eerie and caused them to glisten, and something about the way they moved over one another, as if vying for precious space, told Nate they weren't the island's typical bees.

These bees were larger.

Because everything grew larger on Crow Island.

And then the bees swarmed him.

CHAPTER

45
Sheriff Kilbourne

LAWRENCE HEARD A gunshot from somewhere on the island.

Caleb Jones, walking beside him with his shotgun, had flinched—he'd been extra jumpy since pulling the trigger on the Boo Hag he'd trapped in his garage—but it didn't slow their progress toward the McBrides' house. It was too early for it, but the sky was full dark now, and his flashlight was faint and flickering.

They approached the McBride property from the backyard and immediately saw the dozens of birds circling above their in-ground pool, flittering in and out of the moonlight.

Caleb said, "Sheriff?"

Lawrence was too focused on the pool, because he could swear he was seeing two figures lounging on sun chairs on the far side. Had the mayor come home early after all?

Caleb said, "Sheriff, those are crows circling the pool."

Can't be crows, Lawrence thought, refusing to look at them. Crow Island hadn't had any crows for almost five hundred years. He adjusted his sheriff's hat and unlatched the metal gate to the McBrides' backyard oasis. He felt a little weird being with the man who'd cuckolded him but was truthfully glad now for his company.

Because maybe those *were* crows up there.

At the wrought iron fence, he called out, "Mayor McBride? Mrs. McBride?"

Neither answered back.

Shit, thought Lawrence. They hadn't even moved. He approached the swimming pool with Caleb behind him, hoping they might be asleep. One of the birds from above flew down and rested along the pool's edge. Lawrence shined his light on it. It was a crow, and not a black one, but a bright-red bird unlike anything he'd ever seen before.

It was like the birds Reverend Dodd had scribbled across that page before he'd died.

Lawrence looked up at the circling birds, followed a few with his flickering light, and damn if they weren't all as red as the one watching him from beside the pool.

A murder of crows, he thought, with a short laugh.

He heard the blowflies buzzing before he saw them, forced himself to look at the two bodies in the sun chairs. It was Chip and Beverly McBride, their torsos cleaved by gaping wounds and smattered with dried, crusty blood.

Caleb turned and vomited on the concrete and nearly fell over a third lounge chair, but Lawrence forced himself to take it all in. By the number of flies and the smell of decomposition in the thick, humid island air, he guessed they'd been dead for days.

He'd checked the inside of their house yesterday and found what he'd found inside Mitchell's bedroom and bathroom but had neglected to walk around to the back of the house. He'd been distracted by the earthquake, and then the call for him to run to the Winslows' house. Had the mayor and his wife been back here rotting even then? *A good sheriff would have reconnoitered the rim, Lawrence.* A good sheriff would have checked the backyard and pool, especially with how he'd found the massive hole in the bathroom floor, the outline of an axe in the mud.

Lawrence forced himself to look again at the two corpses. They'd been murdered for sure, and he knew from experience that an axe had been the weapon. The mayor's chest had been thwacked from collarbone to belly, while Beverly had been slashed straight across the stomach, east to west, both of them propped like a pair of vacation sunbathers, complete with sun hats and fancy cocktails, ice long since melted. And whoever had slain them—something told him it was likely their son, Mitchell—had clasped their hands together in the open space between the chairs and tied them together with twine. Below their hands were two cell phones, one atop the other, of course now both dead as all of their phones were, and Lawrence just knew that Mitchell had been the one to respond to his text to Mayor McBride yesterday. Mitchell who had responded so immediately that they were all hunky-dory on the mainland when they were in reality cut up in the backyard.

Lawrence backed away, wondering where the son might be. An on-campus nervous breakdown was one thing, but violence was another. But was it so far-fetched? Just ask school shooters about their motive. The boy had apparently needed help a long time ago and never gotten it.

Lawrence grabbed Caleb by the arm, and they hurried from the yard and out the gate.

Had Mitchell McBride begun his own killing spree with the axe he'd unearthed beneath his bathroom floor? Had it begun with his parents, or with Reverend Dodd's right hand? Could it be Jericho's axe? The indentation in the mud was evidence of the same shape. But the reverend had sworn he'd buried that axe inside Jericho's coffin. Lawrence needed to send out a warning to the island, but his radio was as dead as his phone and his car, and with everything going as wrong as it was, a warning was almost laughable.

He thought back to Jericho's massacre. As wildly and efficiently as the boy had been wielding the axe that sunny Fourth of July afternoon, they were lucky he didn't kill more—and he would have, had the offensive line from the high school football team not gotten him to the ground.

But what was his motive?

That had never truly been settled. With Jericho dead and in the ground, it was a thread Lawrence had let drop. There wasn't going to be a trial. The *Why did he do it?* had been chalked up to what everyone had always assumed of Jericho—that he'd finally become the full-fledged monster everyone thought he was.

But now Lawrence wasn't so sure that was all of it.

Had Jericho, from the grave, channeled through Mitchell McBride to finish what he'd started?

CHAPTER

46
Amy

AMY'S MIND WAS reeling, and no matter how many deep breaths she tried, she couldn't calm the nerves jackhammering through her system.

After running to Mr. Passafume's house and finding him gone, she returned home even more panicked than she'd been after fleeing Matt Folsom's house in the seconds after he shot himself. She opened the fridge—which was quickly losing its cold—and drank straight from the bottle of Moscato. She paced the dark kitchen until she'd nearly finished the bottle, thinking, *Why me?* First Thomas Dodd. Then holding Mr. Torrence on his front porch while he bled out. Comforting Deputy Clampus during his final breaths after he'd jumped from the crashing chopper. And finally, the Folsom brothers, one of whom she'd dragged out of the ocean and the other whose brains she'd seen splatter across the glass of his living room window.

Why me?

Because you've been there, Amy.

You comforted victims on the day of the massacre, even while you grieved for the loss of your own.

She'd gripped Joey Keplar's hand as he bled out on Bull Street. She'd not known the young man well, yet she'd run her hand over his hair as he breathed his last breaths, attempting to calm him by telling him of her own experience over there, on the other side, in the place she at first had thought was heaven but then quickly realized wasn't.

. . . it's beautiful . . .

. . . do you like colorful things . . .

Johnny nodding, staring into her eyes as people screamed all around them.

. . . everything is vibrant and alive and full of sunshine . . .

. . . can you see it . . . on the other side . . .

Him still nodding, the hint of a grin on his lips as he died on the sidewalk in a pool of his own blood.

. . . it's a good place . . .

It's a good place *sometimes*, she thought now, hunting her kitchen for candles. But it was a bad place too. There were bad things there. Evil things with horns and thorns. *And it's an island over there, just like here, but even worse . . . it's the Island of Horns.*

She struck a match and lit three candles on the kitchen island. The flames flickered. One went out, as if breath-blown by an unseen presence, a thought that should have shaken her but didn't, because she knew the feeling in the air. She knew it intimately. She'd felt it inside the swamp water. She felt it when she'd been . . .

Say it, Amy.

She'd felt it on the other side. She'd felt it when Samantha Dodd was pregnant with *him*. She'd felt it when Jericho was born. She'd felt it every time Jericho was in the room with her when he was alive. And she'd been feeling it now for weeks, starting around the time everyone on the island had begun digging, opening the ground, which, she knew now, had started well before the sudden death of Thomas Dodd.

She felt Jericho.

Now.

Everywhere.

And it was getting stronger by the day, by the hour.

She wanted to scream to the entire island *STOP DIGGING!*

"Is that you?" she asked aloud, with an anxious quaver in her voice. "Is it you, Jericho? If it's you, blow out another candle."

She waited, heart racing, for ten seconds, and then a second candle went out.

Christ.

She backed away from the island, left the remaining candle flickering, and left the room. *What now? How do I explain to Nate what I have never been able to explain to myself?* That his brother, while dead, was still somehow out there. His brother . . . had somehow come from that place?

"What do you want?" she asked the darkness inside the living room.

Keep digging . . .

Whether the words were her own or Jericho had somehow put them there, they were right. *What's the damn passcode on Chad's cell phone?*

What did it matter now? She laughed, maniacally almost. Jericho had already shut the power off across the island. Even knowing that, Amy found herself in Chad's home office. Moonlight shone through the window beside his desk. She didn't know what she was looking for, but the more she moved files and papers around, the more frantic she became, before clearing the desktop with two angry sweeps of her arm, revealing a small stack of the trifolded, full-color brochures she'd paid for and had printed before Chad's business, McGovern Maritime, got off the ground. On the front was a picture of one of their deep-sea fishing boats. The center of the trifold read *MEET THE CREW!* Chad's face—he was the owner—was at the top. Next was their general manager and Chad's best friend, Greg Banks. Below him was James Wright, another high school friend of Chad's who, with Greg and Chad, piloted most of the boat trips. Last was the lone female in the crew, Ella Finlay, who ran most everything at the office, from phone calls and scheduling to reservations and paperwork and legalities.

And while Amy had never given Ella's presence around Chad much thought, now she homed in on her with a ferocity that made her eyes fill with sparks. Ella was pretty. She'd always been pretty. And that smile, Amy thought, those perfect white teeth, and come to think of it, her overall flirty nature . . . *Maybe it* has *always bothered you, Amy, and you trusted Chad so much—perhaps* because *everyone else didn't—that you overlooked what maybe was happening right in front of your stupid, gullible face.*

Chad had to have been screwing Ella. Amy had always doubted herself in bed, her lack of experience when Chad married her, the constant feeling she was never enough, never *all* that Chad wanted. Ella had always had boyfriends in high school. She was experienced, more experienced than Amy for sure.

Amy stared at Ella Finlay's face on the brochure and punched it hard, swearing she could hear Jericho laughing. "Bitch," Amy said, as she counted out the letters in Ella's name. One, two, three, four.

E-L-L-A.

Amy stormed from the room and into the kitchen, where the lone candle flame flickered. With whatever Jericho had done to the air, she doubted Chad's phone would turn on, but when she touched it, the screen came to life—like Jericho was allowing her this one quick look—the four empty spaces for the passcode facing her like a crossword puzzle temptress. She typed in *E-L-L-A* and the screen opened. So did her tears—how could he? He had used her, just like everyone had said, for her money. She thumbed through his texts, found the last one she'd sent her husband: *Where r U Chad I'm worried.*

Amy didn't have to look far to find his text chain with Ella Finlay, and she had to know.

She saw a selfie of Ella stretched out on the berth of one of their boats, smiling in a pink bikini, making a duck-lips kiss toward the camera. And then the phone powered off. As if Jericho had somehow given her just enough, and in fact just finding out Chad's password had been enough. Her vision swirled; the disorientation was more than the alcohol. She braced her hands against the island's marble top and closed her eyes for a few seconds. When she opened them, she could see more clearly, and her focus was on her wedding ring. The couple times she'd attempted to take it off since Chad's death, when gardening or doing the dishes, she'd been unable to remove it.

You haven't tried hard enough, Amy.

She twisted the ring and turned it, but it wouldn't go over her knuckle. She went to the sink and tried dish soap, but that didn't work either. She squeezed out more liquid soap, twisted and turned the ring, but it wouldn't come off and now her knuckle was red and swollen and throbbing. She surveyed the kitchen, her vision stopped on the butcher block next to the sink. Even as her mind screamed *Don't do it,* Amy stormed across the kitchen, grabbed the sharpest knife, and placed the blade against the skin of her ring finger, just past the ring itself and before the biggest knuckle. She clenched her jaw and applied enough pressure to feel the blade against her finger bone. Her eyes pooled with tears. She screamed and at the same time lifted the knife from her finger and hurled the knife across the room. It clattered against the counter and landed on the floor. She screamed again, into her hands, until her throat felt raw. She straightened, forcing deep breaths, wanting so badly to hurt her husband like he was hurting her now, from the grave.

"What do you want?" she asked aloud.

The final candle flame snuffed out.

Just to let her know he was still there.

She stormed out the front door, walked deep into her yard, and felt Jericho there too.

A thought struck her, and she grinned. *An eye for an eye,* she thought, as her run turned into a sprint toward the Dodd House. *You cheated on me, so I'll cheat on you.* She'd always wondered, especially after Bridget and Nate had become intimate in the months before the massacre, what it would feel like to be her twin just once. To be with Nate like that. *Nate thought I was Bridget come back to life when he first saw me off the docks, so that's what I'll give him.* But when she arrived at Dodd House, she found it empty. Completely torn up inside the kitchen and library but otherwise empty. She called his name to no avail. She found candles lit inside the parlor, the room Reverend Dodd had turned into a memorial for Samantha, and on the floor just inside the room rested an open photo album. A picture had been removed from the clear sleeve and left on the floor next to the album.

Amy picked it up.

A much-younger Thomas and Samantha Dodd held hands, standing atop the bee barges, and in the background loomed the honey house, light-blue walls and apple-red roof so luridly colored that it reminded her of her dreamland.

She felt breathless for a moment and didn't know why, but as much as she was glad Nate wasn't around, giving her time to come to her senses, she was equally afraid of where he'd gone. And most likely alone. Just when she placed the picture down atop the open photo album, she heard a voice call out from the foyer.

"Hello? Is anyone home? Nate?"

The voice was female, but not familiar.

Amy approached the foyer, and when she turned the corner to face the front door and the petite brunette standing there with her hands clasped together, they both stared at each other.

The young woman was pretty, but above all—and Amy couldn't quite put a finger on how or why she knew—she could tell she was untainted by the island. Unsoiled by the digging.

"I'm sorry," the woman said, eyes moving around, no doubt noticing the lack of power, the condition of the house, the condition Amy was in. "I'm looking for Nate Dodd. I knocked."

"It's okay," Amy said, realizing now how soiled and dirty she was, that her appearance alone should have sent this girl running. "I'm a friend of Nate's, from before. I'm Amy. Amy Barnes."

The girl didn't step closer or offer her hand but said kindly, "I'm Lauren. I work with Nate, at school, back in Atlanta. Lauren Jenkins."

CHAPTER

47
Sheriff Kilbourne

LAWRENCE HADN'T RIDDEN a bicycle in years.

He'd nearly fallen off pedaling away from the McBrides' house, but it didn't take long to gain control, one hand on the bike's handle while aiming his flashlight with the other. After rechecking the interior of the McBrides' house, he'd found it no different than yesterday—aside from the lone honey jar with the yellow sticker resting amid all the pried-up boards beside Mitchell's bed. He saw nothing to convince himself that Mitchell was inside the house or even sleeping there at night.

He and Caleb had found the two mountain bikes propped against the side of the house. They assumed one belonged to the mayor and one to Mitchell, both of whom had three to four inches on Lawrence and Caleb, so they'd had to adjust the seats.

The evening was darker from the lack of streetlights and power. With a murderer on the loose, he needed to shut the island down, but with no way to communicate, he biked to the docks in person.

Both island ferries were gone, and Duff Hollaway was nowhere to be found. Even most of the private boats were gone, and the few that were left appeared to be sinking. Someone was sabotaging the remaining boats. The rest, he assumed, had been taken by islanders trying to escape, risking navigation on the water between Crow Island and Ossabaw and Tybee or even attempting to get to the Georgia coast itself in the dark. Without the ferries, without bigger boats and their emergency helicopter, and without a way to alert the mainland, there was no getting off the island.

Even after the last earthquake, which had been the longest yet, at nine seconds, he'd been unable to use his text chain to communicate with the other islands.

He'd sent Caleb on a similar mission to the docks at Chad McGovern's Maritime and Fishing Company. Caleb had returned moments ago and revealed that there were no boats there either.

"What about Blue Bottles? Did you check on him?"

"He wasn't home."

"Cripes," Lawrence said. "Amy Barnes?"

"Gone as well."

After chewing his lip for a minute and thinking hard, he told Caleb to start going door-to-door looking for any signs of Mitchell McBride.

After telling Caleb to report back to the sheriff's station and watching him go, that's exactly where Lawrence biked next.

He propped the bike against the hedgerow and hurried inside.

Eight years ago, he'd led Jericho into this same building, both of them soaked with the blood of victims, Lawrence saying, "What did you do, Jericho? What did you do?" over and over while Jericho looked equally shocked, no longer resisting as he had on Bull Street.

Lawrence felt the same trepidation now as he entered the dark jailhouse, flashlight in hand. He pulled his gun and called out, "Clare."

Something wasn't right here.

He then shouted for Steven Delacroix, who should still be inside the cell. Lawrence shined the flashlight beam into the cell, up and down and side to side and back again, and saw that it was empty. The door was open, and the keys rested on the floor.

Someone had let him out.

And that's when he saw a hand on the floor, behind Clare's desk. He approached it, saw her arm, her shoulder, and then a puddle of blood oozing around her crumpled body. Her head was connected to her neck, but only barely.

Lawrence had almost thrown up earlier when Caleb had, but now he let loose and retched until his stomach was empty. Holding Tina and David was the only thing that mattered to him now. He'd make sure they were safe and then figure out what to do next. He hurried from the jailhouse and pedaled through the night toward home. The case of Jericho Dodd had been labeled closed only because they'd wanted it to be. They'd captured him. The case was closed because he was dead, because he killed himself inside Sheriff Kilbourne's own jail cell while they were all meeting outside, in shock, trying to calm the island down, trying to figure out what best to do with him.

The case shouldn't have been closed, because we never investigated why.

And then he'd allowed Nate Dodd, who still had Bridget's blood all over his hands and face and neck, to enter the cell to speak to his brother, only to hear Nate screaming soon after that Jericho was dead, Nate's eyes so wide it was as if his last thread of sanity had just left him.

You never should have left him in there alone, Lawrence.

He was eighteen.

You knew damn well that Jericho was prone to hurting himself, to knocking his head against the wall, complaining about the bee buzz. You'd seen him do it, Lawrence—you'd even, as you escorted him into the cell, said it in your mind.

Beat your fucking head against the wall for all I care, Jericho. Do us all a favor . . .

Lawrence closed in on his home, wondering now, as he had many times before, if he'd said those thoughts about Jericho aloud.

Beat your fucking head into the wall for all I care, Jericho. Do us all a favor . . .

Was he partly to blame for that boy killing himself like he'd done?

Yes.

He deserved it, Lawrence.

No, nobody deserved that.

Lawrence brought the bike to a stop and let it fall to the grass before his front yard sidewalk, ran to his boy and his wife, both of them hurrying from the dark house to greet him.

CHAPTER

48
Nate

NATE STUMBLED THROUGH the cemetery, balancing himself on headstones and tree trunks, as he made his way back to the Dodd House, his body in shock from having been stung so many times.

Just as he'd hoped, the memory of that night as a boy, when he'd followed his father to the tupelo swamp, had returned to him. Something had taken Thomas Dodd over that night, and the reverend had unknowingly brought it home.

But where had Mr. Passafume gone?

Nate swore he'd seen him inside the honey house seconds before he'd encountered all those hideous hives, swarming with bees.

Nate exited the cemetery woods, entered the clearing behind the Dodd House. His skin was on fire from stings. His flesh felt swollen. He wasn't allergic, but could this many stings kill him?

He staggered, wheezing, on his way to the house, where two women hurried toward him from the veranda, one slightly taller than the other.

"Nate," one of them called.

He collapsed in the grass, rolled to his back, felt hands on his cheeks, directing his face toward her own.

"Nate," she said. "Look at me."

Fighting dizziness, he saw Lauren's face hovering, her green eyes wet and curtained by curly auburn hair.

He'd never texted her back.

He wanted to tell her he was sorry, but instead he grinned and said, "Hey, dummy."

And she cried.

CHAPTER

49

Eight Years Before the Sudden Death of Reverend Thomas Dodd

NATE PLACED HIS hand over Bridget's mouth to stifle her giggle. "Shhhhh . . ."

Her eyes probed, but from her position in the tall grass, Nate doubted she could see much. He lay atop her, so close their noses touched and he could see the tiny flecks of gold in the sky blue of Bridget's irises. Amy had them too, and swore they were the color of tupelo honey.

Bridget had called those specs eye freckles.

Amy had corrected her—they were called nevi, or choroidal nevi, caused by a buildup of melanin pigment. That was Amy.

Nate, now, as he lay atop Bridget, both stripped to their underwear, stayed as still as possible. Seconds ago, he'd heard someone in the trees, and then thought he'd seen Jericho watching them. Nate wanted so badly to move his hand away from Bridget's mouth and kiss her.

Her tongue teasingly flicked against his palm, and she whispered beneath his loosely clamped hand, "Is that a missile in your pocket, mister?"

"Shhhhhh . . . quiet," he said. "I think Jericho's out there."

Bridget's face grew serious, which made her look a lot like Amy, not to mention that Bridget was still *dressed* like Amy, and was, in fact, wearing Amy's clothes. Or had been before he'd helped remove them a minute ago. She'd even had on Amy's extra pair of glasses, and she'd kept them on during their jaunt up the hill of the Backbone to their secret spot on the island's eastern ridge overlooking the ocean. Amy and Bridget had joked with Nate on numerous occasions that he wouldn't be able to tell them apart if they dressed like the other. He, of course, claimed nonsense, so they'd decided to test him—they'd fooled him for five minutes, until, on their way outside, Nate grabbed Amy's hand, and Amy, instead of interlacing her fingers with his (what Bridget called the waffle grip), had held his hand palm to palm (which Bridget referred to as the pancake grip). And just as Nate grew suspicious, Amy had burst out laughing and yanked her hand from his. Then she playfully smacked Nate across the arm and went inside to change, while Bridget smacked Nate across the other arm and took off running.

Nate had followed and caught her at the top of the ridge, at their secret spot in the trees, but Jericho had followed them. Nate could see him standing in the shadows of a tall live oak.

He shushed Bridget beneath him, and now that she was aware of Jericho's presence, she lay still and quiet.

A few seconds later, Jericho left.

Nate slid his hand from Bridget's mouth.

She said, "Do you think he saw us?"

"I don't know," he said, thinking *Yeah, he saw us.*

But did it matter? It wasn't like he was going to tell the reverend. But it had killed the mood; even though Jericho was gone, Nate still felt like they were being watched.

Bridget must have felt it too. She sat up, gathered her clothes—Amy's clothes—and said, "We better get back." She kissed Nate quickly on the mouth, gestured toward her half-clothed body, and winked. "I'll give you another chance after the celebration tomorrow."

"What celebration?"

"The Fourth of July Parade, dork. We'll make it the best one ever."

CHAPTER

50
Amy

AMY HADN'T INTENDED to slap Nate across the face.

It had been a knee-jerk reaction. He wasn't being rational. He wasn't thinking straight.

None of us are, she'd thought, *myself included*, although her head had begun to clear upon Lauren's arrival, and for the first time in days she *was* thinking straight, and it had taken an outsider, a "come here," to accomplish that.

But Lauren's calming words, in that moment, after Nate managed to make it to his feet, his skin swollen and blotchy from all the beestings, were not working. Not as determined as he was to find his shovel and start digging again out by Oak Alley.

"Because I have to know," he'd shouted.

"Know what?" Amy had asked.

And then he'd turned on her. "Why did he cut off his hand, Amy? And why didn't you tell me?"

Amy didn't know the answers, but she and Lauren had been more convinced than ever that they needed to get him inside, Lauren, with tears in her eyes, asking, "What's wrong with him?"

"Same thing that's wrong with the island."

Amy had said it softly, trying to physically hold Nate back from going after the shovel as he screamed, "Move, Amy! He told me to *dig*!"

And that's when she slapped him.

It wasn't the force of the blow that knocked Nate to one knee but his utter exhaustion, and he'd stayed there for a few seconds, face lowered, tears dripped from his chin to the grass, and then he started sobbing, as if an emotional dam had just been broken. Amy hadn't seen Nate cry since his mother died. There'd been tears the day of the massacre, when Bridget was killed so savagely and in broad daylight by his brother during the Fourth of July parade, but that was shock and rage and panic. This was an outpouring of emotion she'd never before seen from Nathanial Dodd.

The women each took one of his arms over their shoulders and led him into the great room, onto the couch, Amy thinking, *Enough digging. Now it's time to fight what we've unearthed.*

And that's when Lauren had gone into teacher mode, as if Nate had just hurt himself on the playground and it was up to her to patch him up. And now, an hour later, with Nate sedated from a Percocet and some antihistamine they'd found in Reverend Dodd's medicine cabinet, Amy and Lauren rested on the two reading chairs facing where Nate lay on the couch, softly snoring, his body (they'd counted twenty-two beestings on his arms, legs, and neck) covered in toothpaste, a remedy Lauren swore had always worked on her as a girl.

Lauren's mother claimed it helped draw out the venom.

Lauren's father said it helped to dry out the wound and speed up the healing.

Amy could tell with how Lauren had so lovingly mentioned her parents that she'd been raised in a strong, compassionate household. Amy had always done this, analyzing someone so thoroughly by first impressions that they immediately became the truth to her. And she was usually right. In this case, she could easily see what Nate loved about Lauren, and in just this short time, Amy could tell how deeply Lauren cared for Nate. She'd feared Nate would never be able to move on from Bridget, but it seemed he had.

Amy looked over the coffee table that separated them. "Do you drink?"

Lauren laughed. "I'm a middle school teacher, so yes, at least every Friday."

"A double it is," Amy said, standing, legs sore from tension. "What will you have?"

"Anything."

"Coming up." Amy followed her flashlight beam through the dark house. Reverend Dodd kept a stocked wine rack in the kitchen, but with how thoroughly Nate had ripped apart the floor in there, the wine rack, resting on the far counter, wasn't an option. Amy tried the library's liquor cabinet next, and while Nate had destroyed that floor as well, there was a clear path to the liquor next to the bookshelves. Amy aimed the light toward the hole Nate had dug through the floor and into the ground, glimpsing a portion of the large bone running through the soil down there, and that's when she realized how much the library smelled like upturned soil and how Jericho's presence was stronger in here, just like it was in the kitchen.

She opened the liquor cabinet and pulled out a bottle of Old Sam ten-year. She removed two rocks glasses from a lower shelf, poured what she thought might be enough to settle their nerves, carefully balanced both glasses in her upturned hand, held the flashlight in the other, and returned to the great room. She handed Lauren her bourbon and took her seat again in the reading chair. She clicked off the flashlight, rested it on the floor at her feet, and held up her drink for a toast. "Lauren Jenkins, welcome to Crow Island." Her eyes had adjusted to the dark enough to see Lauren's uneasy grin. Amy sipped the Old Sam, and it burned her lips, her tongue, and then rolled like liquid fire down her throat. She coughed, laughed, and then laughed harder because Lauren had a similar reaction to her first sip and was rapidly waving her hand in front of her face as if trying to put out a fire. Maybe laughter was what they'd both needed. Amy said, "Not a bourbon drinker?"

Lauren wiped her eyes. "I'll manage."

Amy's second sip went down smoother. She watched Nate sleep on the couch, his skin covered in dried blotches of toothpaste. The redness around the wounds seemed to be retreating, less angry. Amy said to Lauren, "Would you believe I've never been stung?"

Lauren folded her legs beneath her rear end on the seat. "Not sweet enough?"

"I suppose not." Having already explained who Blue Bottles was while they'd ministered to Nate's wounds, Amy said, "But I guess I can thank Mr. Passafume for that. Most the time I was around the bees, he was with me. He claims to have never been stung, which is quite the feat, seeing he practically lives with them and he's, like . . . ancient years old."

Lauren laughed easily, sipped bourbon. "Ancient years old. Nice." It was quiet for a minute. They took turns shielding yawns, and then Lauren asked, "What's happening here?"

"I wouldn't know where to start," Amy said. "But I feel like I owe you some truth. It's not safe."

"I've gathered that much."

"Yet here you are."

"Here I am." Lauren finished the rest of her bourbon and placed it on the coffee table. "The power shut off within minutes of me stepping off the ferry. I saw that helicopter going down, over the trees."

"It crashed in the water," Amy said. "I was on the beach. The pilot died."

"Did you know him?"

Amy nodded. "It's a small island."

"I'm sorry," Lauren said. "And the holes? All the digging?"

Amy finished her bourbon, rested the glass between her legs. "How much has Nate told you about his brother?"

"Nothing, really."

"But you do know . . ."

"Yeah," she said. "I know what he did eight years ago. But that was the extent of it. Nate seemed too ashamed to tell anymore. Only that he fled the island to escape it all. To start over."

Amy scoffed. "And how's that working out for him?" And then, "Sorry. That was crass."

Lauren waved it off. "I was the only one on the ferry, Amy. I had to beg the guy to make one more trip. I paid him double."

"Double. That sounds like Duff."

Lauren said, "The ferry headed back to the mainland right after he dropped me off. Something about his demeanor said he had no plans of coming back. And I hadn't heard from Nate. He said he would check in. He never did. He wasn't answering his phone."

"He crushed it with a shovel blade."

"Why?"

"Not because of you." Amy shifted in her chair to better face Lauren. "Can we wait until the sun comes up? Then I'll explain what I can."

"That's fair." Lauren leaned her head back and closed her eyes.

Amy watched her. "How long have you and Nate been dating?"

Lauren laughed, said with her eyes still closed, "None months."

"Nine?"

"No, none," she said, opening her eyes. "As in, officially we've never been out on a date. We've never kissed. We've never held hands."

"And unofficially, you've been dating how long?"

"Two years," she said. "We just never realized it until lately."

"By the look he gave you, I would have thought you were practically engaged."

"You know what they say about looks . . ."

"They can be deceiving?"

"They can also say a million words," Lauren said, glancing at Amy, specifically at her hand, which was still bloody and scabbed around her wedding ring. "Married?"

"Widow."

Lauren straightened in her chair. "Shit . . . open mouth, insert foot. I'm sorry."

"It's fine," Amy said. "I'm young to be a widow. He passed away six months ago. Boating accident. Never should have married him in the first place." She twisted the ring on her finger, winced when it scraped against the bloody scab. "I found out earlier today he was probably cheating on me."

"Damn . . . I'm sorry."

Amy smiled warmly. "You've apologized to me more in the past minute than Chad did in two years we were married." She held up her left hand as if to show off the wound. "I almost cut my finger off earlier, because I can't get the fucking ring off." Lauren, for the first time since they'd met, seemed like she didn't have anything to say or know how to voice it. Amy said, "A bit of important advice about Nate?"

"I'm all ears."

"When you do hold his hand . . . do you waffle or pancake?"

Lauren look confused.

Amy explained, "Do you like holding a man's hand palm to palm like pancakes, or interlaced like waffles?"

Lauren, after a beat of contemplation, said, "Waffle . . ."

"Then you'll do fine." Amy read the next question before Lauren could ask it. "No, we never dated, but he dated my twin for years."

Lauren nodded, like perhaps she'd known this, but then a look of solemnity crossed her face, more out of overall sadness, Amy mused, because she knew what had happened, and that made Amy want to get up and hug her. Instead she said, "But I've known Nate Dodd my entire life, Lauren. And he's the type of guy who . . ."

"Who what?"

"Who . . . the longer he waits to ask someone out, the more he likes them."

CHAPTER

51
Sheriff Kilbourne

Lawrence lay restless in their queen-size bed, staring at the ceiling fan that wasn't spinning.

The power across the island was still off, but the battery-run clock on the wall showed four in the morning.

Maybe Mitchell McBride had cut the power before going on his rampage, Lawrence thought, but that wouldn't explain the chopper going down or the strange pulse he'd felt in the air seconds before everything went out. That, he thought, had more to do with what he felt hovering across the island like an airborne virus, becoming stronger, he feared, with every turn of the shovel blade. Which was why, on his last trip out, after he'd checked to make sure his wife and son were okay, he'd shouted out to anyone he saw digging to stop. Even in the middle of the night, half the islanders had been out digging like their lives depended on it, like they had a deadline to meet. Some had listened to him, setting their shovels aside. Others had stared at him like they were too far mentally gone to understand his orders. Or stared at him like it was Sherif Kilbourne who'd lost his marbles.

And maybe he had, he thought now, after returning home again and craving just a few minutes of rest before going back out.

He knew Tina was awake too. He'd hugged her earlier on instinct, but there was still clear tension between them. He hadn't told her he'd spent the last several hours with Caleb Jones, like the two of them were the bicycle version of Starsky and Hutch.

"Lawrence," Tina said, suddenly.

"Yeah," he said, eyes closed.

"I'm sorry."

He let that settle and was surprised how easily it did on his soul, on his heart, because he immediately felt the warmth from the simplicity of her words.

I'm sorry.

No excuses. No *please forgive me.*

They'd known each other long enough to communicate without words, and it was the lack of her words that got him now, that had tears running down his cheeks and wetting his pillow. "Tina," he said.

"Yeah?"

"Why were you looking at my laptop?"

"Because I felt I needed to dig," she said. "Because you were."

"Did you find anything?"

If it were possible to hear a smile, perhaps in the subtle catch in her throat, he did when she said, "No."

"Good."

"Because there's nothing to find, Lawrence."

They were both lying on their backs, David asleep between them. Lawrence scooted his hand toward hers and clutched it. She squeezed his hand back. He could have fallen asleep in seconds but knew he couldn't. He had to get back out there.

"I think we need to all gather at the Dodd House," he said. "All those I can convince to come. It's the biggest house on the island. Centrally located."

"I'll pack some essentials," Tina said. "Lawrence, I don't want you to go back out there."

"I have to."

"I know."

They both jumped and spun from the bed when they heard someone knocking on the front door.

Lawrence grabbed his gun from where he'd left it on the dresser and told her to wait in the bedroom with David and lock the door.

At the front door, Lawrence called out, “Who is it?”

“Dennis Wagner,” the voice said. “Can you open up?”

Lawrence opened the door, ushered the old man inside.

Dennis coughed into his fist. In the other hand he held a tube of what had to be rolled photographs. “I need light.”

Lawrence led him down the hallway to the kitchen and found a candle Tina had had going earlier. He lit it as Dennis smoothed out several eight-by-eleven-inch photos across the kitchen table, and by then Tina had joined them in the room.

“Hey, Dennis.”

Dennis stepped over, hugged Tina, and let go. “Beautiful as always, even in a crisis, Tina Kilbourne.”

She ignored his flattery and studied the pictures just as Lawrence was.

Dennis moved the light closer, holding it over one picture at a time. In his eyes, Lawrence saw clear fear, and as Lawrence analyzed each picture, he understood it.

They were arial shots of the island taken by Deputy Clampus before the chopper went down.

All Lawrence could say was, “Dear God.”

CHAPTER

52
Amy

AT SOME POINT in the middle of the night, Amy watched Lauren fall asleep in the neighboring chair.

Nate snored softly on the couch across from them.

Only then did Amy allow herself to close her eyes.

And slowly, she drifted away.

And within minutes, she was . . .

. . . walking toward the barn of skins, her bare feet ankle deep in yellow grass. Grass that became more painful with every step, the thorns on each blade scraping and scratching and cutting her ankles and toes as she moved toward the open barn doors. The floor of the barn was coated with honey, and stuck to the honey were thousands of bees, most of them dead but some still moving.

When she reached the rows of skins hanging like suits on hooks from a ceiling of shadows, she realized she knew these skins. There was her sister Bridget, spinning in a subtle breeze, her body shriveled like a raisin, with no bones or muscles to give it substance. There were her parents, side by side in separate rows, her father's mouth grinning, his eyeless face like a mask with nothing inside it but a deep, dark void. And there was Reverend Thomas Dodd in another row. That skin rotated on its hook, like a heat-dried cornstalk, and now shadows moved around the floor because something had entered the barn.

Reverend Dodd's skin began to inflate with . . . something, first the arms and then the legs and then the chest, and it wriggled on the hook, and she took off running . . .

Amy found herself running down Oak Alley, through the thick haze of moonlit motes, periodically glancing over her shoulder because Reverend Thomas Dodd was coming after her. As impossible as it was, she could hear his voice.

Tell Nathanial . . . Dig . . . Amy . . .

She ran through the woods, had to get home, where she had marbles to protect her, had to get to her bedroom where she had her broom and hairbrush and colander to protect her.

She heard Thomas Dodd behind her. He was gaining. He was too fast. It wasn't Thomas Dodd, though, she knew that . . . it was one of *them* wearing his skin.

Thomas Dodd was good, and this thing was bad.

She hurried past her empty swimming pool, refused to give it a glance, even as Jericho crawled from it, ground roots in one hand and a muddy axe in the other.

Hello, Amy . . . Could you give me a hand here?

Amy slammed her door closed, locked it, and hurried to her bedroom and locked that door too. She hid beneath the covers and closed her eyes as the wind hugged her house and darkness pressed atop the roof and someone pounded on her bedroom door.

CHAPTER

53
Amy

GLASS SHATTERED . . .

* * *

Amy's eyes flashed open, and she gasped, sure that she'd just been pulled from the tupelo swamp.

Sure that the sound of shattered glass had not been real.

Sure that the barn of skins had all been a nightmare.

Sure that Reverend Dodd had not chased her through the woods to her home.

Sure that she was sleeping on the chair inside the Dodd House with Lauren beside her and Nate on the couch and that she hadn't fled last night in a panic.

She sat up in bed, to familiar surroundings, her bedroom at home, but that terrified her even more because it meant that she *had* fled last night. Fled the safety of a house where she'd had friends, and now she was alone again inside her own home.

In the middle of the night.

And a breeze circled her bed.

The window to her right was shattered. Glass littered the floor. She heard movement to her left, in the shadows on Chad's side of the room.

She screamed.

The white-haired Boo Hag looked up from what it had been doing in the dark, sitting on the floor, legs crossed, and counting every bristle of the broom it must have grabbed from beside the door. Two black beady eyes watched her as she slid from the bed and moved—bare feet atop broken glass—toward her bedroom door.

The Boo Hag stood, dropped the broom. Amy noticed then that the hairbrush and colander had already been discarded to the floor next to the broom, as if it had already counted those bristles and those holes and the broom was all that was left. And now she wondered if it had just finished with the broom when she'd awakened. Because she was sure she was awake now. She couldn't afford to pretend not to be.

She gripped the doorknob, and the Boo Hag stood to full height: well over six feet and slender. She turned the knob slowly, and the Boo Hag stepped closer. She flung the door open, stepped out into the hallway, pulled the door shut just as the Boo Hag slammed into it, hard enough to crack the wood.

Fuck, she thought. *It's real. Think, Amy, think.* She let go of the knob, hurried down the hall toward her living room, and within seconds the Boo Hag was after her, taking up the entire hallway with its length, its footfalls wet on the hardwood, its curled toenails clickity-clacking as it moved.

On instinct, she ran toward one of the glass jars of marbles she kept inside each of the other rooms and hurled a full jar to the living room floor. Glass shattered and marbles sprayed in every direction, bouncing and rolling and finally settling, and the Boo Hag paused, as if confused, or possibly struck dumb with excitement at the prospect of so many things to count.

And begin counting it did.

And Amy, on the floor, crab-walked back toward the window and wall, where she grabbed another jar of marbles from the TV stand. She kicked any marble she could find away from her and closer to the Boo Hag, hoping sunrise would come before it finished counting.

CHAPTER

54
Amy

AMY WAS SWEATING profusely, mostly from fear but also from how much heat that *thing* seemed to be radiating.

It had to have been going on two hours now that the Boo Hag had been counting. Picking up one marble at a time, analyzing it briefly—perhaps studying the unique colors of each one, or maybe making sure it never counted the same one twice—before dropping it to the floor and hunting out the next one. When it appeared it was about finished with the first jar of marbles, she'd upturned the next, and the hag never broke stride. At one point, hoping it would be distracted enough by the marbles to not stop her from escaping, she'd attempted moving past it, making a run for the front door, but as soon as she moved, it had moved, as if it could read her mind, like maybe these marbles were fascinating but not so much that it would not bypass counting to devour her whole.

And now Amy feared it was about finished counting again. It had begun to slow between marbles, and as soon as Amy thought it, the Boo Hag focused fully on her again.

For the first time in the past two hours of her watching it count, it spoke. "He's coming, Amy. The horned one is coming . . ."

She was a kid again on the bee barge, the shadow moving beneath her, below the decking, horns clicking on the boards as it moved . . .

. . . *click-click-click-click-click* . . .

She felt the slightest increase in heat on her neck and prayed it was the sun in the window behind her.

The Boo Hag had moved closer, its gnarled claws clicking on the floor.

But before it could grab her, she yanked the curtain open, revealing what little sun the hazy morning could provide.

The boo hag shrieked, covered its eyes, just as someone knocked on the front door.

Amy screamed, "Help!" even as she ran toward the door, swearing she heard part of that Boo Hag searing like steak on an oil-hot skillet. "Help!"

The door opened.

Sheriff Kilbourne stood on the threshold with a group of islanders clustered behind him. He opened the screen door and raised his gun. At first she thought he was firing at her, but then she felt the Boo Hag behind her, and then the bullet from Kilbourne's gun whiz past.

The Boo Hag was blown across the room and lay writhing on the floor, sizzling in the sunlight.

Amy ran into Lawrence's arms.

He embraced her, said, "Come on, we're all heading to the Dodd House."

C H A P T E R

55
Nate

NATE SAT ON a porch rocking chair, staring out toward Oak Alley, at the eerie orange mist that had overtaken the island.

He knew it was the sunlight mixing with all the dust motes in the air that was creating the bizarre illusion, but knowing it made it no less bizarre. They had to stop. *He* had to stop. He felt sure Lauren had brought him out here to test him, to see if it would trigger his urge to dig.

Earlier, he'd awakened, startled, on the couch, mumbling about the bees, confused by how he'd gotten home last night, curious as to why he was covered with dried toothpaste. At which point he'd gotten agitated again, pleading with them to understand that Mr. Passafume had disappeared inside the honey house last night. Amy had assured him that wasn't the case—although Nate could see she was at least entertaining the notion. But now, sitting next to Lauren on the porch rocking chairs, watching the Spanish moss sway in the breeze, he felt no urgency to dig. He craved coffee, but without electricity he'd settled for a warm bottled water from a fridge that was no longer cold.

He hadn't seen Amy all morning. When he asked about her, Lauren said she'd assumed Amy had gone into one of the bedrooms to sleep.

Lauren sat in her rocking chair with her feet reeled in beneath her, her auburn hair pulled up into a loose topknot. Now, even without the little bit of makeup she typically wore, she was prettier than ever.

She caught him staring. "What?"

"I'm sorry."

"For what?"

"For how we left it at my apartment," he said. "I was an asshole."

"You were grieving, Nate."

"Still, you wanted to help, and I pushed you away."

"Evidently not far enough." She grinned, but Nate sensed a hint of fear in it. "I know what you're thinking, so stop."

"What am I thinking?"

"I'm where I need to be." She lifted her eyebrows, just as she would to her students when waiting for them to agree with her. "Okay?"

He scratched at a cluster of stings on his left arm.

"Stop scratching," Lauren said. Then added, "Dummy."

He smiled, watched the trees. "Lauren."

"Nate."

"I'm probably going to be suspended at the beginning of the year," he said. "That's why I was so—"

"I know."

"You know?"

"I made her tell me," Lauren said. "I knew something was up. I told Bates if you go, I go, and that the Roarks could go fuck themselves backwards."

He laughed. "You said that?"

"Exact words," she said. "Their son is a piece-of-shit bully, and they need to know that."

"I bruised him."

"You grabbed his arm."

"I pulled him across a desk."

"Nate . . ."

"Yeah?"

"Stop," she said.

"I snapped, Lauren. It was like I was younger . . . with Jericho. I saw Roark picking on another kid, and I came to the kid's defense. But I shouldn't have touched him."

"Stop making them sound justified for using their power, their money." She focused on him, and he couldn't look away. "But you have some anger in you, Nate."

This wasn't what he'd expected. He knew it. Of course he knew it—he'd been angry since his mom died. But the truth of it being verbalized by someone he cared so much about hit him hard. "Does it scare you?"

"No," she said definitively. "It doesn't. What scares me is that you've buried the reasons why."

He stared at Oak Alley "That's what everyone said that day Jericho snapped. *Why, why?*"

"You afraid you're gonna snap, Nate?"

"No."

"I'm not either, but I am afraid one day you'll break."

"What if I already did?"

"You can fix broken."

"That why you're here?"

"No," she said. "Just to help."

"Jericho . . . he used to . . . I don't know . . ." Nate interlocked his fingers to disguise how much his hands were shaking. "He was so . . . off."

"I only know what I've read in the papers," she said. "And online."

"Like any of that could be believed."

"That's all I've had to work with, Nate."

"Well, no 'come here' newspaper reporter could even begin to explain Jericho," Nate said, biting his lip. "I hated him."

"Because you feel he stole your mother?"

"Yeah, there's that, but he was also just easy to hate, Lauren."

"And on the other hand?"

Nate choked up. "He was my brother." Nate rocked slowly in the chair. "I got suspended from school once. Got in three fights with kids who were picking on Jericho." He laughed. "Same kid who made my own skin crawl. I still felt the need to stick up for him."

"Because you're a good big brother."

"No . . . I'm not. And I wasn't." He almost told her what he'd learned from Dr. Cheevers last night, but it felt wrong telling her before he had a chance to tell Amy. If she didn't wake up soon, he was going to wake her up. "Jericho . . ." He tapped his temple with an index finger. "He always complained about the bees in his head. And when the bees got bad, he'd beat his head against the wall. Hard. The first time I heard it, I came running. I put my hand in between his head and the wall. I'd talk him down. Over the years, it just became my job. But I hated it. Jericho, according to the story his teacher, Mr. Johnson, later told my dad, he said Jericho clamped his hands over his ears during class one day. That's how those episodes usually started. He'd put his hands over his ears. Except this time—and these rarely struck Jericho in school—he started pushing with his legs, making his desk go backwards. Pushed himself out of his row and kept going, driving his desk backwards."

"Looking for a wall?"

"Yeah, or something hard. But when he gets to the back wall of the classroom, he starts talking. 'Mr. Johnson is a son of a bitch.' And then *bam*. Hits his head. 'Mr. Johnson is a son of a bitch.' *Bam*. Over and over and in between, he says, 'Mr. Johnson is a son of a bitch.' And keep in mind that Jericho, like, never talked. We didn't even know if he could."

Lauren looked like she didn't know whether to be horrified or laugh, but when Nate smiled in the telling of it, she joined him.

"And for whatever reason, on that day, Jericho calmed *himself* down. Maybe it was after Mr. Johnson, who was as mild-mannered and chill as you can get, put his hand on Jericho's shoulder and patted it. But Jericho stopped. And you know what Mr. Johnson says?"

"What?"

"'Jericho Dodd, congratulations, that was the first full sentence I've ever heard you say.'"

Lauren covered her mouth.

"Laugh, it's funny," Nate said. "That's why I told it. It had a subject, a verb . . ."

"I know what a full sentence is, Nate."

"Yeah . . . right . . . But that right there, Lauren, is one of the biggest reasons I wanted to be a teacher. Because of Mr. Johnson. Because of that. Here you have a freak like Jericho doing—"

"Nate," Lauren said, interrupting him. "Can you stop calling him a freak?"

"Yeah, but . . . okay . . . fine, but what Mr. Johnson did," Nate continued, "in a classroom full of nine-year-olds who were a third of

Jericho's size, completely freaked out over what Jericho did, and he comes up with that?"

They rocked silently for a minute, and Nate could tell she was waiting for more, because it wasn't the only reason he'd told it. He'd only peeled off one layer.

Lauren looked like she was about to ask another question, but then something in the distance caught her attention. She walked toward the edge of the veranda and Nate joined her. A group of islanders was walking down the middle of Oak Alley on their way to the Dodd House.

As the cluster approached through the tunnel of trees, Nate saw Sheriff Kilbourne with his wife Tina and their son David, and behind them Rose Bower, Dennis Wagner, Caleb Jones, Easy Perkins, and at least a dozen more islanders in the distance.

And then Nate said, "Amy's with them? When the hell did she leave?"

"I don't know," Lauren said in obvious confusion.

But no Mr. Passafume, Nate thought, going down the veranda steps toward the arriving guests to meet them at Oak Alley.

Nate said, "What's going on, Sheriff?"

The sheriff held what appeared to be enlarged photographs in his right hand. "Have you seen Blue Bottles?"

Trying to mask his concern, Nate said, "No. We haven't." Nate made eye contact with Amy, who looked away; she stood with her arms folded, looking like she'd been through ten kinds of hell overnight.

Sheriff Kilbourne said, "We've been gathering all those who still have their minds intact. We need a bigger place to stay while we figure out a plan."

Nate nodded toward the Dodd House. "Of course you can stay here. Dad would have had it no other way."

Sheriff Kilbourne held the photos out toward Nate. "We got a bigger problem than I even thought. Go on, take a look."

Nate saw what the photos revealed, and his heart lurched.

Lauren said to Sheriff Kilbourne, "What is this?"

"Aerial shots of the island. Taken last night before sundown."

Nate could barely wrap his mind around what he was seeing. It wasn't possible. A skeleton that big? A fossil that big? He'd known that many of the islanders had been digging, and it had been going on for much longer than they'd previously thought, but the entire island had been transformed into an excavation site. The island they'd all referred to as the Devil's Backbone, specifically where the eastern ridge curved atop the beaches like a rugged spine, had become just that. Had hidden just that. Because whatever this thing was that had been unearthed, its backbone was curved into the landscape as if it had been born there.

As if something has grown into it, Nate thought.

Amy walked away like she might get sick—except she was staring at the air, as if she could feel something out there—and then seconds later she vomited into the grass beyond the line of live oaks. Lauren hurried over to her, just as Dennis Wagner began to throw up on the opposite side of Oak Alley, and then Rose Bower and a few others got sick in the middle of it.

Nausea coursed through Nate's system, but he couldn't take his eyes from the photos, all shot from different aerial views but clearly of the same monstrous underground *thing.*

Because that's what it was.

A thing.

They'd dug out and uncovered a monster.

The islanders had been unknowingly doing their parts, digging out what would become small pieces of the much-larger whole, and it was staring Nate straight in the face, curled up on its side like the skeleton of an island-sized fetus. He'd seen pictures in science and history magazines of dinosaur fossils uncovered, the skeletons still partially embedded in dirt and rock, but nothing close to the scale of this discovery, which was the size of an entire island.

Nate finally looked up, saw most of the arriving crew getting sick all around him.

Little David Kilbourne pointed to the sky and said, "Look, Daddy. A crow."

They all looked up, eyes following the bird David had spotted as it circled above them, wings stretched wide, before settling on the gnarled branch of a nearby live oak.

Nate couldn't believe what he was seeing, and Amy looked equally stunned as they shared a glance.

Just as Nate surveyed wider, broadening the scope of his vision, thousands of island birds, of all kinds, flew from their respective treetops in a collective whoosh of flight.

Of fright.

And then the ground started to shake.

And a bright-red crow, oily eyed and completely unfazed by the shaking ground, watched them from a nearby tree.

CHAPTER

56

Four Weeks Before the Sudden Death of Reverend Thomas Dodd

From Reverend Dodd's Diary

I've never kept a diary before, and I'm not sure how this works.

But there's a restlessness inside me now that demands it.

These earthquakes.

It's been seven years since the first one, but our minor earthquakes now have become as common as summer storms.

Although not a joking matter, many of the islanders, after the shaking is finished, jokingly say to the air, "Well, hello to you too, Jericho." And then go on their way.

I'd be lying, though, to say it doesn't sting.

Because deep down the truth always hurts.

Sheriff Kilbourne formed a text chain with scientists from the other islands and in Savannah, and as of yet, not one of our earthquakes has registered anywhere but on our island. Think of it what you will, because I've yet to form any conclusion other than Crow Island has always been known for its oddities.

Needless to say, the morning got off to an interesting start, yet again, with another brief rumble from below, just as I was fixing coffee.

But what was more unexpected was the visit soon thereafter from Mitchell McBride, Mayor McBride's son, not knocking on our door but desperately pounding . . .

CHAPTER

57
Nate

"SECOND-GUESSING YOURSELF?" NATE asked Lauren as she picked up a Freddie Freeman Atlanta Braves bobblehead from the dusty desk inside his childhood bedroom.

She placed the bobblehead down and faced him, arms folded like she tended to stand when she was nervous. "No. I'm not."

"I can find a boat, Lauren. I can find something and get you off this island. We can go now, when it's light."

She looked out the window and laughed softly. "That's not light out there, Nate. I don't know what that is. The sun just came up and it already looks like it's dusk. And you heard Sheriff Kilbourne. We can't get caught out there in the dark. And what he said about . . ."

He approached her, held her, hugged her. This was an embrace he never wanted to break, but he couldn't allow her to stay here. He pulled away, held her at arm's length. "You came here thinking you'd be supporting me through a funeral, Lauren. Not this. Look at me, please."

She did, almost sheepishly, and then she smiled, had that carefree look on her face he'd wanted to kiss for two years now.

He said, "What? What's so funny? What could possibly be funny about any of this?"

"Just that I wish my phone worked so I could snap a picture of you right now."

He looked at his arms past the sleeves of his T-shirt and his legs beneath his shorts—he was covered in dried blotches of toothpaste and still swollen and red in places.

"The other teachers would love it," she said. "Instagram would love it."

"And I can't stop thinking of what your parents would think of me if they knew what kind of situation you were in right now."

At the mere mention of the current situation, her smile melted away. "That earthquake, Nate. I mean, this is Georgia. What were these earthquakes? I overheard the sheriff downstairs hinting that it was your brother causing them? Jericho? I saw those pictures, Nate."

He heard each one of her questions, and somewhere in his brain he'd begun to formulate answers, but his drifting mind had made it hard to fully listen to her, because the word *dig* kept coming back to him. His father's last word . . . dig.

Tell Nathanial to dig . . .

"My father had his hand cut off days before he died," he said.

"What? Why?"

"I have a feeling he'd been driven insane," Nate said, adding, "From guilt. Some kind of guilt." He started pacing from his bed to the window and back again, thinking, *Dig. Dig, Nate.* And he said, "We need to dig, Lauren."

"No." She moved in front of his open bedroom door. "No. You're not going back out there, Nate. You've already done enough of that, and look at you."

He opened his arms. "I'm looking hot, right?"

"It's not funny," she said with her serious *Don't mess with me* teacher face.

"I know." He paced again. The old house's floorboards creaked underfoot. "My father was a deeply religious man, but for a time it wavered. He did something and he got tired of living with the guilt and maybe he was crazy by then, but he cut off his hand because of it."

Dig, Nate.

Mom had a nightmare, he thought, *and it went away. She buried it, Nate. She buried it just like you said.* He stopped pacing. "The garden."

Lauren said, "What garden? What are you talking about? I don't like that look in—"

"My mom, she was tortured by nightmares when she was pregnant with Jericho," he said. "Especially after she was bedridden. Every night. Bridget told me if you write down your nightmares and bury them that they'll go away. It was stupid, really, but maybe not. I told Mom this one night at her bedside. She smiled and patted my cheek, like she was listening but deep down thought it was stupid, but . . . I think it worked. I think she must have done it and it worked." He approached Lauren at the door; she didn't move but no longer looked like she might stop him. "It got so sad near the end of the pregnancy, it never occurred to me that she'd stopped screaming at night when she slept. Or napped during the day. I think one night she got out of bed and went outside. I remember one morning near the end, there was dirt on the floor and Dad blamed me for tracking it in. I swept it up and didn't complain because I was a kid and maybe I did track it in, but . . ."

"Now you think she got out of bed one night and actually did it?"

"Yes," he said, thinking of the small holes all over the yard and wondering if his father had been digging for the same thing.

"And there's no place she cherished more than her garden," Lauren said.

"Yes."

Lauren grinned. "Let's go get some shovels."

CHAPTER 58
Amy

THIS IS STILL my island, Amy said to herself as she stared out the great room window, thinking about the Boo Hag that had nearly gotten her overnight, thinking about the last earthquake and the conversation she'd just had with Sheriff Kilbourne in the kitchen.

The last earthquake lasted fifteen seconds.

It had happened right after many of them began getting sick on Oak Alley. Had they felt the earthquake coming? Or was it the air growing increasingly bad?

In the distance, Sheriff Kilbourne and a crew of four volunteers headed off down Oak Alley. After a meeting of the minds inside the drawing room earlier, the sheriff had decided to go on the offensive and hunt down Mitchell McBride and Steven Delacroix instead of waiting until nightfall for them to come to them. After going out on quick runs to various nearby houses to secure guns and ammunition for the mission, Sheriff Kilbourne, Dennis Wagner, Caleb Jones, and Rose Bower were not only armed but now, due to how toxic the air had gotten, each wearing masks Nate had found stashed in a drawer, left over, apparently, from COVID.

Amy watched until the crew disappeared into the trees beyond the Dodd House's property.

She still felt like she had digging to do.

Minutes before they'd departed, Sheriff Kilbourne had pulled Amy aside to discuss the latest earthquake, which had also been the longest and, as Kilbourne had warned at the beginning of explaining his newest theory, marked the shortest span of time yet between earthquakes.

"Everything is accelerating, Amy."

And then he'd explained what had come to him on his way over to the Dodd House earlier in the morning.

"Jericho is out there," he'd told her.

He looked relieved when she said, "I know. I can feel him too." And she told him she'd somehow communicated with Jericho inside her kitchen last night when he'd blown out her candles.

"Tina and I were discussing freak accidents on our way over," he told Amy, then showed her a pocket diary he kept as a logbook for every earthquake that had happened since Jericho died. "Because we all know that's when they started," he added. But after Sheriff Kilbourne saw those aerial shots of the island, he said, he had become convinced more than ever that everything happening to the island now had to do with Jericho. "Not only Jericho," he continued with a flint of fire in his eyes, "but the land itself, the bed in which Jericho now rests."

"But he's not resting," Amy said.

"He's never rested," Kilbourne said.

And all kids eventually outgrow their beds, Amy thought, before Kilbourne begged her forgiveness for mentioning that Chad's boating accident had occurred out at sea, roughly the same time as one of the earthquakes. He showed her the very one in his diary, tapping it with his finger. Amy had known this, but when Kilbourne said Chad's death hadn't been the only freak accident since the massacre to coincide with an earthquake, she was all ears, and listened, rapt, as he explained two other examples when they both knew there were probably more.

Pat Musso and Aiden Wurst had each died in bizarre accidents. Chad's had been the most recent, and therefore the most memorable. But Pat Musso had died when the golf cart he'd been driving hit a street curb and flipped, and Pat, in the awkward, one-in-a-million way he'd landed, broke his neck against a nearby lamppost. That had been a year and a half after the Fourth of July Massacre and not long—Kilbourne showed her in his book—after an earthquake. But three years after the massacre, Aiden Wurst had been hunting deer in the old cotton fields when one of his bullets missed the large-antlered target and ricocheted *twice*, once off one of the front metal legs of Ken Rutherford's deer stand and then off the side of Rutherford's metal dragon-shaped weather vane, before returning for a one-in-ten-million path into Aiden Wurst's right temple and ultimately killing him three days later in a Savannah ICU, after Deputy Justin Clampus had hurried him to the hospital in the island emergency chopper within minutes of his having been shot. That occurred an hour after another tremor.

"Jericho may not have pulled the trigger of Aiden Wurst's rifle or flipped Pat Musso's golf cart," Kilbourne had explained to her in a hushed whisper in the kitchen, "but I think somehow, from his grave, he caused those once-in-a-lifetime accidents."

Now Amy turned from the window and surveyed the room, thinking, *What do you want, Jericho?* The idea came to her that the monstrous boy had been put here on this island to cause destruction, to kill. But why? And why had he not started earlier?

You're not done digging, Amy.

That voice was Bridget's, and it was somehow loud and clear.

Suddenly she found herself ascending the main stairwell to the second floor, where a tall hallway window at the middle landing gave a magnificent view of the orange haze hovering over the backyard. She stepped closer to the window, looked down because she saw movement below, and inside Samantha Dodd's overgrown flower garden, Nate and Lauren appeared to be digging through the weeds.

As intriguing as this was, Amy continued up the remaining stairs and took a left down the hall toward Jericho's locked bedroom door.

But first, she entered Thomas Dodd's bedroom to retrieve the key in the drawer of the bedside table, the key to Jericho's old room.

She pulled it out slowly.

She screamed when she saw what else was inside the drawer—a dead crow, lying on its side, feathers bright red with thin swirls of orange, pinned to the bottom of the drawer by a sharp steak knife.

And behind it, a small black book.

A diary.

CHAPTER

59

Nate

LAUREN STOOD FROM her crouch, where she and Nate had been digging in his mother's old flower garden, repositioning the mask above her nose. "I hate these damn things."

Nate agreed, but it was better than inhaling the toxic air. "Keep looking," he said, undeterred by having found nothing in thirty minutes of digging. "Please."

Lauren drove her shovel into a fresh patch of green weeds and wildflowers. Nate took a moment to scratch at the bandaged beestings on his left arm, and Lauren, words muffled through her mask, said, "Stop scratching."

"Sorry, they itch like a motherfucker."

"Oh, then by all means," Lauren said with the sarcasm he'd come to adore, plunging her shovel into the new hole she'd started. And then Lauren, from her hands and knees, shouted, "I got something." She scooped dirt and then pulled from the hole a sealed jar.

Inside it was weathered, folded paper.

Lauren handed it to him, but with trepidation, he could tell.

CHAPTER

60

Two Weeks Before the Sudden Death of Reverend Thomas Dodd

From Reverend Dodd's Diary

I can't sleep anymore.

With so many sounds about the house at night, the footsteps, the creaks upon these old floors, the windows open after I'm sure I'd closed them.

I can't turn my mind off from the—what did that boy say?—from the urgency that I dig. That he knows what I did? That I need to confess? And now it consumes me.

I preached about it the other day, that it was time everyone on the island started doing the same. That they start digging . . .

Just as I've been digging.

Because I buried him alive.

He was no longer breathing but I buried him alive.

I know I did, and now it's up to me to free him.

To help him breathe.

The very words Mitchell McBride whispered into my ear that day he knocked on my door. Because the Boo Hags told him all about it. The Boo Hags said it was time to let him breathe. He was full grown now and ready to flower and flourish and open that door.

He wasn't supposed to have feelings, Mitchell said. He wasn't supposed to develop feelings. But he did. Somehow, he did, and oh, these damn delusions. The thoughts I'm having.

But I've been digging. Oh, have I ever been digging, because once that first bit of thread unravels, you just have to pull and pull until it's free, and if pulling doesn't work, you YANK IT! And so I went digging, my love, my dear Samantha, and when I say digging I mean into my own past. Because THAT kind of bad business can't be killed, my love.

Guilt.

It grows and grows and sometimes it can be put on pause, but the reemergence, the resurgence, is as inevitable as the next ocean storm, the next earthquake—

I'm coming out of my skin with anxiety. And I'm so tired. I can't sleep. Ever since that McBride boy pounded on my door, claiming nonsense about the honey house and the bees and the Boo Hags speaking to him—I've been on a downward spiral.

I just want it to end. I just want it to end.

I just . . . Ah, there it is, that damn bird that showed up a week ago. It flew right up to the open library window and perched there on the sill, watching me. It flies through the house and it shows me things. It points out things I've missed over the years, and I found your secret stash of pain pills, by the way—I just knew you were taking something to make you so distant and loopy.

But that crow. That damn red crow. It shows me the way. At first, I didn't think it was real, red crows don't exist outside the imagination! Outside my imagination. I figured it was part of the delusions. But this red crow not only showed me your stash of pain pills, but also where you kept your cigarettes—I knew you'd been secretly smoking. The red crow showed me things and now I can't shake this desperate urge to learn MORE.

To know MORE.

To DIG!

CHAPTER

61
Amy

Amy slammed Thomas Dodd's diary closed as quickly as she'd closed the drawer minutes ago, because she just couldn't stand seeing that red crow stuck to the bottom of it with a knife.

She'd only flipped through and read one day's passage, but she could already tell it was mostly incoherent ramblings, hastily jotted down by a man who, in his life, had been anything but incoherent.

Anything but rambling.

He'd always spoken with thoughtful purpose.

But this . . .

. . . thorns on boards, Amy . . .

Reverend Dodd had known all about the Boo Hags.

She refused. Just because Reverend Dodd mentioned the Boo Hags didn't mean he believed in them. *Of course he did, and quit stalling.*

She looked at the key in her hand.

Dig, Amy.

She closed her eyes and felt and heard and saw the planks of the bee barge under her feet as a girl, heard the horned Boo Hag below, following below her like a shadow, his horns scraping across the wood down there . . .

. . . thorns on boards, thorns on boards . . . now open up wide and let me in . . .

She stepped from Reverend Dodd's bedroom and worked at slowing her heart, but Jericho's closed bedroom door loomed large, and it pulled her, closer, closer, and she walked, the key out in front of her as if magnetized by the doorknob, her hand jittery, the reverend's diary in the crook of her other arm.

She stuck the key in the lock, turned it, opened the door to weird sunlight and dust motes and wide-open windows and walls that shook her to the core. If Thomas Dodd had created a memorial garden downstairs in the parlor for his late wife Samantha, what Amy saw inside Jericho's room was something more akin to a shrine.

To her.

Pictures of Amy covered every inch of Jericho's bedroom walls. Pictures ranging from Amy at roughly age fourteen to the weeks leading up to the massacre when she was eighteen. She couldn't recall seeing Jericho with a camera, or a phone, but then again, how often had she felt Jericho watching, only to turn around and find nobody there? And as she studied the pictures, all stuck to the wall by colorful thumbtacks, in none of them was she looking at the camera, and if she'd come close to looking it had been an accident, because it was clear these had all been taken without her knowing.

He has a thing for you, Amy, both Nate and Bridget had always kidded her. *He loves you, Amy,* they'd say whenever they spotted Jericho carrying a book.

Until she'd begged them to stop because it wasn't funny, because nothing about Jericho was funny.

Cold chills surged up and down her spine and across her skin.

A born monster who'd developed human feelings.

A monstrous boy the size of a man caught in the middle of trying to adapt.

She turned slowly, trying to process what all these pictures meant.

Jericho, for years, had been following her. He was infatuated with her.

She stopped at his desk. It was dust covered like everything else in the room. On the desktop were plastic figures. Farm animals, all seemingly painted black. The horses and deer and cows and elk. They'd all been painted black, and their horns and antlers . . .

Amy looked away, forced her eyes back. The antlers were painted in carefully detailed swirls of red and orange.

The birds had been painted red. The chickens, bright yellow. The roosters, apple green.

Amy was shaking, trembling.

Beside the painted figures was a diorama made from a large shoebox, and inside was a scene of an island with a black beach and a crescent sun and yellow grass complete with thorns and purple snakes and black-barked trees with white leaves and . . .

Amy turned away, fought the nausea coming up.

He's been there, she thought, between panted breaths.

Where is Mr. Passafume?

"Oh my God," said a male voice at the open bedroom door.

But Amy was too focused on her own thoughts for it to fully register.

He's been there, to the other side, she thought, recalling how many times they'd found Jericho staring at the honey house door, how many times he'd had to be lured away from it and led home like a lost dog on a leash.

"What the hell is this?" It was Nate she'd heard at the door. "Amy . . ."

But Amy was still thinking of Jericho. *He's been there. He knows of that place,* she thought. *The other side* . . . And then it hit her. *He's* from *there.*

She snapped from her thoughts and faced Nate and Lauren, both of them studying the walls and room and desk with the same shock and horror she still felt even minutes after the initial gut punch of first opening the door.

Amy saw the old, dirty jar in Nate's hand, inside which rested a folded paper, like the jar was an unopened time capsule. "Nate, what is that?"

But his wide eyes still surveyed the room. "He saw us," Nate said. "Oh my God. Jericho saw us."

CHAPTER

62
Sheriff Kilbourne

"LAWRENCE," ROSE BOWER said from the sidewalk in front of Joe McCutchin's doughnut and coffee shop. She tapped the store's display window with the barrel of her Glock G19. "Found another one."

Lawrence was already making his way across Bull Street, from the body of Jasper McKinley, who lay dead, strewn across the curb in front of Ruth Tulliver's Boutique Shoppe, from a wound he and the rest of his crew had yet to figure out. It seemed Jasper had been gored under his sternum by something the size of an elephant tusk and had bled out before he could crawl more than a dozen feet. Lawrence adjusted his mask, eyeballing the deserted street, the island's main thoroughfare, the orange haze that had settled across the island like a dry mist.

Bright-red crows circled above.

A trail of blood, starting from the middle of the cobblestone street and across the sidewalk, led to the front door of the coffee shop, which was propped open by an unmoving foot. Lawrence asked Rose to step aside. He pulled his flashlight, aimed it toward Joe McCutchin's dead, twisted body at the entrance. He'd been gored too, but through the back, and the evidence was still in there, the tip of an antler protruding through his chest, at least a foot of it visible.

"Christ on a cross," Rose said behind her mask, closing Joe's eyes. Joe's hands were dirty and blistered, clear evidence he'd been digging. She looked up at Lawrence. "What is this?"

He knelt beside her. It wasn't like any antler he'd ever seen; instead of ivory, this one was swirled with deep tones of red and orange. Not painted, Lawrence thought, but the antler's true color. "I don't know, Rose."

But from where it had broken off, this antler was easily four feet long and more than likely longer, because it hadn't been pulled from its base in whatever animal it had belonged to but rather snapped like a broken femur somewhere down the length of it. He imagined Joe being carried by it, clinging on and fighting for his life before finally breaking free, only to realize he'd taken the murder weapon with him. Mitchell McBride and Steven Delacroix and the Boo Hags weren't their only problems out here. Lawrence and the others had gone out as a foursome to hunt them down, but they'd wasted their first hour confronting stray islanders, unmasked and sickened by whatever was in the air. Some refused to stop digging until Lawrence threatened arrest. Some were delirious. Others confused. And while none, so far, had agreed to accompany them back to the Dodd House for shelter, they'd all stopped digging, if only temporarily.

Lawrence knew his threat of arrest was empty, but he hadn't expected to find this carnage. He sensed there were more dead out there, and now their mission had changed from offense to defense—in other words, to stay alive. Assess the damage and regroup, because Mitchell McBride might be a mere nuisance compared to what was coming out of that swamp. The digging had done it. Jericho, somehow, had done it. By the looks of those aerial photographs, they'd unearthed him. That axe had moved underground along with Jericho as he grew. Had he really continued growing all along? Lawrence had no other way to rationalize the earthquakes.

A gunshot echoed out on the street.

Lawrence moved out of the coffee shop with caution. Dennis and Caleb stood in the middle of Bull Street, handguns pointed southward. Lawrence motioned for Rose to stay back as he inched down the sidewalk toward the animal, if that's even what it was.

"What the hell is that thing, Lawrence?" Rose said softly behind him.

Lawrence didn't know but could tell it was what had gored the two dead bodies. At first he thought it was a deer, but it was way too big. It was an elk, but as black as an abyss, with a full rack of antlers marked by vivid swirls of red and orange. One was broken off from the coiling, twisted rack, protruding from a head that huffed and snorted as it eyed the four of them with bloodlust. Plumes of steam escaped from its flared nostrils, as if whatever world this thing had come from had been cold.

Sweating profusely, Lawrence crept closer, and from the side of his mouth, he warned the others to stay put. The black deer eyed their positions on the street and the sidewalk, back and forth, as if determining which to attack first. Meanwhile, the red crows had centralized directly above, as if preparing an attack of their own. *They're working together,* Lawrence thought, slowly inching forward, finger on the trigger, fighting the same tremble in his grip that had stunted him eight years ago, him hesitating during the two brief moments when the crowd had dispersed enough for him to have pulled the trigger on Jericho.

And then he saw someone else emerge from the trees on the other side of the street.

It was Mr. Passafume; he hadn't gone AWOL.

He hadn't disappeared inside the honey house.

Blue Bottles moved slowly, cautiously, just as Lawrence was doing on the opposite side of the street, but somehow without the obvious fear.

"Don't move," Blue Bottles told them, fifteen yards away from the animal. "Don't. Move."

Lawrence couldn't help thinking the old man was on a suicide mission. But at the same time, Mr. Passafume appeared familiar with this thing. Lawrence imagined any minute the elk would lower its rack of antlers and charge, but it didn't. It stood still, eyeing Blue Bottles just as he was eyeing it, like they were playing a game of Don't Blink, and then the elk scampered back a few yards, huffing steam from its nostrils, cracking cobbles as it moved its massive, heavy hooves.

Mr. Passafume slowly removed a gris-gris bag strapped over his shoulder, then the amulet around his neck. He discarded both in the center of the street and continued his approach toward the elk, who no longer appeared afraid of him, because that's what Lawrence was seeing—the massive deer was afraid of *him*. Or, Lawrence noticed, of what Mr. Passafume had dropped onto the street, the remedies the Geechee on the island had always worn or carried to ward off the island spirits.

The red crows squawked above.

Now only a few feet from the elk, Mr. Passafume held out his old, arthritic hand and allowed the beast to sniff it. It recoiled slightly and then sniffed again. Blue Bottles then placed his palm and fingers beside the elk's head, as if petting it, softly, gently, and it even appeared as if he was whispering words to it, but then Lawrence saw the gun in Mr. Passafume's other hand, and he was just as carefully raising it higher, higher. . . .

Rose, behind them, said, "Oh Jesus . . ."

And then Blue Bottles placed the barrel of his SIG Sauer to the elk's head and pulled the trigger. Blood splattered. The red crows overhead scattered. The elk staggered backward, wobbled, and fell in a heap, antlers clickety-clacking on the cobblestones like something brittle instead of deadly. Blue Bottles knelt beside the elk and affectionately rubbed his hand on its head as it died, the steam coming from the nostrils dissipating into whisps and then gone. The elk's massive chest finally stopped moving.

It was dead.

Mr. Passafume stood, faced them, retrieved his amulet and mojo bag from the street, and said, "Come on. Let's go. There's more out there." He looked over his shoulder. "And that was one of the gentler ones."

CHAPTER

63
Nate

NATE COULDN'T GET out of Jericho's bedroom fast enough, not after what he'd seen on the walls and rationalized in his brain and especially now with the honey jar they'd just dug from his mother's garden burning hot and wet in his hands.

Or maybe that was the blisters opening again, which, on his rapid descent down the stairs, he noticed had happened, as blood and blister fluid now smeared the dirty jar.

Behind him on the stairs, Lauren said, "Nate, your hands . . ."

He ignored her. He was on a beeline toward the parlor, the same room where he'd seen his father crazedly dance that night with the ashes swirling out of the fireplace and hearth.

The parlor was empty now, and that's why he'd chosen it. He wanted to be left alone to read what had been sealed inside the jar, but Amy and Lauren entered the parlor with him and closed the door behind them.

Amy—oh, poor Amy, what had Jericho done?—was the first to speak, and it had everything to do with the words he'd meant to keep inside upstairs in Jericho's bedroom.

He saw us . . .

Because she hadn't let it go. "Saw who, Nate?" Amy asked in a panicky desperation that made Nate so sad tears came to his eyes. "What do you mean, he saw us?"

"Me and Bridget," Nate said. "We took him to that picnic on the Backbone. Bridget, you remember?"

Amy stared, wide-eyed. "I remember."

"She invited him," Nate said. "Neither of us wanted him to go. You remember?"

"Yes, Nate, I remember. But what are you talking about?"

"I'd never seen Jericho smile. But he did, after that picnic. He never showed emotion, like ever. You know that. But in those days, Amy, he smiled."

Amy closed her eyes as if to quell nausea. "He thought it was like a double date."

"But then, a few days after that picnic, the day you and Bridget decided to trick me, you dressed like the other and you had me for a few minutes, until I held your hand, and you held it differently than Bridget would have. After I figured it out. You went back inside to change."

"And Bridget, dressed as me . . ."

Nate chewed his lower lip. "She ran up the hill to the Backbone, and I chased her. We went to our spot in the field, and we . . . we . . . we started . . ."

Amy said, "I get it." She glanced at Lauren. "And she gets it. Spit it out, Nate."

"He saw us," Nate said. "I know he saw us."

"And he thought it was me," Amy said, horrified. "And the next day he bought that axe."

It was silent while they let that sink in, but it didn't last long, because Nate couldn't wait to open the honey jar.

"Nate, don't," Amy said.

The blisters on his hand made it hard for him to get a grip, but he twisted until it turned. Dirt and rust sifted to the floor.

For some reason Amy didn't want him to open it. Part of Nate didn't want him to open it.

But the main goal of digging was to find something, right?

You didn't fucking dig for the fun of it.

With his back against the wall, Nate slid to the floor and sat with his legs extended out before him. He nodded toward the diary in Amy's hand. "What's in that?"

She made as if to start telling him, but stopped and said, "Just open the jar. I'll get to this later." Amy sat beside him for support.

Lauren sat on the other side of him, rested her head on his shoulder. "Read it."

Nate pulled out the paper. Parts of it crumbled as he unfolded it to reveal his mother's perfect penmanship.

CHAPTER

64

Eighteen Years Before the Sudden Death of Reverend Thomas Dodd

Samantha Dodd's Nightmare

Out of desperation I write this.

I was not of sound mind in the time after you were born, Nathanial. Postpartum depression, four subsequent miscarriages, and then the stillbirth. It buried me.

And then I became pregnant again, this time with the boy I carry now. The boy I call Jericho. Part of me—most of me—doubts I will survive this delivery. This baby inside me is too large. He grows too quickly and even the doctors are baffled. He is not right, and my nightmares are desperately trying to tell me so. Deep down, I've known since the night he was conceived that he wasn't completely human. Thomas entered the honey house uninvited. I know he did. He made a deal with the devil that night. With good intentions, perhaps. For me, yes, he did it for me, but it was not him inside our bedroom that night. Not ONLY him, I should say, because while it might have been Thomas's body, it was not completely his . . . form, and certainly not his mind. Those were not his eyes hovering over me, that was not his tongue, those were not his fingernails, and that shadow . . . that shadow he wore like a cloak was laughing, it had arms and legs and a faceless head, and it was laughing. Never had I been so terrified. Never had our coupling taken so long. And I don't even think he remembered the morning after, or the morning after that, and then on and on the days and weeks and months went, me growing larger and Thomas growing more inward, more guilty it seemed, even though I don't think he truly remembered from where that guilt had come. And now every night that memory visits me in the form of a nightmare. Every night Bad Thomas visits me. Every night Bad Thomas crawls atop our bed and I'm frozen with fear. He crawls atop me and I'm helpless. He puts his mouth to mine and sucks the breath right out of me and with those eyes that aren't his eyes, he glares, and those lips that aren't his lips, he laughs, and Bad Thomas rides me like the Boo Hag he was that night.

I hope you never find this, Nathanial, and I certainly hope you never have to read it, but I can't take the horror anymore, and so I've taken your advice. I'm writing this down and I'll bury it in the garden and sneak back into bed and pray it goes away as you suggested. You were always so smart and handsome, my sweet boy. If my determination to have another baby was driven by anything, it was you, it was so that I could maybe have another child as loving and caring as you, and I was an only child, and I didn't want you to grow up the same.

I must confess that Bad Thomas—oh how silly that sounds, but that's what I called him in my nightmares—was not the only nightmare that has plagued me during this pregnancy. There's a place I began going to in my mind, when Bad Thomas was riding me, and at first that place was beautiful. It was so colorful I knew right away it was not real. It was my fantasy land. My escape from reality. My splintering, as some psychologists might say. The grass was sunflower yellow there and the crows were red and black trees had white leaves larger than magnolia blooms, and inside those leaves were threaded veins of bright red. The sand was magnificently fine and black as coal and the waves, the ocean waves moved away from the shoreline toward the pocked rocky wall over the horizon.

This place was beautiful . . . until it wasn't. Until Jericho began to grow inside me. Because once he started growing inside me, I saw a boy over there, sitting in the grass and staring at the vast yellow field before him, as if waiting for something to open, for something to HAPPEN. And as he sat there, and even those dreams became nightmares, and in each one of them he was bigger and bigger, and growing and waiting . . . I know it was Jericho sitting in the grass in that place. Somehow, it was my future child, and I was afraid of him even before he was born.

The island spirits took advantage of Thomas.

I know that now.

They tricked him.

And now things have been done that can't be undone.

This baby, I fear, will be a monster, just as Thomas was briefly a monster that night.

It's as if my mind—my imagination—is creating a monster and I'm physically growing him inside me. But in that land where Jericho sat in the yellow grass and grew and waited, Bad Thomas eventually arrived there too. Looking for me. Every nightmare I had as a girl found me there. Scarecrows in closets. Massive spiders coming to eat me. Boo Hags and plat-eyes and haints grew by the dozens. And those red crows perched on the crooked branches, the murder of crows flying through purple skies, I realized, after some time had passed, that they belonged to Thomas. Those had been his nightmares as a boy, and they were in this place, on this island, because that's what it was, an island from another land.

The Island of Horns.

Because as I looked closer, there were tiny thorns on everything—the grass blades and tree bark and rocks and flowers, and the thorns there grow into horns, and then antlers, and all the black deer and black cows and black elk and black caribou have them. Even some of the dogs there have begun to grow horns.

Now, as I write this, and my hand grows tired from the effort, I'd be remiss if I didn't write down the most peculiar occurrence early on in my dreams of this place, when they were still pleasant dreams and not yet nightmares. I was atop a bluff overlooking the field of yellow grass, and all of a sudden, I saw a young girl emerge, like magic, from nowhere. One second the space was empty and the next, she was there, as if lost. Lost and confused and taking in this place much like I had at first. As she walked through the field toward the shoreline, I recognized who it was. It was Amy Barnes. She reached down to the tall blades as she walked and then quickly brought her hand up to her mouth, as if she'd been nipped by a thorn and she was sucking the blood from the wound. And then she froze.

She stared off in the distance, and approaching her, hunkering low in the field at first, was a red-fleshed Boo Hag, and from its stringy white hair protruded a set of hooked horns, and suddenly it started running toward her. She turned and ran, screaming the words HORNS ON BOARDS . . . HORNS ON BOARDS . . . I didn't know what she meant and was too far away to help her, but then, just as she'd appeared out of nowhere, there stood Mr. Passafume with his hand out . . . I'VE GOT YOU, AMY. I'VE GOT YOU, I heard him say, and then just like that, Blue Bottles and Amy were gone and the horned hag looked confused.

That entire scene took no longer than thirty seconds. I know I saw that in my dreams around the same time Amy drowned in that swamp. And when I later learned that she'd stopped breathing or had lost consciousness for nearly thirty seconds while Blue Bottles beat the water from her lungs, I feel like I know where she went. I told no one, because she was alive and no one would have believed me, but it has proven cathartic to write it down now.

I don't know how else to explain these feelings other than this place is real, and it's coming, and I fear Jericho is somehow the vessel. He's somehow their Trojan Horse.

Bottomless anxiety and dread grows inside me with every waking day, and all I want is for this to end.

For Bad Thomas and for this strange place to go away.

This place Bad Thomas calls Lalaland.

CHAPTER

65
Nate

TEARS ROLLED DOWN Nate's cheeks.

On either side of him, Amy and Lauren cried silent tears.

Nate's hands trembled, but he managed to carefully fold the pages and slide them back into the old jar.

Near the end of Samantha Dodd's confession, it was clear Amy had pulled inward. Nate had offered to stop, but she'd insisted he read all of it.

Amy, now that the letter had been read, and without looking at Nate, said, "Do you believe me now?"

"Yes," he said, so softly it barely registered.

Amy walked toward the windows of the parlor, facing Oak Alley, her back to them.

Nate stood, offered Lauren a hand off the floor, and they stood behind Amy at the windows. In the distance, Sheriff Kilbourne and his crew were walking down Oak Alley, emerging through the orange hazy mist like weary survivors in an apocalyptical movie. Their group of four had grown to what looked like six or seven.

It was clear to Nate that they'd picked up stragglers along the way.

Nate stepped closer, stared directly over Amy's shoulder toward the long, meandering gravel road of Oak Alley. "It's Blue Bottles."

"I told you he was fine," Amy said. "He's always fine."

Yeah, Nate thought, *and he's the only one not wearing a mask.*

C H A P T E R

66
Sheriff Kilbourne

SHERIFF KILBOURNE CALLED the meeting in the dining room, with the intention of gathering, at first, with only a few. And then those few would spread the word to whoever they saw fit to hear it.

But Mr. Passafume had insisted everyone in the house be invited to attend. Before Lawrence could argue, Blue Bottles had said, "Because everyone is scared, Sheriff. They deserve answers."

Amy was the first to take a seat at the dining room table. Nate brought chairs from around the house and lined the dining room walls with them, and soon twenty-one adults and three teenagers filled the room, where Blue Bottles had already lit four candles. The weird orange haze outside had brought about a premature sunset, and Lawrence wondered how long it would take for full dark to set in.

He called the meeting to order after Blue Bottles took his seat and Lauren, God bless her, had taken the five younger children into the living room to play games and Caleb Jones had volunteered to stand guard outside with Dustin Gibb.

Lawrence filled them all in on the threat of Mitchell McBride and Steven Delacroix.

Easy Perkins said, "I thought that damn axe was buried with the body."

"It was," Nate said. "I put it down there myself."

"Then how did it end up in Mitchell McBride's hands?" Rose Bower hissed. She hadn't meant it as accusatory, but it came out that way and Nate responded in kind.

"I don't know," he said, his emotions just as raw.

Lawrence got the feeling something had gone down with Nate and Amy while he was gone, because they both seemed extra agitated.

Most of the islanders now eyeing Nate Dodd still probably looked upon him with disdain. Like a prodigal returned, because although the digging had been going on for weeks or more, shit hadn't really started hitting the fan until he arrived home on that ferry.

Lawrence said, "Mitchell dug through the floor of his bathroom and unburied it from the ground."

"How did he know it was down there?" asked Dennis Wagner.

"I don't know," Lawrence admitted, watching as Blue Bottles stood from his chair and left the room. "And I don't know how it made it the quarter mile underground from where it was buried to where he dug it up, but somehow it did. And something urged him to go down after it."

"We know what that something is, Lawrence," Tina said, but as if she were treading water lightly, gently tiptoeing around the elephant they all knew was in the room.

"It's the earthquakes," Easy Perkins said. "We need to stop beating around that bush and admit what we're all thinking." She eyed everyone in the room. "That that boy, that monster, just like he was doing when he was alive . . . he kept growing after he died. He kept growing underground."

"And he's out there," James Wright said.

"I can feel him in the air," one of the teenagers said. "Just like I did when I was little."

"Because we dug him up and let him free," said Tiny Henderson, who, in his dirt-covered overalls, barely fit in his chair, his big hands restless on his lap, fingers caked with dried dirt.

Rose Bower said, "Question is, what does he want?"

Lawrence noticed how quiet Amy Barnes was at the end of the table, opposite him, and next to Nate. The two of them had been sharing glances the entire meeting—Amy with what looked like a diary on the table in front of her, Nate with an old honey jar Lawrence had seen him rest on the floor beside his chair when he sat down.

They both seemed on the verge of revealing something when Amy said, "I unlocked Jericho's bedroom earlier. And I went inside." Gasps of disbelief moved like a wave over the room, and after they settled, she explained what she'd found on the walls, and then what Nate had described that day on the Backbone when Jericho must have thought he'd seen his brother with Amy when it was really Bridget.

And Easy Perkins said, "So he murdered my husband because he was *jealous*. Because of some kind of unrequited love." She looked at Amy. "For you?"

Nate stood up. "Don't go pointing fingers, Easy. Jericho was messed up and some wires got crossed."

Everyone started sharing their opinions, talking over one another with increased urgency, until Dennis Wagner shouted, "I think we can all agree that—"

But his voice was drowned out.

Just as Lawrence was about to stand and call everything back to order, Mr. Passafume returned with an armful of bourbon bottles and, one by one, placed them on the table, landing the bottom of each down harder than the next—*bam*, *bam*, *BAM*—and with each one he placed, the chatter in the room decreased, and all eyes fell on him. By the time Mr. Passafume finished placing the bourbon bottles around the table, Nate had left and returned with a tray full of rocks glasses.

The tension dissipated.

Nate placed the tray in the middle of the table. "Sorry, no ice."

CHAPTER

67
Amy

THE BOURBON HELPED.

Blue Bottles didn't even hesitate to pour when the three teenagers held out their glasses for a splash of Old Sam.

Amy downed hers in one swallow, and the bourbon trailed like fire down her throat.

Sheriff Kilbourne told them the unpleasant news that Duff Hollaway had left them high and dry and they had no safe way off the island. Sending up flares at nightfall would be the best option left, with hopes that the other islands, or even the mainland, might see. Tiny Henderson not only volunteered to help retrieve the flares from the jailhouse but also offered his stash of illegal fireworks, saying, "I'll light that sky up like a fucking war zone."

Tired of Tiny's macho bravado, Amy asked Sheriff Kilbourne for the floor, then said bluntly, "If anyone in this room is still clinging to what they'd previously considered reality, I'd ask you to step out right now."

Nobody moved.

She eyed Nate on the far end of the table. He shook his head, but she felt the urgent need to bring it up anyway, because hiding what Samantha Dodd had written inside that jar for even another day was wrong. The islanders deserved to know. With what was happening outside, they deserved answers. Nate must have had a sudden change of heart, or maybe it was the quick glance he and Lauren shared, because right before Amy started talking, he placed the jar on the table and unscrewed the rusty lid and, without any preamble, read his mother's letter out loud for the second time in as many hours. Amy didn't know how he managed to do it, but Nate made it through without shedding a tear this time, and when he finished, the room was so silent the sound of him folding the paper and replacing it in the jar was almost palpable.

"Lalaland?" Tiny Henderson said with a chuckle.

No one laughed along with him, and Amy would have scolded Tiny had she not heard the obvious nervousness in his laugh. Next to her, Blue Bottles stared at the tabletop, rubbing his rough, calloused hands together; he was pissed about something, and she had a strong feeling it had everything to do with Thomas Dodd and the reason their relationship had gone south.

Amy hadn't had time to completely allow her emerging theory to breathe, but she let it out anyway. "Jericho was put here on this island for a reason. I think it was to do exactly what he did that Fourth of July day. And we've already thrown out a possible reason why he did it when he did. The history of this island is a violent one." She took a few minutes to recite the correlations with the high honey purities and cotton and indigo yields and used Mitchell McBride and Steven Delacroix and Matt Folsom as the most current examples. Mitchell had stolen a crate of this year's 100 precent purity, and he'd at least given bottles to the other two men. And she was convinced that while most everyone on the island had lost their minds digging, the only ones to become violent thus far were the ones who'd eaten the honey. When no one argued her point and most nodded in agreement, she continued, "The island gets thirsty. For blood. And this other place Samantha Dodd wrote about, I know this place. Many of you all have heard me speak about it at some point in our lives together, and I hope you can understand how real it is. She was sleeping when I drowned. She was in the middle of a nightmare or dream when I drowned, and she says she saw me there during the exact amount of time I was out, when I was chased by what has been witnessed now by at least three people"—she pointed out the window—"out there, on our island, right now. Some of them have gotten through."

"That's crazy talk," Tiny said, but still with the anxious quaver in his voice.

Amy hit the table with the bottom of her fist. "Is it? Have you seen what's going on out there, Tiny? Have you? That elk Sheriff Kilbourne described. The dead Boo Hag in Caleb's garage? The one Mr. Wagner got a picture of inside the bank? Red crows flying all over the place." She sucked in a deep breath to calm herself down. "Jericho was born a monster, but he was a monster with a mission. I don't think the plan was for him to start developing human feelings, as misguided and confused as they were, but he was their Trojan horse. He was somehow made flesh through what Reverend Dodd did inside that honey house and then with his wife that night, but he was put here to grow and grow until he was big enough to open the door and let the other side in. But he died when he was ten." She leaned back in her chair. She had no other way to explain it. She turned to Blue Bottles. "Mr. Passafume, you were not at the parade that day. You might have been the only one on the island not in attendance. You were at the honey house. What did you see that day? What did you see when Jericho started killing?"

She'd asked him the question too many times to count over the years and prayed under these circumstances he'd finally give an answer. And he did, but not before allowing his eyes to run across the dining room, taking in all their nervous faces as they anticipated his answer.

"I was on the bee barges that afternoon, doing some summer cleaning after the harvest." He downed the rest of his bourbon in one gulp. "As soon as the screaming started, I saw the door to the honey house rattle. It was locked, like always, if I wasn't in there. And as the screaming intensified, so did the rattling of that door, like someone was on the other side shaking it, violently."

"And as more blood was spilled on Bull Street," Amy said, leading him.

"Yes, Amy," Blue Bottles said, but with obvious regret. "The more blood was spilled, the more that door moved. The closer it got to opening."

"But not necessarily the honey house door," Amy said. "The *other* door. Inside the honey house." She glared at Blue Bottles. "If Jericho hadn't been stopped that afternoon, did you fear that door might fully open?"

After a pregnant pause and a loud, dry swallow, he said, "Yes."

"I don't think I'm alone in that I feel Jericho out there right now," Amy said to the entire room, and they all either nodded or said soft words to concur. "He's in the air. We dug him up. His job was never finished because he killed himself in that jail cell. But he never stopped growing. He wasn't fully dead, and we let him out and that door has opened. I know this place, and I know you do too, Mr. Passafume. And you *knew* what Jericho might be even before he was born. You knew Thomas Dodd entered the honey house."

Before he could respond, Rose Bower said what Amy knew was on most of their minds. "What door are you talking about?"

Blue Bottles said, "The place Amy speaks of . . . is real. And it's here. And I'm going to do my best to get everyone off this island safely. And at the same time continue doing what I've been doing since before any of you were born."

Rose Bower said carefully, "And what exactly is that, Earl?"

"Guarding that door." He took in their confused stares. "I've been doing a lot more than making honey these past decades."

Amy thought of the black-and-white picture she'd shown him. "Or longer."

Blue Bottles said, "Yes . . . even longer."

Lauren asked from the dining room entrance, "What exactly is in that honey house?"

Mr. Passafume answered, "*That* door has been there long before the honey house was even built. And to explain *that*, we all need to know what really happened to Adeline Drew."

Tina Kilbourne said, "How? It was a legend. And it happened over a hundred and fifty years ago."

Mr. Passafume nodded, because she wasn't wrong, and then his eyes bored straight into Amy when he said, matter-of-factly, "Because I was there."

CHAPTER

68
Blue Bottles

Part I

Blue Bottles held up a hand to stop the questions before they came.

"Let me first explain the true parts of the legend," he said, looking directly at Amy. "William Honeycott Barnes—your great-great-grandfather, Amy—was an evil man. After the Civil War, when many of the freed slaves came back here to claim what the government had given them when the white landowners were run off, only for President Andrew Johnson, after Lincoln was assassinated, to give this island right back, Honeycott Barnes led the charge. He was brutal. He and his pals beat those former slaves into submission and killed too many to count. They were dead set on bringing slavery back to this island. By that time, Honeycott had claimed the island as his own, purchasing it outright through a bank he owned and with lawyers in his pocket. But don't ever tell me apples don't fall far from trees, because with Amy here, and with her twin sister Bridget, the buck stopped," he said with clear emotion. "You are not your family. But unbeknownst to many on the mainland, Honeycott Barnes secretly started the transatlantic slave trade again."

Mr. Passafume allowed that to sink in. "He held meetings in Savannah with those still pissed off about the abolition of slavery.

Secret payments were made. And in the winter of 1869, the first slave ship landed on a shore steeped with mist, at what we now call the Rocks, and seventy-five men and women stolen from the western coast of Africa were marched off that ship and taken into newly built slave quarters a hundred yards from Crow Island Sound." Blue Bottles surveyed the room. "Off that boat came the woman now known as Adeline Drew, although her true name has been lost in the lack of official records. Adeline was the name given to her once they removed the shackles. Drew, because she was good at drawing on parchment paper. Not just good but great. She drew pictures to communicate, since none of them could speak the language. She was a conduit, of sorts, between her people and theirs. Keep that in mind." He held up a crooked finger. "She was a conduit. She was an artist. She was what I call a *creative*. Anyone with a vivid imagination. Like Amy. Like Samantha Dodd was a creative with her garden. And in creatives, the imagination thrives. Adeline Drew was a strong, pissed-off woman, with child, who sought revenge for having been stolen from her homeland, from her husband, her family. And for months, while these men and women were forced into labor for this cruel, futile attempt to grow King Cotton again, Adeline Drew plotted. Even as the baby in her grew and her back ached and her fingers bled in the field, she plotted her revenge. Vowed to kill them all. But while she never lacked the courage, she found, over time, that she didn't have it in her to take another life, no matter how badly she wanted it done.

"Until one evening, when she was more than eight months pregnant, she went on a walk, like she was prone to do, and she ended up in the swamp. Folks said she often was drawn there, to those cypress and tupelo trees, to that deep, dark, mysterious water."

Nate said, "Jericho would walk to the bee barges and just stand there, staring at the honey house. Like he knew . . ."

Sheriff Kilbourne fidgeted in his seat. "Knew what?"

"That somehow he . . . or at least part of him . . . wanted to go back there," Amy answered, looking to Mr. Passafume for affirmation, for validation, and he gave it with a nod. "Like he knew there was a thin line between here and there, inside that honey house—"

Blue Bottles said, "Except in the time of Adeline Drew, there was no honey house. There was only the swamp. But Adeline knew better. She sensed there was something more and walked deeper into that swamp. And that's when the Boo Hag took her. Used her. Burrowed under her skin and gave her the strength to do what her mind had not allowed. I used to think the island spirits were brought across the Atlantic with the slaves, through their folklore, but now I believe the evil spirits have always been here, lingering on either side of that unseen door. One took Adeline Drew for a ride. And in the coming days and weeks, as she neared the delivery of that baby, she carried a newfound strength. She carried boards into those woods at night. Hammer and nails she'd stolen from the owners' sheds. And she worked. She hammered and nailed and built that shack, what would become the honey house, by herself, around that door, a door that couldn't be seen by the common eye. And then she did it. She took an axe one night from a nearby barn and killed one white owner after the next, saving William Honeycott Barnes for last. She took off his head. By then, half the island was up in arms and the hunt was on. They lit torches, got on their horses, and chased her into the swamp, which was exactly what she wanted. She entered that wooden shack she'd built with her own hands and locked herself in. The islanders were set to burn it down, but then they heard Adeline screaming. And the next thing they knew, all went quiet, and then they heard a baby crying inside. Adeline Drew had given birth, alone, inside the walls of that little hut. The islanders busted the door open, stepped inside, thinking they'd find Adeline and the baby. They found the baby, a boy still covered with a caul, and crying, but Adeline was gone."

"Bullshit," said Tiny Henderson.

"Which part?" asked Mr. Passafume, daring him to answer.

"All of it."

Rose Bower said, "Shut your face, Tiny."

And he did. Sheriff Kilbourne said, "Go on, Earl. Finish it."

"They left that baby to drown in the swamp, left him on the banks, just as the legend goes," he said. "But where the legend *doesn't* go was that the boy, soon after the last men walked away, started crying again.

A local white woman with a kind heart, along with a kind husband with the surname of Passafume, swaddled that baby and took him home."

Rose Bower said, "How do you know that baby lived? Earl?"

"Because that baby was me," he said, pointing in the direction of where the honey house was outside. "Because I was the boy born at the door."

CHAPTER

69
Nate

NATE SAT STUNNED like the rest of them.

He looked across the room toward Lauren. She raised her eyebrows at Nate, body language he took as *So this is Blue Bottles? Born right after the Civil War?*

Nate held up his hands to Lauren like *I don't know.* And then looked at Amy, who was staring at his father's diary on the tabletop, at the black-and-white photograph she was pulling from the middle of it, but nobody was talking. Nobody moved. Had Nate not known Blue Bottles all his life, he would have thought him a whack job. Problem was, nobody on the island was more respected and loved than Blue Bottles. And now that Nate thought on it, now that he was studying his face, the dude hadn't aged a wink since he'd known him.

Not knowing how else to break the weird silence, Nate said, "Well . . . have a wonderful day, Mr. Passafume."

It hadn't been meant as an attempt at levity, but the room breathed a little.

And when Blue Bottles said, "You too," a few people closed their eyes in relief, because maybe something was still right with the world.

If there was ever a time for someone to say *just kidding*, this was it, but instead the old man went on. "I was a boy when I first came into contact with the door inside the honey house."

Sheriff Kilbourne must have seen what Nate was seeing, that half the room looked pale and wide-eyed, and maybe all this truth syrup was making things worse. Kilbourne said, "Should we save some of this for a smaller audience, Mr. Passafume?"

Blue Bottles considered this for all of two seconds. "No. If you all are going to somehow make it off this island, you have to know exactly what you're dealing with."

Nate said, "What do you mean, you all?"

Blue Bottles leaned forward, elbows on the table. "Because I'm staying here."

CHAPTER

70
Blue Bottles

Part II

"THE PASSAFUMES RAISED me from the time I was born until the day I moved out on my own at age sixteen."

Rose Bower said, "A Black boy living with white parents during that time?"

"It didn't come without tension," he said. "I'll grant you that, Rose. And there were suspicions from the start. Where did I come from? Why did the Passafumes take on a Black child when they had three perfectly healthy children of their own? Their story was that they'd found me abandoned on a doorstep, in a bassinet, during a day trip to Savannah. I was crying, so they nurtured me. And the Passafume family was so well respected on the island that, over time, few still questioned them."

"Nobody questioned where . . ." Amy paused, as if to gather her thoughts. "That baby born at the door and left in the swamp—nobody questioned where that baby went?"

"Initially, yes, there were theories, most of them nonsensical. I was too young, of course, to remember those times, but as years passed, even though common knowledge said an islander found the baby and buried him, that story had already become legend. And what makes for a better legend than snippets of untruths? It became more of a story if not only Adeline disappeared but the baby as well. Like my birth mother, I was infatuated by that hut, the place where Adeline Drew disappeared. Mother and Father Passafume forbade me to go to the swamp. They believed the stories of evil spirits. They believed Adeline Drew had been possessed by a Boo Hag and feared something similar would happen to me. But by age seven I began sneaking out there. I felt connected to it. It was, after all, where I was born. The Passafumes kept it from me until I was fourteen, but by then I'd begun to figure some things out. That I was the son of Adeline Drew, that I was the boy born at the door." He pulled out a small, centuries-old laminated paper from his shirt pocket. "As I said before, Adeline was an artist. One day—this was late 1870s—I entered the old quarters where she'd lived, which had been abandoned since she'd died—"

"Disappeared, you mean," said Nate.

Blue Bottles pointed at him, as if to say *Exactly*, but continued with his thread. "I found some of her drawings she'd left behind in an old dresser drawer." He flipped the laminated picture over and displayed it on the center of the table. It showed a Black woman, presumably Adeline Drew, from behind, standing atop a small hillside over a tree-filled swamp. "We all know where this is. Imagine my bee barges, and that's about where we're at in this picture. Except Adeline here had yet to build the hut that would become the honey house. But where she's standing in this picture would put her inside the honey house now."

Tiny Henderson leaned forward for a closer inspection. "What's she doing?"

"She's discovering," said Mr. Passafume, tapping the picture where Adeline had drawn herself reaching forward with her right arm, the fingers on her right hand splayed out as if raking the air. "Look close." Blue Bottles passed the picture around the room. "Might look from afar that she's raking at the air with that hand, but you can see what she drew inside the finger trails. Snippets of birds. Of trees, of grass. She's showing us what she saw when she first did it. Little sneak peeks." He glanced at Amy, who was staring at him intensely.

"Little sneak peeks of what?" Amy said, although he could tell she already knew and just wanted him to say it.

"Of that other place," he said calmly. "The other side. Lalaland."

"Bullshit," said Tiny, but his voice was weak, like he couldn't even convince himself. "And if you've been alive since way back then, why did you stop aging? It's like you've been in a holding pattern of . . . old."

Rose said, "Shut up, Tiny, and let him finish."

But even Blue Bottles didn't have an answer to that question, and before he could give one, Nate spoke up.

"Let's get back to that place," he said. "What is it exactly?"

"It's where we go when we dream," Mr. Passafume said. "When we have nightmares. It's where we go when we sleep, although when we wake up, most goes unremembered. When we have nightmares often enough, like your mother did, Nate, they have staying power. They become real, over there."

"Christ on a cross," Rose mumbled again, and poured herself another finger of Old Sam.

"But what was he?" Tina Kilbourne asked. "What *was* Jericho?"

"I think *is*, in this case, Tina, is more appropriate than *was*. Can we agree on that?"

Amy looked around the room. "I can feel him in the air."

"And he never stopped growing underground," Nate said, looking at Sheriff Kilbourne. "That's how the axe ended up underneath the McBrides' house. Those earthquakes . . . that was him, growing, shifting . . . and we dug him up. We did this. And there are some out there still digging."

"Which is why the air keeps getting worse," Sheriff Kilbourne said.

"So what?" Rose Bower said. "We start filling the dirt back in?"

"Too late for that," Mr. Passafume said. "We already let him out. Can't put air back in a jar." He looked at Principal Tina Kilbourne. "And to answer your question, what is Jericho? He's everything. Nate's right. He's a baby born from a Boo Hag. I know of two other instances where this nearly happened. Or, at least, I believed it to be true. One to a woman in 1906, but the baby only lived five days. The second time was to a woman in 1923, and that baby only lived two days."

Nate shifted uncomfortably in his seat. "I talked to Doc Cheevers last night." He looked around the room and spotted Doc Cheevers leaning against the wall, pale and tired. "Jericho, when he was born, was hidden for five days by my dad and Doc Cheevers. They wouldn't let anyone see him." He said to Doc, "Do you want to tell them or me?"

Doc Cheevers swirled the bourbon in his rocks glass, finished it in a deep swallow, and said, "I will," as if entering a long-needed penance stemming from this very matter. "To say I was shocked when I delivered Jericho was an understatement. I shouldn't have been surprised by anything at that point, with how the pregnancy had gone until then, but I knew we had a problem from the start, just because of his color. At first, I thought it was the normal fluids, but after Jericho was cleaned, his skin was . . . it was red. He looked burned all over. Yet he never cried like he was in pain. And his veins, you could see them, distinctly, like tiny blue rivers all over his body."

"Like the Boo Hag," Amy said.

"Yes," Doc Cheevers said. "I showed Reverend Dodd, who . . . looked horrified, of course, but also deeply strung out with guilt. A guilt I'm only understanding fully now," he said to Nate. "After your mother's letter. But for days, your father and I, we monitored Jericho." His voice caught in his throat, like he might choke up. "We even entertained . . . ending his life. With that skin, those eyes, his size, he didn't seem human. But then, right around the third day, his skin started to change. To acclimate. I've no other way to describe it. So we continued to monitor him, and by day five, his skin looked like any other newborn. We decided it was okay to let others see him." Doc Cheevers looked like he might get sick. "Excuse me." And he left the dining room.

Blue Bottles watched him go, and on his face, Amy saw that perhaps some of his own questions had been answered by what Doc Cheevers had just divulged. "Now Jericho is an evil entity made angry from a bad death," he said. "He's growing in spirit just as he grew in life. And that's what we're dealing with." He gave that a few seconds to settle in with the room. "But if you want my opinion, and I think by now you do, Jericho was a vessel. He *is* their Trojan horse, just like Amy said."

Tiny said, "Whoa, what?"

Dennis Wagner, thinking out loud, said, “A program designed to breach the security of a computer system.”

Mr. Passafume said, “The Greeks concealed themselves inside a hollow wooden horse in order to secretly enter Troy.”

“I know what the Trojan horse is,” Tiny said. “But how does that apply here?”

“Who creates dreams and nightmares? Who creates folklore and legends?” asked Mr. Passafume.

“We do,” Amy said. “Man. Woman. People.”

“This altered but real state of mind. Everyone adds to it. Every time they think, every time they imagine, every time they dream and have nightmares . . . let me just say that Lalaland has become overpopulated, and it needs places to grow.” He looked at Amy. “You’ve had nightmares of Boo Hags since you were a girl. Do they grow in numbers, the Boo Hags you see over there?”

“Yes,” she said.

“Because you’re so invested now, every time you have one of your reoccurring nightmares, you create a new one over there.”

Nate shifted in his seat, leaned forward. “You’re saying Jericho was made flesh over here, to what? Open the door?”

From the dining room entrance, Lauren said, “And keep it open.”

Mr. Passafume nodded. “To let the inhabitants of Lalaland in.”

Sheriff Kilbourne downed the rest of his bourbon and placed his glass down with a pop. “If it didn’t make so much damn sense, I’d call bullshit too, but it does. It just does. I’ve seen it with my own eyes. But what’s your role in all this? How are you still alive?”

“I was born at the door,” Mr. Passafume said, like that alone would appease them.

“You mentioned a caul?” Rose asked. “You were born en caul. I’ve heard those referred to as mermaid births.”

“Or veiled births,” said Easy Perkins.

“One in eighty thousand,” Mr. Passafume said. “Yes. Very rare. And folklore suggests that possession of a caul brings its bearer good luck.”

“That’s what this is?” Nate asked.

"And it protects that person from death," Mr. Passafume said. "Specifically, from drowning." If he hadn't grabbed their attention by now, that seemed to do it.

Amy tapped the laminated picture on the table, now that it had made its way around the room. "Finish this story, please."

Mr. Passafume retrieved his picture. "After finding this picture, I entered the swamp the same day, around dawn. I stood around where Adeline had drawn herself standing, and I reached out just like she'd drawn herself doing. I opened my fingers . . . and I . . . I raked the air. Like one might rake their fingers through sand, and in the grooves I'd made in the air, I saw glimpses of what was on the other side. Grass as yellow as egg yolk. Black trees with white leaves."

"Some of the trees at the swamp are starting to look like that," Dennis said from the back corner of the room. "All around that honey house."

Blue Bottles nodded as if he already knew and then continued. "I raked the air again," he said. "Saw birds and animals in the distance, unlike any animals I'd ever seen before. The sun was crescent shaped. The sand on the beach was the color of dark chocolate, and the waves . . ."

Amy said, "They move away from the shore."

"Yes."

"Everything is wrong," Amy said.

"Just like everything here is turning wrong," Lauren said.

"Ever since I was a girl," Amy added, "I'd called it the Island of Horns."

"Because that's what it is," said Mr. Passafume. "Lalaland is vast. It has mountains and oceans and rivers and land masses of its own, and they somewhat mirror our world here. And it has many islands as well." He tapped the laminated picture again. "The one on the other side of the door here is *called* the Island of Horns."

Sheriff Kilbourne said, "Are you telling us there are more doors than this one?"

Blue Bottles folded his hands. "All over the world. Most are inactive. Cave systems. Islands, because islands are seen as stepping stones to the mainland. Most are found in abandoned tunnels. A few years ago, inside an old, abandoned tunnel in Harrod's Reach, Nebraska, there was a major breach. It has mostly been covered up, but if you dig deep enough there are remnants of evidence. But Lalaland has been trying to come through for centuries."

"And you've been guarding our door since the late 1800s?"

"More or less. But it seeps through the cracks. Like water, it finds a way."

Amy said, "The crops here . . . that's why they've always . . ."

"Yes," said Mr. Passafume. "The indigo. The cotton. The blue crab and fish and wildlife. The vegetables. The fruit. And the honey."

"No place has ever grown it better," Tina Kilbourne said. "Or bigger."

"Like Jericho," Nate said beneath his breath.

Mr. Passafume nodded. "There's always been something in the water."

Rose Bower said, "The honey is special because our trees are special? Because they've been drinking the same water our island's crops have been drinking since who knows when?"

Mr. Passafume shook his head. "No. Maybe a little. But it's not the trees, Rose. It's not the blooms. It's not the honey itself that's wrong here."

"Then what is it?" Rose asked.

"It's the bees," he said. "It's always been about the bees. Without the bees, there is no honey."

"What about the bees?" Rose asked.

Nate looked at all the bandaged wounds on his arms from having been stung. "Because they're *from* the other side."

Just as Mr. Passafume was about to expand on what Nate had said, two gunshots sounded.

C H A P T E R

71

Sheriff Kilbourne

THOSE GATHERED IN the dining room hadn't had time to process what Mr. Passafume had told them when the gun went off outside. Two pops in quick succession—*bam, bam*—before half the room ducked and the other half scattered, leaving Blue Bottles sitting alone at the dining room table, not smiling but seemingly at peace with himself, Lawrence thought.

Before Lawrence could exit the house through the foyer, David came out of nowhere and latched on to his left leg. "Daddy!"

Lawrence patted his back. "Daddy's gotta go, buddy. Let go now."

David laughed when Lawrence took a couple of steps toward the door with him still plastered to his leg like a cast. "Daddy's gotta go, David." He opened the front door.

"David, there you are." Tina hurried down the hallway and helped peel their son off his leg. She picked him up. "Daddy's gotta go to work."

David stared through the screen door. "Why's it look so funny out there?"

"Just a quick storm coming through," Lawrence said.

"Where's the rain?"

"No rain yet," he said. "More like dust."

"It smells funny."

"Yes, it does. And I need to go." He kissed David's forehead. David used that moment of proximity to wrap his arms around Lawrence's head.

At first he thought his son was giving him a hug, but then he felt warm breath in his ear, and David whispered, "Daddy."

Lawrence whispered back in David's ear. "Yeah?"

"Unicorns are real," David said softly, his lips touching Lawrence's ear.

After hearing what Blue Bottles had just confessed in the dining room, Lawrence wasn't about to tell his son they weren't. And then David did that eye tic thing, two in rapid succession. Lawrence did it right back to him and David grinned, as if a moment of solidarity had passed between them. Lawrence kissed Tina on the lips, touched her face lovingly, longingly, and then forced himself out the door.

Caleb Jones stood at the trees at the beginning of Oak Alley, waving him over. Lawrence positioned his mask on his mouth and nose and scanned the area as he approached Caleb, thinking *Where is Dustin Gibb?* And then he spotted him twenty paces to the left, hunkered under the shade of an old cypress, his mask around his neck like he'd just gotten sick.

"What happened?" he asked Caleb.

Caleb shook his head as he watched Dustin stand, weak-kneed, fidgeting with his own mask with one hand while still holding his gun in the other. "He saw something—hell, I don't know what. Got spooked. He panicked. Fired twice. Then got sick."

Lawrence moved toward Dustin. "You good?" Dustin nodded, but he was deathly pale. Lawrence stopped short of reprimanding the man for firing, remembering that Gibb sold island knickknacks and memorabilia at his surf shop down at the Sands. And Caleb was a CPA. They weren't trained soldiers. Even Lawrence hadn't been trained for this. He patted Gibb on the shoulder. "What'd you see?"

"I saw one of the Boo Hags, out there in the trees," Dustin said. "They're real. It looked at me, Sheriff . . ." He lowered his mask, got sick again.

Lawrence winced at the retching, looked to Caleb. "We need to get him back inside."

Caleb watched as red crows circled through the orange haze above, not like a normal black crow would, maybe hunting for something small down on ground level, but more like they were hunting *them*. "Look at the sunset, Sheriff. It's the middle of the day. It's already going down."

Lawrence agreed. The sunset looked like a smashed rainbow under a thick purple ceiling stretching across the horizon. They'd have to gather again quickly and make plans before total nightfall. *Nightmares come alive in the dark,* he thought.

Caleb coughed, rubbed his eyes. "Air's getting worse." He did his eye tic thing.

Lawrence put a hand on Caleb's shoulder, patted it. "You need a break, let me know. I'll get somebody else out here."

Caleb shook his head. "I'm good."

Lawrence saw Blue Bottles and Amy Barnes walking side by side toward the woods on the opposite side of Oak Alley and wondered what they were doing. Then he saw Nate Dodd and his girlfriend Lauren coming his way, and that made him think he'd missed something. He started toward Nate.

Caleb said, "Sheriff?"

Lawrence turned.

"What was decided in there?" Caleb asked. "In the meeting? What'd I miss?"

Nothing was decided, thought Lawrence. *And everything. You missed everything.* But he said, "I'll fill you in later. And Caleb?"

"Yeah?"

"Call me Lawrence."

C H A P T E R

72
Amy

"COME," MR. PASSAFUME SAID to Amy, on the veranda. "I've something to show you."

Caught between watching Nate and Lauren approach Sheriff Kilbourne in the distance and trying to process what Mr. Passafume had just told them inside the foyer—that they needed to make a trip back to his house for something necessary inside his garage—Amy followed him, but with reluctance.

She adjusted her mask. "Why don't you have to wear one of these?"

He watched the woods they were closing in on. "I'm acclimated."

"So this," Amy said, gesturing toward the orange haze and floating motes, "is the air over there?"

"Partly. But this"—he grabbed at the floating haze—"is also Jericho." He stopped within a few feet of the woods and faced her. "When I entered the honey house as a boy and raked my hand through the air, I saw, inside the invisible grooves, the land over there. But I also witnessed something else. A bee came through the opening I'd made with my fingers. The rip, you might say. A single honeybee. It crawled through the opening in the air, with reluctance, I think, at first, and then flew all the way in, buzzing around the walls of that hut, and then out the door. I followed it. It was larger than any honeybee I'd seen, and its colors were more vibrant.

Almost cartoonish, it was so striking. The tupelo trees were blooming. It flew to one of the white blooms. The next day I returned to find at least a dozen of those bees flying inside the hut, and even more buzzing around the tupelo blooms. The next day, hanging from the rafters inside the hut was a beehive the size of a football, and it was covered in bees. The color, Amy . . . never had I seen black and yellow with such real depth, such lurid richness. The bees were wet with it."

"You started making honey when you were a boy?"

"Yes," he said. "I painted that house the color it is today, haint blue. The roof, apple red. I took a jar to the Barnes family, your ancestors who owned the island after my mother's murder of Honeycott Barnes. Ellington and his wife Beatrice. They each tasted it. Dipping their fingers in. They asked me where I got it, and I told them I made it. They asked for more."

"And the rest, as they say, is history. You made my family rich."

"Your family was already rich, Amy."

"Richer."

"Yes. Much richer. Their corruption took care of itself. The money made them worse."

"Mr. Passafume?"

"I thought I said to call me Earl."

"How are you still alive?" she asked.

"I was born at the door."

"That's not good enough."

"Some things don't have explanations, Amy."

"I don't buy it."

"I first entered the honey house when I was a boy," he said. "Until then, I'd just occasionally raked the air to catch a glimpse of the other side. But one day my curiosity got the best of me. I raked with my fingers. I pawed like a dog might digging a hole. Those grooves became wider and wider, and within minutes I'd opened it enough to step through. I didn't stay long. Just a minute or two. It was hard to breathe. Whatever weather people have dreamed up over time, it has all added to the climate over there."

Amy watched the woods. Leaves moved on branches like something unseen had passed through. "Your age?"

"It wasn't until my twenties, when I'd earned enough to purchase a pocket watch, that I realized time was different over there." He pulled out the old watch and chain she'd seen him wear for as long as she could remember. He showed her the clock face, the second hand ticking. "When I first took this watch over there, to the other side, it stopped. Time literally stopped."

"And let me guess," Amy said. "It started working again when you came back?"

"Yes. But that wasn't all. The air . . . it took me a few times to get used to it, but every time I returned, I felt . . ."

"Refreshed?"

"Yes."

"Rejuvenated?'

"Yes."

"Younger."

"Yes, Amy, yes," he said. "But let me tell you. That's not the way of the world over there. Most age quicker than normal. There's less time in between sleeps."

"Because everything is wrong."

He stared into the woods. "Everything is indeed wrong. It's all made-up. We sleep here, our minds go there. And it's fleeting. But Amy, people who are in comas here . . . especially prolonged comas . . ."

"Their minds are there?"

"Yes," he said. "And just as I've been guarding this door for nearly my entire life on this side, they are guarding the doors on *that* side. We call them seers. And there are very few people who have entered through a doorway, physically entered through a doorway, and disappeared—"

"Like Adeline Drew?"

"Yes, like Adeline, my mother. Over there they call them elders."

"Is Adeline still alive? Mr. Passafume?"

"No," he said with sadness. "She died a long time ago. On the other side. You were right the other day, Amy. I take flowers to this cemetery and then leave some over there."

"And that's not a distant relative," Amy said. "That grave where you leave the flowers . . . Hannah Jane Jones Passafume . . ."

"My wife," he admitted. "God rest her soul."

"And the rest of the flowers you take into the honey house?"

"For my mother's headstone on the other side."

Amy gripped his arm, turned him. "You speak of seers, elders. What exactly are you?"

He smiled. "The baby at the door, Amy. Born at the threshold of both sides. Over there they call me The Wanderer. The Man on the Island. The Middle Man. Mister In-Between. Over here I'm just Blue Bottles."

"And you keep us safe."

"I tried," he said.

"You did," she said. "You do."

"Until now," he said, resuming his gaze into the woods. A red crow landed on the ground between a cluster of live oaks. "Adeline died on the Island of Bones. They brought her to me. On the shore over there, so that I could bury her properly. Lalaland is full of bad things, Amy. Sometimes they get through, but not like this. Never like this. For as long as I've been Mister In-Between, they've tried to breach us here at Crow Island."

"You hinted earlier that you'll help us off the island, but you won't go with us."

"Right," he said. "But it's more that I can't."

"Can't what?"

"Leave the island," he said, grinning. "I've never left the island on that side either. I've tried, but like a fish out of water, I can't breathe."

"You've never been off this island?"

"No."

"You've tried?"

"Yes," he said. "I tried for the first time, with my wife, in the summer of 1902. For our anniversary, we'd purchased tickets to Savannah. I started feeling sick even before boarding the ferry. And within fifty yards of the shore, symptoms began hitting me like little heart attacks. It was torturous, the pain, I couldn't breathe. My wife insisted they turn the ferry back to shore."

"And they listened?"

"I oversaw the island tupelo, Amy. I had, what would you call it . . . street cred? But I tried again in the 1950s. And again in the seventies, with similar results."

"And over there?"

"The same," he said. "You see now why I rarely venture close to the docks."

"I just assumed you were afraid of the water."

"I'm not really afraid of anything, Amy." He winked. "Not at my age."

"Except dying."

"Well, there's that," he said. "There is that." He beckoned her closer. "But hurry, let me show you something." He reached his arm out toward the trees, opened his hand, fingers splayed wide in the orange haze, and raked at the air, and in those air grooves Amy saw her dreamworld. She glimpsed yellow grass and black sand. "This used to be possible only inside the honey house," he said. "Because that structure was built *around* the door. But a few days ago, I felt it larger. The doorway had expanded onto the bee barges. And now this—it reaches the outskirts of the woods. It's slowly turning inside out." He nodded at her. "Go on, give it a try."

"Me?"

"Go on. Hurry."

Amy reached out and raked her fingers through the air, and even though she felt nothing at her fingertips, she saw what her movement had revealed on the other side. She jumped back. "How did I do that?"

"Because you've been there, Amy." He looked sternly at her now. He turned her away from the woods, from the scratches she'd made in the void, grooves that had already filled themselves in by the time he'd turned her around. "And I fear that you want to go back. That has always been my greatest fear for you, Amy. That you'd want so desperately to go back that you wouldn't stop to think what it would take to get you there."

C H A P T E R

73

Seven Days Before the Sudden Death of Reverend Thomas Dodd

From Reverend Dodd's Diary

It's dead.

Finally, after three days of following that red crow through the house, it's dead, and by my hand. By my knife, my dear wife. I know, I know what you're thinking, thou shalt not kill. Thou shalt not murder. Thou shalt not put a knife we received at our wedding through the ribcage of a poor, defenseless bird.

This crow.

But it wasn't just any crow. It was red. At first, I paid that strange detail very little attention. I followed it. I listened to it. I DUG and now I can't stop DIGGING.

It was that damn boy Mitchell. He told me to dig. He told me he knew all about Jericho because the Boo Hags told him. He told me Jericho was still alive. That we'd buried him alive and if I ever wanted any peace, I'd dig him out and set him free.

Now I wish I would have stopped and thought.

Red crows don't exist, Thomas. Ignore it. It'll go away, just as your nightmares did as a kid. It's just your imagination at play. I know from experience now, unfortunately, that there's no other path a red crow can take you other than astray. I should have known that the instant it first perched on my library windowsill, cawing, those deep oily eyes peering right through the heart of me. Its gaze might as well have been saying, "Remember me, old pal?"

Because oh boy do I!

In my childhood nightmare, red crows chased me, shitting blood on me like acid rain. Isn't it amazing what our minds can conjure at night, when the imagination is most active? I was a curious boy living inside this very house, always intrigued by God, yes, even then, but curious about so much else. I'd been so intrigued by the fact that the island had been named after a bird that may have never lived here that I spent hours researching it. Studying it. Studying them. Until one night I dreamed of the crows. I dreamed of the crows, and THEY became MY nightmare. And as time went on and my dreams evolved, the crows became red and violent and angry and then BAM! One arrives on my windowsill!

I listened to it for too many days when I should have been hunting it down. I know that now. Because red crows aren't real! Are they?

And nightmares can't come to life! Can they?

Regardless, it's dead as a doornail. Maybe now I'll get some badly needed sleep.

But I must say, as dead as it is, as close as I am to it now even as I write this—I must admit I've been carrying it around on a platter with me for hours, determined to remind myself it is real—that it hasn't lost its luster. In death, it hasn't lost its color. It hasn't lost its ability to watch me. So, in a drawer it must go.

Because I can't bring myself to bury anything ever again.

And what was that noise?

Back to digging I go.

C H A P T E R

74
Nate

TWO HEAVILY ARMED parties went out simultaneously.

One party, led by Sheriff Kilbourne and also including Caleb Jones, Dennis Wagner, and a set of twins, Sally and Wren Grisham—two middle-aged women Nate didn't know but who apparently ran a beauty parlor on Bull Street—was tasked with retrieving flares from the jailhouse. Blue Bottles led the second party, along with Nate, Lauren, Amy, Rose Bower, and Tiny Henderson, but they'd been kept in the dark as to their specific mission.

Armed with a shotgun, Nate walked between Amy and Lauren and behind Blue Bottles, Rose, and Tiny. "You got no idea what we're doing?" Nate asked behind his mask; the air, he could tell, was growing worse by the hour. People were still out digging.

Amy said, "No," and kept her eyes straight ahead, on Mr. Passafume's house fifty yards through the trees. She'd been extra quiet ever since Mr. Passafume had taken her over toward the woods earlier.

Nate asked, "You okay?"

"Never better," Amy said with sarcasm, following the flight of one of the red crows across the sky. "Nate . . . your father left a short diary. Of his last few weeks."

"Have you read it? I don't think I can, not after Mom's letter."

"Just a few entries," she said. "But it's clear he'd lost his mind at the end. Guilt tortured him. I think he was tricked somehow back then, and Mitchell McBride tricked him all over again about a month ago."

"What does Mitchell have to do with it?"

"He visited your father. He somehow knew what he'd done . . . in regard to Jericho's existence. He convinced him to start digging. One Sunday your father must have preached it from the pulpit, and then that was the last anyone saw him at church."

"Is that why he cut his hand off?" Nate asked, trying not to imagine the axe cleaving through his father's flesh and bone but unable to stop the vision. "Or did Mitchell, with Jericho's axe, cut it off?"

"Yes," she said. "I believe so."

Nate stopped, but Amy continued walking.

Lauren waited for Nate to catch up. "What's going through that head of yours?"

"Nothing. Everything." He couldn't stop thinking of his father now.

"Earlier," Lauren said, "Mr. Passafume said something about a spirit created from a bad death."

"Jericho's death . . . it wasn't pretty." Nate could tell she wanted to ask but wouldn't, so he said, "He beat his head into the jailhouse wall."

Lauren looked horrified, but not completely surprised.

Their arrival at Mr. Passafume's garage saved him from any further explanation.

Blue Bottles told them to wait in front of the roll-up door while he went in through the side. Seconds later, a latch unlocked, and then the garage door rose a couple of feet off the concrete. Passafume's fingers showed on the underside of the heavy door, gripping the bottom edge, so Nate hurried over to help him hoist it, as there was no electricity to open it mechanically. He and Tiny helped lift it the rest of the way, revealing stacks and rows of wooden crates, dozens and dozens of them.

"Blue bottles," Amy said beside him.

At first Nate thought she was calling out Passafume's nickname, because he'd disappeared behind one of the rows, but upon closer inspection of the crates, he saw that they held blue bottles and were stacked to the ceiling, every bottle painted various shades of blue.

Mr. Passafume emerged from between two of the rows. "We ready to get to work?"

"Doing what?" asked Lauren.

Mr. Passafume said, "Turning the island blue."

CHAPTER

75
Sheriff Kilbourne

SHERIFF KILBOURNE WISHED he'd double-masked upon entering the jailhouse, because Clare Barnett's rapidly decomposing body in the dark corner made the air more difficult to breathe.

If they made it through another night, he would bury her, but their mission was to get the flares, which he'd secured minutes ago from storage. As he passed through the jailhouse lobby again, he heard something moving near where he knew Clare's dead body to be. He shined his light in that direction and saw Clare's golden retriever, Max, on the floor next to her, paws resting atop a dried puddle of her blood. When Clare hadn't come home as expected, Max must have gone out to find her.

He couldn't leave the dog here. He patted his leg, called him over, but Max didn't budge. Lawrence moved closer and Max growled protectively.

For now, Lawrence let the dog be and backed his way out of the jailhouse. The sun was mostly hidden behind a smear of strange, wispy clouds, and an encroaching line of dark loomed over the horizon like a dome.

"Got 'em," he told the rest of his crew, patting the heavy satchel over his shoulder. They seemed eager to get back to the Dodd House—the sky directly above was full of red crows and their squawking was deafening.

Wren Grisham held her ears. Her twin Sally held her gun like she was prepared to fire should any one of those birds come lower. Caleb and Dennis stood poised and ready for whatever might come at them from the woods, from the deserted streets, from so many doorways and storefronts that appeared to have been left open.

A gunshot sounded. They all ducked, surveying in every direction, guns poised.

Catty-corner and across the street, a second-floor window opened above Ned Gleeson's fruit market. Lawrence feared someone was about to open fire, but instead, Ned, who lived above his fruit market with his wife of many years, climbed into the open window frame.

Lawrence thought *Jesus, Ned, don't* . . . And then Ned did. He jumped.

A rope unraveled, and then his body jerked to a stop, feet dangling above the sidewalk, the noose holding him suspended as he choked to death out in front of his own store. Wren Grisham screamed. Her twin hugged her. Lawrence started toward where Ned's body swayed, Caleb and Dennis in tow, but then, out of nowhere, something came out at them from the narrow alley between Stan Lowenstein's gaming shop and the law offices of Gilbert, Davies, and Stein, blocking their path.

It was a Boo Hag. One of Amy's nightmares made flesh, Lawrence thought. Just like the one he'd seen in Caleb's garage, before Caleb blew it away with his shotgun. This one was small, closer to four feet tall, but with distinctive red, skinless flesh and blue veins and long, dirty white hair. The whites of its eyes were stark, the dark pupils small but menacing.

Just as Lawrence raised his gun, another emerged from the trees to their left, joining the first in the middle of the road. It was taller, closer to six feet, and thicker boned, like this was an adult and the other was not yet full grown.

In the background, Ned Gleeson finally stopped moving, his legs no longer twitching. Lawrence realized they'd maybe witnessed a murder-suicide, sure now that Ned had probably shot his wife right before he jumped.

"Easy now," Lawrence said softly to both his untrained crew and to the Boo Hags now hunkered down and slowly approaching them.

Steam jetted in plumes from their nostrils as they breathed.

Where was Blue Bottles now, Lawrence thought, to talk these things down as he had that elk in the middle of Bull Street? And if they shot, Lawrence thought, they'd better hit them flush or they were goners. Because those teeth were sharp as daggers.

Lawrence heard movement to his right, from the trees beside the jailhouse, and feared a third Boo Hag was coming, or maybe more.

The taller Boo Hag raised its head, as if sensing something dangerous in the air, and then, quick as a gunshot, a horse darted toward them from the trees. The horse was bright white, with a long, flowing mane, and moved with the force of a steam train—not toward them, Lawrence noticed, but toward the two Boo Hags, both of whom had gone into defensive fighting positions. But not in time, because the horse's horn—yes, that's what it was, a goddamn single horn swirled with a dozen different lurid colors, protruding from the top of its head, three feet long, at least, and coiled—entered the chest of the taller Boo Hag, burying it like a drill bit down to the thick shaft, and the Boo Hag's squeal was monstrous.

Lawrence and his crew backed away in quick retreat. Dennis fell and Caleb helped him up. It was as if they were in the middle of Jurassic Park and the dinosaurs had gotten loose. The horse, head lowered, haunches flexed, bore down and drove the stuck Boo Hag toward the street curb, pinning the beast against a wide-trunked live oak, the Boo Hag squirming like a stuck moth. The smaller Boo Hag lay dead and unmoving on the street, having been trampled in the process.

The horse wrestled its horn free and then plowed it into the Boo Hag again, and finally the thing stopped moving.

The intensity of the attack was almost too much to bear—not to mention the horrible sound of it; the sheer, thunderous force from the horse and anguished pain from the Boo Hag—but Lawrence couldn't look away, even as the horse drove the horn into the dying hag again, dropping it to the ground in a bloody heap.

Ribbons of bright-blue blood from the Boo Hag had spurted across the horse's bright-white coat and long mane.

Lawrence made sure his crew was all behind him.

The horse's three-foot-long horn dripped haint-blue blood like a faucet. Plumes of colorful mist escaped its flared nostrils. It had saved them, yes, but had it been out of protection, or did it want them now for itself? As Lawrence backpedaled, he told his crew, "Keep walking. Don't run. Just walk. Casually walk." The white horse—no, unicorn—turned and snorted colorful mist again, spraying sky-blue blood as it whinnied and stomped. It shook its head, and hag blood flew from the horn. And then it took off down the street in the opposite direction, in a full gallop, powerful hooves echoing off the pavement like gunshots.

Within seconds it was gone.

Lawrence knew he should cut Ned Gleeson's body down but couldn't risk it. Ned was dead and his crew wasn't. He needed to get them back safely, so he ushered them as a tightly clustered group toward the Dodd House a half mile away. They moved quietly, stunned speechless, Lawrence's heart racing a mile a minute.

They startled at the innocent sound of paws on the street behind them, and then Clare Barnett's golden retriever, Max, caught up to them, mouth open and tail wagging. Lawrence ran a hand over his fur. "I wouldn't have wanted to stay back there either, pal."

Dennis looked over his shoulder. "That Clare's dog?"

"Max," Lawrence said.

Dennis seemed to be eyeing the jailhouse in the distance. "Is she . . . ?"

"Yeah," Lawrence said in acknowledgment. "Dead." He felt the emotion ball up in his throat.

Sally Grisham said, "Welcome to the team, Max."

Max barked, then ran up and took the lead.

CHAPTER

76
Blue Bottles

Nineteen Years Before the Sudden Death of Reverend Thomas Dodd

BLUE BOTTLES SAT across his kitchen table from Reverend Thomas Dodd, as they had so many times since they'd known each other, but this time, Earl knew, was different.

Never had he seen Thomas Dodd so desperate.

He knew Thomas and Samantha were struggling—Samantha from depression and Thomas at his wits' end on how to comfort her.

But Thomas, who was typically groomed and put-together, was unshaven, his button-down shirt wrinkled and his eyes red. He'd admitted he hadn't slept for forty-eight hours.

What troubled Mr. Passafume most was the fact that Thomas had hinted he'd been visited by something two nights ago. And then, finally, Thomas said, "You believe in them, don't you? Boo Hags. I think I was visited by one. He told me—"

"Stop, Thomas." Earl leaned over the table and touched his friend's hand to calm the shaking in it. "Stop. It's folklore. You weren't visited by a hag."

But I was his eyes cried—demanded, almost. "It told me . . . it whispered in my ear."

Mr. Passafume shook his head. Thomas had told him the same thing last night. Two nights in a row he'd come by, claiming the same thing, asking for the same thing.

"I will not give you the key to the honey house, Thomas. You know that."

"But it said it could help," Thomas said softly, so pathetically Earl wanted to scream at his friend.

Instead, Earl said, "Continue praying to your God, Thomas. It's the best you can do."

"But . . ."

"But what, Thomas?"

"He's not listening," he said. "The Boo Hag is." And here Thomas was, all over again, for the second night in a row. Earl felt the question coming and then Thomas asked it. "Just this once, Earl. For a friend. For Samantha. Give me the key to the honey house. I know it's a magic place. I've always known. And I know that magic is the opposite of what I'm supposed to believe, but please . . . I'll come right back."

Earl swallowed a gulp of the whiskey Thomas had poured for each of them while he'd been in the bathroom minutes ago. Suddenly Earl felt woozy. He blinked, but that didn't work; it only made him dizzier. And then he said to Thomas, "What did you do?"

"I'm sorry," Thomas said with sincere tears in his eyes. "You left me no choice. The Boo Hag had horns . . . he told me I had to come . . ."

Earl's head hit the table, his eyelids fluttering.

Thomas's footsteps trailed down the hallway and returned. "I'm sorry. I'll bring them right back."

Earl felt paralyzed as he watched Thomas leave the room.

The front door opened and closed.

Blue Bottles blacked out.

CHAPTER

77
Amy

AMY PUSHED A small wooden cart stacked with three crates of bottles toward the Dodd House.

On the surface, Mr. Passafume's plan—to hang the nearly three thousand bottles he'd painted blue over the past decades on trees all over the island—seemed impossible, given their circumstances, but the more she thought on it, the more it made sense. If it was Jericho out there in the air, created from whatever mind-warping ingredients had come together to form him, they needed to treat him like the biggest, most dangerous, out-of-the-bottle Boo Hag spirit any mind could ever conjure. And if blue-bottle trees were what the Geechee culture believed caught and trapped these spirits, holding them until the next morning's sunlight could burn them up, then Amy was on board. But the hanging of them would take days, Amy thought, as Oak Alley and the Dodd House loomed in the distance, and they didn't have days. Nor did they have the manpower.

Daylight vanished quickly under heavy, dark clouds. Dozens of red crows circled above, casting red shadows on the ground as they flew. It had to be a trick of the waning sunlight, Amy thought as she walked beside Mr. Passafume, with Tiny Henderson pulling one wooden cart full of blue-bottle crates in front of them, Nate and Lauren pulling another, and Rose Bower with a smaller one in between.

Even with the number of crates they now had in transit, it was only a fourth of the load. The red crows circled lower, no more than twenty feet above their heads, and by their increased level of noise, they seemed to be communicating. The ground was littered with their red droppings, like they were shitting blood.

Amy walked side by side with Blue Bottles, her with her cart, him with a shotgun propped over his right shoulder and a wooden box big enough to fit a pair of shoes in the crook of his left arm. He too eyed the birds, but more out of curiosity, she thought, than fear. He didn't seem to be afraid like the rest of them.

"These crows," Amy said. "They're the reverend's nightmares," she said, watching the sky. "He had nightmares of red crows as a boy."

"Nightmares are born from fear, Amy," he said knowingly, yet his focus stayed on the birds. "They're smart. Calculating. And when there's ever a chance for a nightmare to . . . to meet their host, to confront their creator, they do it. But nightmares have found other ways to become real. To be made flesh. Have you ever heard of the Bookman family?"

"No," she said. "I don't know, maybe. I've heard of Ben Bookman, the writer. I've read his books. Same family?"

"Same family," he said. "Ever wondered why he stopped writing?"

"No."

"Ever heard about the scarecrow murders?"

"No."

"The Nightmare Man?"

"No."

"Mr. Lullaby?"

"No."

"Mr. Dreams?"

"Jesus, *no*!" she said so loud the red crows shifted their collective pattern and perhaps dropped even lower. She said under her breath, "What are you talking about?"

"Look into the Bookman family," he said. "And look into Blackwood Mansion."

"Sure, I'll get out my phone and Google that right now."

"When you reach the mainland," he said. "Do it then."

"And when will that be?"

"Hopefully, if all works in our favor—"

"Nothing is working in our favor."

"If all works in our favor," he repeated, undeterred, "then we'll have you all off the island and on the mainland by midmorning."

"I'm not going anywhere," she said. "This is my island." But she hoped for the sake of the others he was right. "Did you predict all of this?"

"This exact situation? No. But this," he said, nodding toward the crates of blue bottles, "has always been my security plan should Jericho ever become fully Jericho and that door open. And you'll get your internet back soon enough."

"I don't care about the internet."

"Your cell phone, then," he said. "This generation and their cell phones."

"*Your* generation, and your *invention* of the telephone," she said. "Or was it electricity?"

"Touché."

She eyed the box cradled in his left arm. "What's in that? The box you're carrying?"

"My life insurance policy."

"You're kidding, right?"

"Yes, I'm kidding."

"You're not going to tell me?"

He drummed his fingertips on the box. "Letters of great import." It was clear he wasn't going into further detail. The birds squawked overhead, red wings unfurled. "Something's about to happen."

"How do you know?"

"They're no longer in pattern."

Amy watched the woods on either side of them. She didn't sense an earthquake but felt like they were being watched, and then a gunshot echoed and Tiny Henderson's head exploded in a red, gory mist, spraying Rose Bower next to him, and Tiny's large body toppled, upturning Rose's cart.

The rest took shelter behind their carts, just as another bullet whistled and a crate of blue bottles off Tiny's cart exploded. Covered in Tiny's blood, Rose stood, sharply racked her shotgun, and fired into the trees. Nate and Lauren fired from behind their cart, and while the gun looked right in Nate's grip, it was clear Lauren had never fired a gun in her life, and the size of it looked silly in her small hands. Amy's arms shook violently, making it impossible to properly aim, but she fired anyway. Blue Bottles, beside her, remained calm as he placed his mystery box on the ground and readied his shotgun.

"He's aiming for the bottles," he said. "He knows what we're doing."

"Who?"

Another crate of bottles exploded, shards of blue glass scattered in shrapnel-like jewels across the dirt road. Mr. Passafume shifted his position on the ground. "Steven Delacroix. I just saw him through the trees."

Rose Bower fired at the trees and screamed, "*Come get me, you coward motherfucker!*"

Passafume grinned—maybe at what Rose had just yelled, Amy couldn't tell. But then he calmly said, "Have a wonderful day, Amy Barnes," and then stood and walked out into the open, scanning the trees with his shotgun leveled. A bullet whizzed past, and he didn't so much as flinch—he was too focused on a target Amy couldn't see.

"What's he doing?" Nate hissed at Amy.

Blue Bottles fired into the trees.

A man screamed. Passafume held out a hand, as if to say *Give it a minute.* Amy gave it more like thirty seconds before she joined him out in the open, a fourth of their crates obliterated into blue shards all around them, crunching underfoot as they all followed Passafume toward the trees, where Steven Delacroix lay dead in the weeds forty yards away, a bloody, lung-sucking hole in the middle of his chest.

Blue Bottles closed Delacroix's eyes.

Something moved through the trees ahead, and again through the trees to Amy's left. She followed the sounds, the movement, saw white hair and red flesh, and then it disappeared into the shadows.

A red flare streaked the sky over the Dodd House.

Sheriff Kilbourne and his crew must have made it back with the flares.

And darkness had come sooner than they'd realized.

CHAPTER

78
Sheriff Kilbourne

FULL DARK COVERED the island by seven pm.

There would be no more parties sent out.

"It's too dangerous," Lawrence had told the forty-six islanders now seeking shelter inside the Dodd House, six more than when he'd led his party out for flares, of which they'd already fired three into a sky that seemed to swallow them. They'd use their remaining four sparingly throughout the night and pray someone on the mainland or neighboring islands would see them. Lawrence watched out the great room window at the ten men and women taking their shift hanging blue bottles on the trees up and down Oak Alley.

The air was bad enough now that they'd all double-masked.

Lawrence was due out there in two minutes for the next shift. He hoped Delacroix had been a lone wolf out there and not part of something more systematic, but to be safe, while ten volunteers hung bottles from the trees, eight more stood guard, two at the end of Oak Alley and three more on each side.

Tina arrived in the foyer with a cluster of masks hanging around her neck. Lawrence kissed her on the lips. She was taking her turn outside like the rest of them. "Where's David?"

"With Lauren somewhere," she said. "She's great."

"Maybe you should hire her."

Tina's silence was answer enough. They both knew there'd be no school to return to. She seemed preoccupied by something and said, "Lawrence, what did you see out there earlier?"

"I don't know, Tina. I do, but . . . hit me with this in the morning when I'm fresh. I don't think my mind could do it justice right now."

She squeezed his arm lovingly, and then he masked up. But to mess with her—and this had been one of her pet peeves as a principal during COVID masking—he pulled the mask up to just below his nose.

She slapped his arm. "Jackass." She masked up—triple-masked, he noticed.

He fixed his masks over his nose and followed his wife out the door.

Outside on the veranda, he felt no wind blowing. No breeze. Nothing.

Yet the blue bottles already hung were swaying and clanking together like wind chimes.

CHAPTER

79

One Hour Before the Sudden Death of Reverend Thomas Dodd

From Thomas Dodd's Diary

It's back.

The goddamn thing is back.

I killed the fucker.

I stabbed it with a knife and stuck it in a drawer, but it's back, right there on the library windowsill, watching me.

Red like the last one.

I swear it has Jericho's eyes.

Somehow.

Just like the windows I open every night. I fall asleep and they're all closed. Sometimes I wake up and the house is rearranged. Someone is fucking with me.

Maybe it's the honey. That McBride boy brought me some of the newest batch like Blue Bottles used to do before he stopped talking to me.

Seems even more potent than last year's batch, and I can't stop drinking it.

I don't feel right.

I think my stump is infected. There's pus . . . and blood. I can still feel my hand, even though Mitchell took it with him. God knows what he did with it. He's strange, that boy.

The hand is gone yet I still feel guilt.

He was wrong.

I was wrong.

Removing the hand of sin did nothing but cause even more pain.

I have phantom pain in my fingers, in my palm, but the stump, good Lord, it throbs all day and all night, and how did those windows get closed? And how did the living room furniture get moved around? I lock my doors at night, yet still someone is in here with me.

I'm still amazed that boy was able to lop it off with one swoop of that axe.

Jericho's axe.

Somehow, he'd dug it up.

Oh, the pain.

The honey.

I've been resisting the notion for hours, but I think I'll try it.

I think my stump will fit into the jar.

C H A P T E R

80
Amy

WITH THE FIFTY-SIX people they now had staying inside the Dodd House—people trickled in by the hour—Amy began to grow more restless.

She hadn't intended to enter Jericho's bedroom but found that she'd migrated there.

It was the only room where fellow islanders hadn't dropped sleeping bags for the night. But once she was in there, she knew what she needed to do. She felt exposed just looking at the photos, and even now could feel Jericho in the room with her.

She plucked the pictures Jericho had taken of her from the walls. What started as a one-by-one removal ended five minutes later with her frantically pulling and swiping them from the walls, tacks and all. When she finished, she turned in a slow circle atop the strewn and scattered and ripped pictures.

She felt better now that the pictures had been taken down but could still sense Jericho out there. She heard the blue bottles whistling on the trees outside, much louder than they had an hour ago.

CHAPTER

81
Nate

"LAUREN . . ."

"Yeah?"

They were in Nate's childhood bedroom, on his childhood bed, atop the covers. He was resting with his back against the headboard and Lauren leaning on his chest.

He had his arm around her.

Innocently.

Every so often his fingers touched her bare arm. When he didn't say anything after he'd prompted her by saying her name, she looked up. Tears rolled down his cheeks. He'd silently started crying.

She turned, sat up in bed to face him. "Nate? What's wrong?"

He smiled. "What isn't wrong, Lauren?"

"This," she said. "Us. Right now."

And he couldn't deny that.

Nate wiped his cheeks, felt stupid for being emotional. Knew she'd think he was stupid for thinking it. "Was any of it ever his fault? Jericho, I mean. Did he ask to be born? I think he spent his entire life trying to get back . . . to that place . . . but I didn't stop him. I could have stopped him but I didn't, and that's what really keeps me up at night, Lauren."

"What are you talking about, Nate?"

"Inside that jail cell," he said. "After he did what he did. Sheriff Kilbourne let me inside the cell with him, maybe hoping I could get some answers. Maybe calm him down. That's when Jericho started hitting his head against the wall. Hard. Like, even harder than usual, and it was a hard, cinder block wall to begin with. I put my hand between his head and the wall, taking the impact, like usual, but . . . but then I pulled it free. His head collided, hard. I heard something crack, Lauren. It was awful. He must have thought it was funny, because he was smiling. Grinning, and I hated him for it. After all he'd done out there on Bull Street, right in the middle of that parade, and he's grinning." Nate closed his eyes, opened them. "I saw Bridget lying there on the sidewalk, nearly cut in half. Everyone knew what Jericho did when he got stressed. When the bees got too loud. In my head, I'm screaming *What did you do . . . What did you do . . . What did you do . . .* and I just watched him." Nate choked up, wiped his face. Lauren scooted closer, put a gentle hand to his face, crying along with him now, maybe because she'd known for two years that he was hiding something and here it finally was in all its hideous glory. And she wasn't running. "He said . . . he said, 'I'm sorry, Nathanial. I'm sorry.' But I just stood there, frozen. He never talked, and he . . . he called me Nathanial. And there was blood on the wall, and I heard his skull cracking, and then he stopped blinking. I was still yelling, I think . . . *What did you do, what did you do . . .* but he was gone. I think a light went out of everybody's eyes that day."

"Nate," Lauren said, her face inches from his. "It wasn't your fault."

"How could it not be?" Nate asked. "I didn't stop him."

"You were a kid."

"I was eighteen."

"You were *a kid* . . . who'd just watched his girlfriend die," Lauren said, and then softer. "You were a kid."

CHAPTER

82
Sheriff Kilbourne

By the middle of the night, Lawrence had taken five trips through the house, not so much for security—they had four adults standing guard outside the house, rotating in one-hour shifts—but more to keep himself awake.

If he laid down, he'd doze off, and he wouldn't be able to live with himself if something were to go down under his watch. But many had managed to find sleep where they could get it—on couches and beds and in sleeping bags. Peter and Tracy Cronin had fallen asleep atop the pool table in the billiards room. Iain McCarty had fallen asleep on the dining room table. One of the kids had passed out on one of the great room's oversized ottomans. Exhaustion had won out. But this was still a fraction of Crow Island's residents. He wondered what the rest of the islanders were doing out there. Were they even alive?

Were they still digging?

He looked out the window toward Oak Alley, where the bottles glistened like blue crystals in the eerie moonlight. They'd sent the final flare up less than an hour ago, their last hope.

Four masked, armed adults stood by the front door, ready for their shift as soon as the four heading up the veranda steps came back inside. The switch was made. Pats on the back accompanied muffled words exchanged, and the front door closed again. The night sky might appear clear, but by the residue on the shoulders of the four who'd just come in, like they all had dandruff disguised as tiny dirt particles, it was clear the air was getting worse.

Rose Bower removed her masks, brushed debris from her shoulders, and approached Lawrence. "Not sure how much longer we can do this. The masks are hardly working." Rose winced, smacked at a bee that had just stung her right elbow. "Damn it."

The bee buzzed on the floor.

She was about to step on it when Lawrence stopped her. He knelt for a closer look. The stinger was still attached. It was longer than any stinger he'd seen. And the colors of that bee—although black and yellow—were stark and bright, like straight out of a coloring book done with fresh markers. He pointed. "Look at that."

"I'll be damned, Sheriff," Rose said, acting like she gave a shit, before stomping on it. It crunched under her boot.

Just then, something small hit the window, buzzing against it with reckless abandon—another bee trying to get inside with them. And then another hit the glass. Seconds later the sky swarmed with them, like he'd seen before with cicadas, but nothing like this.

The air droned with buzzing.

The four who'd just gone outside for their shift all came running back toward the veranda, swatting at the bees that had come out of nowhere.

CHAPTER

83
Crow Island

AMY WAS RESTLESS again.

She was exhausted but afraid that if she closed her eyes she'd sleepwalk outside again, and she couldn't have a repeat of last night.

She roamed the house, spying out the windows, waiting for sunrise to see if the blue bottles had done *anything*.

And where was Mitchell McBride? What was he waiting for? How many had he already killed with Jericho's axe out there?

She remembered Thomas Dodd's diary and how Mitchell had somehow gotten inside the house to mentally terrorize him.

But how did he get in?

And then it dawned on her. The basement. The coal chute. The tunnel to the old cotton fields she and Bridget and Nate had run through as kids.

And then she thought *Oh no, has he been living under the house the entire time?*

* * *

It felt good to close his eyelids, if only for a few seconds.

Lawrence lay down on the floor with David and Tina underneath the dining room table, because that's where David agreed to settle. The swarm of bees outside had left him overly excited and too stimulated to sleep, but the boy had finally closed his eyes and appeared to be drifting off. Despite his intentions to stay awake no matter what, Lawrence began dozing as well, but then felt a soft tapping on his forehead. He opened his eyes and found David, inches away, staring right at him.

"Daddy," he whispered.

"Yeah, buddy?"

"You're my daddy," he whispered, staring.

Lawrence teared up immediately. "You're my boy."

"Yup," David said. "And Captain Swirls will protect us from the bees too."

David closed his eyes.

Lawrence watched him with a warm heart. After a minute he tapped David lightly on the forehead and David's eyes opened. Lawrence whispered, "You were right."

"About what?"

"Unicorns are real," he said. "And Captain Swirls . . . I've seen him."

* * *

Nate awakened to someone shaking his foot.

Amy stood by his bedside.

"What happened?"

"Nothing," she said in a whisper. "I mean, maybe nothing."

Lauren was asleep beside him in the crook of his arm, her head on the inside of his shoulder, her right hand on his chest. He didn't want to move. Didn't want to wake her. If their world weren't so fucked, he could have stayed in this position with her until eternity. He'd drifted off earlier, hoping that when he awakened it would be sunrise, but darkness still reigned outside.

"Have you even kissed her yet?" Amy asked.

"What? No . . ."

"But you've already slept with her?"

"No . . . we . . . she—"

"I'm joking, Nate." She waved for him to come on.

"What is it?"

"Mitchell McBride," she said. "I think he's already in the house."

* * *

The basement door off the old servants' hallway was wide open.

Nate aimed his flashlight down the narrow stairwell, and Amy followed him down. And while it had been well over a decade since she and Nate and Bridget had ventured down into the old supply tunnel, the creak in the wooden steps hadn't changed.

As kids, the three of them would start in the coal room, run through the tunnel and out the grated opening into the fields, and then climb the rope ladder up the small rock wall beneath where Jericho was ultimately buried, sprint back across the yard to the front of the Dodd House, hurry back inside, and then go back down into the basement again. The circuit could be completed in just over three minutes, although Nate, on several occasions, had done it in under three.

Halfway down the stairs, Amy said, "You smell something?"

"Yeah," Nate said, and then he stopped abruptly at the bottom of the steps. "Oh shit." He turned. "Oh fuck. Oh my God. Go back up. Get back upstairs, Amy, go, go."

As she turned, her shaky light beam revealed at least three bodies down there on the basement floor, limbs and torsos hacked and stacked in a heap. Random townspeople, but she swore she'd seen her seventh-grade homeroom teacher, Mr. Tisdale, among them. Amy climbed the stairs, heart in her throat, with Nate right behind her. But before they could reach the landing, the door slammed shut in Amy's face. The bolt latched, locking them in.

Soft laughter sounded from the other side of the door, and Mitchell McBride said, "Sorry, can't help you out this time, Amy."

* * *

Somewhere inside the Dodd House, people had started screaming in terror, and Lawrence immediately thought *Mitchell has made it inside.*

How did he get in here? Lawrence thought. Eyeing Tina on the floor—she was awake now like several others in the room—he mouthed the words "Take David and hide. Now."

She didn't need to be told twice; she grabbed their sleeping son and ducked off into a room to their right, in the opposite direction from the screaming.

A sliver of sunlight emerged through the dining room's bay window, and outside the blue bottles chimed with a fierceness he hadn't heard all night.

Maybe those blue-bottle trees had trapped something after all.

Burn, baby, burn, Lawrence thought as he inched out into the hallway, just as a chain reaction of screams sounded from the great room.

* * *

Nate thought his shoulder might be broken.

After plowing into the basement door several times to no avail, his arm hung limply as he navigated the stairs toward Amy, who looked frozen in shock.

He gently shook her. "Amy." And then louder, "Amy!"

She blinked, followed his voice. "Do you have a gun?"

"No," he said. "You?" She shook her head. "Damn." He hadn't known what to expect entering the basement, but he hadn't expected this. And now everyone in the house seemed to be screaming, running, fleeing, their panicked footfalls like thunder bursts above.

All he could think of was Lauren's safety. Gunshots fired upstairs, followed by more screams.

Nate grabbed Amy's free hand and moved her away from the bodies and toward the old coal room. "Come on."

"Where are we going?"

"Through the tunnel."

For the first time since he was a young teen, Nate entered the old supply tunnel, and after panning his light from wall to wall and spotting candy bar wrappers and processed-food wrappers and a crate of tupelo honey—most of the bottles missing—it was clear Mitchell McBride had been living inside the old supply tunnel, right under their noses, even before the reverend's death.

* * *

For Lawrence, the chaos brought back tremors of PTSD.

Mitchell McBride appeared to be wearing a mask of stitched human skin, and with each violent swing of the axe, the messy mask shifted loose on his face.

Lawrence, slowly closing in as half the room scattered—bumping into one another, tripping over slain bodies, a few nearly trampled as others fled—had him in his sights.

Eight years ago, Lawrence had hesitated, but he didn't hesitate this time.

* * *

Amy flinched at the sound of another gunshot.

The pop was muffled by how deep she and Nate were now inside the tunnel but audible enough to remind them of the urgency as they closed in on the rusted metal grate ten yards ahead. An eerie Lalaland sunrise showed in swirls of red, orange, and yellow over the horizon.

They moved with their shirt collars pulled up over their mouths, but the air was still hard to breathe. Nate kicked open the gate and helped Amy outside to the rock landing, now overgrown with weeds and moss. Across the acres of fields below, which centuries before had been white with cotton, a black Lalaland deer sprinted across a stream and up a barren hillside. Three Boo Hags sprinted through the field in a small cluster and disappeared into the trees.

Amy stood mesmerized as a sunflower-yellow seagull's flight bent with the wind above them and then it soared down toward the field. Nate grabbed her hand and pulled her along toward the rope ladder and rock wall thirty yards to their right. She couldn't see the blue bottles in front of the Dodd House, but in the distance, they not only whistled but screamed and hissed, like something inside them was in pain.

* * *

Sheriff Kilbourne hit Mitchell McBride flush in the chest.

The impact blew him against the wall. The gunshot had prompted another level of screaming, and more people scattered throughout the house. A few had run outside only to run right back in, remembering quickly that *out there* might be even more dangerous now that the bees had arrived.

So where was the blood? How did Mitchell, after only a few seconds on the floor, get right back up and hurry from the room? And then Lawrence saw it beneath the unfurled buttons of his shirt—a bulletproof vest—and cursed himself for having not aimed higher, at his neck or face, or lower, to take out one of his knees. But with as little experience as he'd had firing his weapon during real chaos, he'd gone for the largest fail-safe target.

And now he'd lost him.

Selfishly, finding his wife and son were priority number one now. Gun poised for another shot, Lawrence eased past two islanders, both of whom silently pointed toward where Mitchell had gone. Lawrence motioned for them to go take cover and hide, and then up ahead he saw Mitchell flash across the hallway, from one room to the next.

Lawrence fired again, took a large chunk of drywall and door frame.

He checked one bedroom, then the next, found both empty.

Screaming lured his attention toward the parlor that was now Samantha Dodd's memorial garden. Lawrence followed, but as he moved past the kitchen, he saw Mr. Passafume out the window, standing in the grass outside the veranda, allowing himself to be covered by bees.

* * *

Nate couldn't get inside the house fast enough.

The sun was almost fully up now, the layer of dark slowly being squeezed out by the weird, ominous sunrise. Leaves on every tree were turning white. As he and Amy ran, a brittle leaf veined in red skittered across the grass, and up and down Oak Alley, the blue-bottle trees whistled and screeched. Was Jericho inside them? If Mr. Passafume was right and blue bottles did trap evil spirits, Nate guessed it would take the thousands they'd hung from the trees to fully catch Jericho, but even then he hoped they'd hung enough. The rising sun seemed to be doing its thing, burning up whatever had been trapped inside those bottles. Had he not needed his hands to help cover his mouth, Nate would have used them to protect his ears, the noise was so loud.

The bottles rocked like streetlights caught in hurricane-force winds, except Nate felt no wind. Whatever was trapped inside those bottles was trying desperately to get out.

Nate rounded the corner of the Dodd House, Amy behind him. Another gunshot sounded from the house. He looked over his shoulder to find that Amy had veered off toward Oak Alley, walking catatonically between the two rows of live oaks, staring up toward the sea of sun-dappled blue, the bottles sparkling like magic crystals. Nate called her, but she didn't stop, didn't turn, and that's when, from his periphery, he saw someone walking up the porch steps toward the house, completely covered in bees.

* * *

Lawrence's worst nightmare was playing itself out in front of his eyes.

Inside Samantha Dodd's memorial garden, Tina crawled across the floor between two rows of flowering plants and hanging baskets, leaving a smear trail of blood behind her from a leg wound. Across the room, Mitchell held David in one arm like a shield while holding Jericho's axe in the other, the bloody blade inches from David's neck.

Lawrence desperately needed to help Tina, but he couldn't take his aim from Mitchell. Lauren entered the room to Lawrence's right, with bandages, and dived toward Tina on the floor. Lawrence could now focus his full attention on Mitchell, the monstrous homemade mask even more hideous in the daylight, his clear blue eyes watching through crudely cut eyeholes like they were saying *What now, Sheriff?*

It was like the boy was trying to transform into a Boo Hag.

In Mitchell's grasp, David pinched his eyes closed, like he was praying hard, or wishing for something even harder. Or summoning something, Lawrence couldn't help thinking, noticing for the first time that little unicorn figure clenched in David's tiny right hand.

* * *

Blue Bottles walked slowly through the Dodd House, coated from head to toe in Lalaland honeybees.

Islanders inside the house parted for him as he moved carefully through the foyer, toward the hallway, calmly, knowing that if he made a swift, frantic movement the bees might finally sting him.

They weren't just Lalaland's honeybees but *his* honeybees. Mr. In-Between. And they listened.

* * *

Lawrence heard the drone of the bees but refused to take his eyes off Mitchell.

Mitchell saw what was coming and shifted David in his arm.

Mr. Passafume was ten feet away and slowly approaching, but with each step he took, clusters of bees flew from his arms, his legs, his head—they'd completely covered him—peeling off in clumps and layers, swarming toward Mitchell.

Mitchell dropped David and swiped at the thousands of bees buzzing into the room, coming directly toward him, as if they'd been directed. Still clutching the unicorn, David ran toward Lawrence, who opened an arm to his son and caught him when he jumped. David buried his face into his chest and wept. With his free hand, Lawrence kept his gun on Mitchell, who by this point had dropped the axe and was so covered in bees he could no longer stand. He dropped to his knees, screaming, clawing at the crudely made mask on his face, swiping at the bees still covering him in torrents, stinging and buzzing and crawling, and Lawrence whispered into his son's ear, "Don't look . . . don't look," because now the bees were entering Mitchell's open mouth and Mitchell, from his knees, dropped face forward onto the floor, barely moving as the bees continued to swarm him, covering him completely, and behind Lawrence, Mr. Passafume stood completely free of the bees he'd ushered in.

* * *

Amy might have heard gunshots.

Might have heard Nate calling desperately for her to get inside. Might have seen Mr. Passafume enter the Dodd House covered in bees. But she couldn't take her eyes off the loud, sparkling bottles.

He was in there, she could tell, trapped and desperately trying to get out. She imagined one of Jericho's eyes inside one bottle, an ear in another, his brain smashed into yet another. But where was his heart? she thought, standing in the center of all the beautifully glistening blue.

She turned, saw Nate at the end of Oak Alley, but the singing bottles swallowed his voice, and then all of a sudden—as if called to attention for a miliary drill—every bottle on every tree swung parallel to the ground, held there for a beat, glistening in the sunlight, and Amy watched, mesmerized.

By the time she realized what was about to happen, she didn't have time to run.

* * *

Nate screamed, "*Amy!*"

Just as the blue bottles simultaneously and by the thousands exploded in a burst of sunlight and brilliant blue.

Nate dropped to one knee, shielding his face as the bottles splintered out like shrapnel.

Amy, through the sea of shattered blue glass, had dropped to the ground just in time.

He hoped.

Nate, throat burning and eyes watering, sprinted toward Amy's unmoving body in the middle of Oak Alley, noticing, as he ran, the dozens of tiny blue shards sticking in his arms and hands from the blast. He could feel them in his neck. Blood oozed down his face, but he didn't care—he was alive, and Amy was starting to move on the ground.

Mr. Passafume hurried down the veranda steps, followed by Sheriff Kilbourne and Rose Bower and Lauren—thank God she was still alive—all of them masking as they tore through the alley of live oaks toward Amy.

Nate got there first, saw Amy's flesh, damn near every bit of it covered in shards of blue glass that had penetrated her flesh during the blast. What wasn't covered in blue was bleeding red.

She sat up, looked dizzy and disoriented at first, and then suddenly alert.

They looked up toward the sound of distant footsteps coming from the wooded road leading to Oak Alley. At first Nate thought it was other islanders coming to check on them, to see what had happened here—the grounds and the grass, for acres, was covered in shards of sun-shimmered blue.

A sea of broken glass.

But then Sheriff Kilbourne said, "The flares worked."

And Nate knew that help had arrived.

* * *

Evacuation off the island wouldn't be easy.

Multiple ferries had arrived from Tybee and Ossabaw and Savannah. The Coast Guard had been sent, along with a couple dozen Marines.

Lawrence didn't know what strings had been pulled, but he would ask questions later.

The flares had been seen by many, but it was the earthquake text chain he'd started on a whim years ago that had convinced the powers that be to send what looked like an army. Apparently, Crow Island wasn't the only island that had felt the last earthquake. If Lawrence's phone had been working, he would have seen the responses from all his contacts, one island after the next, for the first time, saying *We felt something here* or *We felt that one* or *Something registered here* or *Are you good out there, Sheriff Kilbourne?* It was the fact that none of them heard from him this time that put them on alert—Crow Island was in trouble.

A dozen military-style transport vehicles had come along with the ferries, but seven of them wouldn't start once they'd docked, and the five they'd managed to drive onto the island had all petered out before reaching Bull Street, which told Lawrence that even though the threat of Mitchell McBride had been eliminated, the island still wasn't safe—unless Jericho had exploded inside the blue bottles after those military vehicles failed.

The wounded would go first on stretchers carried by brave men and women in uniform, who, despite their training in combat, all had fearful looks in their eyes as they moved about the island, watching the red crows circling overhead and spotting strange animals in the woods.

Lawrence gripped his wife's hand. Tina's face was ashen, her eyes weary, but he could tell she smiled beneath her multiple masks. She would make it. He promised to see her and his son soon on the mainland; as sheriff, he would be the last one off the island.

He hugged David next. "You keep watch over your mother."

"Okay," he said, doing his eye tic thing two times.

Lawrence gave it back to him, ruffled his hair, and told him to get going. By then, David had lowered his mask. Just as Lawrence was about to reprimand him, he noticed how readily his son was breathing the air. Lawrence lowered his mask; the air was already improving. David showed Lawrence the unicorn in his right hand. He grabbed Lauren's extended hand with his left.

Lauren lowered her mask, breathed freely, and said to Lawrence, "I'll keep them safe until you arrive."

Nate emerged from the house with his father's box of ashes. He hurried down the veranda steps, and when he noticed everyone's masks down, he lowered his. "It worked?"

Lawrence nodded, although with caution, and shook Nate's hand. He told him to get going and that he'd hopefully see them before nightfall.

* * *

Nate said, "You all go on. I'll catch up in a minute."

The soldiers carrying Tina Kilbourne's stretcher didn't argue—they were in a hurry to get the wounded off the island. It was Lauren who argued with him, not with words she didn't want to say in front of David but with a glare that said *If you die, I'll come hunt you down and kill you again myself.*

David tossed Nate the unicorn in his hand. "It's a unicorn. They're magical."

"Thanks, champ. I'll bring it back."

Nate scanned the area for Amy. The last he'd seen her, she'd been helping the wounded out of the Dodd House despite the fact that she herself was wounded and had yet to remove all the tiny blue slivers and shards that had embedded in her skin after the blue bottles exploded.

Nate still had tiny blue glass slivers stuck in the skin of his hands and arms. He'd pull them out later. Convincing himself that Amy could take care of herself and would get off the island with everyone else, he entered the woods running, carrying his father's ashes. Minutes later he approached his mother's tombstone with trepidation and quickly spread his father's ashes atop her grave. He promised he'd return to the island, that his time away wouldn't be as long as last time. He left the wooden urn atop the soil and hurried back to Lauren and the crew.

* * *

Amy told no one where she was going.

They would have stopped her had they known. They would have made her go along with the wounded. Her flesh was speckled with blue glass and trickling red blood, but she wasn't going anywhere without confronting the honey house. Not without closing that door for good. Not without making sure the hag with horns never stepped foot on her island.

She hoped whoever owned the shotgun she'd grabbed from the veranda of the Dodd House wouldn't realize it was gone until she was where she needed to be.

And she'd made it.

All around the swamp, everything dripped with color. Leaves had turned white. Strange vines blooming with full red blossoms wrapped the blackened trunks of the cypress and tupelos and live oaks. Coiled silver and gold vines grew around the bee barge's posts and handrails and floorboards. The honey house was so enveloped by them that only a few spots of the sky-blue exterior were visible, and the same went for the roof. Beyond the honey house, the grass had turned buttery yellow, and even the swamp below, typically dark and murky, had taken on a slightly purple hue as something bulky moved within.

She thought of the Loch Ness Monster and refused to look down over the rails. She thought of the hag with horns she'd seen as a girl, walking beneath the decking, its horns clipping against the boards as she walked, and refused to look down. Refused to give in to her fear.

The honey house door was gone, and from the opening, bees buzzed and colorful butterflies fluttered. Something larger moved within the darkness of the small house.

"Ma'am." A male voice sounded behind her. She looked over her shoulder, saw a uniformed Marine coming up the bee barge's steps and onto the decking. "It's not safe, ma'am. We need to get you off the island."

"It's my island." She kept her shotgun leveled at the honey house.

He didn't argue that point but said, "Even so. We need to go. Please."

She looked over her shoulder again. He was dark haired under his helmet and handsome. She focused back on the honey house. "What's your name?"

"Charlie."

"Hi, Charlie," she said. "Amy Barnes."

She saw movement to her left, in the trees. A Boo Hag was coming down the hillside thirty yards away. And then two more showed themselves. They'd been hiding behind trees, Amy assumed, lurking in the shadows, trying to stay out of the sunlight.

"Amy, can you stand behind me. Move slowly," he said. "Whatever these things are, they're fast, and I've already gunned down six of them."

Amy moved behind him but kept her weapon on the honey house.

"Might want to cover your ears," Charlie said. Seconds later he fired his weapon, something that to Amy sounded like an automatic, or maybe he was pulling the trigger that fast—she didn't know much about such things—but he dispatched all three Boo Hags within seconds.

Right about the same time, something began to emerge from the honey house's open door. Amy saw the shadow first, a head with horns stretching across the inside wall of the honey house. A long-fingered red hand gripped the doorway, as if it were pulling itself through, and then the horned hag emerged in full.

It shielded itself under the morning sun and screeched, as if in pain. It locked eyes with Amy and started sprinting directly at her. Amy stood her ground, and just as Charlie told her to "Get down," she fired and blew the horned Boo Hag in half. Blue blood sprayed across the bee barge. The force of the shot knocked her backward onto the decking, and she dropped the shotgun to the floorboards.

She took Charlie's hand, and he helped her to her feet. She asked him, "How many more bullets do you have?"

He smiled at that, said, "Plenty."

"Then do me a favor, and then we can go."

"Sure."

She nodded toward the honey house. "Level that to the ground."

"My pleasure," Charlie said, firing and firing and reloading and firing until there were no walls left and the honey house was a heap of collapsed shingles and fallen, bullet-riddled boards.

Amy said, "Now we can go."

* * *

With the Savannah skyline growing larger by the minute, Nate stood at the railing with the wind in his hair and clean sunlight on his skin.

He reached out toward Lauren, who was talking to David Kilbourne about something.

"What?" Lauren asked.

"Come here."

She told David she'd be right back and approached Nate, who gripped her hand and gently brought her close.

"What?" she asked again, laughing this time.

"This." And he kissed her.

* * *

The final ferry rested at the Crow Island dock.

Amy and her new Marine friend Charlie boarded the near-empty ferry and turned toward the loading ramp. Sheriff Kilbourne was the last to board, and soon the ferry was floating west toward Savannah.

Amy watched the island's shoreline at the Sands grow smaller and could have sworn she saw a unicorn running across the beach in pursuit of a black deer. Her heart ached for Mr. Passafume. He'd be stuck on the island, alone, until they could regroup and come back with help. She would build the island back again and start anew, she thought.

Amy closed her eyes, leaned back against the railing next to Charlie, and let the wind blow her hair. She opened her eyes at the sound of approaching footsteps.

She was startled to see Blue Bottles standing in front of her. "What are . . . Mr. Passafume, you can't leave the island."

She didn't know how far away they were from Crow Island, but Mr. Passafume already looked sick and frail.

"Stop the ferry!" she screamed.

Charlie said, "What's going on?"

"He can't leave the island," she said, and when she saw Sheriff Kilbourne coming toward them, she yelled, "Stop the ferry! Tell them to turn the ferry around!"

Blue Bottles looked at Sheriff Kilbourne and shook his head. "No."

Sheriff Kilbourne said, "What's going on?"

He doesn't know, Amy thought. She was the only one who knew. Why had he knowingly stepped onto the ferry? It was suicide.

"Mr. Passafume, you've got to go back."

He shook his head. "Amy . . . I'm tired." He coughed, wobbled on his feet. Charlie held him up on one side and Sheriff Kilbourne took the other. "I want to see the mainland, just once . . ."

His knees buckled, and they virtually carried him to a nearby bench. Tucked under his arm was the box he'd taken from his house on their first trip gathering the crates of blue bottles.

"What's happening to him?" Sheriff Kilbourne asked.

"He's dying," Amy said, trying to hold it together. "He's never been off the island. He'll die if he gets too far away from that swamp." She screamed to no one, to everyone. "Stop the ferry!"

"Amy . . . please . . . let me do this." He must have used every bit of strength he had left to grip her forearm, and when he did, she could feel his resolve, she could feel his plight, his lack of fight . . . she could feel his weariness. He handed her the box.

"What's in here?" Amy asked.

"Letters," he said. "Open it."

Amy unlatched the lid, and inside the red felt-lined box was a stack of sealed envelopes. The top one was addressed to Matthew Janks.

Sheriff Kilbourne looked at Amy, then at Blue Bottles. "That's the director of Homeland Security. That Matthew Janks?"

"Yes," Mr. Passafume said, so tired now that Charlie had to help prop him up as he sat. "You'll notice it's marked urgent."

Amy fingered through a few more of the envelopes, reading off the names above the addresses. "Brianna Bookman. Detective Samantha Blue. Gideon Dupree . . . Maddy Boyle . . ." She looked up, said, "Mr. Passafume, what is this?"

"Just see that they get them, please."

She closed the box, set it aside. "What do you want us to do?"

"Just let me sit here." His voice was weak. His breathing was raspy and uneven, but otherwise he seemed calm and content, if not peaceful.

The three of them held him as the ferry coasted through the water toward Savannah.

Tears dripped down Amy's cheeks, but the wind quickly dried them. Sheriff Kilbourne was teary-eyed too, and Charlie, who'd only known Blue Bottles for a few minutes, looked like he was on the verge of a dozen different emotions, with confusion at the top of the list.

Blue Bottles must have sensed it.

He was good at that.

He pulled a pen from his pocket, slid it into one of Charlie's uniform pockets on his chest, patted it, and smiled briefly. He said, "Have a wonderful day."

One after the next, they answered, "You too."

And then Blue Bottles closed his eyes, smiled, and stopped breathing.

Amy looked back toward the shrinking island in the distance and wondered if she would ever return. If anyone would return.

Charlie placed a gentle hand on her shoulder, and the warm gesture played as if they'd known each other for years, not minutes. He asked, "You okay?"

She looked at Blue Bottles, the smile on his face.

A peaceful death.

She stared out over the water, Crow Island no longer visible. "Yeah. I'm good."

After

ON A SUNNY September afternoon, Lauren and Nate, who'd driven down from Atlanta for the weekend, sat with Amy and her boyfriend Charlie on the lawn inside Oglethorpe Square in Savannah's Historic District, all of them still admittedly feeling the effects of the drinks they'd consumed last night at several River Street bars.

It was a reunion, Amy thought, that they'd all badly needed, not only for closure but to talk out whatever confused thoughts still lingered between them.

From the numerous scientists now studying Crow Island from afar, they understood that no earthquake had occurred in that area since the day they'd fled three months ago.

Amy had done her best during her new courtship to fill Charlie in on everything, and he'd believed all of it, because he'd been there at the end, he'd seen it firsthand, but he also trusted everything Amy said. They'd begun dating in the weeks after they met and had been inseparable ever since; he'd told her only days ago that he was leaving the Marines, eager to—as he'd explained it—start a more normal life. They'd kept in close contact with Sheriff Kilbourne and his family, and without saying it, Amy got the feeling Charlie one day wanted what Lawrence and Tina had and what they shared in their son, David, to the point where Charlie had begun talking about becoming a cop or a sheriff himself.

Last night, in response to the question Amy had saved until everyone was buzzed enough to answer—"Do you think Jericho is really gone? Finally gone?"—Nate had wasted no time saying yes.

He would have felt it otherwise. He just knew it.

And that answer seemed to appease them all, because Amy thought she would have felt Jericho too. The blue-bottle trees had worked—they'd trapped the boy who was never human and burned him up in the sun.

They all wondered what was left of the island, an island that belonged to the state of Georgia, and for the time being, the United States government was in charge.

Although a strict no-fly zone had been established over the island, several drones had managed to go in and out unscathed, bringing back pictures of an island that looked postapocalyptic at best and unworldly to those who allowed their minds to go there . . . to the stories that had been circulating since that day the survivors arrived on the mainland in Savannah.

Stories of real Boo Hags and red crows and black elk and strange deer with antlers not born of this world.

Any pictures taken by the drones had been quickly confiscated, and the few that had made it briefly online had been swiftly taken down.

Amy insisted to her friends she'd be the first to return to the island, as soon as they were allowed. She'd found a note in Mr. Passafume's pants pocket, stating very simply that he wanted his body cremated. And that if the island was ever safe again, he wanted his ashes scattered atop whatever was left of the honey house.

Amy told their group—as they sat in the shade of a sprawling live oak on Oglethorpe Square, with Spanish moss swaying, breeze blown, above the four of them—that no matter what it took or how long, she would get Blue Bottles' ashes where they needed to be.

And the three of them quickly made it clear that she wouldn't be alone in her return.

The honey might not be the money anymore on Crow Island, but in the months since being gone, the honey had been what Amy craved most.

THE END

James Markert
DIG
July 3, 2025

ACKNOWLEDGMENTS

WE MEET AGAIN at the end of another novel, which means I'm still somehow living out my dream of being a published author and writing for a living, not only writing but writing books people are apparently reading! And for those readers who finished this book and are still reading into the Acknowledgments, thank you, thank you, thank you—writers can always write, but without readers, we wouldn't be able to make careers out of it. And for my current success and hopefully ever-rising career—and I'm promising myself and the readers I'll keep digging and digging until all my goals are reached—I'd like to begin with Matt Martz and everyone at Crooked Lane Books for taking a shot with *The Nightmare Man* and for continuing to drive the bus (maybe even the Lullaby Express) for these next however many novels. *Dig* is my 5th Crooked Lane novel, and *I Am Mallard Malone* will be my 6th, in the Fall of 2026, and I'm hopeful for many more. For a decade I wrote historical fiction under my name, James Markert, publishing 6 novels during that time (and I promise I will soon return to that genre, with one ready to roll as I type this), but I made the decision to rebrand and go in a different direction, and I couldn't imagine a better publishing family than everyone at Crooked Lane. So, at the risk of leaving someone out, I'd like to thank everyone at CLB for all the hard work and dedication put into my scribblings, from cover design and book design to foreign rights and sub rights and production and editing and marketing and promotion and sales—Thank You! To all the booksellers out there, from Barnes &

Nobles and Indie stores to libraries across the country, thank you for continuously stocking my books and for supporting me. Very few got to read DIG early in the process, and I'd be remiss if I didn't say a thank you to my cousin Shawn Lockhart for trudging through an early draft of this one, hopefully we're in agreement that the finished product was better than what you read! I'd also like to thank Emma Markert and Roy Foster for their early reads and notes on *Dig*. A special thanks to my agent, Alice Speilburg, and my editor, Sara J. Henry, for challenging me on this one and encouraging me to dig just a little deeper for the answers they both knew were in there, however deeply buried they'd been at the time. To my kids, Ryan and Molly, keep digging, but stop growing up so damn fast! To Tracy, my wife of 26 years, thank you, as always, for the support. *DIG* is as close as I've gotten to setting a book in Savannah, one of our favorite cities, and all the more reason now to go visit, again, and maybe even sign some books while we're down there. I fell in love with tupelo honey while writing this book, and for those wondering where to buy bottles of this glorious gold, my go-to is the *Savannah Bee Company*. Their tupelo is amazing, and their Tupelo Golden Reserve (98% purity!) is pretty much a party in your mouth, and I highly recommend it! Until next time, loyal readers. Go get yourself some honey and keep digging, continuously onward and upward…

James